FICTION
Escalada, V.
$26

D

SEP − − 2017

HALLS
of
LAW

DAW is proud to present
V. M. Escalada's novels of
The Faraman Prophecy

HALLS OF LAW (Book One)
GIFT OF GRIFFINS (Book Two)*

*Coming soon from DAW

V. M. ESCALADA

HALLS
of
LAW

BOOK ONE OF
THE FARAMAN PROPHECY

DAW BOOKS, INC.
DONALD A. WOLLHEIM, FOUNDER
375 Hudson Street, New York, NY 10014
ELIZABETH R. WOLLHEIM
SHEILA E. GILBERT
PUBLISHERS
www.dawbooks.com

First printing, August 2017
1 2 3 4 5 6 7 8 9

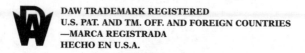

DAW TRADEMARK REGISTERED
U.S. PAT. AND TM. OFF. AND FOREIGN COUNTRIES
—MARCA REGISTRADA
HECHO EN U.S.A.

PRINTED IN THE U.S.A.

For Paul

Acknowledgments

My first thanks have to go to my agent, Joshua Bilmes, and my editor and publisher, Sheila E. Gilbert, who, as of this writing, has just won the Hugo for Best Editor, Long Form. They have both been especially helpful, and especially patient, in shepherding me down the long path that led to this novel. There are many people in both the JABberwocky and DAW offices who deserve my thanks as well.

Thanks to my good friend David Ingham, who functioned as beta-reader for this manuscript, and who gave me some great advice, and some equally good pointers for book two. Thanks also to fellow Canadian writers Marie Bilodeau and Derek Kunsken, for the superfantastically productive writers' weekend we did during the final draft of this book. Not only was a great deal accomplished, but morale was well-bolstered.

Finally, the right to have a character named after him was purchased at silent auction by Nathan Primeau. I changed the spelling a bit, Nate, so I hope you're okay with it. And last, but not least, the right to have a character named after him was won in a contest by Paul Weimer. I said "Human or griffin?" and he said, "Griffin, please." I didn't know the griffin was going to become such an important character, but I'm glad that he did.

Prologue

KERIDA Nast stood at ease outside the Cohort Leader's tent, trying hard not to look as though she was listening to the discussion inside. That the Cohort Leader was her older sister Ester wouldn't make much difference to her punishment if she were caught.

"You people checked her every year from ten to fifteen—like everyone else in the Polity—and never found anything," her sister was saying. "Talents just don't manifest this late."

"It is rare." The dry voice of the Talent Inquisitor sounded familiar. Kerida held her breath. "But rare is not impossible. We have the right to investigate every reported occurrence of Talent, no matter the circumstances."

"Explain." Ker had heard that tone often enough to picture her sister's narrowed eyes. That tone usually meant trouble for someone.

"You wouldn't be the first to believe they could hide Talents from us. We don't waive our rights over any. Not at any age, nor in the highest places." The man's tone clearly showed he didn't consider a temporary camp of the Eagle Wing to be any such place.

The pause that followed was quiet enough for Ker to hear the surf on the other side of the dunes. Long enough that the cold knot in her chest had time to send out tendrils. Guilty of hiding a Talent— At the very least her family would be fined. Money, land, and probably livestock, though Mother, Daughter, and Son knew there was none of that to spare. The Nasts were of the old nobility, long on honor and military service, short on ready money. So much for her parents. As for her sister Ester? She'd be lucky if she were only demoted. If the Halls of Law decided that the Cohort Leader had really been hiding Kerida from them, Ester could be stripped of her command and dishonorably discharged. Such things had happened before, to Battle Wing Faros, no less, and no one in the military ever forgot it. Or forgave it.

"We have hidden nothing." Ester's voice was stony.

Another pause, in which the Inquisitor must have made some gesture that acknowledged her sister's words. "Undoubtedly, my examination will reveal this."

"Examination of a military officer requires a royal warrant." Ester was clutching at straws, and the Inquisitor must have known it. Ker was only a Barrack Leader, in charge of ten soldiers, the lowest official rank in the Wings. She shifted her weight from one sore foot to the other. Drill hadn't gone so well this morning. And now this.

"You know that such a warrant would be granted. The suspected party, yourself, and your entire Cohort would have to remain here until the warrant arrived."

Still another pause. Would Ester make him do it? The Ruby and Emerald Cohorts were due to rotate back to Farama the Capital the following week, leaving coastal patrol to the Onyx and Pearl. Ker had been looking forward to her first visit to the Capital as a soldier; her first chance to spend her pay on more than extra food.

"Very well." Ester's tone was as harsh as the reality they all faced. "You may examine her."

Ker straightened and edged away from the wall of the tent, just in time to avoid being caught by her sister's runner when he came to the entrance and signaled to her. She tugged her green tunic straight with fingers grown suddenly cold and followed the girl in, coming to attention in front of Ester's traveling desk, and giving her salute.

"Barrack Leader, Black Company, Emerald Cohort, reporting as requested," she said. She kept her eyes fixed firmly on her sister, as if the man in the black tunic, with the griffin-shaped emblem of the Halls of Law on his left shoulder, wasn't even in the tent.

"At ease, soldier." Ker saw the little muscle at the corner of Ester's jaw jumping. She was angry all right. There was no love lost between the military and the Halls of Law at the best of times, and whatever happened today wasn't going to help.

"You will submit yourself to Talent High Inquisitor Luca Pa'narion for examination." Ester looked Kerida right in the eyes, unflinching. Her sister was facing this head on, and Kerida knew she was expected to do the same.

She turned smartly to her left, bringing herself face-to-face with the Talent—and swallowed. No wonder his voice was familiar. Talent High Inquisitor Pa'narion was the one who'd done her final examination at fifteen, so it was less than a year since she'd seen him. Like the majority of people, Kerida hadn't shown any Talent. The Inquisitor was lots older than either of her sisters, though not nearly as old as her father, who was at least ten years retired from his post as Faro of the Panther Wing. The Inquisitor's eyes were a most unusual shade of pale lilac, though they turned gray as he bent his head away from the light.

"Please open the neck of your tunic." He gestured toward his own collar, and came a step closer.

Gritting her teeth, Ker undid the braided closure of her

collar and spread it open. She swallowed again, and shifted the twisted leather cord that held her military identification plaque to one side.

Inquisitor Pa'narion moved closer still and placed his hand so his thumb rested on Ker's right collarbone, and his fingertips on her left; his left hand he placed across her forehead. At first, Kerida felt nothing, but then a creeping cold spread from the places of contact, pleasant at first in the heat of this summer afternoon, like a wet washcloth when she had a fever. But this cold didn't fade, it grew. Grew until Ker started to hiss with the pain of it. No matter how many times this happened, Ker thought, a person would never get used to it.

"Relax, it will pass." It sounded enough like a command that Kerida instinctively obeyed it.

And the cold faded, replaced by a tingling warmth. This warmth spread through her, and gradually Ker's muscles loosened, and she felt as though she were somehow floating. She wanted to resist, to turn away, but the warmth was comforting . . .

Images began to form.

. . . Ker is sorting the weapons. "What about this one?" Viki asks, handing her a short sword with a worn leather grip. "It's the right weight," Ker says, hefting it. "I wonder—" Suddenly she falls to her knees, sweat starting out on her brow. She hears her voice from far away. "This has blood on it." "I don't see any blood," Viki says. "It has Ju-an's blood." Her own voice, still distant. "Ju-an's and Tikor's and Soni's. Too much blood. Too much." She drops the weapon and looks up. Viki's eyes are wide with shock. "What?" Ker says. The sweat on her skin turns cold when she realizes what's happened.

Viki saw me, she thought now, as the images faded. And though Viki hadn't said anything to her at the time, she must have said something to someone later. And that something had reached the ears of the Talent assigned to the Emerald Cohort—no knowing how, because surely no soldier would have gone to a Talent directly and reported on one of their own. Even a rumor would have been enough for the Talent to act, however; otherwise why would the High Inquisitor be here?

But he was still taking her back.

. . . she wins another hand of Seasons, this time because she knows when the Luqs of Winter will turn up in the deck.

That was—four years ago? Ker remembered the faces of her father and her grandmother, half-pleased at her skill, half-annoyed that she'd scooped up the pot. She'd been Winter, and they'd had to pay her double.

There were more instances, just as insignificant, some she'd forgotten herself, like:

. . . she touches a tarnished cloak pin in her mother's box of jewels and sees an older woman, straight-browed, with a wide, firm mouth. She can tell from the resemblance to her oldest sister, Tonia, that this is the grandmother none of them ever knew, their father's first wife's mother. But the Inquisitor isn't finished with her. *He's looking for all of it.*

"No," she says, and she knows she's spoken aloud.

"We must," he says, but his voice was kind. "Breathe deeply."

His hands on her throat and face were like cables pulling her back, though she struggled to resist. Pulling her into the dark where she never let herself go. Back to the light and sun that were worse than any darkness.

Late in Griffinmonth. Sun burning hot in a sky the color of her father's eyes. Her brother Fraxim, the one who went to the university and became a doctor, racing her through the meadow, and letting her win, because he didn't really want to play with his little sister when he could be reading in the shade.

She hadn't known that at the time; she'd thought they were really racing, and she'd run with all her strength, despite the hot sun and the scratchy stubble of the hay, into the dark copse of wood on the far side of the field, through the trees, over the stream, jumping it easily because it was already shrunken down to its summer trickle. Landing in what she thought was dark ground on the far side, but sinking into what turned out to be mud, falling forward, hands out to catch herself.

. . . her left hand lands in the mud, on something hard and round, and she grips it instinctively, like a railing. But it's a leg bone. Ker knows this immediately, though it's still covered with mud, and she's never seen a human bone before. Let alone the bone of a murdered man, struck over the head, again, and then again, and his throat cut, and his money taken and his body stripped. He'd been so frightened, and his family would never know what became of him, and she could feel it all, the terror, the pain, and the blood. She thrusts the bone away, scrabbling backward into the water behind her, but the Flashing doesn't stop, and she pounds on her head with her muddy fists, squeezing her eyes tight and *pushes*. . . .

Pushed it all away into the darkest corner room in her mind and slammed shut the door.

Kerida opened her eyes and found she was sitting down, the Talent on his knees in front of her, her hands held tight in his. His expression was very serious, with his gray-flecked eyebrows pulled together above his long nose and his lilac eyes. Ker's lips trembled, and her eyes were wet. She swallowed. Over the Inquisitor's shoulder was Ester's stricken face, her sister's eyes wide with shock and concern. Suddenly realizing she was seated in an officer's presence, Ker braced her wobbly knees and tried to stand.

"Sit quiet, girl." There was kindness, and a certain edge that might have been respect in Inquisitor Pa'narion's voice. "Rest easy. If we know nothing else, we know you won't be staying here, so your niceties of military courtesy no longer apply. Sit quiet, and don't worry; his family will be found and told."

Tears spilled over and rolled down Ker's cheeks. The body, he meant. His Talent was so great that he knew who the body had been, even though he'd never touched a bone of it himself.

"There is no doubt, then?" Her sister came around the Inquisitor, leaned over, and brushed Ker's hair back from her forehead with rough soldier's fingers. Ker blinked back fresh tears. Her sister hadn't done that since Ker had been little, and Ester already grown and gone off to be a soldier. More than anything else, that gesture told Ker that her own life here was over.

"It's true?" Ester said now. "A late manifestation?"

"Yes and no."

Her sister glared up at the Inquisitor, now standing at his full height, his brows still drawn together. "What, then? Don't play with us, man."

"It's not a late manifestation," he said, his voice soft. "It was an early one. *Very* early. It terrified her, and she blocked it. As powerful a natural block as I've ever seen. Powerful enough to last a good ten years."

"*Ten years.*" Ester straightened, her hand staying warm on Ker's shoulder. "But she would have been only four years old, five at the most."

"Manifested early, as I said." Talent Inquisitor Luca seemed pleased now. "It doesn't happen often, but when it does, it's usually the sign of a great Talent. Griffin Class, she will be. Your family has reason to congratulate itself."

Ester's upper lip lifted. "No offense, Inquisitor, but none of us is going to feel that way." Her voice was cold again, and in that chill Ker felt the width of the gulf between the military and the Halls.

The Talent High Inquisitor turned to pick up his black cloak from the corner of Ester's desk. "Have her things brought here, if you please."

"But surely, a visit home, a leave-taking—"

"She has no home outside the Halls of Law. Not anymore." He gestured with his long-fingered hand. "Come, Cohort Leader, do I have to tell you what the whole world knows? I'm satisfied that you knew nothing about this—not only from your own behavior, but from what I Flashed from the Candidate." Another gesture, one which made it clear to everyone that he meant Kerida. She was a Candidate now, a Talent, not a Barrack Leader. Not anymore.

"Must I examine the rest of your family?" the Inquisitor continued. "Make certain none knew and kept silent? Shall I interrogate the servants, to see if any has guilty knowledge? Or shall I go, taking my Candidate with me?" The kind, soft-spoken man of a few moments ago was gone.

Ker took in a deep breath, her nose stinging from the salt air. She'd have given odds no one at home knew—gods, she hadn't really known herself—but there had been that quiet look on the head shepherd's face, that one time, when she'd gone to help with the lambing, and she'd known the unborn lamb was still alive. Genron was an old man, but they'd examine him anyway, wouldn't they?

Ker got to her feet, and tugged her plaque from under her tunic, lifting the cord over her head and letting it dangle from her hand. "Don't, Ester. I'll go."

Her sister held her gaze for a long moment before nodding slowly and putting out her hand for the plaque.

KERIDA pushed a loose strand of hair off her forehead
with the back of her wrist, trying not to get any more
grease on her face. She dipped the damp cloth into the bowl
of sand, and resumed scouring the pot in front of her. Sand
for scouring. Water for rinsing. Oil to prevent rust. Kerida felt
as though she'd been cleaning pots for weeks, not just two
days. She looked to her right. Only three pots left, but they
included the two biggest, the two that somehow—as if the
two Candidates smirking on their way out the door didn't explain exactly how—had been left for last. At her station.

Ker bit down on her anger, tugged the next-to-biggest pot
into position, and scooped up another handful of sand. Normally there'd be three people doing this job. One to scour, one
to rinse, one to oil, so they wouldn't be constantly wiping either oil or sand off their hands to do the next step . . . and
they'd trade off every so many pots, so as not to get tired
and . . .

"Kerida." The sharp whisper startled her back to herself

and she set down the sand pad. Good thing it was Cana who'd seen her daydreaming and not one of the other kitchen serfs. Cana was a decent sort who would rather give Ker a chance to collect herself than use the advantage that reporting her might bring.

Three weeks of kitchen duty, that's what Matriarch had said, and no one, not the Instructors, not even an Inquisitor, could say anything once Matriarch had made her decision. Three weeks to teach Ker discipline, to give her time to think. To make her appreciate better that she was a Candidate in the Halls of Law, and what that meant.

And what could happen if she chose to reject it.

Ker lugged the last pot closer, wrinkling her nose as she glanced inside. Just as she thought. The oatmeal pot, and all the leftover scraps had hardened into something that more closely resembled the mortar between the bricks of the kitchen walls than anything anyone had been eating lately. No point in asking why no one had put it to soak. No point in asking why this particular pot had waited until now, after supper, to appear, instead of after breakfast.

When Matriarch decided you were to be taught humility, everyone had their parts to play. Yesterday afternoon there had been teasing, some sharp, some friendly, from the kitchen serfs. Someone had put a stop to that, and today, except for directing the dirtiest pots to her station, everyone pretended she wasn't even there. Ker didn't know which was worse.

She pushed her hair back again and wondered, not for the first time, whether things would have been easier if she'd come to the Hall younger, if she hadn't started down the path to what she still—after close to two years of Hall training—thought of as her real life.

Most Talents were found between the ages of ten and thirteen, with boys tending to be a little older. Ker hadn't been found until she was almost sixteen, which made her a good four years older than most of the other Candidates in her year.

She'd thought it was a late manifestation—you did hear about such things—and she'd hidden it, determined not to spend her life in seclusion and meditation. *Stupid.*

And part of her—just as stupid—must have gone on thinking that one day she'd be back with her sister in the Emerald Cohort of the Eagle Wing, angling for promotion like the other junior officers. Until yesterday morning's meeting, that is.

It wasn't the first time she'd seen Matriarch, of course. The old woman reviewed every Candidate's progress regularly, and her cold assessment was recorded. Yesterday, Matriarch had been sitting sideways in her chair, looking out the window of her workroom, the morning sunlight showing every fold and wrinkle in her face. Ker had been marched in, and left standing in front of the desk. She'd been hopeful this might be just a surprise examination—until she'd seen exactly what was spread over the books and papers on the desktop.

There were the stones she'd chosen and fetched out of the stream to use as training weights. The long stick of ash she'd used as a practice sword. Three arrows badly fletched with goose feathers stolen from the kitchen. The bow she'd been in the process of smoothing into shape. The creased deck of playing cards. Ker laced her fingers together to keep them still.

"Do you know how many disciplinary lines a Candidate must receive before they are seen by me?"

Ker blinked and looked up. She knew a question that had to be answered when she heard it. "No, Matriarch." She kept her eyes resolutely focused just to the right of the old woman's shoulder. A spiderweb was forming in the upper corner of the window, though Ker couldn't see the spider.

"Twenty." The old woman had brought her sharp gaze round to skewer Kerida directly. She'd waited, but Ker only lined up her feet more carefully. She'd learned the hard way that Candidates—or soldiers—could get themselves into more trouble by ill-considered remarks than by standing still and quiet.

"Once I become involved, the delinquent Candidate either redeems herself, or himself, from that moment, or not at all." If anything, the old lady's eyes were even harder now. "Most Candidates pass their whole tenure here without accumulating twenty lines. You have managed it in slightly less than eighteen months."

Matriarch paused again, and again Kerida decided it was better not to speak, though she gritted her teeth.

"Great concessions have been made for you already. I see from the report that High Inquisitor Pa'narion chose not to question your family at the time you were found." Matriarch lifted her left eyebrow, the movement barely visible. "Luca Pa'narion has always gone his own way. Had I had the judgment of it, he would never have been an Inquisitor."

Ker's ears grew hot. The High Inquisitor had never been one of her favorite people, but if Matriarch disliked him this much, maybe she should change her mind.

"Perhaps your family conspired to hide your Talent from us. Perhaps they did not." Matriarch shrugged. Then her eyes narrowed, and Ker braced herself against taking a step back. "But with you, there is no doubt."

Now Kerida did start to speak—but Matriarch held up her hand, and Ker subsided.

"Not at first, no. The trauma you suffered at your premature Flashing was real, and the block you instinctively created, strong and deep. But afterward?" Here, the old woman turned one hand palm up. "Understandable, perhaps, that your experience should make you fear the Talent, and hide yourself from it. We understand the difficulties that the onset of the Talent can bring, particularly one as powerful as yours. As we understand the force that family traditions and expectations can have.

"But that was there, and then. And this is here, and now."

Ker's ears had begun to buzz. This was the first time anyone here at Questin Hall had ever spoken to her about that terrible day in her sister's tent. Gods knew how hard it had been when she'd starting Flashing so late, watching to make sure it wouldn't show, that no one would suspect. And it *had* worked. At least for a while.

Matriarch was still looking at her, dark eyes opaque, but Ker hadn't moved, though the sweat trickled down her back. Matriarch's room was always kept hot. The old woman looked back at the pages on her desk, turned one.

"Four disciplinary lines in as many weeks," she observed. "Bringing you to twenty."

Ker pulled her shoulders back, determined not to squirm under the scrutiny of those glittery black eyes. She was almost eighteen, for the Daughter's sake. Her sister Tonia had been the standard-bearer of her Company at that age. But Matriarch had a way of making your years, whatever they might be, dwindle into insignificance. Ker swallowed.

"A review of the lines and reprimands in your history displays a pattern, as does this." Matriarch gestured at the items on the desk. Kerida shrugged. She'd thought her things had been well hidden. *Stupid.* "Your attempt to run away, early in your training, was to be expected, perhaps, under the circumstances. This was followed by a period of relative obedience and submission."

Matriarch leaned back against the cushions of her chair, bringing the tips of her fingers together. Ker braced herself. "You seemed to be settling down, finally, until these last weeks. Why is that?"

A direct question. Ker cleared her throat, determined not to show the older woman any fear. "It was the news of the signal fires, Matriarch. You know they're only lit for some emergency, and the Battle Wings are so far away, beyond the Serpents Teeth, with only the five Cohorts of the Eagle Wing in the Peninsula. I felt—" Ker took a step forward. "I'm not doing anything useful here, and I . . ." *And I have a sister in the Eagle Wing.* Just in time, Ker had stopped herself from saying that aloud. Talents didn't have family outside the Halls. No family, no friends. No ties. No allegiance other than to the Law. "You know I was in the military, Matriarch, before I came here. I could be helping—"

The old woman held up her index finger. "What do you imagine will happen to you, Junior Candidate Nast, if you do not complete your training with us?"

Ker blinked at Matriarch's abruptness. Another direct question. Unfortunately, not one she had an answer to. Her cheeks had grown hotter, and her ears started to burn. Why didn't the old woman come to the point? "I don't know, Matriarch," she finally managed to say.

"Surely you did not think you could be allowed to return to your family? To your land and your military traditions? You are not the first who wished to reject the Talent, thinking to put their own preferences before the choice of the Mother. Nor would you be the only Talent in our long history who could not submit themselves to the discipline and training of the Halls of Law. Have you never wondered what is done with Candidates whose discipline fails them?"

Kerida pressed her lips together tightly over her clenched teeth, as cold spread through her body. *Dampened.* That was the word whispered when Candidates met for midnight feasts—not that she'd been included in many of those. That's when the old stories came out, the ones the youngsters loved to frighten themselves with, about the evil Feelers, and how they had to be dampened before they could be killed. Even Kerida had been told, when she was little, "Behave, or the Feelers will get you."

Feelers were put to death and their bodies burned when Talents in those old tales came to the rescue. *Feelers.* Not . . . Ker took a deep breath and swallowed past the lump in her throat.

Matriarch leaned forward again, her palms flat on the tabletop. "Let me make this plain. Even should you fail your training, you would not be returned to the world. You would remain here." Matriarch tapped the surface of her desk with one bony finger. "The Inquisition would be summoned. Your Talent would be dampened. You would never leave this Hall again. Is that what you wish?"

Talents do not live in the world. That was the old saying, and Ker had never thought about what it meant. No Talent. Not even the ones judged unworthy of training. Maybe especially not them.

Ker had looked away right then, afraid for the first time. Afraid of what she saw in the old woman's face. The worn wooden griffins that made up the legs of the huge desk seemed to stare back at her with the same cold emptiness in their carved eyes. Matriarch had actually used the word "dampened" in speaking of Kerida herself. Used it as though it was something she'd ordered done before.

Ker lifted her hand to her throat, to the place where Inquisitor Pa'narion had rested his hand. She remembered what his Talent had felt like, the cold, piercing shock of it.

"Well, Junior Candidate?"

With an effort, Ker moved her head right and left, feeling her fear and her resentment in the stiffness of her neck and shoulders.

The look on Matriarch's face didn't change, but was there some disappointment mixed into the satisfaction in the old woman's tone? "In the Talent itself, you show yourself capable of great self-control, Junior Candidate. Redouble your efforts in that area. Yours is a great Talent, profound. It is there, whether you like it or not. You must master it, as you must master yourself. For our own sakes, the Halls of Law cannot allow any other option."

This time Ker forced herself to nod before baring her teeth. "So if I'm good, I might be Matriarch someday?" She'd meant to be sarcastic, but even her own ears told her she hadn't managed it. If it was submit or be dampened, she knew which one she chose, but was submission alone going to be enough? Would her anger betray her?

Still with no change in her expression, Matriarch tilted her head to one side. "I do not usually speak so plainly to Junior Candidates, but it is important that you understand exactly what your circumstances are, and that you give up your childish notions of another life."

Ker suddenly had an overwhelming feeling—almost like a Flash, but it couldn't be, could it?—that Matriarch didn't like her and wanted her to fail. Ker clenched her jaw and managed to nod again without speaking.

"Very well." Once more the sheets of paper were consulted. "Let me see. We might have overlooked the physical exercise, as it did not interfere with your studies, but the rest? Possession of personal arms. Forbidden. Instructing fellow Candidates in games of chance. Forbidden."

"No money changed hands, Matriarch."

"Practicing hand-to-hand combat. Forbidden." The old woman looked up. "Attempting to teach those techniques to others. Forbidden."

Ker pressed her lips tight. She should have known those girls hadn't really wanted to be friends.

"Three weeks of disciplinary work will give you time to reflect. You may meditate at the Mother's shrine to achieve a state of calm before reporting to the kitchens."

Noises of running feet and slamming doors in the corridor outside the kitchen brought Kerida back to the present, and the cleaning of pots. This was what she could expect if she didn't complete her training. She'd trade her Talent in a heartbeat to get back her old life. But if that road was closed . . . Ker glanced around at the kitchen serfs, seeing them with new eyes. Matriarch had been quite clear. If she didn't become a Full Talent, they'd dampen her. Then she'd be given some menial job in some Hall somewhere that would free a Full

Talent from having to do it. A kitchen or garden serf, maybe. But she'd never leave the grounds of a Hall again.

Had any of the people around her right now once been in her shoes?

Ker rested her forehead on the back of her hand, squeezing her eyes tight. She didn't want to be a serf in the kitchen or garden—or a clerk in the offices for that matter. But what was she going to do about it? She knew what her sisters would say just now. "Straighten up, soldier." Kerida took a deep breath and obeyed.

She had just put the freshly oiled oatmeal pot in its proper place when Senior Candidate Barid Poniara stuck his head in the door. "General assembly in the great room," he called loudly enough to be heard through the whole kitchen. "Sharply, everyone. You, too, Kerida." Barid waited for her, holding the door open until she reached it. He took care to abide by the strict rules, and didn't meet her eyes, but he coughed and brushed at his forehead with his fingertips. Ker blushed, rubbing at the sand there with her rolled-down sleeve.

As he drew the door shut behind her, he leaned in and breathed, "Here. One hour after the last bell." She lifted her right hand as a sign that she'd heard him, and proceeded down the corridor.

Barid would be a Passed Candidate by the spring, and a Full Talent as soon as he completed the last of his solo assignments, but in the meantime, as a Senior, he presided over Ker's dining table, there to answer the Juniors' questions, give advice, and maintain order. He was her own age, part of the year she would have been in, if age alone decided such things. Barid was like Cana, one of the few who'd always treated her as though they believed she belonged with them.

Ker and Barid might have been friends, even good friends, if the differences in their ranks hadn't been so great. She'd thought there was no one who would risk a disciplinary line of their own to speak to her, but Barid had just proved her wrong.

Here. Meaning the kitchen. Not very risky, even an hour after the last bell, when every Junior Candidate had to be in bed, and every candle out. If they were caught, easy for Barid to say it was part of her punishment. Barid was well thought of; no one would doubt him.

Ker found herself quite eager to hear what he had to say.

She stayed right on Barid's heels as he went down the short flagstone corridor that led from the kitchen wing into the great room. Like a similar space in a noble's holding, the great room served the Hall of Law as the area for dining, assembly, and the greeting of outside visitors. Matriarch was already seated at her place among the Senior Staff on the raised platform at the far end opposite the main entrance. Not all of the Senior Staff sitting with her were Full Talents, and for the first time Ker considered what that meant. The Senior Cook, and the Gardener, for example . . . could *they* be Talents who had somehow not measured up? Chafed too much under Hall discipline? How, exactly, did dampening work?

Ker hurried to her own table, one of the two for second-years, close to the raised platform, and to the Matriarch's left. She arrived at her seat just as the signal for silence was given. Like everyone else in the assembly, she remained standing, and turned her eyes to the head table, expecting Matriarch to speak. Instead, the old woman signaled a waiting steward who threw open the side doors of the great room. Ker turned her eyes toward the opening—and promptly forgot everything that had been worrying her.

What, or rather who, she saw moving into the clear space in front of Matriarch's chair and falling into parade rest certainly explained why they'd all been called back to their tables so soon after supper. Matriarch would want to put on as big a show of strength and numbers as she could.

Soldiers. More precisely, a Cohort Leader of the Eagle Wing, in her green tunic and cloak, with five of her Company in support. For a moment Ker's heart rose, but these were all wearing the pale green sleeves of the Opal Cohort. There was no one from the Emerald Cohort, no one who served with Ester. The soldiers shifted place, and Ker realized they weren't all Eagles, after all. A second Cohort Leader was wearing the purple of the Bears. What was someone from a Battle Wing doing here in the Peninsula?

Ker automatically sat down when the signal was given. The Candidates, whether Juniors, Seniors or Passed, took longer than usual to come to order. The Wings had their own Talents assigned to travel with them, and it was very rare for military personnel to come to a Hall.

There'd never been any great friendship between the military and Talents, even though some of the newer provinces called them the Twin Hammers of the Polity. At best, each treated the other as a useful tool; at worst, a necessary evil. The relationship wasn't helped by the fact that the Halls had the same powers of Law over the Military that they had over everyone else.

Ker licked dry lips. The common soldiers were scanning the room, the two Cohort Leaders stood shoulder-to-shoulder, eyes on the high table. Matriarch lifted her hand, and the silence finally became complete. Canlor, the Hall's Senior Administrator, rose from his seat on the Matriarch's right and took her hand in his. The older woman no longer had the lungs to be heard throughout the room, and the contact meant he would speak for her.

"You are welcome, Cohort Leaders. You have news?"

"Opal Cohort Leader Jen Sha'na, Matriarch, and yes, we do." Like most officers, the Eagle knew how to pitch her voice to be heard. "Farama the Capital has fallen."

It was not so much the silence, Kerida thought, as the wash of buzzing in her head. She was sure the noise was coming from inside, not out. The *capital* had fallen? Ker couldn't feel her hands and feet, though her heart seemed to be thumping in her chest. Administrator Canlor had called for order, and the Seniors were bringing their charges into line by pounding their fists in unison on the tables in front of them. Gradually, the familiar rhythm steadied the younger Candidates, and the great room was quiet again.

"Impossible." Canlor repeated Matriarch's words, and echoed the thoughts of everyone else present, Kerida was sure. "We have heard about the signal fires, of course." Ker shook herself and tried to focus. "But that was less than three weeks ago. How has this happened?"

A good question, and the Cohort Leader had an answer.

"Treachery, Matriarch." Jen Sha'na kept her eyes on the old woman, as if she'd been the one who was speaking. "There were simultaneous landings on the coast, by Algrade, by Leb-sos, and at Lavensa. And while we rushed to stem that tide, two more ships were already in the capital, disguised as scows from Tolnida Province. By the time word could be sent, it was already too late."

Ker pinched herself, dredging her brain for military strategy that she hadn't had to think about in ages. So the signal fires—they had been to say the enemy was already in the capital.

It was clear from Canlor's reactions, and the looks on the faces at the high table, that this was news to the Senior Staff. There was regular communication between Halls. Obviously, however, no such news had arrived from the Hall of Law in Farama the Capital. Matriarch's grip on Canlor's hand seemed to have tightened, almost as though it was the only thing holding the old woman upright.

"They were in the city by the time the signals reached Camp Oste," the Cohort Leader said, confirming what Ker had thought. "What little we know now, we've learned from those of the Emerald and Ruby Cohorts who managed to escape."

The Emerald Cohort? Ker inched forward in her chair, fingernails biting into the palms of her hands. Had her sister's Cohort had the duty in the capital this month?

"This is grave news, indeed." Canlor's voice was colorless. "Thank you for bringing it to us." There was real appreciation in his tone, an acknowledgment that Jen Sha'na had set aside whatever rivalry she might have felt in order to bring this important news.

"There is yet more." The Cohort Leader paused as if she were considering how to proceed. Then the woman squared her shoulders and took a deep breath before continuing. "The reports that have reached us say that the Luqs and all her family have been taken."

Murmuring spread through the Hall, but Ker didn't move, except to become even more quiet and still. Finally, control was asserted once more, and the exchange at the front of the great room could be heard.

"You have some proof of this?" Canlor was saying. "We all know how easily rumor can take wing." Those words, more than anything the Seniors might do, helped to settle the younger Candidates down to something resembling normal discipline.

"I have something which may help us to proof, with your aid, Matriarch." Jen Sha'na stepped up to the table and pulled a chain out from under her uniform tunic, separating it from the leather thong of her plaque. She lifted it over her head and set it down, along with the round object hanging from it, on the tabletop in front of the old woman. Kerida peered around the soldiers who stood in her way, but could only see that the object was small. Barid, in a better position, laid his left hand on the table where all could see him and tapped the index finger. A signet ring.

Kerida nodded. That, of course, was the real reason the Eagles had decided to stop here and beg an audience at a Hall of Law. If the situation wasn't as serious as it was, Kerida would have grinned. She wondered whether this thought had occurred to anyone else, or whether it was her own military background that made her think of it.

"It was given me by Prince Halnor," Jen Sha'na was saying as she took a step back from the table. "I've had it some time, but it came from his own hand."

Nothing more likely. Ker saw the exchange of glances among Tutors and Seniors as others came to the same conclusion. The prince's preference for military women was as famous as his generosity. The Cohort Leader was a handsome woman, and just the prince's type.

Matriarch had picked the trinket up in her own hand, not letting so serious a Flashing be done by someone else. It seemed the whole great room didn't breathe while the old woman held the ring. Ker pressed her hands hard between her knees. She'd give anything to be able to Flash the thing herself.

"They *are* captives," Matriarch said. "They are together. The Luqs has a small injury, but she is otherwise well." The silence that followed these words when Canlor had repeated them was more frightening than the uproar Kerida had expected. But the soldiers had relaxed, ever so slightly, now that they knew the Luqs was living.

"Can you tell us anything more, Matriarch? Can you Flash where they are being held?"

The old woman shook her head, but slowly. "I do not know the building myself as it is new since I have been in the capital. It fronts on the southwest, and has two towers and red doors." She closed her eyes again, waited, and gave the tiniest shake to her head. "The prince has not worn this in some years. That is all I can Flash." She held out the ring.

The Bear Cohort Leader leaned forward and murmured in Jen Sha'na's ear. She nodded as she stepped up to retrieve her ring. "We know the building, Matriarch, thank you."

"May we ask what is planned?" Talents lived apart from

the world, objective and neutral, but that didn't mean they weren't curious. And precisely because of the objectivity, and the neutrality, their curiosity could be safely satisfied.

"We are mustering in Bren's Ford, along with the Onyx, Ruby, and Pearl Cohorts of the Eagles." Jen Sha'na gestured at the Bears' Cohort Leader, who gave Matriarch a short bow. "Three Cohorts of Bears have joined us from the transit camp at Oste. Together, we'll rescue the Luqs." Jen Sha'na's tone was very quiet and serene, for all that she spoke loudly enough to be heard by the whole assembly. There was certainty in that tone, and Kerida sat up a little straighter. That's the way her sisters would have spoken.

"We must travel as quickly as we can. May we ask food of you? Whatever is already prepared and can be easily carried would be welcome."

The Senior Cook and two of his assistants were on their feet, but when both the Head Cook and Matriarch held up their hands, they sat down again.

"You know that if we grant you help, then we must help the invaders also, should they ask it of us."

"Matriarch?"

Canlor took up the task of speaking. "If these invaders are from Tolnida, as you suggest, then they have received the benefit of the Law. There are Halls there, from which you would—and will—be able to ask for provision and aid. We are neutral and apart, and we must show ourselves as such. That is the Law."

Tolnida. Sometimes the Halls of Law sent Talents into new areas before the military got there. Tolnida had been such an area. Another source of conflict and rivalry between the Halls and the Wings.

The Cohort Leaders exchanged a look, clearly unhappy, though how they could have expected a different answer Ker didn't know. How could the Halls serve everyone equally, and fairly, and be trusted, if they took sides? Ker hadn't thought about it this way before she came to the Hall herself. Of course, they would help if they were asked, and if they could, but now that request would also have to be honored if the invading army asked it.

"We understand." This time Jen Sha'na's tone left little doubt that while she understood, she didn't like it much. Ker had to confess she felt the same way.

"Then if you send to the kitchen, the staff there will see to it."

This time the Senior Cook and his assistants were allowed to leave their places and head for the kitchen.

"Kerida." Barid jerked his head toward the doorway. "Go and help them."

Ker tried not to look too eager as she shot to her feet. Anyone else would think his order was part of her punishment, but Barid understood how much she would value a chance to speak with the soldiers who would be sent to fetch the food. She couldn't thank him aloud, she could only hope her gratitude showed in her eyes as she scurried to obey. A small taste of her old life and maybe a chance to learn something about her sister.

Minutes later Ker stood ready at the door to the storeroom to fetch and carry as needed. The Senior Cook and his first assistant were walking through the storage area consulting with each other, nodding, making notes on their lists, and pointing out what was wanted. Ker carried the selected items out to the big worktable in the center of the kitchen, cleared off now in preparation for the morning. The second assistant cook had brought Cana to help her, and the two of them stayed in the storeroom to set aside exact duplicates of what Kerida was carrying out. That, of course, was what made the Senior Cook's discussions with his first assistant so complicated. The exact amount of whatever was given to the Eagles and Bears had to be set aside for the invaders, in case they also asked for help. That was the only way everyone could be sure that the Hall remained scrupulously neutral. It was a testament to the Senior Cook's organization that the decisions on what could be spared were made so quickly.

The flow of food and supplies piling up on the big worktable slowed and finally stopped. Ker ran her eye over the result and calculated. Ten soldiers to a Barrack, ten Barracks to a Company, five Companies to a Cohort, five Cohorts to a Wing. There was enough food here to feed a whole Cohort for two days, though that wasn't likely to be the way it got parceled out. Packs of hard travel cakes wrapped in oiled cloths had come out of the storeroom first, followed by small sacks of flour, corn and oat meals, and a dozen jars of preserved fruit. The Senior Cook and his two assistants counted over everything again, finally stopping to discuss the six fat, round clay pots, well-sealed with wax, that had come out of the storeroom last. From the markings, four of them contained roasted peppers preserved in oil, and two held cooked sausages congealed in their own fat. Neither would last anywhere near as long as the travel cakes, or even the jars of preserved fruit, but they wouldn't last any longer here in the Hall. At least this way the officers of the Eagles and Bears would have a few days' treat before they went back to eating the same travel cakes as everyone else.

Ker's stomach growled, and Cana smiled. "Me, too," she murmured, her eyes carefully looking elsewhere. She could have been talking to herself.

"They should bring their own sacks." This was the Senior Cook, coming out one final time from the storeroom, leaving his assistant to close up behind him. "If not, they may use these." He indicated a pile of very worn hessian sacks that had been used for bringing kindling into the kitchen.

Ker nodded; she knew better than to speak, but the others were already on their way out of the room. She grinned at their backs. They thought they were leaving her to the most menial part of the job, dealing with the soldiers who would complain about how little they were given, and perhaps even show their resentment, depending on what kind of officer came with them. But Ker found her spirits lifting. This would be a chance to speak to someone from the outside world. Perhaps even someone who knew her sister.

Finally, a knock came at the courtyard door. Smiling, Ker went to open it. The squad who arrived with their own packs to collect the food were led by one of the tallest men she had ever seen, wearing the purple tunic of the Bear Wing, the left sleeve red/brown for his Cohort, and the right sleeve green to show which Company he belonged to.

This soldier couldn't be much older than she was, but he was at least a head taller. His skin was dark, but his hair was sandy, bleached by the sun to the color of a linen shirt that had been washed too many times, and his eyes were a pale gray, almost as colorless as his hair. Kerida knew the look of a broken nose when she saw one, and there was a scar along the outside of his left cheek.

He had to be an officer of some kind, but not important enough to have been one of the people with the Cohort Leaders in the great room—if he had been, Ker would have remembered him for his height if nothing else. No, he'd be some Barrack Leader, or a Third Officer at most. Someone more or less on her own level, in fact. At least the level she had when she wasn't being disciplined.

He smiled at her when he walked in, and Ker smiled back. "These are your supplies," she said. "On the table."

The officer stayed close to her, letting the three soldiers with him go up to the table by themselves. "It's not very much, is it? But I suppose that's not your fault." He smiled at her again. She hadn't thought eyes so pale could look so warm.

"No, it isn't. I mean." Kerida cleared her throat. It really had been a long time since she'd spoken to anyone not in the Hall, but surely that wasn't enough to tie her tongue? "I meant, it's as much as we can spare to you."

"A village would give us more than this." One of the soldiers spoke without looking up from the goods he was packing.

"But they need your protection, and we don't." The last thing Ker ever expected was to find herself defending the Hall. "What we give, we give freely."

"And to all." The officer's tone neither approved nor disapproved. His words were more a reminder than anything else. He turned to smile at her. "We weren't able to bring a lot of supplies from Oste, so it's good the Hall is in the mood to share."

Ker leaned her hip against the station where she'd been cleaning the pots earlier and folded her arms, watching the officer out of the corner of her eye. The style of harness he wore was familiar to her; she'd had one like it herself. Straps of leather as wide as two fingers went around the waist and up over the shoulders, held in place by thinner straps and buckles. To this harness could be attached short sword and dagger, and the waist pouch that any traveler would carry. The harness was set up in such a way that mail could be worn under it, or body armor attached to it, depending on the wearer's rank, and on the contents of his purse.

"Yes, it's a brand-new harness."

It had been days since anyone had spoken to her in such an open manner, and Ker started, taking half a step back before she realized what that might look like, and stood her ground. She wouldn't want the soldier to think she was afraid of him. He smiled and moved a little closer.

"I think it looks rather fine, don't you agree?"

Ker snorted and rolled her eyes. Now she was on comfortable ground. "Don't hate yourself, do you?" She was pleased when his grin grew wider and his face even more open. She grinned back. "Anyone could tell your harness is new," she told him. "It looks stiff as a billet of wood. Don't you have any grease to soften the leather?"

"What do you know about it?" But still the tone was friendly.

"I've got two sisters in the field," she answered. "One with the Emerald Cohort of the Eagle Wing. The other with the Panthers in the Battle Wings." She felt a bit shy of mentioning her sisters' ranks and, now that it came to it, Ker was afraid to ask about Ester. Not that this Bear would be likely to know anything, she told herself.

"Really?" His interest seemed genuine and his face even friendlier. Ker was not surprised when his shoulders relaxed further and he stuck out his hand. "Tel Cursar," he said. "At the moment, Third Officer, Green Company, Carnelian Cohort, Bear Wing." Just what his sleeves had told her.

Ker grasped his wrist in the military way. His skin was warm, and his grip on her own wrist firm. Already Third Officer? He was young for that, but the Battle Wings promoted quickly, everyone knew that. "Kerida Nast. At the moment, fourth assistant kitchen serf, Questin Hall of Talent. I know where there's a pot of grease no one will miss." It seemed to her that Tel let go of her wrist more slowly than was necessary.

Yup, really doesn't hate himself, she thought as she reached into the shelves under the cleaning stations. But she smiled as she thought it. "Here you are."

Tel took the pot from her and tucked it into his pouch. He didn't seem in any hurry to leave, and Ker leaned on her wash-tubs once more.

"So with all your family connections, did you never think to come into the military?"

"I did, I was." Ker frowned. She was acting like the kitchen serf he thought she was. "In fact, I had almost thirteen months with my sister's Cohort after I left school."

"Wait a minute. Your sister is Ester Nast? Emerald Cohort Leader of the Eagles? What happened? How did you go from that to, to ah . . ." Tel cut short his gesturing at the kitchen, as if he realized that any such reference could be offensive, and lose him any points his smiles and friendliness might have gained. "Were you injured?"

"No. I told you I was only the fourth assistant kitchen serf 'at the moment.' The rest of the time, when I'm not being disciplined, I'm a second-year Candidate here." Now, since he knew who her sister was, it seemed a good time to ask. "You wouldn't be able to tell me—"

Tel Cursar straightened abruptly to his full height. "You're a Talent." His tone had hardened, his face had stiffened, and his eyes had gone cold. For a moment Kerida thought he was going to say something harsh to her, and she braced herself, ready to give as good as she got. "I thank you for the hospitality we have been given," he finally said. The most formal words he could have chosen.

"You are welcome." She gave the answer courtesy required. She couldn't ask him now. He wouldn't tell her. Talents do not live in the world.

He turned on his heel, very crisp, very military, signaled to his waiting men, and was gone without saying another word.

Ker blew out her breath, blinking away what she refused to acknowledge was the burn of embarrassed tears. She was a Talent. Her old life was gone, really gone. If she'd needed any proof, she'd just been given it.

Was *that* why she'd been allowed to speak to them? She rubbed her face, breathing deeply through her nose. Something to ask Barid when he showed up.

Ker looked around the kitchen for something that would give her an excuse to stay where she was. If she went up to her room now, she'd just wake up the others, without getting any sleep herself. Finally, her eyes rested on the water reservoir to the left of the bread ovens. Unlike the water barrels, the reservoir was made from tin, nothing more than a large square pot, really, filled with water kept warm by its spot next to the stove. Picking up two pads to protect her hands, she inched the container away from the oven wall until she was able to pull it out and push it over completely. She danced out of the way as the water splashed over the floor, stopping short of where the stone turned to wood.

She released the breath she'd sucked in. That was lucky. She fetched the mop and clean rags from the cupboard next to the outer door. If water had gone down into the storage cellars, she would have been in trouble.

K ER was bringing the final pail of water from the well in
the courtyard when Barid let himself into the kitchen
from the corridor.

"What are you doing?" He frowned at the wet floor, the
mops and rags.

"Giving myself an excuse to be here," she said, tipping the
pail into the reservoir. "And you an excuse to come looking
for me."

"You emptied out the water on the floor?" Barid still looked
puzzled.

Ker shrugged. She tossed the damp rags into the pail and
picked up the mop. "I was planning to say the soldiers made
me do it, if anyone asked." The rags she hung from the han-
dles of the oven doors to dry, and the mop and pail she stuffed
back into their cupboard. Drying her hands on the front of
her tunic, she sat down on the stool usually reserved for the
Senior Cook.

Mopping up the water and fetching more in from the well

had given Ker time to think. Whether or not her encounter with Tel Cursar had been planned, it had shown her, in a way even Matriarch's lecture couldn't, that there was no turning back. She was here to stay, and as much as it rankled, she'd better find a way to deal with it.

The only consolation was that her success would really annoy Matriarch.

"Well?" she said now. "You had something you wanted to say to me?"

Barid nodded, frowning, as if he didn't know how to begin. "You remember High Inquisitor Luca Pa'narion?" he said finally.

"How would I possibly forget him?" Not only was he the Inquisitor who'd taken her away from her life, and her family, and brought her here, he was the one Matriarch didn't like.

"There's an opportunity he wants to offer you, something that could start as early as the spring."

Ker started, her interest sharpening, and crossed her arms to cover the movement. "In the spring, I'll only be a third-year Candidate, if I'm not still here in the kitchen."

"You really don't know?" Barid shook his head, leaning back against the worktable and gripping the edge with his hands. "With your gifts, if you put as much work into your studies as you've been putting into pretending you were going back to the Eagles one day, you'd be finished your training in six months. You and I could graduate together." His teeth flashed white against his dark skin.

A Passed Candidate—maybe a Full Talent—in six months. Ker shivered, suddenly aware of the late hour, and how cold it was here in the kitchen. That would really get up the old woman's nose—an old woman who'd been very careful not to say anything about this when she'd gone on and on about how great Ker's Talent was. She straightened her spine.

"Are you interested?"

"What do *you* think? Maybe the Halls of Law weren't my

first choice, but at least as a Talent I'd be doing something besides hoeing potatoes all summer and then peeling them all winter." She frowned. "Is *that* Luca's 'opportunity'? To graduate early?" She had another thought. "I could be a Talent *for* the Wings—" Ker broke off when Barid shook his head. "They wouldn't want me," she said. "Or the Halls wouldn't let me. Neither one could ever be sure where my loyalties were." She took a deep breath, squared her shoulders. "What's this opportunity, then?"

"Ordinarily someone with your gifts would be training to be an Inquisitor—"

Ker straightened completely. "I could be an Inquisitor?" She grinned. That was better than being Matriarch. *Inquisitor Kerida Nast*. No, *High* Inquisitor.

"That's what Luca is hoping for, though there's something more."

Of course, there was. Ker stayed quiet. Everyone had their own plans for her.

Barid pressed his lips together, and concentrated on a wet spot on the stone floor. "There's a reform movement within the Halls, it's been working in secret for—well, a long time anyway. Working against exactly the kind of things we all worry about—the narrow thinking, the rigid ranking—"

"The way that by the time you're high enough in rank to make changes, you're too old to care anymore? Don't look so surprised. That happens in the military as well." Her own father used to complain of it; he'd liked to surround himself with younger officers for that reason.

"Fine." Barid grinned at her. "There's a small group of Talents working against the worst abuses of the Halls, working to establish a different system, a better system."

Ker laughed out loud. "And Luca thought this was something I'd be interested in, did he? Well—" She sobered. "He'd be right. But tell me, how can a conspiracy like this stay hidden from examination by the Halls of Law?"

Again Barid's teeth showed white. "Easily, if the people doing the examination are part of the conspiracy."

"The *Inquisition?*"

"Shh! Keep your voice down. Not all of them, no, but some."

"Luca, for one."

"Luca, exactly. He's had his eye on you since he first saw how powerful your Talent is."

Her powerful Talent that for the first time seemed to be working for her rather than against her. "Still, it couldn't always be the same person examining you all the time, why the Tutors check us regularly . . ." She let her voice trail away as Barid just kept smiling and nodding.

"The people here are the best teachers, and they're very good Talents," he said. "But they're not necessarily the *best* Talents."

Not Griffin Class, Ker thought. *Not like me.*

"The best become Inquisitors—" Barid began.

"Who do our final examinations, the out-of-hall examinations, so if the wrong one examines me, she Flashes that there's a conspiracy, and that I'm part of it."

"Not after I show you how to block it."

A block that was effective against an Inquisitor? She could rebel and be safe. Submit and not submit. Ker licked her lips. "You could have started with that."

The soldiers came back on Kerida's last day of discipline. This time they arrived long after the evening meal, when most of the Candidates had gone to their dormitories for the night, and Ker and Cana, the only ones left in the kitchen, were returning clean plates, bowls, and spoons to the stands in the great room where only the lamps on the head table, and the fat beeswax candles in front of the shrine for the household gods, were still lit.

Kerida should have been doing this by herself, but there had been a problem with two leaky water barrels in the kitchen. It was now very late, and when Cana had started to help sort the platters and bowls onto the wheeled carts, no one in the kitchen had stopped her. As soon as they were finished unloading the cart, Ker sent Cana back to the kitchen with it.

"Go on," she said, when the other girl hesitated. "I'm almost through here. There's no need for both of us to be this late, and you've helped me so much already." Cana had given her a swift smile, and a short nod, and headed back for the kitchen.

As Ker was restacking the last of the dishes, Barid came in from the outer corridor, stopping short when he saw her. "Kerida, can you finish later? There's need of the room."

"But—" Kerida stood ready to argue, but the stricken look on Barid's face stopped her. He'd given her so much secret coaching in the last few days to help her catch up, Kerida reminded herself. She put down the bowls she still had in her hands. "Get me up early," she told him. "I'll finish then." His smile was almost worth the sleep she'd lose.

Kerida crossed the great room briskly, but once she was in the darker shadow of the service corridor leading to the kitchen, she stopped and turned back, curiosity getting the better of her. What could require the great room at this time of night? The Senior Staff would meet in Matriarch's apartments, where the old woman had a small conference room. The great room was a public place, far more likely to be used for the reception of someone from outside the Hall.

Now came the sounds of footsteps, the murmurs of voices, and Ker shifted, making sure she was beyond the light from the great room lamps, but still close enough to hear and watch what was going on.

"I regret having kept you waiting." Matriarch must have come in by the main doors, but she hadn't gone up to the head table, to her regular chair. Instead, she had to be sitting at one of the Candidates' long dining tables. Standing between Ker and the old lady were several other people, blocking her view. They wore military cloaks, these others, some even with hoods up, and Ker shivered. It seemed they brought the chill of early winter inside with them.

She took a half step forward. One of the strangers was very tall.

"You have news for me?" Matriarch was still speaking.

"Matriarch, please." This was a voice Kerida hadn't heard before, breathless, and not under the best control. "Please, you *must* listen to me. You must flee the Hall now, tonight."

Kerida's heart leaped into her throat.

"Whatever do you mean? Where is your Cohort Leader?"

"Dead, Matriarch—or worse—and what's left of us Eagles and Bears, we're in flight. We were routed at the plains of Farama. We only stopped here to warn you." The speaker took a deep breath, the sound ragged, and Kerida inched closer to the edge of the light. She couldn't make out colors clearly. Were any of *these* soldiers Eagles? Any from the Emerald Cohort? What about Ester? Was her sister safe? "The Hall in Farama's destroyed, and the Talents murdered. The invaders from the sea are torching the Halls as they find them, and they're heading this way."

Kerida put both hands over her mouth, sure that someone must have heard her suck in her breath.

"You are mistaken, I am sure." Matriarch's quiet voice was calm. "You have suffered great losses, this is clear, but think what you say. Halls have been burned before this, even Talents killed or injured. Accidents of war can happen, but it is not possible that invaders from Tolnida would deliberately destroy Halls and Talents."

That's exactly what Ker—what anyone—would have said. The Halls were the foundation of the Faraman Polity, the basis of the Law. For all their differences, Talents had been

working alongside the Battle Wings since the very beginning—
since Jurianol, the first Luqs, created the Polity—bringing
Law with them wherever they went.

The speaker scrubbed his face with his hands. "Listen to
me, old woman. Don't you understand? *It's not the Tolnidas.*"

Shock almost allowed a bark of laughter to escape Ker's
mouth. But the laughter didn't last. If anything, the man's disrespect showed how far out of patience he was.

"The invaders are foreigners, for the Mother's sake! They
call themselves Halians and they're not bound by the Law!
I'm telling you this for your own good, though why I should
bother when you wouldn't lift a finger to help any of us, I
don't know. They're coming *here*. They're not so very far behind us, maybe five days. Get your people away."

"Impossible. Halians!" Ker could almost see Matriarch
shake her head. "Halia is on the other side of the world. If you
are trying to get my help, young man, you are going about it
the wrong way."

"Listen to me—"

"How can I listen? Nothing you say makes sense. What
have the Halians to do with any of us? And if they are Halians,
how could they be so close behind you? They can be no great
force so far inland, not and keep a corridor open to their
ships."

That made good sense. Kerida found herself starting to
relax.

"I don't know how, Matriarch." Tel Cursar. The voice and
the height together were unmistakable. "I only know the numbers I've seen with my own eyes. I only know they have weapons I've never seen before—arrows that explode when they
find their marks, lights that follow those who are trying to
retreat."

Tel paused to draw in a breath. Exploding arrows? Lights
that moved of their own accord? That sounded like something
out of Feelers tales. Ker shook herself. He was still speaking.

"I only know that people I trust, people my Cohort Leader trusted, told us the Grand Hall in Farama was torched, and those in Caldil and Kender as well. This Hall will be next." His voice was strained with more than exhaustion.

For the longest time, Ker thought Matriarch wasn't going to respond. Finally, she said, "Will you submit to examination?"

Ker's throat loosened as relief flooded through her. There was the answer; the soldiers would be examined, and the truth found out. That's what Talents did, after all.

"That's your answer?" The bitterness in the first man's voice was so strong Ker could almost taste it herself. "We endanger ourselves to help you, and you won't even take our words?" He drew himself up straight. "No. I won't submit. And neither will any of my people."

Tel shifted and reached out to touch the other man's sleeve. "Fedna—"

"No!" Fedna, the officer who'd been speaking, shook him off. "I won't—I'm in command, and we can't . . ." In the pause, Ker could see him visibly taking control of himself. "After all we've already been through—a pox on them if they can't believe us."

"Examination is your choice, but you realize I will draw the inevitable conclusions if you do not submit." Matriarch held up her hand. "Even without examining you, I know you mean well, and that your offer comes from your genuine and sincere belief that what you tell us is true. But, with nothing more, I must trust my own judgment and my own knowledge of the world. I cannot toss aside centuries of law and tradition because you ask it of me."

"Then we're wasting our time here." Fedna turned and walked back down the central aisle toward the main doors without any kind of leave-taking. That alone told Kerida just how serious the man was.

Ker didn't know she'd moved, but she must have, that or made some sound, because as Tel Cursar turned to follow the

Eagles officer, he looked toward the corridor where she stood, looked right at her. His feet faltered, but he caught himself, and anyone seeing him would take it for the clumsiness of exhaustion. Before she even knew she was going to, Kerida made a fist and tapped herself on the left shoulder. "Come to me" was the signal, or had been when she'd been a soldier. "Meet me." She was sure he could figure out where.

As silently as she could, she raced back to the kitchen. The place was now deserted, though Cana had left a lamp burning on the worktable. Kerida went first to the outer door, the one that opened into the stable yard. She lifted off the short stave of wood that acted as a bar, though it was used more to make sure the wind didn't blow the door open than to keep intruders out. Then she took up the lamp and carried it into the storeroom.

Here Ker hesitated, lower lip between her teeth, scanning the shelves, the baskets and chests, and the net bags hanging from the ceiling. The inventory was so carefully kept that it would be known almost immediately if any food stores were missing. Her glance fell on an old, moth-eaten tapestry in the far corner of the room. Then she smiled. All the stores *were* carefully accounted for, even those already set aside, that balanced what had been given to the Carnelian Cohort twelve days ago. Those stores were already out of the inventory. She eyed the tapestry, committing its contours to memory, taking note of how the edges of the cloth lay on the floor. All she had to do was make sure this cover looked undisturbed, and Tel and his fellows could take away all they could carry. It might be days, or even weeks, before the theft was noticed.

She set the lamp down on a chest full of jars of spices and reached for the corner of the cloth covering the supplies. With her hands mere inches away, she froze, trembling at what she'd been about to do. If she touched it, if she touched *anything*, she'd be caught no matter how much time passed. Any Talent could Flash the tapestry and know who'd touched it and taken the food. She clasped her hands together, pressing them against her mouth. She couldn't believe how close she'd come to giving herself away. Her heart was thumping so fast Ker thought it might explode.

"Deep breaths," she told herself. "There's nothing to worry about." She picked up the lamp and crossed back into the main kitchen, glancing around again at the pots set out for the morning and the utensils hanging above the banked fires. She'd touched the lamp, but that was all right, she'd handled it tens of times. Likewise the bar for the door. She could say she thought she'd heard a noise, that she'd stepped outside and then forgotten to rebar the door behind her. What was the worst that could happen? She'd be punished for carelessness? She could handle that. Ker leaned against the table and folded her arms. What if they questioned her more closely? Examined her?

It wasn't very likely, she decided. She'd get Tel to leave plenty of trace, and she'd have to hope no one looked any further than that. If she *was* suspected? She let out her breath in a silent whistle, finally shrugging tight shoulders. It would give her a chance to really test the blocks Barid had been teaching her. She pressed her lips tight and nodded.

The light flickered, and Ker hurried to adjust the wick in the lamp. What was taking Tel Cursar so long? Had the army's hand signals changed so much, or hadn't he seen her after all? She was just wondering whether to put the light out or leave it burning to explain the missing oil, when she heard a noise outside. She stayed where she was, watching as the latch lifted and the door swung slowly open. The lanky form of Tel Cursar slipped inside. Before she could move, he had her wrist in his grasp. His fingers, as warm as she'd remembered, were long enough to wrap completely around.

"Still on kitchen duty?" A ghost of the grin she remembered so well flitted across his face. He seemed thinner, and there were stains on his purple tunic.

"Luckily for you. Are you alone?"

"There's not so many of us now that we can spare more than one." The matter-of-fact way he spoke sent a chill up Kerida's spine.

"It's just that I can't help you," she said, motioning him to follow her into the storeroom. "All this, back here, you can take, just leave enough to make it look like the pile is still intact. But you'll have to pack it up yourself. If I touch anything, they can Flash my trace on it."

Tel caught on right away, taking measurements with hands and fingers, and examining the drape of the cloth. "Have you any sacks I can use?"

Ker showed him where the hessian sacks were, and stood holding the lamp as he filled two of the larger ones with travel cakes. He hesitated over a couple of the pots of sausages, but finally shook his head, taking dried meat instead.

"The dried stuff will last us longer," he said aloud. "I don't know how to thank you for this. We had to leave most of our supplies behind. I wish there was something I could give you in exchange, but all I have is my sword."

"Keep that, whatever you do. I won't need it."

"You don't believe us, do you? No more than the old woman did."

Kerida looked away, a little surprised by the question, but more surprised by her own response. No, she realized she *didn't* believe them. If she did, she wouldn't be worrying about getting punished for helping them. She'd have other worries on her mind. "How can any of us believe you if you won't be examined? What you're telling us—it's like saying the rain falls up, or mice hunt cats."

"You'd have to see it to believe it?" She nodded. "Well, I've seen it, Kerida. I saw what was left of the Hall in Kender. The bodies . . ." His eyes focused on something far away.

"Tel, do you think—look, I'm military, and I know what I've heard soldiers say, what they'd like to do with the Halls and

the Talents, if only the Luqs could be persuaded to allow it."
Ker grimaced. "My father never let anyone talk that way,
never in his hearing anyway, but my sisters used to say talk
like that was fairly common. Do you think, knowing the Luqs
is captive, that some of those soldiers who think that way
about Talents might have . . ."

Tel Cursar's face went stony, but he lowered his eyes as he
shook his head. "If you feel that way, why are you helping us?"

"Do you have any news of the Emerald Cohort of Eagles?
My sister . . ." Ker's throat closed and her eyes stung.

Immediately, Tel's face softened, and he touched her shoulder with his right hand. "I'm sorry. I don't know. But, Kerida—"
He remembered her name, and this was a really stupid time
to notice that. "There was something we didn't tell Matriarch,
something we didn't get a chance to tell her. Some of the
troops we fought at the end—they were *our* troops. From the
Jade and Onyx Cohorts, the ones that were in the city."

She couldn't have heard that right. "Traitors?"

He shrugged. "What else?"

Pain made Ker realized she was biting down on her lower
lip. "I'll have to trust my sister's alive." She looked at the sacks
of food. "And that wherever she is, someone is helping her."

"You aren't like any Talent I've ever known."

He surprised a huff of laughter from her. "Not like any Talent anyone in here has ever known either."

It was when he went to lift the first pack that she saw the
look of pain cross his face.

"Are you injured?"

"It's nothing." He sounded as though he meant it, not like
he was showing off. "I strained my shoulder a bit; it will pass.
We're all close to the end of our strength. That's why we were
hoping for shelter here. Even a day would have helped."

Kerida nodded. People who didn't heal quickly weren't
likely to find a life in the military. They were likely to find a

death; she almost grinned at the old joke. "Do you know the Rija Vale at all?"

"Our Cohort Leader did. The rest of us, not so much. This is my first time this side of the Serpents Teeth."

Ker nodded. She thought she'd heard a trace of an accent in Tel's speech. If he'd never been south of the mountains that separated the Peninsula from the rest of the Polity, that would explain it.

"Keep to the main road then, and head north toward the pass. About halfway there, maybe a day's march, you'll come across a grove of old oaks, real old monsters, maybe twenty trees, all spread out. There may still be pigs feeding under them."

"Not for long."

Kerida grinned back at him. "Leave the road there and go west, straight up into the hills. West and a little south. You'll go through some rough pasture land, at first, but it turns rocky pretty quickly, and you'll start seeing pine trees. Keep a look out for a tall white pine, with a double crown. You'll find a cave close by. Should be empty this time of year."

"Should be?"

Ker shrugged. "They say it used to be a mine. Shepherds use it now, but only during the summer months. You should be safe there for a few days at least. There might even be bedding, firewood, other supplies, left for the spring."

Suddenly Tel snatched up her hand and pressed it to his throat, so her fingers spread across his collarbones, where she would touch him if she was Flashing him. She could feel the hard muscle under the thin linen of his shirt. Why was his heart beating so fast?

"Come with me. I swear what we said to Matriarch is true. You're all in terrible danger here. Can you Flash it? Come with me."

For a moment she saw herself doing it, she saw herself

grabbing her cloak and her spare boots and following this young officer into the night. But only for a moment.

"I can't Flash you," she said. "I don't—I'm not good with people." Except she could tell his injury was more serious than he'd said. "Besides." She drew her hand away from him. "They'd know. The first week I was here I ran away, and it took them about as long to find me as it takes to tell you about it. This is a Hall of Law. All they have to do is touch my bedding or something else of mine to know exactly where I've gone. You're better off without me."

"I'm not so sure, but we're better off than we were, at least." He patted the sacks of food. "I wish you could come. Keep your eyes open, please. Best of luck to you, Kerida Nast. I'll never forget your help."

"Best of luck to you, Tel Cursar." She helped him sling the sacks over his left shoulder, mindful of the unhealed arrow wound that was paining him in his right. "Mother watch over you."

And then he was gone.

Company Commander Fedna turned out to be wrong about one thing. It took the Halian invaders only three days to reach the Hall, not five. He was right about everything else.

Kerida's kitchen duty was over, but it was the time of year when every able-bodied person, even some of the most Senior, were recruited to help with the harvests of the last apples, cabbages, and chard, the digging up of carrots and turnips, and the heavy mulching of the parsnips and of the asparagus and artichoke beds against the coming frosts. They'd drawn lots, and Ker was considered lucky to be down in the root cellars under the kitchen, trapdoor swung open above her, lantern hanging on a hook over her head.

Ker hadn't thought herself very lucky to be back in the kitchen, though she quickly discovered that everything was changed now that she wasn't under order of discipline. Now others besides Cana smiled at her, talked to her. Even the Head Cook nodded at her in greeting, calling her by name, and Ker would have given oath that the man hadn't even been aware of her existence.

There was a part of her, Ker thought, that would still rather be out on the march with her pack on her back and a sword at her side, but it was a much smaller part than she would have expected. In the last few weeks she'd seen the possibility of an entirely new future, one well worth reaching for. She couldn't go back, and she was beginning to think she didn't really want to.

Tonight, after the evening meal, she was going to meet with Barid again, this time officially and in one of the teaching rooms. He was giving her extra tutoring, to accelerate her studies. Ker grinned. Matriarch had pressed her thin old woman's lips tightly when asked, but she couldn't actually forbid extra study. And maybe they'd have time, now that Barid had taught her how to keep the special block in place, to talk about the things Inquisitor Pa'narion had in mind for them.

"Wind's picked up," was the comment passed down by Devin—who turned out to have a very nice smile, now that he was allowed to use it on her. Kerida grinned back at him, picturing the reddened noses and chapped hands of those whose lot had set them outside. The next load of carrots darkened the opening above her, and she reached up to steady it as it was lowered down. As gently as she could, she dragged it to the far end of the cellar, where a round copper lamp hung from a hook on the square overhead beam.

Once she reached the shallow wooden trays set aside for them, Ker began laying the carrots out on damp sand, trying to achieve the most economical use of the space. She was placing the last layer, concentrating on getting the sand an even thickness, and didn't register the soft thump from behind her until she turned and found the trapdoor shut.

"Daughter curse you barren." Kerida climbed up the ladder, taking a firm grip on wooden rungs worn smooth by the touch of many hands. "Hey, Devin! What are you doing? Open up!" No response. "Come on, this isn't funny." And here she'd thought they were treating her better. She applied her shoulder to the trapdoor, but it didn't budge. Though it was thick and solid enough to walk on, she should have been able to lift it, unless something was weighing it down. "Devin!" she called again, then stopped, straining her ears. She could just make out a murmur of sound, a sense of movement, of thudding weight. She glanced at the rafters above her. Nothing. No light, no dust falling through the well-fitted planks. These cellars were cut into the same rock as the foundations of the main building, the kitchen floors partly stone, partly wood, thick and strong either way. She was lucky to hear anything at all.

A quick search through the cellar confirmed there was nothing she could use as a lever. Finally, frustration more than any hope of a different outcome made Ker push against the door once more. This time, it gave a little. Encouraged, she climbed higher on the ladder, for a better angle, and heaved. The door lifted free of the opening and with it resting heavy on her shoulders, Ker climbed higher still, managing finally to push it over onto the floor.

"Devin? Cana?" Ker heaved herself out of the cellar and got to her feet. The kitchen was empty. No one was waiting to laugh at her. No one was waiting at all. She stepped away from the trapdoor and looked around. Nothing in the kitchen looked different. There, near the opening in the floor, was the next basket of carrots, waiting for someone to pass it down to her. But where was everyone? And why had they shut the trap?

She headed for the door that led to the service corridor, but stopped halfway, looking down at a mark on the flagstones. Kerida knew these stones. She'd scrubbed them at least once a day for the last three weeks, and there had never been any mark like this on them. She squatted down, and reached out. A part of her mind must have known what the stain was, because when she brought her finger to her nose and smelled blood, she wasn't shocked. Someone had cut themselves, that was all. This was a kitchen, such things happened all the time.

But a knife cut wouldn't have emptied the kitchen of its staff. She'd seen blood from knife cuts, how it dripped, or fell, or got wiped off on the nearest apron. This was too much blood for a knife cut. And it was smeared, as though whatever had bled had been dragged. She noted the direction of the dragging and flipped the trapdoor closed. Whatever had bled had been resting on the door. That was why she hadn't been able to open it.

Now Ker heard muffled sounds and a scream, rising to painful pitch, suddenly cut off. She was halfway along the passage leading to the great room before she was aware she'd moved. Something, however, made her slow as she approached the end of the passage, and creep to the opening instead of rushing out. The sounds were clearer now, sounds Ker hadn't heard in almost two years. Blows, weapons striking wood, striking flesh. Crying, sobs, and more screaming. The smell of blood and of viscera. She edged closer to the opening, almost to the spot where she had been standing a few nights before, watching Tel Cursar and the other soldiers.

Horses. It was there her mind stuck, on the extraordinary sight of men on horseback in the great room. Men with swords, axes, and even some spears, leaf-bladed and bright in the glow of the fires. Some part of her mind wondered why the soldiers were wearing the wrong uniforms, until she shook herself, realizing with a sick clenching of her stomach that the people on horseback were Halians.

Tables and benches had been broken and tossed aside. Walls, windows, furnishings, flickered in the light of a fire burning fiercely on the dais, just where Matriarch's chair should be. The Mother and the Daughter had been pushed from their shrine, and lay smashed on the floor, though the Son was still intact. A man in a quilted vest pulled on over what looked like a red Polity tunic was tossing pieces of statue into the flames, where the pottery was starting to glow hot. The smoke made her eyes water, and, what with the shadows thrown by the fires and the moving horses, it took a moment for Kerida to see Devin and Cana almost directly across the great room from where she stood. The girl's face was bruised and smudged, and she was holding her left wrist in her right hand, as if it were injured. A dark stain down the front of Cana's tunic told Kerida where at least some of the blood on the kitchen floor had likely come from.

There were others against the wall, all of them people she knew, people she'd been eating with, studying with. There to the left was Serinam, one of her Tutors, trying to calm the youngsters around him. Everyone Ker knew was lined up against the far wall, held there by the men on horses, men in motley outfits made up of quilted clothing along with bits and pieces of Polity uniforms. They were being brought forward to the cleared space in the center of the room one by one, and made to kneel, before an ax swung.

Kerida's knees shook under her as she leaned against the wall for support. It was true. What Tel and the other soldiers had tried to tell them. All true. The invaders were killing Talents.

Standing next to the invader with the ax was the only other person on foot. This was a taller, darker man, with a tattoo on his face. The others were mostly bareheaded or wearing light leather helms, but this one wore a kind of chain mail hood, close-fitted, that left only his face bare. When he turned, his black cloak swung open, revealing a blue tunic with a red emblem Ker couldn't make out. This taller man was directing the others, that much was clear. Especially the axman. Ker saw the tall man point to the people huddling against the wall. As he pointed, the ones on horseback would herd someone forward.

The next one pointed out was Cana. Cana with the soft smile and friendly whisper. Cana kneeling under the ax. Kerida wanted to call out, tell them the girl wasn't even a Talent. Then the ax fell, and Kerida was running back down the corridor to the kitchen, covering her mouth with her hands, to keep her own scream in.

Go back, said a voice in her heart. *Go back, you coward, and help your friends. Don't be stupid,* said the other colder, harder voice in her head. *You can't save them.* But she could save herself. She could carry the word. She was a Talent. Unlike the soldiers, she would be believed.

Once in the kitchen, she grabbed up a pack and began to thrust food into it. The slab of bacon waiting to be sliced for luncheon. The part of the wheel of cheese that always sat on the sideboard. She dashed into the storeroom and grabbed up travel cakes, shoving them as quickly as she could into the pack, tears sparking her eyes. Was it only three nights ago that Tel Cursar was doing this? A waterskin. A carving knife almost the length of a short sword—even now she was afraid to touch the Head Cook's knives. A cloak someone had left tossed over a stool. The sight of the pepper grinder sent her back into the storeroom, where she flipped up the lid of the spice chest and, acting as quickly as she could, thrust a half dozen packets of dried herbs into the pack.

Back in the larger room she stood biting her lip, taking time to look around her. The trapdoor was closed. She hadn't moved anything else of consequence. If the enemy came back to the kitchen, they'd find it exactly as they'd left it.

Afterward, odd snippets of things came back to her when she thought about the next few minutes. How the wind blew the corner of the borrowed cloak into her face as she ran across the stable yard. How her boots slipped on the cobbles—

and how grateful she was to Barid for suggesting she put boots on that morning.

Barid. She hadn't seen him back in the great room. Was it possible he'd escaped? Or was he already dead? She pushed that thought away. Too much time spent thinking like that, and she'd be dead herself.

Once out in the yard, dodging from outbuilding to outbuilding, Kerida headed for the stables. The regular mounts were still in the paddock, but there was no chance she could catch one of the loose horses. With the smell of blood and burning in their nostrils, they were already nervous, trotting from side to side, corner to corner. Besides, those were the regular mounts and work horses. Ker wanted something with more speed, and those horses she'd find stabled.

Inside, it was quieter, the animals less disturbed. A bay horse had come in the day before, ridden by the factor of a nearby holding. He'd eaten with the Senior Staff last night, and Ker wondered where he was now, and whether he was one of those in the great room. The bay was in the third stall down, but Ker stopped before she got that far.

Most of the stalls on this side of the stable buildings were boxes, closed off with doors that actually shut, but the door to the bay's stall was standing open, held open, in fact, by the weight of a battle-ax. It seemed that she wasn't the only one who recognized a good horse when she saw one. Ker had frozen when she'd seen the open door, now she drew her dagger and crept forward, mouth dry, careful to place her feet quietly, and to keep her balance. Afterward, she shivered, thinking over what she had done, how risky it was, how she should have just turned around and left. Taken her chances on foot. But at the time, things moved so quickly she didn't even stop to think about how long it had been since she'd trained to do this.

The man inside the stall was standing with his back to her, smoothing his hands over the bay's head and neck, crooning to it. He was about her height, maybe just a little taller, and wearing the same rounded leather helm she'd seen on the others in the great room. Thinking of that made what she had to do easier. His raised arms had lifted the edge of the leather cuirass he was wearing, leaving a gap where his skin showed. Which made it easier still.

That was where Kerida slipped her dagger. It slid in like a warm knife into butter, but the man did not cry out. As his arms came down, Ker reached up with her other hand, taking hold of his chin, and dragged him backward. She pulled the dagger out of his kidney and sliced it across the front of his throat.

The bay horse didn't take kindly to being sprayed with blood, but once Ker had brought it out to the saddling area, the familiar movements, and the soothing noises that came automatically out of her throat, settled it enough that she could finish saddling. She had nicked her own finger, and smeared blood on everything she touched, but she hadn't time to deal with that. As she was about to mount, she had another thought and returned to the body. The rounded helm had fallen free of the dead man's head, showing close-cropped blond hair turning to gray. She picked it up from where it had rolled into a corner, cramming it onto her own head. The ax she took as well, finding a loop on the saddle that would do to hold it for now.

She mounted easily, old habits from childhood coming back, so long as she didn't think too much about them. If only she could stop shivering. The wind wasn't *that* cold, was it?

Once outside, she opened the paddock gates and rode in. The loose horses clustered around her, finding some comfort in the familiarity of a horse with a rider. She urged them toward the open gate, and it didn't take long for them to see this as their chance to escape the bad smells that were disturbing them. Ker leaned as low as she could over the bay's neck, riding out into the fields west of the stables, using the other horses as cover. There were no fences on this side of the property, only hedgerows and fields, empty now of the grain that was meant to feed them all, humans and beasts alike, over the winter. If she could get to the other side before anyone noticed her—if she could get to the road—she would head for the safe place she'd told Tel Cursar about.

She'd head for the cave.

KERIDA crouched down on her heels, peering up at the dark tops of the trees silhouetted against the brighter night sky. Still no sign of the double-crowned pine. The previous afternoon she'd ridden the bay horse all the way to the oak grove she'd told Tel Cursar about. She'd gone up into the trees straight from the horse's back before letting it go, walking along the branches of the great mother oaks, jumping from tree to tree, and not coming down until she was at least thirty spans away. With luck, anyone tracking her would follow the bay horse, calmly proceeding down the road, going home to its own stable.

Ker had thought about keeping the horse, but once she was well away from the Hall, the beast was more useful as a decoy. He'd be easier to track than a person on foot, and she couldn't fit him into the cave anyway. Without the horse, however, Ker had to stop more frequently to rest; she judged it to be close to sunrise now, which meant she'd gone a whole day without sleep. She told herself she couldn't sleep until she was safe, but she wondered if she wasn't afraid to—afraid of who and what she might see if she closed her eyes for too long.

The moon was waning, but the sky was clear and there was still more than enough light to make walking easy. She'd bound up her sliced finger with a few strips torn from the bottom of her shirt. Though the wound was not serious, it was sore enough to distract her. She was stopping every ten paces to check the skyline for the silhouette of the pine tree, and finding it harder each time to keep going. All those good meals and soft beds at the Hall hadn't been offset by the small amount of exercise she'd done in secret, and the discovery of her flabby condition frightened her more than a little. If she didn't reach the old cave soon, she'd have to find some other place for a long rest, even if she didn't sleep.

The sky was lightening with the approach of the sun when Kerida finally saw the pine's distinctive silhouette and took what felt like her first easy breath since swinging back the trapdoor in the Hall kitchen. Just past the forked tree the footing became much rockier and rougher, no longer the carpet of dried grasses and old needles there'd been under the pines. In spring and summer, scrub trees, weeds, and wildflowers grew rampant around the entrance. Even dead and drying in the winter air, the growth helped to disguise the presence of the cave opening so much that Ker wasn't sure she could have found it if she hadn't known it was there.

As it was, she had to feel her way to the darker patch that was the actual entrance, stubbing her toes and bruising her sore finger against rocks hidden in the frost-killed growth. One minute she was feeling her way along the rock, and the next her hands met nothing but air and she fell forward. She didn't bother to stand up, but crawled into the opening on her hands and knees, feeling the twitches of muscle exhaustion in her legs. Once inside, she sat back on her heels, rubbing at her face, the relief almost too much to bear. Finally, she could sit down and rest. Maybe eat something, even make a fire, if she could find the hearthstones and the kindling the shepherds were sure to have left, if Tel and the others hadn't used it all.

She was getting to her feet again when something heavy slammed against her. Old training automatically took over, and she wriggled sideways, raising her arms and turning away from the hands that were reaching for her throat. The same half-forgotten training brought her knees up as she was pushed down, and she managed to wedge one in against her assailant as she clawed at his face, her fingers brushing against skin that felt unnaturally hot.

"Hah, thought you'd kill me, did you? I could hear you coming a mile off, clumsy fool."

That voice again. Ker stopped clawing and concentrated on keeping the hands away. "Tel? Tel Cursar? It's me, it's Kerida Nast. Hey!" She braced herself and shoved as hard as she could with her knee, but his arms were so long, it hardly made any difference to his reach. "Tel, you idiot! IT'S KERIDA!"

"Kerida?" The hands with their long steely fingers stopped trying to choke her and clutched at her instead, dragging her upright. "Kerida, is it you?" And then he was crushing her in a hug that shoved her face against the hard planes of his chest. He thrust her away almost as roughly, turning her to face the dawn light that ghosted its way into the mine entrance.

"Is it really you? You're not a fever vision?" There was a shakiness to his voice that told her all she needed to know. That and the heat she'd felt in his skin.

"It's really me," she said. "Not your fever. What happened? Where are the others?" She led him deeper into the cave, away from the entrance. She didn't think there was anyone out there, but then she hadn't thought there'd be anyone *in* here either. "Do you have any light?"

He did. The cave had originally been a long straight tunnel shape, but the shepherds who used it had filled in a portion of it with rock, enough to give themselves a windbreak, and to cover the light of a fire from the outside. Once around this, Ker could see embers glowing in the ring of hearthstones, and the pile of blankets Tel had been sleeping on.

She saw a candle perched on a convenient shelf of rock and managed to get it lit, even though Tel was still holding on to her, touching her face from time to time as if he couldn't believe she was real.

"Where are the others?" she asked again.

"Had to go on without me." The words were barely out of his mouth before Tel's legs failed him and he sat down, dragging Kerida down with him. For a minute, she thought he'd fainted, but he was still gripping her sleeves fiercely, as if afraid that if he let her go she would disappear. She managed to shift him around so that at least they both had room to sit, and not too close to the fire.

"They left you behind?" Did she hear a bleakness in her own voice? Tel hadn't been the only person left behind. She shivered, and again pushed away images of the Hall's great room.

"Had to," he repeated. He swallowed, grimacing. "Wound got worse. Slow them down. Not my Wing, anyway," he added. They were Eagles, he meant, while he was a Bear.

Ker opened her mouth, and closed it again. Nothing she could say to that.

Instead she looked around, taking in what she could of the place in the meager light from the candle. The space was about four paces across, perhaps twice that in length. The shepherds had made good use of small rock ledges as spots to set supplies and utensils. There was indeed firewood ready to hand, either left behind by the shepherds, or by Tel's friends when they'd abandoned him. There were also a couple of packs of travel cakes, and a waterskin, now half empty. It must have hurt the others to leave behind food and water, but they'd done it.

What would have happened if she hadn't come along was something Ker tried not to think about. The others might have been kinder to cut Tel's throat than to leave him with a festering wound, waterskin or no waterskin. A shiver ran up her spine like mice on a curtain as she picked up the skin. Cutting throats was something else she didn't want to think about just yet. She handed the water to Tel. "When did you last drink something?"

"Rationing," was his answer. Not unexpected, but Kerida rolled her eyes.

"Well, drink something now, there's plenty of water around here. Hey! Slowly, don't choke on it."

When she saw that he was obeying her, she turned her attention to the fire, building it up until she had a fair blaze going. She found Tel gazing at her with fierce concentration, his eyes shinier than the firelight alone would account for. She could see signs of pain and fever on his face, and he seemed thinner even than he had been only a few days before.

"Have you been eating at all?"

Licking his lips, Tel nodded. "Tried to."

"You were keeping the food down?" He nodded again. That was all to the good. At least the bad wound hadn't poisoned his stomach. Yet.

"Come sit here, between the fire and the candle. Let me have a look at that wound." She managed to pull off tunic, under tunic, and shirt, although with much clenching of teeth and hissing from Tel and much apologizing and eye-rolling from her. The wrapping around his right shoulder had been neat and tidy once, but Kerida wrinkled her nose at it now, and not just because of the smell. Their struggle by the entrance had dislodged it, and that looked to be a good thing.

"Did they leave you any medicines?" she said. "The bandage is loose *and* dirty, so at the very least the wound has to be cleaned again."

"It was boiled when it went on."

"And how many days ago was that?" Getting the bandage off was going to be trickier even than the shirt and tunics. Disturbed as it was, it had stuck in places where the wound had bled and the blood dried. On the other hand, if the wound had started to go bad—and from the faint smell she thought it might have—there was no real need to be gentle. She made a face.

"Bite on this," she told him, handing him a wadded-up corner of his own shirt. When she was sure he had a good wad of cloth between his teeth, she took a firm grip on the bandage and yanked it off as quickly and as cleanly as she could.

But not so quickly that Tel didn't scream into the cloth and grab her wrist in a grip that made her fingers numb.

"Let go of me," she said. She wanted to slap him. Her eyes felt gritty with fatigue, her own cut finger throbbed, and dealing with Tel's wound was draining the last reserves of her strength. She probably should have waited—for more daylight if for nothing else, but she couldn't leave the wound undressed at this point.

"Well, that's not so bad," she said once the filthy dressing was cleared away. "The wound's definitely inflamed . . . edges red . . . and the skin hasn't started knitting—"

"*That's* 'not so bad'?"

"As I was about to say, it's a nice clean slice, straight and even along the line of the muscle, not a puncture, and there's not as much discharge as there might have been. If someone had only cleaned the wound properly in the first place, and perhaps stitched it up, you'd be well on the way to mending." Ker chewed on her lower lip. As it was, it would all depend on the herbs she had in her pack. "The arrow must have just grazed you."

Tel licked his lips. "Lucky it wasn't an ax."

Ker winced, glancing at the weapon lying next to her pack. "Here. Lie down on your side. That's it, back to the fire." The shepherds had left two cooking pots, one larger than the other, along with a collection of mismatched cups and two wooden spoons, carved by someone who was no expert. Ker filled the smaller of the two pots with water from Tel's bag and set it on the fire to boil while she looked over his shirt for a good edge to cut fresh bandages from. She wrinkled her nose. The shirt didn't smell any too clean.

"Do you have any cleaner piece of clothing than this?"

The sound Tel made wasn't in the least helpful, and Kerida sighed. There was no point in looking into Tel's pack for any more dressings. Every soldier carried a single set of bandages; the theory was that if you needed more, your wound was too serious for you to be helped in the field. Tel's bandages would have been the ones she'd pulled off his wound. Ker sighed again, and hauled her own tunic and under tunic off over her head. *Her* shirt had at least been clean the day before. If she needed more dressings, she would have to cut strips off Tel's shirt and boil them. The old ones she pushed into the fire.

Once the water was boiling, Ker added two careful pinches of dried yarrow out of one of the packets she'd brought with her. She waited until the sharply aromatic steam rose up before pulling the pot off the fire. First, she scooped up a small amount in one of the cups and set it aside for Tel to drink later. Then she folded up one of the pieces of cloth she'd cut from her shirt, dipped it into the cooling liquid, and began cleaning Tel's wound, dabbing at the mess gently but firmly. Tel hissed again, and tried to shift away from her, and this time she did slap him, gripping him firmly with her free hand above the wound, where his neck met his shoulder.

"Hold still. Do you *want* to die from this?"

He murmured something from which Ker could only make out the word "bossy." "This is nothing," she said, smiling. "You're lucky it's not my sister Tonia doing this." Tonia was Ker's oldest sister, and had been their father's Laxtor, his second-in-command, before she herself became Faro of Panthers.

Once the wound was cleaned to her satisfaction, Ker pressed the edges together as closely as she could, sprinkled some of the dried yarrow directly on it, and wrapped the shoulder up again with clean bandages. Fresh leaves would have been better, or a salve made from the dried herb, but this was the best she could do under the circumstances. It was better than Tel and his fellows had been able to manage on their own.

"Didn't any of you get medic's training?" Never mind her sister Tonia. In Ester's Cohort, everyone who expected to advance had to receive all the basics of training, and it was lucky for Tel that she had. *And lucky I thought to bring medicines with me.*

"Next time I'm on the run from an invading army, I'll make sure to run with someone who did well at his studies."

Ker ignored him, picking up his shirt again. It would do for a sling, if nothing else. "Here, lean forward. I'm going to bind your arm."

"What? Come on. It's not that bad."

"It *is* that bad." He might protest, Ker thought, but Tel was leaning forward all the same. She tucked his forearm into the folded shirt, wrapping the sleeves around his torso. "I've nothing to stitch the wound with," she added as she tied the sleeves off. "You've got to move it as little as possible."

"Good thing I can fight left-handed."

"You sound better already." Ker helped Tel to sit up, laid his military cloak over his shoulders, and one of the blankets across his legs. Fever or no, it was too cold for him to be sitting there without a shirt, even with the fire.

"I feel better."

"Here, drink this. It should make you feel better still." He took the cup of yarrow tea from her with his left hand. She only had to steady it a bit. "I'll look around for wild yarrow tomorrow, or fever bark if that's the best I can find."

"What now?"

Ker's stomach chose that moment to growl. "I don't know what I want more, to eat or to sleep. Sleep, I guess."

"Both of us?"

He was right. Someone should keep watch. But if she didn't sleep soon, she was in danger of falling face-first into the fire. She was tired enough to take a chance that she might have unpleasant dreams. "If you can stay awake, you can take the first watch. I've been on my feet since dawn yesterday, and I'm all in."

There was only the one set of blankets, but Ker was beyond caring. She rolled herself in her own cloak, and pulled the remaining blanket almost completely over her head. For a moment she wondered what Tel Cursar had done about keeping watch when he was alone. For another moment she thought that sleep wouldn't come after all, that she'd reached that strange level of exhaustion where she was so tired she couldn't drop off, but just as she was formulating the thought, the world drifted away.

The afternoon was well advanced when Kerida woke up to the smell of roasting meat. She squeezed her eyes shut, almost afraid to open them. But she'd slept like a stone, with no dreams. Maybe she would be all right after all. She rolled over, every muscle protesting, and blinked at the fire. Or rather, at what was on the skewer suspended above the fire.

"You went hunting?" She didn't exactly call him an idiot, but it was all there in her tone. If this was how he rested, it was no wonder his wound had become infected.

"Didn't have to. We set snares when we first got here, and when I went out to check them, I found this rabbit." He grinned at her. "And I was careful to use only my left hand."

"Uh-huh." Ker would have been happier about it if the glint of fever wasn't still in his eye. She rolled upright, stretching as much as her sore muscles and the confined space would let her, and rubbed at her face. She focused on the rabbit, her mouth watering. "Not dead *too* long, I hope."

"What do you take me for?"

"I take you for somebody who doesn't know how to keep his wound clean, and who, instead of resting to make sure his fever doesn't get worse, pretends he managed to gut and skin a rabbit with only his left hand."

Tel's face hardened, but almost immediately, he nodded. "Fair enough," he said. "I admit I haven't made much of a showing. But roasting rabbits is a skill I definitely do have. Here." He had cut a travel cake in walnut-sized pieces, and now handed her two of them. "Something to take the edge off, if you haven't eaten since yesterday."

Everyone called it travel cake, but the fact was that even people who never journeyed farther than the nearest market kept some on hand, especially large groups like the military or the Halls. Kerida had only the vaguest idea how it was prepared. Made properly, however, travel cakes could be kept for years before they would go bad, and a person could live on them safely, even when they could get no fresh food of any kind.

Too bad she'd never gotten to where she liked the taste.

She washed the first chunk of cake down with several swallows of water before putting cake and waterskin aside. "Let's have a look at your shoulder while we're waiting for that rabbit."

With only his left arm through the sleeve hole, Tel's tunic pulled off easily. Once she'd untied the shirt-sling, Ker was happy to see the wound had lost its fiery redness, and felt much cooler to the back of her hand. She wiped it clean again with the yarrow water she had saved from the morning, re-wrapped the dressing, and restored Tel's arm to its sling.

"How do you feel?" She laid the inside of her forearm against his forehead. She could vaguely remember her mother doing this to her as a child. Or perhaps it had been her brother.

"Much better, I'm glad to say."

"You still feel warm to me, but not as hot as you did when I got here."

"Which reminds me, just what is it that brought you here? Or do I need to ask?"

Kerida had no way to know what her face told him, but it clearly told him something.

"Never mind," he was quick to say. "There's only one thing that would have a Talent on the run for a whole day." He prodded the rabbit with the point of his knife, clearly needing to look away. He was trying to keep his tone level, but he wasn't doing all that well. "Did many escape?"

Kerida shook her head, trying to dislodge the images of what she'd seen in the great room. "No one." She swallowed, her mouth suddenly dry and her throat tight. She picked up the waterskin, but couldn't make herself drink from it. "No one else, that I know of." Once more, the enormity of what had happened swelled up out of the darkness to overwhelm her. Once more, Ker pushed it back.

"Hey." Tel's hand was on her arm; she blinked at it before looking up into his face. His pale gray eyes were still too bright, but there was a warmth in them that reminded her of the first time she'd seen him in the kitchen at the Hall. "Don't be too hard on yourself," he said. "You did what you needed to do."

Her glance fell on the ax she'd left leaning against the far wall. But he didn't know about that. "I didn't go back, I didn't help anyone. I didn't even check to see if there was anyone to help." Kerida shut her mouth tight, clenching her teeth together, before the rising note of hysteria she'd heard in her voice could get any worse.

"You did what you needed to do," Tel repeated. "Just like those Eagles did, leaving me behind. Getting killed along with everyone else wouldn't have helped anyone." He gave her arm a little shake. "It wouldn't have helped me, that's certain."

All of which was true. None of which made her feel any better. She made her lips smile. "Is the rabbit burning?"

The rabbit was fine, and if Kerida had to force herself to

finish her share, at least it was an improvement over travel cakes. Neither one of them had much appetite, but both understood the necessity of eating. Once they'd finished, and Kerida had made Tel drink another cup of yarrow tea, she got him to lie down, spreading both blankets and his cloak over him.

"You'll be cold," he said, shifting to find the position where his shoulder would hurt the least.

"I've got my cloak. And I'm closer to the fire."

"Sing out if you need me."

"Of course," she lied. Pulling the hood up on the cloak, she went out of the mine entirely, needing to feel the fresh wind on her face, trying to gauge whether it was getting colder. Snow hadn't fallen yet, but from the smell of the air, it wasn't far off. Eventually, she went back inside, settling in a spot where she had a good view through the entrance. She set Tel's sword down on her right, the ax she'd taken from the Halian on her left, hoping not to have to use either. It had been a long time.

I can't always be lucky enough to cut someone's throat from behind while he doesn't even know I'm there. She stroked the handle of the ax with her thumb. She done exactly what she'd once trained very hard to do. Kill the enemy. It was never easy, and should never be done lightly, but it was necessary. The Faraman Polity was still expanding, and even on the Peninsula there was still order to be kept. The first time, though. The first time was hard. She sighed, wishing she could use the flames in front of her to meditate, to empty her mind of the thoughts that whirled there, and keep it empty.

"Talk to me." Tel's voice startled her, its warmth pulling her back from her bleak thoughts.

She sat up straighter, easing her shoulders and lower back. "You should be resting."

"I *am* resting. It's just that I can't sleep."

Ker cut off a sour laugh. "Aren't we a pair. I don't think I'll be able to sleep either."

"Well, you did sleep most of the day." There was an edge of irritation in his voice that Ker put down to the fever.

"I was exhausted. Now I'm not."

"And you're still brooding about leaving your mates behind you. I've already said you shouldn't feel badly about that."

Ker shook her head. "Easier said than done. But it's not just that. I don't want to see . . ." Why shouldn't she just say it? Every soldier had a first time when it came to killing. If he was going to laugh at her doubt and queasiness, she'd better get it over with. Not that she cared what he thought.

"I'm afraid of what I'll see if I try to sleep. The images." She swallowed, focusing her eyes on the fire. The way the wet blood on the ax caught the flicker of the flames as the blade fell onto Cana's neck. "The way the horse shied when the spray of blood hit him in the face," she said aloud.

"Someone killed a horse?" Tel sounded interested.

"No, I killed a man to get a horse. That's how I got these." She indicated the helm and the ax. "I killed him while I was getting away."

Fever still flushed Tel's face. But not laughter. "Your first?" he said, nodding back at her when she nodded. "So. Somewhere every soldier has been. You already know the truth of this. You had no choice. If you'd stayed to help any of your friends, you'd have been killed, too. Running was the smart thing, the right thing. Tell me, which was harder? The killing or the running?"

"Running." Ker blinked. She'd answered without thinking, and she'd surprised herself.

"So you've learned a lesson that every soldier learns sooner or later. Running is the hardest thing you'll ever have to do." He nodded his head at the ax. "Killing someone's far easier."

Kerida felt a tightness deep inside her suddenly loosen. "It didn't bother me when I did it. Like you said, it was something I had to do. But now—when I shut my eyes, I keep thinking I see his face, accusing me, glaring at me from under this helm." She tapped it. "Except I never saw the man's face. Never turned him over to look at it."

"That will pass, trust me." He took a deep breath, and his tone changed. "You must have gone in for training while you were still in nappies, to have had any at all before your Talent came."

Kerida was never sure what prompted her to tell him the truth. Perhaps it was the loss of everything she'd known for the last two years. Perhaps it was the shock of their world, of which the Halls of Law were the backbone, falling to pieces around them. Perhaps it was because he understood how she felt.

"I hid my Talent," she said. "The Halls of Law didn't find out about me until a couple of years ago."

Tel shifted up onto an elbow. "You *hid* it? How? Why? That's supposed to be impossible."

"Remember how you guessed that my sister was Ester Nast? Well, if you thought about it a little more, you'd realize that means my other sister is Tonia Nast, Faro of Panthers, and my father is Elidon Nast, who was Faro before her, like my grandmother Fermina Nast before him. Not to mention some of my aunts and uncles and cousins, scattered through the Wings." Ker scrubbed at her face with her hands. "I grew up in a military household. We're one of the old Shield families. We've born arms for the Polity for generations. Since before there was a Polity, if you listen to my grandmother. I never expected anything else, I never wanted anything else."

"But when your Talent came?"

"When I got caught, I told everyone that it had only just come. It hadn't." Ker blinked. Apparently, once she'd decided to tell the truth, she was going to tell all of it. "Exactly the opposite, in fact. My Talent came early. Much earlier than it's supposed to."

Tel shook his head. "Why didn't they find it when you were examined?"

Ker pulled the cloak a little closer around her. Whose was it? And why hadn't she thought about that until now? She took a deep breath and let it out slowly. Tel Cursar was still looking at her, apparently willing to wait, his pale eyes fixed on hers, until she told him.

"I was alone when it happened the first time." She hesitated again, feeling the warm mud, and the cold smoothness of the old bone under her fingertips. "I found the bones of a murdered man. The Talent High Inquisitor said it was such a shock," she finally managed to say, "so horrible, what I Flashed, that I somehow blocked it all away: the images, the Talent itself, everything."

"But how could it have been a shock? Didn't you get the lecture?"

Ker raised her eyebrows at him. "How old were you when you first got the lecture?"

He shrugged, wincing as his wounded shoulder moved. "I don't know. Nine? Ten? Oh!" The light dawned. "You were *younger*, you said. Your Talent came so early you hadn't heard the lecture."

"I hadn't heard it. And you know no one talks about it in front of you, until you've had it."

He was nodding. "Like it's too frightening for children to know about, until they have to." He drew his brows together. "But when you *did* get the lecture, you must have realized then what had happened to you?"

"By then I thought I'd imagined it. I convinced myself that it was a dream or something." *And I was hoping it was*, she said to herself. Aloud she added, "I think that's why no one ever found it when I was examined."

"But it *did* happen again. And you hid it."

His fever must be getting better, Ker thought, for his thinking to be so clear. "It did, and I did," she admitted. "It only flared up once in a while, so I thought I could go on hiding it."

"How did you slip up?"

"That's just it. It takes training to use it, to make it come and make it go. Otherwise, we'd be Flashing everything, all the time, we couldn't touch anything or anyone." She shuddered, remembering again the shock of that first time when the Talent had hit her like a blow from a war club. "Looking back on it, I suppose it was inevitable that one day I'd Flash when there were other people around." She sat up straighter, hands on her knees. "So that was that. The end of my military career."

"But the start of another one."

Ker shot him a look. Sure, easy for him to say. Everyone respected Talents, but nobody *liked* them. "Yes, well. It's only just recently I've started to look at it that way," she said finally. *Now that it's too late*, she realized with a sinking to her stomach.

"And your family being military couldn't have made things any easier." Tel was lying once more on his back, his uninjured arm tucked under his head. "Did you ever hear from them?"

Ker moved her head slowly to the left, to the right, and back again.

He rolled over to face her again. "What did you think about that?"

She looked away, shrugging. "What was I going to think? 'Talents do not live in the world.' Everyone knows it." But she'd expected something, even if just her childhood books. But they'd sent nothing, not even a farewell note. Ker rubbed at a spot of dirt on her breeches.

Tel grunted his understanding, and she looked at him sideways. He was breathing faster than he should be, and his color was up again. He needed to calm down.

"You'd better go to sleep," she said.

Tel looked into the fire for a long moment before he nodded and settled back again. Kerida thought he'd fallen asleep at last when he spoke again.

"How far along in your training are you?"

"Why?"

"I was wondering if you could Flash that ax you have, or the helm."

Startled, Ker looked down at the ax as if seeing it for the first time. "I hadn't thought of that," she said. Though now that she *was* thinking of it, Ker knew perfectly well why. She'd killed the man who used this ax. She didn't want to learn that he had a family, people he loved and who loved him, back wherever Halia really was.

And she didn't want to know what the ax had been used for before she'd taken it.

"Do you think you could? We might get useful information."

It would be very easy to say no. To say that her Talent wasn't trained enough. The fact was that remnants of her original block still prevented her from Flashing much from people, though she and her Tutors had been working on that. But she could Flash objects better than most. And Tel was right; they might very well be able to get something useful from the ax and helm.

Suddenly the fire seemed very small, and the dark very large.

"Let's wait until the morning," she said finally. "It's easier when I'm rested. Now get to sleep. It'll be your watch soon."

"Yes, Mother. Kerida?"

"*What?*"

"What happened to the horse?"

WHEN Kerida woke up the next morning, the sun was clear of the horizon, and the air was crisp with frost. Tel Cursar had been out already. That was clear from the amount of wood available for the fire. He was squatting now on his heels, the fingers of his free hand wrapped completely around one of the small clay cups. Ker could smell the distinctive aroma of kaff.

"Can't you sit still for more than two minutes?" She sat up, rubbing the sleep out of her eyes and wincing at her still sore finger.

"I only went out for wood—which I tucked into my sling, so don't give me that look. I think I found some fever bark, but maybe you should see it for yourself." He studied the liquid in his cup as if it carried a message. "Time I should be moving on, anyway." There was a sudden bleakness in his tone that Ker hadn't heard before. What dark thoughts had Tel been thinking while he gathered wood?

She threw off her blankets and rolled slowly to her feet.

Her muscles still felt every single one of the steps she'd taken to get here. "If you don't give yourself a chance, your fever will get worse, and then where will you be? Alone with no shelter and no medicine."

"Alone? Aren't you coming with me?"

The plain question silenced her, and sat her down on her heels. She *had* to carry the word. Matriarch hadn't believed what the soldiers had told her—and Ker silently cursed the officer who'd refused to let the old woman Flash him, even though part of her understood why. But, as Matriarch had said, Halls had been destroyed before, Talents killed by accident. Now that was all changed. Ker herself had been a witness to what had happened at Questin Hall. She would be believed.

There were things about the Halls she didn't like, ideas she didn't believe in. But there had been good people. Cana. Barid. Devin. Even Matriarch, in her way. She'd had a future there, even if it hadn't been the one she'd expected. And whatever else might be wrong with the Halls of Law, Ker thought, they didn't go around slaughtering people.

She realized she hadn't thought beyond getting away, but now that she had, where *was* she going?

"Temlin Hall's just on the other side of the Serpents Teeth," she said finally. "I've got to let them know what happened to us. On foot, we can reach the pass in two, maybe three days."

Tel sipped at his cup and made a face. "You figure they'll believe you where your Matriarch didn't believe us?"

Ker nodded. "I'm a Talent, like it or not," she said, and heard the echo of Matriarch's words. "They're my people, and I need to warn them."

"I can see you safely as far as Temlin, but after that I've got to rejoin my Wing."

Ker thought about pointing out that he wouldn't be joining anyone if it weren't for her help, but managed to keep the words unsaid. She hadn't helped Tel Cursar in order to put him in her debt, and it was wrong to think that way.

But oh, so tempting.

"So where will you go?"

"My Faro's at Oste Camp, along with the Opal Cohort she kept to garrison the place, and that's where any—where anyone who escaped will go."

The word "survivors" hung in the air between them, silencing them both. *That's where Ester will be heading, too.* Ker wondered if there was anyone Tel was particularly worried about. Strangely, she was feeling better than she had a few minutes before. If soldiers like Tel Cursar and his group had gotten away, maybe she wasn't the only Talent to escape. There would have been some on the road, and if so, they might be heading for Temlin Hall as well, now that the Peninsula was death to them. She wouldn't be alone for much longer.

"So are you rested enough, or should you eat something first?"

"Huh?"

"The ax? The helmet? You were waiting until this morning to Flash them?" Tel drained his cup and set it to one side. "I have to admit I'm curious about how you do it. Except for the Talent examinations, I've never actually seen one of you at work, not from up close anyway."

"There's not that much to see," Ker admitted.

"What? No trance? No eye rolling?" Tel grinned. "I always thought there'd be at least some magical words."

"Well, not exactly." Ker wondered how much to explain. "You remember I told you yesterday how my first reading shocked me so badly? I put up a natural block somehow, without knowing that was what I was doing?" Tel nodded. "Well, that turns out to be what Candidates get taught first, how to block the Talent, and leave the block always in place."

"Otherwise you'd go crazy from Flashing everything all the time." He held up his hands, palms toward her. "I understood it when you told me yesterday."

Ker took a sip of her own kaff, far more slowly than the

watery beverage deserved, and swallowed. "All right. What we do, then, when we *want* to Flash something, is temporarily remove the block, using a trigger word to release it, and then another one to recall it again."

"What if someone said your trigger word by accident?"

Kerida set down her cup and crossed her arms, tucking cold fingers into her armpits. "It's more complicated than just the word."

Tel nodded, frowning. He must have picked up on her reluctance. "You said you were far enough along in your training to manage this."

"It's not that." Ker scrubbed her hands on her trousers. "I can do it." She was very good with objects, better than many of the more advanced students. *I just don't want to.* "How much do you know about the first person you killed?"

"What? Nothing. Nothing personal, anyway." Tel's eyes widened. "Oh. I see." He nodded. "Maybe there *is* something harder than running away."

Ker blew out the breath she hadn't realized she was holding. He understood. Somehow, that made what she had to do much easier.

She took another deep breath and closed her eyes. In her mind, she pictured a sturdy wooden door, studded with decorative nailheads. She put her hand on the latch and as the door swung open, she said *Paraste*. Her skin felt flushed with heat, though she knew her color wouldn't have changed. She opened her eyes.

"It will snow tonight," she said. She kept her hands raised, careful to touch nothing.

"By the gods."

"Very funny. You know perfectly well any experienced farmer in the Polity can do exactly the same without Flashing the air. Move the helm here in front of me," she directed. "I'll try it first." At least it wasn't a weapon.

"The thing closest to his head might give us more of what

he was thinking, eh?" Tel said as he placed the object on the rock floor in front of her.

Ker raised her eyebrows.

"Doesn't work that way, huh? So maybe I'll keep quiet now."

Ker took several deep relaxing breaths, and released her lower lip from between her teeth, before picking the helmet up in both hands. As usual, it took a few moments to sort out the jumble of information as she slowly turned it over in her fingers.

"It was made by Sveren in the city—" She shook her head. "No name, just 'the city.' He was an armorer who sold it to a trader. Bvorak bought it from the trader just before setting out on board. Bvorak lost it in a dice game to Dvenik. Good." It wasn't Bvorak she'd killed. "Bvorak has a wife he loves very much and two young children. I wouldn't have wanted to kill their father." Ker stopped speaking with a grimace. She'd rather have kept that last observation to herself. "Dvenik cheats at dice and his Tekla can't do anything about it because Dvenik knows what his Tekla did to the sister of—oh!" Kerida let the helm fall to the ground. She looked at Tel and then quickly away, scrubbing her hands once again on her trousers. "Mother and Daughter help us, that's awful."

"Did he kill her?"

"No, but I think she might have preferred that." Ker swallowed. "He caught her in a garden one afternoon and forced her."

Tel's mouth dropped open. "But how did he get away with it? Any Talent could have backed her story."

"She didn't tell anyone, I'm not really sure why. It seems incredible that she wouldn't, but—" Ker waved her hands in the air, as if to clean them. "That part's all confused, as if there was no one for her to appeal to. And yet, he *would* have been in trouble—" Why would people let a rape go unpunished? And why wouldn't the girl have fought her attacker? Or at least accused him? The man seemed to take it for granted she would hide it.

"They don't allow women in the military." She knew suddenly.

"No, but they'll use a piece of filth like that—" Tel broke off. "Is there such a surplus of men?"

"That I can't tell. This Dvenik was low ranking, and they don't use the same words for ranks as we do. Tekla seems to be the equivalent of our Company Commander, but this one—" She tapped the helmet with her forefinger. "He was something like a Barrack Leader."

"Even our new recruits know who the officers are, and who outranks them," Tel protested.

Ker nodded. "They seem to divide everything into twelves, instead of tens like we do. I don't know what that means, though, or how useful it might be."

"Wiser heads than ours will have to figure that one out. Is there nothing else? What about the ax?"

Ker looked down at the weapon and made a face. She *really* didn't want to touch it. But it had to be done. They couldn't risk passing up a chance at useful information. She took hold of the haft with her left hand, and laid the fingertips of her right on the blade. "This has always been Dvenik's weapon. At least . . ." She frowned and lifted her hands away, turning to Tel. "It's as though the weapon was owned by two different people, one after the other, but they were both Dvenik."

"Father and son maybe? That's not unusual."

Ker curled her lip. "I can tell the difference between two owners, thank you very much, even if they are father and son and have the same name. No." She drummed her fingers on the haft of the ax. "This is more like he was changed somehow, like there's a mist or a shadow over him." She frowned. The change had something to do with colors, but that didn't make *any* sense.

"People do change when they become soldiers." Tel's voice

had a serious note. "Especially after the first time they kill someone."

Ker pressed her lips together, nodding. She wished she didn't know exactly what he meant.

"That could be it." But even as she was saying it, Kerida didn't think so. "It's like he became more focused, but as though he knew less, if that makes any sense."

Terestre, she thought, restoring her block as she set the ax down.

Tel grinned. "Like when my buddy fell in love with a girl at a dance and couldn't remember he had the duty next day?"

"For the gods' sake, this is serious."

"All right, all right. No offense meant." Tel shrugged, and then winced at the pain in his shoulder. "Anything else useful?"

"He came here on a boat with twelve twelves of men. All men, no women. There were four ships carrying that number, and then another, larger. That carried twelve twelves of twelve."

"You mean twelve cubed? One thousand, seven hundred and twenty-eight?"

Ker stared upward, doing the sum in her head. "Yes, that's right. Twelve cubed, though that's not how they say it."

Tel was shaking his head, looking a little paler than he had been a moment before. "That's more than three Cohorts— close to four! On one ship?"

"They were met by trading ships." Ker wrinkled her nose. "On the night of the new moon, near the mouth of the Juadal River. They got sorted out into other ships, waiting hidden for the trip up to Farama the Capital." There was something else. "Tel." She was cold despite the fire. "The ships? Some of them were ours."

The house looked much the same as the others in Tailors' Alley, except Talent High Inquisitor Luca Pa'narion knew it was empty. Anyone could see the windows were shuttered over, and that no light escaped the gaps. But Luca knew the hearth was cold, and that mice had already come out to nibble at the meal drying on the table. The house was empty because Talents Pavelon Tallfeather and Q'ar Evet had left it in time, not because they'd been taken away. It was the third such house Luca had checked since the coming of the Halians, but the only one he'd found empty for good reasons.

He managed to stifle his smile. They'd made it all the way to safe house number four. He'd find them there.

"You have a reason to be here, sir?"

Luca made sure to jump before turning around at the guard's words. He'd Flashed the man's arrival, and that of his partner, watchful and waiting in the alley around the two-story house on the corner.

"Other than plain curiosity? Not really." Luca smiled, even though it wasn't a town guard standing to his left, but a middle-aged man in a green Eagle tunic.

"Know the people in that house, do you?"

Luca shrugged. "They've been customers of mine in the past. I'm a spice peddler." He'd lost his Inquisitor's uniform as soon as he could, and wore the good linen-wool trousers, shirt, and tunic that he'd borrowed from the first unattended laundry he'd found. As it happened, he knew the merchant family the clothing belonged to, but decided it was safer for all concerned if he didn't ask them for it.

"Where's your goods?"

"I left my pack in the Spotted Pheasant Inn."

The soldier looked him up and down. "We go there, we'll find it, is that it?"

"I think I just said that." It was the right thing to say, even though the soldier pressed his lips together. Anything else would have been suspicious. As it was, the man *was* annoyed, but not with Luca. Not really. He was just bored with his assignment.

"You'll have to come with me, sir."

"Now, really, since when is it against the law to stare at a house?"

"Since the house was reported full of Talents, and since I don't know you."

"Oh, that's what it is, eh?" Though he'd expected this answer, Luca found it hard to pretend he wasn't shaken by it. He forced his shoulders down as if relaxed by what he'd heard, and stared at the house with his hands on his hips. "I wondered why the place was shut up." He frowned at the soldier. "But there were no Talents here before, not among my customers anyway."

"You can tell your story to the commander. Come on, this way."

Again, Luca shied and cast a widened eye at the second soldier as he came out from his hiding place and fell into step behind him. It wouldn't do to give the impression that he'd known all along the man was there.

Luca's confidence wavered as they approached the town's small administration building. The town leader used one of the four rooms in the long, low building as an office. And one was set aside to house visiting officials. Luca had stayed here himself, once or twice. He widened the focus of his Flash, and breathed a little easier. The Company Commander who looked up from his paperwork when the two soldiers escorted him through the street door was a stranger.

"What's this?" The man cleared his throat, frowning.

"Says he's a spice merchant."

"I said I was a spice *peddler*. If I were a spice merchant, I'd be considerably better dressed, I assure you."

"We arresting peddlers now?" If anything, the Commander was more bored than his men.

"He was watching the house in Tailors' Alley."

"I was looking at the house, I wasn't watching it."

"Well." The officer got to his feet and pulled a ring of keys off his belt. "You'll have to wait and tell your story to the Shekayrin."

Immediately, Luca put up a fuss, demanding that the Commander summon a superior officer, that someone be sent for his pack before the denizens of the Spotted Pheasant made off with it, but it was all for show. Like many people now living in the Peninsula, Luca had learned that once a Shekayrin was involved, there was nothing anyone else could do.

Luca had three days to prepare for his interrogation. The holding cell was small, but not uncomfortable, with a cot, two blankets, a pillow, a chair, a table holding a wash basin and ewer of water, and a waste bucket. Luca had stayed in worse rooms at public inns, even as an Inquisitor.

Three days was time enough for Luca to become bored Flashing everything he could learn about the room's former occupants, the soldiers manning the outer office, and the very few people who came by with questions or concerns. Time enough, almost, for him to welcome the arrival of the Shekayrin. Apparently, the man had been circulating from town to town, much like Talents had been doing only a month ago.

This was the first Shekayrin Luca had seen up close, and since curiosity couldn't be suspicious under the circumstances, he took the opportunity to study the Halian mage. The man was square and thick of build, several inches shorter than Luca, with a northerner's pale winter skin. His hair was completely covered by a close-fitting blue hood. A colorless but perfect rose was tattooed around his left eye in a dark red line. The same rose, in the same dark red, appeared as a crest over his heart.

"I am Garlt Bvelter, Rose Shekayrin for this district. Answer my questions truthfully, and you have nothing to fear. Do you understand?"

The words were polite, but the tone was one of complete indifference. The man had said them so many times they no longer had any meaning for him. Luca sat on the edge of the bed, wiping his hands on his thighs and nodding, the very picture of a man ready to do as he was asked.

"I know you cannot be a witch yourself, but what interest did you have in a house where witches had been reported?"

Luca didn't bother to pretend he hadn't heard the word "witch" already. Over the last few weeks, he'd seen, and heard, more than one of the Halians' proclamations against Talents, and they all used that word. He also knew of the Halians' belief that men did not have the Talent—just as he knew that male Talents had been executed merely for being with their female companions. Luca knew what the Shekayrins could do; he'd even seen one in action from the edges of the crowd in a public square. They weren't Talented, no, but they had a Gift of some sort. The Halian would find *something* if he examined Luca, even if he refused to see it for what it was.

"I've had customers in that house, sir," was what he answered. "But none of them were Talents, I mean witches. Sir. We've got an old saying here," he added helpfully. "'Talents do not live in the world.' They'd have been staying here, in this building, if there'd been any in the town."

"So I have been told."

The Shekayrin took a red jewel out of a small pocket formed by the crest on his tunic.

"Have you seen a jewel such as this one in your travels?"

Luca had seen these jewels twice, but never this close. They had something to do with the mages' Gifts, a focus point perhaps. He leaned forward to take a careful look. It was about the size of a hen's egg, flat on one side, faceted on the other.

"I'm in spices, sir, not jewels, but I'm often at fairs and trade marts, and I've never seen anything with that deep a red color."

The Rose Shekayrin snapped his fingers, and the two soldiers who'd been standing near the door stepped forward and put a hand on each of Luca's shoulders. The mage polished the jewel on his sleeve, leaned forward, and placed the flat side of it on Luca's forehead.

Luca felt the sweat break out on his upper lip. Would he be able to block the jewel's probing? But what if the device could detect that? He breathed in. There was another kind of block, especially created to seem like no block at all. The one that Luca and his fellow conspirators used to keep themselves safe from the Grand Inquisitor, and the conservative element of the Halls. Could that same protection serve him now? Luca swallowed, praying to the Mother that the hope didn't show on his face.

At first, Luca felt nothing but the coolness of the stone. Then a warmth seemed to spread from it, flushing his skin. He became aware of a redness, like seeing the sun through closed eyelids, but this redness was everywhere, all around him like a mist. The mist began to thicken. Quickly, Luca pictured himself standing behind his block that was not a block, like a man standing behind a fine, sheer curtain. He recalled, in the detail only a Talent could recall, a Flash he'd once done of a spice peddler, and he let the substance of that pass through the curtain with a little of his fear, and his worry, and even a touch of the real despair that underlay his own feelings.

Finally, the pressure eased, and disappeared.

"There man, rest and take a breath." This time the Shekayrin's tone was as gentle as his words. "You've nothing more to fear from me." The man studied him, head on one side, as if he found Luca more interesting than he'd expected. "You have just a touch of the magic of the mind about you, did you know that? But you don't even know what I'm talking about, do you? Never mind. Were we in Halia, and if we had found you young enough, we might have made a Shekayrin out of you." He nodded, and smiled, as if he'd said something he thought would please Luca.

Luca did his best to keep his answering smile small, to keep the joy that was washing through him from showing in his face and eyes. Others could do what he had just done. Anyone who, like him, already knew how to use this particular block. Someone, for example, like Pavelon and Q'ar, and whoever else had made it to a safe house.

He mustn't let the renewed hope he felt show in any way. If these two Talents had managed to escape the Halians, there must be others—others who had been on the road when the Halians came, perhaps, and who might still be in hiding. There might even be someone from Questin Hall.

Later that day Kerida mixed the last of the dried yarrow she'd brought with her and made Tel drink it down. She'd done a little exploring around the mine entrance looking for more wood, and about four spans away she'd found the dead and drying remnants of what must at one time have been some shepherd's small herb patch, overgrown and gone half wild. From it, she collected what she recognized, some seeds, some roots, all the time wishing she had paid more attention to the lessons her father's cook had given her when she was a little girl. She was turning to go before it occurred to her to trigger her Talent, and see what Flashing would tell her. This was the first time she had done such a thing, though it was common enough among Full Talents. Most of the herbs she hadn't recognized were for cooking, she discovered, but she did find valerian and added that to the rest of her collection.

Some snow had fallen during the day, a day she'd made Tel Cursar spend really resting, doing no more than minding that the fire didn't go out, and giving his opinion as she went through both their packs and decided what to take and what to leave behind.

"I hope this means we're leaving in the morning," Tel said, watching her over the rim of the cup. He glanced at the strong daylight that streamed into the tunnel and drew down his brows. "If you're right about the snow tonight, maybe we should go now. Tomorrow we'll leave tracks, but the snow would cover any signs we left today."

Ker frowned, wrapping the herbs in the last square of cloth she'd cut from the bottom of her shirt. "It's late in the day to set out now. We'd have to start looking for some place to camp for the night almost right away."

"And then we'd have to make camp with the snow coming down on us." He nodded. "Better we should wait until morning and take our chances leaving a trail. Will they be ahead of us, do you think?"

Ker shook her head. "They're waiting for the others to catch up. This twelve-twelve came ahead with the Shekayrin to deal quickly with the Hall. The other twelves are still on the road."

"And when were you going to tell me this?"

She blinked, frowning down sideways at the ax and helm. "I didn't know I knew it," she said. She looked at Tel and saw the irritation fade from his face as he believed her. "We didn't ask the five questions," she added. "I'm sorry, it's just that I've never Flashed anything without a Tutor guiding me."

"Never mind apologizing. Tell me what you mean."

"We're trained to Flash five classes of information about an object." Ker began to recite in the same voice she would have used in the classroom. "*Who*, as in who owns or pertains to it; *what*, as in what is its nature and purpose; *when*, as in when was it made and when used; *where*, as in from where does it come, where it is going; and *why*, as in why is it here, why are we interested in it."

"So you have to ask these questions to get the information?"

"No, that's just it, we collect the information automatically—it just floods into us. That's why we're drilled and drilled and drilled until we can sort it out just as automatically."

Tel held up one finger. "So if I'd asked you 'when,' we'd have known already that they weren't right on our heels."

"That and where they were. 'Objects have intention,' that's

one of the things we get taught. Sometimes their own, inherent intention, sometimes the intention of the owner or user."

Tel grinned at her. "Remind me not to let you touch any of my things. A person needs his privacy."

Ker raised her right eyebrow. "What person would that be?"

Ker didn't know what time it was when she finally fell asleep, but she woke from dreams of running from a bleeding man into a silence so profound she didn't know at first where she was. Tel was sitting up by the fire, but he was sound asleep, his head hanging down, his hand still holding the stick he'd been using to poke the embers.

"Hey." She reached out of her blankets and shoved at the bottom of his foot—and then pulled back as he swung the end of the stick at her. "Hey! It's me!"

He blinked at her. Then at the stick in his hand. "Sorry. Must have dozed off."

"As long as you haven't let the fire go out." Ker wriggled out of the bedding. "Don't suppose you've looked outside?"

"Not unless I was sleepwalking."

Ker edged past him and peered around the pile of stone blocking the entrance to the cave, then advanced until she stood in the entrance itself. She felt Tel come up behind her.

"Guess we're not going out into that," he said.

"That" explained how quiet it was, and why it was so dark when all of her senses told Ker the sun should be breaching the horizon. At least it wasn't windy.

"How long until it stops, do you think?"

Ker shook her head. "Won't matter," she said. "With this much snow already as far down the valley as this? The pass is closed."

"Daughter and Son save us," Tel said. "What now?"

*   *   *

The last of the kaff was too watered down to taste, but the liquid's warmth was welcome.

"Wind's picking up," Tel said from where he stood near the entrance. "Snow's still coming down, though. Or I suppose I should say, still falling, but sideways now." He came back in and squatted next to her. "So now that we've eaten, what's the plan?" Tel's eyes were clear, the flush in his cheeks gone. At least his wound was getting better. *Something* had to go right for them.

"Since when am I the planner for this expedition?" she asked.

"Since you know where we are," Tel said. He grinned. "Besides, I can always say I don't agree with you once I've heard what your idea is."

Ker decided not to ask him how he knew she had an idea. She put her empty cup into an outside pocket of her pack. "What's at the back of the cave?" It was a safe bet the soldiers would have looked.

Tel shrugged, then winced. "Pile of rubble, like there'd been a rock fall. Why?"

Ker laced her fingers together around her knee. "There are old stories that say this place was really a mine entrance. So there might be tunnels, and if we clear away the rubble, and if any of them go all the way through . . ."

Tel shook his head. "There's two things I don't like about that." He poked at the fire. "When you say 'might be' and when you say 'tunnels.' One single tunnel would make things so much easier."

"Yeah, well, not being overrun by invaders would make things easier still." Ker snapped her mouth shut before her voice could rise higher. She took a deep breath, and cleared her throat. "The old stories about this part of the Serpents Teeth . . ." Stories shared by her fellow Candidates at those late-night gossip sessions, where she was rarely welcome. With her fellow Candidates who were dead now.

"Old stories?" Tel prompted.

Ker pushed her thoughts away. "Some of the shepherds wouldn't bring their sheep up here. They talked about bad luck and animals disappearing and such. I know, I know." Ker held up her hand. "The point is that there *were* stories told of people going all the way through the Serpents Teeth to Bascat. And if there is such a way, I'm pretty sure I can Flash the right tunnel."

"Pretty sure?"

"You have a better idea?" Her voice seemed to fill the whole tunnel, reaching back even into the darkness where they couldn't see. Tel looked at her, but Ker refused to lower her eyes.

The end of the cave was far enough back that Ker was relieved when Tel pulled a glow stone out of his pouch. Ker hadn't seen one of those devices since leaving the military. Made from a natural stone mined in the province of Tavia, they had the quality, after being cut and shaped, of glowing like a tiny sun.

"I didn't know glow stones were so plentiful that Company Third Officers could have one."

"They're not." Tel's response was so curt that Ker was left with her own mouth hanging open. Crap. Of *course*, Tel wouldn't have been issued a glow stone. He must have taken it from a dead officer—or been given it by a dying one. Either way, not something he'd want to chat about.

The rocks, once they'd reached them, were smaller than she'd expected. Nothing larger than her head. It could have been a cave-in, she thought; the rocks were just stacked in a pile, not mortared in any way. Ker placed her hands on the rocks. *Paraste.*

"It's not a cave-in," she said. "These rocks were piled here deliberately by three men—no, two men and a woman. They weren't happy about it, but they were under orders."

"Were they closing something in?" Tel's voice was a bit shaky.

"Not that they knew of," she said. "They weren't happy because the job was so menial, and no one explained to them why soldiers were doing it."

"When was this?"

"More than a thousand years ago."

"You can Flash that?"

Ker dusted off her hands. "The rock's a lot older than that," she pointed out. "And it did come out of here—it *was* a mine, and there *are* tunnels, lots and lots of tunnels."

"But you can find the right ones?"

Ker nodded. "Yes." She tried to sound confident.

"And we can get through this?" Tel tapped the rocks with his fist.

Ker grinned, and patted a spot just to her left. "This is the thinnest spot, right here. Or maybe . . ." Still Flashing, she touched one rock after another until—"Stand back," she said. "Over there." She waited until Tel had moved before wiggling the rock free—and jumped back herself as the rock wall crumbled to an uneven pile of rocks.

They could see a tunnel on the other side.

Tel grimaced and rubbed at his eyes with the fingers of his free hand. "All right, then. We'll have to rearrange the packs." He led the way back to the fire.

Ker had already noticed that they weren't making equal contributions to the supplies. Tel Cursar, like any soldier, had started out with the required minimum of three days' food in his pack, along with his one set of bandages, a fire starter, waterskin, and his spares kit. The food was long gone, and the bandages had been burned, but his tools and weapons were intact.

Ker's contribution consisted mainly of the food she'd snatched up while running through the kitchen. Add to that her knife, the cloak, the invader's ax and helm, and the herbs she'd manage to scrounge. Ker pressed her lips together. It didn't seem like much when compared to Tel's, but on the other hand, she had all the food.

Tel returned the glow stone to the small pouch attached to

his harness, where it would be easy to hand. Sword and dagger were already in place. He hesitated over an oilcloth packet the length of his forearm and twice as thick around.

"I haven't an extra sword for you," he said. "Can you manage a crossbow?"

"Of course." Ker took the package from him. It was heavier than she'd remembered. "Assemble it now?"

He pursed his lips, finally nodding toward the darkness at their backs. "Did you Flash anything in there?"

It was a serious question, and deserved a serious answer. Kerida found herself looking at the darkness as well. "I could only be certain of animals. I didn't Flash anything big, but *something* was taking those sheep."

"Then I guess you should assemble it now," he said.

While she was preparing the crossbow, making sure each section was fastened as tightly as possible with the little tool that came in the package, Tel laid his own cloak on the ground and, one-handed, began piling what was left of the firewood on it.

"What are you doing?"

He squatted back on his heels, his forearm across his knees. "We're going to walk through the mountain range, right? You figure we're going to do that in less than a day?"

"Oh." Ker felt like slapping herself on the forehead. It had seemed so obvious that trying the tunnels was their only option, but she'd never considered how long that might take. It took at least three days just to walk through the pass.

"It'll be warmer," she pointed out finally. "But not by much."

"Exactly." Tel continued laying the cut wood on his cloak, finally drawing up the corners with cords he'd pulled out of his pouch. Ker must have made some noise because Tel looked over at her.

"I'd forgotten that military cloaks have those eyelets," she said. With the addition of metal eyelets and leather cords, military cloaks could become carry sacks in a moment. Or shrouds. She shivered. Best not to let her thoughts go down that path. "It's a pity my cloak doesn't have them as well."

They had so little to pack that a very few minutes more saw them done. They had divided up the food as best they could, and Kerida had managed to make a sling out of her cloak, much like those she had seen parents use to carry small children, and so they were able to take all the available firewood. Like the food, those particular packs would only get lighter.

Ker helped Tel into his harness, adjusting the straps around his bound arm, only to find she also had to rehang all his pouches and weapons, to make them handier to his left hand. They each took a last look around, searching the shelves and crannies of the rock walls, but Ker knew they were stalling. They'd spent three days here; it was hard to leave that feeling of security, even when they knew they had to.

"I'm not taking these," she said, nudging the Halian helm where it sat on the ax. "I can't use the ax *and* the crossbow." That wasn't the real reason, but she wasn't ready to share those particular feelings with Tel.

"Suit yourself," Tel said, starting to shrug before remembering his shoulder. "You want to lead?"

Ker shook her head. "There's only one tunnel just now. Plenty of time for me to lead when it splits." She smiled. "Besides, it's your glow stone."

The tunnel was only slightly smaller than the entrance cave, a good span and a half wide and at least that tall. Unfortunately, Tel was just a little taller. He only needed to bump his head once to learn to crouch over, but he wouldn't be able to keep up that posture for long, Ker thought. Not with his bad shoulder. A surprising amount of light leaked a surprising distance down the tunnel, despite the partial blockage the shepherds had put up. It wasn't very long, however, before Tel got out his glow stone.

Not much farther in, they found their first piece of luck in the form of a miner's sledge. It had been well made in the first place and was still sturdy enough for use; even the hemp ropes were solid.

Tel took advantage of it to sit down and straighten his back. "My Cohort Leader used to say there was nothing like hemp for ropes, but this is amazing," he said as Ker tugged again on the rope nearest him. "We can put at least the firewood on the sledge," he added, trying to massage the small of his back one-handed.

"We can take turns," Ker said. "But will pulling while crouched over be any better for you than carrying?"

"Are you joking? Crouched over is bad enough, but crouched over with a weight on top of me? I was actually looking forward to not having enough wood for a fire."

They ended by putting everything, packs and all, on the sledge. When her turn came, Ker found that once the sledge was moving it was easier than she'd expected. The floor of the tunnel was worn so smooth in this section that the sledge runners glided along almost as though they were on snow.

Still, Ker was glad when Tel announced it was time for them to rest and have something to eat. She'd known he must have a good inner clock; that and a good sense of direction were two things senior officers looked for when promoting juniors. They would have had to stop anyway, however, as they'd come to a place where the tunnel split into three, with one branch going off to the left almost perpendicular to the main tunnel, and another two veering off to the right.

"What do you think?" Tel said. "Either of these two seem to be heading in the right direction."

"Which means nothing," Ker pointed out. "You can't tell from here how they branch later on."

"No, *I* can't, but I think you were suggesting earlier that you *can*."

Ker pressed her tongue against her upper lip. It had seemed like such a good idea at the time. Now she wasn't so sure.

"Let's eat first," she said, and was relieved when Tel agreed.

As they'd thought, it was warmer here in the tunnels than at the entrance to the mine, and they decided to wait until they stopped for the night before lighting a fire.

"Though I might have felt differently about it if we hadn't found the sledge," Tel said.

About to agree, Ker saw a familiar shape in the shadows beyond him. "Don't move," she whispered. As smoothly as she could, she reached for the crossbow she'd laid down to her right when they'd sat on the sledge. With her left hand, she pulled a quarrel out from the pouch hooked to her belt.

Tel went on chewing, only his raised eyebrows showing that he'd heard anything she'd said. Ignoring the small crank, Ker braced the butt of the crossbow against her sternum and pulled back on the string, setting the quarrel in place.

She leaned forward slightly, took careful aim, and let fly. There was a squeak, but she'd hit the rat dead center, and dead it was.

Tel swallowed and then turned his head. "That's the biggest rat I've ever seen."

Ker went to retrieve the animal, and the quarrel. "I've seen dogs smaller than this," she agreed.

"What's it feeding on?"

"That's the thing about rats. If there's any food at all, they'll find it."

"Maybe we should have followed it instead of killing it."

Ker smiled. "We don't need to follow it *to* food. It *is* food."

Tel shrugged. "Looks healthy enough."

Ker nodded, pulling out her knife. "I'll clean it here."

A gasp, high-pitched and sharp, echoed through the tunnels.

"That was no rat." Ker jumped up, knife still in hand.

"Wait here." Tel took off down the left-hand tunnel in the direction of the sound, every inch the soldier instructing the civilian.

"Not likely." Ker dropped the rat, scooped up the crossbow,

and took off after him, cranking in a new quarrel as she went. As if she wanted to wait in the dark.

Tel slowed as the tunnel veered to the left, advancing cautiously around the curve. He had slipped the glow stone into his mouth to free his hand and had been running with his lips slightly parted. Now he opened them as much as he could, raising his sword.

Ker caught only a glimpse of light hair, white skin, and wide open dark eyes before there was another gasp, and the person stepped backward.

Only to disappear completely with a squeal.

"Blast." Tel spit out the glow stone, and it dropped at his feet. In the brightness Ker could see that the tunnel floor broke off in a sharp edge not far from where he stood. Tel ran forward and kneeled, reaching down with his good arm outstretched. "Hold still, you stupid girl. Take my hand."

Ker flung herself on her knees next to him. The girl—no more than six or maybe seven—clung to a thin uneven ridge a half span from the edge. Off to one side, and too far below the child to be of any help, Ker could just make out the remains of what could have been a ladder, fastened somehow to the rock. This was a shaft then, not a collapsed tunnel.

Tears were flowing out of the corners of eyes clamped tightly shut. The child's knuckles showed white with the strain.

"The light," Ker said. "It's blinding her." She snatched up the glow stone from where it had fallen and pushed it into her own mouth, tasting the grit from the floor and, somewhere behind it, Tel's mouth. She parted her lips, letting out barely enough light for them to see. Tel now lay prone on the ground, turning his head to one side, and reaching down with his left hand. He shifted forward awkwardly to lean deeper into the abyss and Ker immediately set down the crossbow to sit on his legs, using her full weight to help hold him in place.

Whether it was the dimming of the light, or just plain fear of falling, Tel was finally able to persuade the girl to hold up one little hand. Tel's was large enough to wrap all the way around her forearm, in a delicate parody of a soldier's greeting. Taking a firm grip on Tel's harness, Ker began to inch backward, letting him do the same, as he pulled the girl up.

Once the girl was secure, Ker was able to roll off Tel's legs. She was panting, and could feel sweat drying on her forehead. Tel was sitting up now, his left arm around the girl's shaking shoulders.

Ker carefully spit the glow stone into her cupped hands. She didn't know what had frightened the child in the first place, but it had certainly been the light which had startled her into stepping back off the edge.

Tel reached out for the stone. As soon as he let go of her, the girl bolted back in the direction they'd come and vanished into the darkness.

"Hey!" Ker got to her feet, but stopped when she realized Tel wasn't following her.

"Let her go," he said. "She's probably more afraid of us than anything else in here, even if we did end up helping her."

Nodding, Ker dusted off her hands and picked up the crossbow from where it had been kicked to one side. "Do you think she's living in here?"

"It explains the miraculous longevity of the hemp rope." Tel wiped the glow stone on his sleeve. "You saw how she reacted to the light." He looked over at her. "*How* long did you say this mine's been abandoned?"

Ker shook her head, looking around her. The darkness didn't seem so neutral anymore. "What do you think scared her in the first place?"

It was Tel's turn to shake his head. "Let's hope it wasn't seeing a couple of strangers killing and skinning her pet rat." He levered himself to his feet. "Come on, let's get back."

"Did you strain your wound?" Ker examined his sleeve. "It doesn't look like it's bleeding again, but I wouldn't mind a closer look."

"When I'm sitting down on the sledge you can look all you want—"

Ker bumped into Tel's back when he abruptly stopped moving.

"Daughter curse that sneaky little brat, she tricked us."

The sledge, their packs, and the bundles of firewood were gone.

So was the body of the rat.

TEL looked from one tunnel opening to the other. "Which one?"

"Step aside, Tel. Let me—" Ker stopped short as a man hefting a spear stepped out into the open space.

"There now, youngsters. Stay so quiet and so steady as hens on eggs, and you'll maybe walk away on your feet." A murmur came from the darkness behind him. "That's right, too. Be so courteous as to pocket that fierce light of yours."

For the longest time Tel didn't move, but finally he lowered the glow stone, pushing it firmly back into his belt pouch. At first, Ker saw nothing except the dark, but gradually she became aware of a soft greenish glow coming from the man's forehead, and his wrists. Similarly lighted shapes appeared in the tunnel behind the old man, and in the one next to it.

The little girl they'd been chasing bounced out, deftly avoiding the old man's snatch at her shoulder. Now, without the brighter light from the glow stone overpowering them,

Ker could see the child wore the same luminescent bands on head and wrists.

"See, I told you she was coming."

The old man lowered the spear, but didn't ground it. "This is her?"

"That's the one." The little girl grinned.

"Then why were you running away from her, Larin?"

Larin pursed her lips. Ker decided that the way the child's shadow seemed to shift in size was due to the unfamiliar lighting. Probably.

"Never saw *him*." The girl pointed at Tel and her face crumpled. "He scared me!"

"But then I saved your life, you ungrateful brat, don't forget that part."

Larin stuck out her tongue and retreated to the old man's side. His wide smile showed even white teeth.

"Put down your knives and belt pouches, so soft and easy, if you please, and back away to that tunnel there." He indicated the one they'd used getting here. "You're a matter for the council, if what the little one says is true—"

"'If?' What do you mean 'if'?" The child stamped her foot.

"Softly, little one, softly. No one doubts you. It's just we like to check things when we can."

"Huh. Sounds like doubt to me."

"Ganni." A woman with a thin scar running white down the left side of her face stepped forward. "Sala says it'll be the whole council, not just the small. We're to go to the great meeting hall."

"Are we now? So, then. This way, if you please, youngsters."

Once their eyes were used to the soft illumination from the Miners' wristlets, they managed a good pace through the tunnels, and it seemed no time at all before they were ushered into a great, round amphitheater. From the echoes it was almost as large as the one in Farama the Capital, where the performances sacred to the Son were staged every Spring Festival. Pots of the same luminescent stuff the Miners wore were set around the clear central area, but most of the vast cavern remained in darkness. Their captors ushered them quickly down uneven steps to the flat, cleared space.

"Do you think this room is natural?" Tel said out of the corner of his mouth.

"I hope so. Imagine how long it would have taken to cut it out by hand." Ker wondered if, like the stage in Farama the Capital, her voice would carry to the unseen roof.

"Well, we *are* in a mine," Tel pointed out. "They'd have the equipment for it."

"It'd be a little of both." The old man, Ganni, rejoined them. "Mostly we cut out the steps, and leveled off this bit. That would have been in my great-grandsire's time."

Ganni directed them to seats on cushions of old worn leather in the center of the level space. Without speaking, they sat back to back. Set around them in a circle were six chairs, each different and each showing signs of use. Larin ran immediately to as fine a carved armchair as Ker had ever seen and hauled herself into it. The others were filled one by one. Ganni sat on a low, four-legged stool. A tall woman with the dark skin and tightly curled hair of a Ma'lakan took a plain wooden chair. Tel elbowed Ker, and she nodded. There was no mistaking that the tall woman moved like a soldier. The remaining three seats were taken by an older woman with dull red hair, and two younger men only a few years older than she and Tel. Behind the chairs rose row upon uneven row of seats cut into the rock face. Ker could see perhaps thirty or forty people, but she had the feeling there were at least twice that many out of sight in the darkness.

"What is it you have, outsider?" This was the younger man with his blondish hair cut like a stiff brush. He was grim-faced, while the others merely looked interested.

"You've taken all our things." Ker pressed her back more firmly against Tel.

"But do you move? Or maybe see?"

A glimmer of an idea made Ker sit up straighter. Moving? Seeing? Those were Gifts out of the old tales of Feelers. But there weren't any Feelers. Not anymore.

"One moment, Norwil." This was the taller, dark woman. "You are new to the council, but you know that we wait until the assembly is complete before we ask questions."

"But she has to have some kind of Gift, some Talent, or she couldn't have found her way in."

Ker coughed, relieved. She must have misunderstood him after all. "I'm not a Full Talent," she said. "My name is Kerida Nast. I was a Candidate at Questin Hall."

A murmuring out of the shadows was quickly cut off by a gesture from the tall dark woman.

"That explains it, Sala," called out a voice.

Sala held up her hand again and this time there was silence. "I am Sala of Dez, Speaker for the Mines and Tunnels. I call this assembly to order," she said. She turned to Ker. "We six are the delegates of the people. We represent them, and speak for them. Is this clear, Kerida Nast and . . . ?"

"Tel Cursar, Third Officer, Green Company, Carnelian Cohort, Bear Wing."

Once more, voices were raised among the people sitting around them in the darkness. Again, Sala lifted her hand, and the voices were stilled. Ker was suddenly reminded of the dining hall in Questin, and she blinked back tears.

"Ganni the elder you have met, and Larin. These others are Hitterol—" Sala indicated the older woman. "Norwil—" The brush-cut man. "And Midon." Sala returned her attention to Kerida.

"How did you escape from Questin?"

"You know about the invaders, then?" Ker said, leaning forward.

"From over the water. Horses of the sea. I told you," Larin said, her voice suddenly serious and firm. But she wasn't talking to Ker.

Ganni's bushy eyebrows lifted. "The longships," he whispered. Even in this light Ker could see he was no longer looking at her but was focused off somewhere in the middle distance.

There was a murmur of what sounded like satisfaction from the people around them.

"So, then," Ganni said, nodding now. "What Larin says may very well be true. This girl's the one the Prophecy speaks of."

A sudden and echoing silence as the entire cavern fell quiet and still. Then everyone seemed to take a breath simultaneously, and Ker felt every eye on her. Tel's long-fingered hand wrapped itself around hers, and she took a steadying breath.

Finally, Sala leaned forward, elbows on her knees. "If you *are* the one the Prophecy speaks of . . ." She pursed her lips.

"Oh, thank you *very* much." The old woman's voice, coming from where Larin was sitting, startled Ker. Someone behind the child must have spoken. She noticed Ganni staring at her with narrowed eyes.

"I saw you," Larin cut in. "They said I was too young, but I did, I saw you." The way she smiled was instantly familiar, the smile of any child who's managed to prove the grown-ups wrong. "I went looking for you." She glanced at Tel, her smile fading. "Not for him. *He's* not in it."

Ker looked from one eager face to another. Even Norwil, the brush-cut man, seemed excited now rather than grim. "I don't know anything about a prophecy," she said. "I don't see how I can help you."

"That is what we must discover." Sala nodded across the circle, and Ganni gestured with his left hand. A young boy, his too-short sleeves showing bony wrists, ran forward out of the shadows carrying a small wrapped bundle cradled in his arms. Ganni took it from him with a grin.

"This was found at the bottom of one of the lower west shafts." The old man's face split in a big smile, showing his perfect teeth again. "What is it?"

These people knew perfectly well what the object was, Ker thought. They were testing her. Tel squeezed her hand and she squeezed back. She let him go, and wiped her palms dry on the thighs of her trousers. "If I can tell you that," she said, "you'll let us go?"

"It is the first step in that direction, yes." Sala did not take her eyes from Ker's face.

Ker nodded. "Pass it over." She expected Ganni to unwrap it, but instead he gave her the bundle intact. The cloth was a piece of old blanket, so faded there wasn't any color left, just shades of a brownish gray. *That's not what they're asking me about.* Tel shifted over to watch what she was doing. He smiled, nodding encouragement, but his eyes were worried.

Ker returned his nod, clenched her jaw, and folded back the edges of the blanket until the object was revealed. It was pale, the length of her hand, and right away it reminded her of an old drinking horn of her father's, something he'd brought home from an early campaign, before she was born. Instead of being round like the horn, however, the thing was hollowed on the one side like . . . "It's a claw," she said.

"That much anyone can see, girl." Ganni's tone was dry. "Do you tell us, what *kind* of claw."

Ker licked her lips, mouth suddenly dry. *Bone*, the shadow in her thoughts said to her. *Danger.* Sweat beaded on her upper lip, and Ker swallowed past a lump in her throat. Again she saw the bright sun, the cloudless sky, the darkness under the bank of the stream where she'd found the bones that had triggered the first fierce explosion of her Talent. She'd been younger than Larin then, and honestly, she didn't feel much older than that now.

What if it happens again? Her fingers twitched on the edge of the cloth.

"Ker?" Tel's voice sounded far away, though she felt his fingers warm on her arm.

Ker took a deep breath. "It's all right," she said. "Just gathering my thoughts." *It's not a human bone.* She took in three deep, steadying breaths. *Paraste.*

"It's not a bird," she said as she stroked her fingers lightly on the claw. Not *Who*, think *What.* "It's a cat." Her fingers brushed against the cloth and she blinked, getting an unusually strong Flash of the weaver, though not of the weaving itself. "It's a cat bird." Ker saw feathers, but she also saw fur, thick and golden, a slashing tail, the curving beak of a bird of prey, the shiny edge of a delicate golden shell. That was *When*—

"Oh!" She opened her eyes. "It's a griffin."

There was a silence so profound it almost hurt her ears, followed by a rumble as though everyone, seen and unseen, had murmured at the same time. Norwil slapped his hands to his knees.

"Griffins aren't real." Tel stretched out his hand, stopping short of actually touching the claw.

"They are so very real." For the first time there was an old man's tremor in Ganni's voice. "So real as starving. And so, it appears, are you, my girl." He moved his head in slow arcs from side to side. "What more can you tell us? How did a griffin get into our tunnels?"

It was curiosity in the old man's voice, not disbelief. Ker turned the claw over in her hands. *How.* "It's a baby," she said. "Its nest . . . its nest was here in the mines, ages ago, before— before everything. A nest with three eggs in it."

"There are *three* of them?" From the rustling out among the crowd Sala wasn't the only one concerned.

"Hmmm?" Ker looked up, finding it oddly difficult to pull her eyes away from the claw. Hurriedly, she spoke her closing word. "No, there's only the one. The first one out of the egg breaks open the others and eats them." Ker looked around at wrinkled noses and unhappy grimaces. "It's natural for them."

"Just thinking my brother would've tasted terrible." Ganni made a gagging face, and several people laughed with him.

The older woman on the council, Hitterol, leaned forward, her brows drawn down. "It must be hungry, and frightened."

"It's a *griffin,* for the Mother's sake," Norwil said. "What's going to frighten it?" There was still a light of satisfaction on his face.

Ker shook her head. "No, she's right. He's just a baby."

Ganni clapped his hands. "See now? We have to help him."

"We should send the Talent, then," Norwil said, turning to Larin. "So far she's only told us what any Talent could. It's whether she can befriend the griffin that makes her the prophesied one. Doesn't it? That's what the Fields and Paths Clan will say, let alone the Springs and Pools, when we claim the Prophecy came to us." From the shuffling and murmuring, there were many who agreed with him.

"Perhaps." When Larin saw that everyone was looking at her, she smiled and shrugged, then swung her feet.

"Just what *is* this prophecy?" For a moment Ker thought no one had heard Tel, then she realized they were all simply waiting. Norwil stood, and cleared his throat.

"Let all the people of the land awake and listen," he said, and it was obvious that he was reciting. "For the day of joining comes. It comes near."

Ker jumped as every voice in the cavern repeated the last three words.

Norwil sat, and Ganni stood. "Watch horses of the sea come clothed in thunder. Longships bring nets of blood and fire. Blood of the earth."

"The First Sign."

This time Ker was ready for it, and the chorus of voices didn't startle her.

Ganni sat and the other woman, Hitterol, stood.

"Hear the runner in the darkness, eyes of color and light. Speaks to the wings of the sky. Speaks to griffins."

"The Second Sign."

Everyone in the small council, and everyone seated close by, turned and looked at Ker.

Hitterol sat, and the next councillor, Midon, stood. Until now, he hadn't spoken, and his deep voice startled Ker again.

"See the bones of the earth touch blood and fire. Net the souls of the living. Bones of the griffin."

"The Third Sign."

This time, Ker almost said it with them.

Midon resumed his seat, and Sala stood.

"See the child eyes of color and light. Holds the blood and the wings and the bone. Child of the griffin."

"The Fourth Sign."

Ganni looked at her again, though no one else did, and smiled.

Sala sat, and Larin bounced to her feet. "The child rides the horses of the sea. Bears the blood and wields the bones of the earth. Brings freedom and light."

"Freedom and light is near; the day of joining comes."

"Not so very helpful now, is it?" Ganni actually looked sympathetic. "Not for you, at least. It's ours, you see, given to us, not yours. At least, not yet."

Sala spoke up. "Do you know where the griffin is now?"

Ker blinked, her ears still ringing with the last words of the Prophecy. What could it all mean? She frowned. She'd been asked a question.

Where. "That way." She pointed off to her left, behind Ganni. Everyone turned to follow the direction of her finger.

Maybe it was the light, but Ker thought she saw an odd gleam in the old man's eye, as he turned back to face her. She could have sworn he was about to smile.

"Good," Norwil said. "Let's have her go to it. Then we'll know for sure she's the one the Prophecy speaks of. Can we vote?"

Sala was nodding. "All in favor?"

Every member of the council put out their hand, palm

down. Sala stood and looked out into the cavern. "Does anyone disagree with their delegate?" There were whispers of conversations, but no one spoke up.

"Then it is settled. The Talent will meet with the griffin."

Hitterol stood, holding out a hand to Larin. "These two are dead on their feet, Sala, and hungry. I vote the griffin waits until morning."

Tel sat down next to Ker with a thump. They'd been shown into an alcove cut out of the rock wall of the great cavern. A thick curtain of woven grasses served as a door; the place was clean, and there was bedding on a sleeping ledge. Relatively fresh bedding. They'd been given back their pouches and their personal knives, but nothing else.

"Can we trust them?" Tel sounded as though he needed to clear his throat. "Have you *any* idea what this is all about?"

"Not a single clue." She wasn't going to share her thoughts on Feelers. He'd think she was completely crazy.

Almost as though he could hear her thought, Tel echoed it. "Son and Daughter, Ker, who are these people?" He blew out a breath through his teeth. "*Griffins.*" He slapped his leg with his left hand. "What next? Feelers?"

It did seem silly, now that someone had said it aloud. "The griffins in the stories are always good, though, aren't they?" *Not like Feelers*, she didn't say aloud.

"That's right." Tel frowned. "Do we know anything that isn't from a story?"

"Not so very much, I'd wager." The voice out of the darkness made them both jump. How easily they'd started to feel secure, because they'd been left alone with a light.

Ganni pushed the curtain to one side and dropped Ker's pack in front of them before sitting down, cross-legged. He squinted in the light of the glow stone, and bowed his thanks when Ker covered it over with a corner of her cloak.

"Still, you ask a good question, soldier boy, and one it so happens I can answer—if so be, you'll then answer some of mine." The old man grinned. He nudged at the pack with his fist. "I've brought your food. Perhaps I can tell you what I know while you eat, eh? Mind you, some of what I have to say will sound like stories, but I assure you, it's history you can find in the libraries in Farama the Capital."

Maybe not, Ker thought, shivering despite Tel's nearby warmth. The libraries in Farama had been kept in the Hall of Law.

"They lived here once, the griffins—no, not in these mines, and you needn't look at me so fierce, youngster. On the surface. In the valleys and on the slopes. There was a stone here, a jewel, precious to them, that we mined for them, we humans. We think that's what the Prophecy speaks of, when it says 'bones of the earth.'"

"And when the supplies ran out, the griffins left?"

"Don't run ahead now. It's me telling this tale. The histories say they were driven away. But they lived here once and had their dealings with humankind. That's fact and not story. Does that not fit what you yourselves know of them?"

Ker exchanged looks with Tel. Were there stories told about griffins in the Battle Wings? She couldn't remember her father or even her grandmother telling any. Tel stayed quiet.

"The Talents have a tradition that the griffins were their first teachers," she said. "That they taught the brightest and the best. We still have a saying 'Griffin Class,' when we mean someone's really excelling." *Griffin Class*. That's what Luca Pa'narion had said about her. That's what had given her hope, for a future in the Halls. She shrugged, suddenly uncomfortable. "Other than that? They're supposed to have the body of a lion, the head and wings of an eagle."

"They taught more than Talents, and were counselors to the Luqs," Ganni said. "That claw now, is it an accurate judge of its size?"

"It's a little larger now, I think." Ker frowned. "This claw came out when the new one grew underneath."

Tel was reaching for the backpack, but hesitated, his hand hovering as he looked at Ganni from under his eyebrows.

"I've told you, go ahead, boy. Don't mind me, I've eaten."

Tel pulled the pack toward him with his left hand and tried to steady it with his feet while he manipulated the closures. Ker ducked and shifted as his elbow came perilously close to her head.

"Here, let me." She reached forward.

"Is his wound so fierce? Let me look at it whilst you hold the light."

"No, thanks," Tel said, before Ker could get in a word. "I can wait."

"It's me that's brought you the food, youngster. If any of us meant you harm, you'd *be* harmed. And are you? No. So don't be foolish. How is tending to your injury a bad thing for you?"

Tel's lips pressed together. "I'm fine."

"Really? So ready as a champion to swing your sword at all comers? If we give it back to you, that is." Ganni smiled, but there was no malice in it.

"Not to worry." Tel wasn't exactly smiling back. "I can fight left-handed."

"If you two are finished showing each other your teeth, let's get on with checking the wound. Yes!" Ker said as Tel began to shake his head. "This is how you got into trouble in the first place. And I've no yarrow left. We can't afford for you to get worse again."

"Listen to her, boy. Your own officers would tell you the same."

Ker didn't know if that was the argument that convinced him, but, jaw clenched, Tel submitted, letting Ker loosen and remove his harness, ease off tunic and under tunic, and untie the sling she'd made of his shirt. She had him sit down in front of Ganni and knelt to one side. She frowned, drumming her fingers on her thigh.

"Could you hold the glow stone for me?" the old man asked her. "So steady as a star in the sky."

Ganni peered through slitted eyes as the light fell full on Tel's back and shoulder. "Dim it a little, my dear one." Ker shifted her grip.

Tel's skin pimpled in the chill air. "Well?" he said.

"It's not worse," Ker admitted. The cut seemed shallower, the edges less red, but that was the most she could say.

"Then what's taking so long? I'm freezing here."

"Patience, youngsters. I'll have seen more wounds than both of you put together, I should think. Hold the light here, to my right. There, that's better."

The new angle was awkward, and tired muscles made her hands tremble. In the wavering light, Ker found herself squinting to follow the movements of Ganni's fingers as they probed and prodded the wound, almost as if the old man was massaging the flesh of Tel's shoulder. Ganni pressed his thumbs along the partially healed cut, as if smoothing the edges, and sat back.

Ker moved the light closer. She blinked, and touched the wound herself, feeling the smoothness of what was now a half-healed scar. She looked at Ganni, and found the old man looking back at her, his eyes bright and his grin wide. He waggled his eyebrows at her and made a slight shrugging motion with his shoulders.

"What? What is it?" Tel twisted, trying to peer over his own shoulder.

"Seems it's better than she thought, boy."

Ker opened her mouth and closed it again without speaking. What, exactly, could she say? The wound had healed. A moment before it had been open and sore, and now it was healed. Her skin tingled, and the air felt as it did before a thunder storm. She chewed at her lower lip. She thought about Tel's reaction when he'd learned she was a Talent, and kept quiet. "It *is* better than I thought," she said, coughing to clear her throat. "Much better."

"I'd leave his arm free," Ganni said. "He's fierce unbalanced with it bound. A man likes to feel square on his feet."

Tel couldn't argue with that, Ker thought, though from the look on his face, he wanted to.

"Turn around," she said, as she shook out Tel's shirt. Not that any mere shaking was going to get the creases out. It was filthy, but he'd need the warmth. She tapped his shoulder, and he raised his arms obediently. She pulled the shirt down over them, following it with both his under tunic and the purple tunic that marked him as a Bear. Finally, she pulled on his harness, adjusting the straps where needed. The half-familiar movements helped to calm the flutter in her stomach, and the hairs on the back of her neck flattened.

"There," she said, once she had the last buckle fastened.

Tel moved his shoulders back and forth a couple of times, gently at first and then with increasing freedom. A smile formed on his lips, as he reached again for the pack, this time with both hands. He took out a travel cake and unwrapped it, cutting it into pieces with his knife before passing her some, using the waxed cloth it came in as a plate.

"So tell us," Tel said, as he settled back with his portion of cake. "What makes the griffins so important now?"

Ganni was cross-legged again, back in his original position. Just an old man making himself comfortable. "You heard the Prophecy. It tells us that the day of joining comes, that freedom and light come. It mentions the longships, you heard that. That's the First Sign."

Ker sat up straighter. "But the griffins? Where do they come in?"

"The coming of the griffins and the one who'll be able to speak and deal with them, why, that's the Second Sign. And it's long been held that this one wasn't one of us, but a Talent. Who else could speak with griffins better than their old students?"

Ker nodded. "So it's the griffins that are supposed to do all this joining?"

The old man's laughter startled Ker so that she almost dropped the piece of cake she still had in her hand. "We've been mulling it over and studying it all this long time, and it's as complicated as a spider's web. It's Larin who knows the hows and whys of it now, since the elder Time Seer is gone."

Tel wrinkled his nose. "Time Seer?"

Ganni laughed again. "What else would you call the one who sees the future?"

Ker chewed on her lower lip, watching Tel as he brought out more food. Now that they were alone, she knew she should tell him about her suspicions, but every time she tried, the word "Feeler" stuck in her throat. Tel was just a soldier—and she never thought she'd say that, but there it was. Soldiers couldn't always be trusted with the finer points of the Law. As the only Talent available, the Feelers were *her* responsibility.

Besides, there was a griffin to deal with. One myth at a time.

"Have you done much hunting?" was what she finally said.

"Some." He shrugged, turning away to unwrap a stick of dried sausage, breaking it carefully in half and handing over her share. Ker accepted, biting into the sausage with her side teeth.

"The sausage may have been a mistake," Tel said, but only after the last bite was gone. "The salt's making me thirsty."

"Sure," Ker agreed. "But I'd rather starve than eat another bite of travel cake."

"You don't like it either?" For a moment their smiles were

exactly as carefree as the ones they'd shared back in the kitchen of the Hall. That thought sobered Kerida in a hurry.

"What is it?" Tel's smile vanished as well.

"Nothing." She shrugged. "Just that I was reminded of the first time we met, when you were sent to pick up the supplies the Cohort Leader asked for."

"That was, what, fifteen days ago? Twenty, since the Halians entered Farama?" He shook his head. "Seems like it should be longer, when so much has changed. It's a different world now."

There were so many things Tel could be thinking of. The loss of the Luqs, the breaking of the Eagle Wing—Ker resolutely put thoughts of Ester out of her mind, only to find them replaced by images of her last sight of the Hall. She'd looked back just once, as her borrowed horse reached the line of trees on the far side of the west pasture. Light from the fires had been visible in the windows of the great room. She managed not to think about what she'd seen inside.

"I'm sorry I took offense when I found out you were a Talent." Tel sounded like he'd been waiting to say that for a long time.

Ker sketched a wave with her hand, shifting her eyes away from him before he could see her confusion. "You were sticking up for your own. I understood." *I didn't like it, but I understood.* "Things have never been easy between the military and the Halls. The blade and the whetstone, my grandmother used to call them. Neither one's any good without the other, but both want to be in charge."

"I suppose we're the blade and you're the whetstone?"

Ker clenched her jaw. So that was how he saw her? Not part of "we," but part of "you"?

And that's why I won't tell him I think they're Feelers, she told herself. "I'll take the first watch."

Tel didn't argue; proof he was exhausted. Ker settled down cross-legged, her back against the sleeping ledge. Tel curled up on the ledge above her, lying on her cloak, and using his own as a blanket. Had they been in a safer place, it was cool enough for them to be lying down together like two spoons, to share body heat.

For a moment Ker imagined lying with her back against Tel's chest, his arms around her, his breath making her hair move—

No. Wouldn't happen. We'd have to keep watch. Ker rested her forearms on her knees. She had the glow stone in her left hand, planning to switch it back and forth at intervals to time her watch. Tel was a soldier, and the light wouldn't affect his ability to sleep. If she should happen to fall asleep herself, her hand would relax, and the sound of the glow stone hitting the rock surface between her feet should wake her up—though she was going to do her best not to put that to the test.

It had been a long time since Kerida Nast had been expected to keep watch and she'd forgotten how boring it could be. Usually there was something *to* watch—gates, the approaches to the gates, the edges of forests, that kind of thing—in addition to things to watch *for*. Here she had nothing to look at but the rock walls and the curtain of their alcove.

"Nothing to see here," she whispered to herself. She wished it was as easy to convince herself that she *hadn't* seen anything after all. That Ganni hadn't healed Tel. She twisted around.

He looked younger asleep, she thought. His beard was growing in, but so lightly he probably didn't need to shave every day. Sleeping, she could no longer see his most remarkable feature, his pale eyes. In some lights they looked a bit green, in others gray, but most of the time they were so pale as to seem colorless, especially when contrasted with the deep tan of his skin, the tan of someone who spent most of his life out of doors. The tan of farmers, of builders, of herders, and of soldiers. His hair must have been blond to start with to have been bleached so white by the sun, much lighter than her own dark brown hair. Ker wondered whether he had siblings with the same unusual coloring. The same long limbs, the same graceful way of moving.

Ker sat down again, and took a firmer grip on the glow stone. Had Tel Cursar ever said *anything* about his family? About where he'd come from or how it was he'd become a soldier? There had to be *some* military background for him to be Third Officer of a Company so young, since junior officers usually rose from the ranks. Sometimes senior officers were idiots from good families, rather than good soldiers, but as her sister Tonia used to say, war had a way of taking care of idiots fairly quickly.

Kerida herself might have been a Third Officer by now, or even a Second, though she was younger than Tel. That's what it meant to come from a famous military family. Ker pressed her lips together. That was all behind her. She had Matriarch to thank for opening her eyes to what her powerful Talent actually meant, and Barid for showing her another and more interesting path.

Much more interesting, she had to admit, than the path that might have led to a Wing Faro's cloak like her sister Tonia's. A Griffin Class Talent? Never mind a Matriarch; she could have been Grand Inquisitor one day. *Could have been.* She shook her head.

As little as a month ago, Ker would have said she was ready to give anything to leave the Hall, to be a soldier again. She shivered. Now? She'd happily scrub pots for the rest of her life if it would bring the old world back. Cana, Barid, the Luqs. Even Matriarch.

"Thinking about tomorrow?"

"What?" Ker was so startled she almost dropped the glow stone. "No. And why aren't you asleep?"

Tel sat up, swinging his long legs off the sleeping platform. "Maybe you're thinking too loud. Maybe I'm cold."

He sat down next to her, dragging the cloaks with him, using both hands now, but still moving his right arm with care. He shifted closer, arranging the heavy folds of cloth over their knees and feet. He put his left arm around her shoulders and pulled her close.

"What?" He grinned as she gave him the sourest look she could. "I'm freezing. You wouldn't want my fever to come back, would you?"

"Uh-huh. Like I haven't heard *that* before. It's not bad enough you're the size of a twillbeast anyway, you have to take up all the space?"

"I feel safer close to you." His tone was laughing, but Ker saw his eyes were not. He'd been quick to say his fellows had been right to leave him, but those few days he'd spent alone and fevered couldn't have been easy.

"Used to having your brothers and sisters around you, huh?" Ker said. As good a way as any to introduce the topic of his family.

"Used to having my Company, at least. So were you?"

"Was I what?" It *was* warmer sitting this way.

"Were you thinking about tomorrow? Can you track the griffin?"

"That's not what's worrying me." Ker thought back to the feel of the claw in her hands. "He's so young, and he's alone and afraid."

"You know how it *feels*?" Tel peered at her, his face inches from hers. "I thought you couldn't do that?"

"Not with people, at least not yet. Maybe it's because he *isn't* a person . . ."

"Or maybe it's what *you're* feeling." Ker stiffened and Tel shrugged, wrinkling his nose as he moved his right shoulder. "Think about it. Maybe you're not alone, but you *know* you're worried about your family."

Ker clenched her teeth. She *had* thought more about Ester in the last two weeks than she had since the day Inquisitor Luca had taken her away, but . . .

"It still seems wrong. He's just a baby, lost, alone, scared."

"They don't want to hurt him." There was certainty in Tel's voice. "And helping the Miners may be our way out of here."

"Uh, I don't think they're exactly 'miners.'" The words were out before she knew she was going to say them.

"No, I don't think so either." Tel's arm tightened around her. "I think—I swear this isn't my fever coming back—"

"Just say it."

"I think they might be Feelers."

"I'd like to Flash the claw again," Kerida said. They'd had a chance to eat, and been shown a place to wash not far from their sleeping alcove, before being joined by about a dozen of what they'd agreed it was safer to call miners. Some were carrying nets, though there were a few spears and a couple of archers as well, carrying heavy war bows. "I could get a more accurate feel for where the griffin is this morning."

As she'd suspected, Ganni had the claw with him. He passed it over to her without hesitation. She took off the cloth and handed it him.

"She must have been very interesting," she said.

"Pardon?"

"The woman who wove this. Karal? Karan? I can't quite catch the name."

The old man looked from Ker's face to the cloth and back again. "She's been dead for years," he said finally. "Since— years anyway."

Ker almost caught what it was the man had meant to say. She nodded. "Sorry to hear that."

"Can you tell—no, never mind." Ganni pressed his lips tight before continuing. Again, Ker caught a wisp of thought. There was something unusual about the woman's weaving. He folded up the cloth and placed it in the satchel at his waist.

Ker looked away from the emotion on the old man's face and focused on the claw. *Paraste.*

"He's scared," she said aloud, turning the claw over in her hands. "Scared and lost. He wants his parents."

Ganni was handing Tel a net, but this made him pause and look over at her, his hand still on the loops of cord. "Somehow, you don't think of them feeling the same as we do."

"Why not? Doesn't a dog or cat feel things?" Tel said. He made a face as the woman with the scarred cheek they'd seen once before hefted her spear. "We seem to be awfully well-armed if we don't mean to kill it."

The woman's smile curled her lip back from her teeth. "And if we have to stop it from killing us?"

"Enough. There'll surely be no need for killing." It was hard to tell who, exactly, Ganni was trying to convince. "It'll speak to us, you'll see."

"And if it doesn't?" Scar-face was respectful, but firm.

"Then we show it a way out. We show it our good faith." He looked around at his fellows. "This may be a test." Her lips compressed, Scar-face nodded, and the others finally did the same. Ganni turned to Ker.

"Girl, do you have a direction?"

Ker turned slowly. Three tunnels opened into this space, and Ker turned to the one on the left. "That way," she said.

"There's branchings up that way," Ganni said. "Maybe that'll be a problem, maybe it won't. You'll have to go in front," he added.

"Not alone," Tel broke in. "At least give her a weapon."

"What do you think *I'm* for, you daft lad?" Ganni twisted his head up to look Tel in the eye. "Did you hear nothing we've said? She's as important to us as she could possibly be to you. Far more important than you are, if it comes to that."

"He's important to me," Ker said into the silence that followed the old man's words.

Ganni took in a deep breath and let it out slowly. "And we'll remember that, Talent. No fear."

Tel pressed his lips together and looked at her. Ker raised

her eyebrows and gave her head the smallest of shakes. Tel shrugged and stepped into place behind her, rolling his eyes a little when two other Miners moved in behind him.

They walked for some time before they reached the first crossroad and Ker stopped. Holding the claw in one hand, she crouched down to touch the floor with the other. Flashing, her awareness of the griffin was like a straight line in her head, but there was no tunnel that went precisely that way. Ganni stood almost over her, with Tel hovering at the old man's elbow. She hoped no one would touch her while she was still Flashing.

She straightened. "It's this way." She indicated the right-hand tunnel with her chin. "Sort of."

Ganni's brow furrowed. "Ennick." A younger man, as tall as Tel but bulkier, came trotting from the group of Miners behind them. "Am I right? This leads to the Rose Warrens?"

Ennick's eyes darted everywhere, never stopping on anything for long. His mouth hung a little open, his lower lip slack. There was a tremor in his left hand, and he looked as though he wasn't sure of his name. "Right, Chief. The Rose Warrens. Two turns, left and right, seven tunnels, Rock Face Nineteen."

"Any shafts?"

"The Clear Water Shaft, but that's past Nineteen, Chief."

"Cross points?"

Ennick frowned, squinting his eyes almost shut, and looking as though he might start to cry. Finally, he tilted his head to the left, and his face cleared. "Three. Tunnels Twelve and Nine, Nine and Eighteen, Seventeen and Thirty-four."

Ganni patted the younger man on the shoulder. "Good, Ennick, thanks. Good remembering." The slack mouth stretched to a smile that showed well-spaced teeth, and Ennick moved back to his position in the rear.

Ker shivered. The boy—which Ennick surely was, regardless of his age—reminded her of Orris back in the kitchens at

Questin Hall. That same slack face, that same absolute lack of focus until someone asked him to recite a recipe. Then, like Ennick with his directions, Orris never faltered.

"I'll want six of you," Ganni said, pitching his voice to the Miners behind them. "Two at each of the cross points Ennick mentioned. Make sure the griffin doesn't come back this way. If we can't communicate with it, we'll need to encourage it to move past Rock Face Nineteen, to Clear Water Shaft."

Ker could hear the sounds of running footsteps as the Miners disappeared into the dark.

Ganni looked between Tel and Kerida. "We'll hope it can get out at Clear Water Shaft. It should fit."

"'Should' seems a large word just now," Tel said. "Could it get above us there?"

The old man was already shaking his head. "Shaft's wider than this tunnel." He indicated the rock above them with a toss of his head. "But it's mostly straight up."

Tel whistled through his teeth, his fingers twisting the net he was holding. "And if it won't go, or it won't fit? Beasts fight more fiercely when backed into a corner," he pointed out.

"It's not driving it out we want, lad." The old man looked at Ker as he said this. "We want the Talent to speak with it."

6

ASHARP sting on his upper right arm and Jerek Firoxi stepped back, lowering his sword. At the look on Nessa's face, he stifled his protest.

"That's what you get for watching the people coming up the road instead of paying attention to the swords. You're lucky we're using black blades, or I'd have had your arm off."

"I don't feel lucky." Jerek rubbed his arm. "How did *you* know anyone was coming? You weren't looking."

"I knew because *you* were looking," Nessa said. This time she grinned and lowered her sword, finally turning to look for herself. "What's interesting enough to take you away from your sword lesson?"

Jerek shrugged. "These people don't look like the other refugees."

Nessa raised her eyebrows, her smile becoming fixed. She nodded slowly. "Explain your reasoning to me."

Jerek twisted his mouth to one side as he thought. "For one, they're all men, and they're all mounted. Their horses move like they're well-rested and have been fed and watered recently. So they've stopped somewhere close. For another, they aren't carrying anything with them but saddlebags, as if they expect to stop at inns. The others we've seen—well, they were all carrying a lot more stuff." He glanced at Nessa. "Should I fetch my father?"

Her eyebrows were lowered, and she studied the men as they approached. "Not yet. Three of them are soldiers. Eagle Wing if my eyes don't trick me. Let me see what they want first."

Jerek drew himself up straighter. Nessa hadn't sent him away, she hadn't even told him to put his sword down. Of course, it *was* a practice sword, but Nessa had told him you could kill people with one, even though she hadn't shown him how. Yet. Point was, Nessa was treating him like one of his father's guards, someone she wanted near her if it came to a fight. Not like a child.

Three of the men *were* wearing the green cloaks and tunics of the Eagle Wing, Jerek saw. One had a round metal helm with a horsehair brush—he'd be the officer.

"Can you see their sleeve colors?" he asked Nessa.

"I don't think it matters to us which Cohort they come from." Nessa lifted her empty left hand in greeting. Her right hand still held the sword. "It's who the civilians are that interests me."

The two civilians were wearing taller boots and longer tunics under their cloaks, one black, one blue. As they rode nearer, the man in the black cloak pushed back his hood, revealing a neat metal cap made of small rings that covered his head and neck. Nessa put her hand on Jerek's shoulder.

"That's not Polity armor, is it?" she said.

"No." Owning the land meant Jerek had no career in the military, but that didn't mean he wasn't interested.

"I didn't think so."

At that moment Black Cloak looked toward Jerek and

smiled. His face was friendly, his smile the same, but though he smiled back automatically, Jerek's stomach clenched a bit.

"Gentlemen," Nessa called out when the visitors were near enough. "Welcome to Brightwing Holding. I'm the Factor, Nessa Grassmeadow. How can I serve you?"

"You confirm this is Dern Firoxi's holding?" That was the Eagle officer.

Nessa hesitated, her mouth set in a thin line. "Well, if we're being all legal about it, Lord Firoxi stands as guardian to his son, Jerek." Nessa nodded at him. "Whose holding it is by inheritance from his mother."

The officer nodded, smiling, and gave Jerek an abbreviated salute before turning his attention back to Nessa. "You won't mind fetching his lordship, then."

"Not at all, once you tell me what brings you here asking for him."

The officer's eyes narrowed, and he glanced at the two civilians before looking once more at Jerek. "You'd best get your father, Lord Jerek."

Nessa's hand on his shoulder tightened, and Jerek hesitated, unsure which of them he should obey.

"Something I can do for you, gentlemen?"

Jerek wasn't usually so relieved to hear his father's voice. The man himself appeared in the main doorway and advanced until he stood close to Jerek's left side.

"Lord Dern Firoxi?" the military officer said. "Of Brightwing Holding?"

It was safe for Jerek to wince, since his father couldn't see him. Dern didn't like to be reminded that the lands had been his wife's. Since her death, some people had started calling the place "Firoxi Holding," and his father had stopped correcting them.

"I am Dern Firoxi." His father's voice was brittle, and Jerek swallowed.

"Fair day, my lord." The officer dismounted nimbly and

tossed his reins to Jerek with a wink. "I'm Kran Luxor, First Officer, Blue Company, Pearl Cohort, Eagle Wing. I've brought a Barrack with me, but I left them in the olive grove. I didn't know whether you'd have room for them all."

That was considerate, Jerek thought, eyeing the horse, who eyed him back.

"Not at all," his father said. "Plenty of room for them in the kitchen, and for the night, if they don't mind the hay barn."

Jerek shuffled his feet.

"They won't," First Officer Luxor signaled, and one of the other soldiers immediately headed back up the track toward the olive grove.

"If I might ask—?"

"What brings me here? Of course."

Jerek kept his eyes on Black Cloak, who'd just dismounted. His father didn't like being interrupted. He wouldn't show this soldier how displeased he was, but the rest of the household might see it later.

"You'll have heard about the recent upheavals in Farama, of course." The First Officer waited until Dern Firoxi had nodded, so Jerek began to relax. "May I introduce Pollik Kvar, a Poppy Shekayrin of Halia, Mage and representative of the Sky Emperor Guon Kar Lyn." Jerek's stomach tightened. The Halian Empire? This *was* one of the invaders, then. What was he doing here with Polity soldiers?

"Now I know what you're thinking, my lord, but let me assure you there's nothing to worry about. There's been a change of rule, that's all, and the Halians are just here to help us restore order, nothing more, nothing less. Disagreement among the royals doesn't need to affect real people like yourself."

Jerek's heart beat painfully in his chest. He knew from his tutors about changes of rule, but there hadn't been one for— why, old Kalnast, Nessa's grandfather who'd been his mother's old Factor, used to tell of something that happened in *his* grandsire's day. Some disruption within the royal family itself, if he remembered correctly. There'd been a civil war, and that was the reason only the Eagle Wing was allowed in the Peninsula. Had something like that happened again?

Jerek looked at the Halian, and found the man looking back. He smiled, quickly, and the man nodded. He had a tattoo around his left eye, a round large-petaled flower, like a poppy.

"There are, however, certain changes with which we expect everyone to comply," said the Shekayrin. His voice was deeper than Jerek had expected, and with very little accent. The First Officer stepped toward them, his hand out for Nessa's sword.

"Women aren't allowed to go about armed," he said. "You'll have to hand that over."

Jerek started forward, but Nessa's grip on his shoulder kept him in place. She looked toward his father.

Dern raised his eyebrows. "Surely you can see it's just a practice weapon, First Officer? Factor Grassmeadow has been putting my son through his sword work."

"You'll have to get him another instructor, my lord."

"I see. Nessa, please be so good as to give me the sword." Nessa immediately reversed the weapon one-handed, as she'd taught Jerek to do, and handed it, hilt first, to Dern.

Jerek looked from his father to the soldier and back. He couldn't believe that his father wasn't going to question this.

"That will be all, Nessa, thank you."

"Very good, my lord." She went, but not without giving Jerek a hard look he recognized immediately. Watchful and wary, it said to him. And that Nessa would expect a full report later. Jerek lowered his eyes and raised them, the closest he could come to nodding in front of these others.

". . . one of the conditions of our aid, Lord Firoxi," the Halian Shekayrin was saying, "that the rule of women, in all its forms, be over. The magic of the body, what you call the Talent, is outlawed, and it is a punishable offense to harbor or to aid any of those known as Talents."

His father was smiling, but Jerek didn't relax. He'd seen

that smile before. "I'm not sure I understand. 'The rule of women?' Without Talents, how will matters of Law be settled?"

Dern Firoxi was playing innocent. They'd already heard of this from the refugees. How the Luqs had been imprisoned, and the council made to swear a new allegiance.

First Officer Luxor was smiling again. "What the Shekayrin means is, from now on, the courts are only going to accept evidence that's plain to anyone. We won't have to just accept what a Talent says." The man shrugged. "I mean, how were any of us to know that they were telling the truth in the first place? Plenty of people outside the Polity don't use Talents, and their legal matters are attended to."

"The Halian Empire has functioned well without the so-called Halls of Law for many thousands of years," the Shekayrin added.

"I see." Dern nodded. "Yes. Well, there's much value in what you say."

His father's reaction was no surprise. Ever since that ruling about the olive trees on the edge of the southwest grove had gone against them, Dern Firoxi hadn't had much good to say about the Halls of Law.

Jerek wasn't sure how trees could tell you who had planted them and therefore who they belonged to, but he believed it just the same. He carefully kept that thought off his face.

". . . make as few changes as possible to the way things are." First Officer Luxor had pulled some papers out of his saddle bag and was looking them over. "In your case, for example, Lord Firoxi, I see that this was your wife's property, which she inherited from her father?"

"Yes, my late wife, the boy's mother."

"Well, not to worry, young lord." The soldier patted Jerek on the shoulder, which he managed to endure without cringing. "The place is still yours. But in future," the man continued, talking again to Jerek's father, "inheritance will pass only through the male line."

"But the property still belongs to my son?"

Jerek knew the other men would hear this and think his father was only worried about him, and they'd think Dern must be a very good and loving father.

"In Halia, the wife's property becomes that of her husband," the Shekayrin said. "I would suggest you make an inquiry to that effect once matters become more settled." The Halian paused, his brow furrowed. "A word of advice, Lord Firoxi. I would give the post of Factor to another, if you would like your inquiries to prosper."

Jerek's stomach dropped an inch, and he swallowed.

First Officer Luxor cleared his throat. "In the meantime, we're asking that everyone just continue going about their business until the new regime is settled."

"Any idea when that will be? My people will want to know."

You mean you want to know.

"At the moment we are seeking a suitable member of the royal family to assume the throne." The Shekayrin's tone left Jerek in no doubt who the "we" referred to. "But there do not seem to be many male candidates."

With the Luqs' second cousin Prince Hanlor also gone, there wouldn't be *any*, none that Jerek knew about anyway. And if there were any to be known about, his tutor would have made sure he'd memorized the names.

"What happens if they don't find anyone?" He flushed as his voice cracked halfway through his question.

His father frowned; later, Jerek would hear about speaking without leave, but that would be later. In the meantime, the Shekayrin was looking at him with interest.

"The Emperor will send a member of his own family, his own blood to sit on this throne. Our prince will marry here, and raise his family here, and become a good king to you, under the Sky Emperor, the father of us all." The Shekayrin bowed his head for a moment.

"Certainly, of course." Dern Firoxi smiled stiffly at the

Halian before turning back to the officer. "Is there anything else just now? Won't you come in and rest before the evening meal?"

"Just two more details, if you will." The soldier turned to the Shekayrin.

The Halian reached into a small pocket Jerek hadn't noticed before, made by the flower crest sewn on the front of his tunic, and pulled out a red stone. Jerek leaned forward to see it better. His father frowned, so he stepped back again.

"Are you familiar with this jewel?" the Halian said. His voice had thickened, and for the first time Jerek noticed the trace of an accent. "Are there any deposits of such a stone on your lands?" The Shekayrin turned to Jerek. "Young boys are great explorers, are they not? Have you seen such a thing, young man?"

"Well, Jerek? Have you? Speak up."

Jerek shook his head, momentarily speechless. "No. That is, there's the old quarry . . ." He let his voice die away. Their neighbors the Salcians might not appreciate him pointing soldiers and Halians in their direction. Olive trees or no olive trees.

"Yes, of course," he heard his father say. "But that old quarry is granite, not a fine stone such as this."

Jerek breathed easier.

"But you said there were two things?" Dern added.

After a glance at the Halian, First Officer Luxor continued. "The Shekayrin needs assurance that there are no Talents in your household, Lord Firoxi."

His father frowned, his brows drawn together. "This isn't a Hall, Officer Luxor. There are no Talents here, I give you my assurance."

"If you personally vouch for everyone else, my lord, then you would only need to be examined yourself."

Jerek's father blinked. "Examined? With no Talents, who, exactly, is going to examine me, Officer?"

"I shall do it, Lord Firoxi. With this." The Halian held up the red jewel again, and this time Jerek thought it looked darker, and as if something moved in its facets. "The stone contains no taint of the magic of the body. Alternatively, I could examine your entire household, but there would need to be compensation for my time."

"That will not be necessary." There was more steel in Dern Firoxi's voice. Steel Jerek was familiar with. "I will be happy to— What is it now, Jerek?"

Jerek must have tightened his grip on the horse's rein without being aware of it, making the horse jerk its head and snort at him.

"Nothing, sir."

But the Shekayrin was looking at him with narrowed eyes, absently rubbing the red stone between the thumb and fingers of his left hand. "Are you sure, little lord? Is there nothing you wish to tell us?"

Jerek clenched his teeth, and tried to keep his eyes away from the red stone. He shook his head, not trusting himself to speak.

"You mentioned a hay barn, Lord Firoxi. I'll send my men to have a look at it now, if you don't mind."

"We have nothing to hide, First Officer."

"Don't hurt them!" The words sprang out of his mouth before Jerek could stop them. They did stop the soldiers, though. "They're not Talents. They're just ordinary people going to their family in West Andal."

"Jerek!" His father's tone cut like a sword.

"I was going to tell you, sir, at dinner."

First Officer Luxor put his hand on Jerek's shoulder. "No harm done, Lord Jerek, but you do see that we need to check? Someone might lie about being Talented, you know."

Jerek gritted his teeth. His father was frowning, but Jerek was more upset by the fact that the soldiers were once more heading for the hay barn, this time with the Shekayrin close behind. It wouldn't take them long to find the three people he'd left hidden in the loft.

"Lord Jerek, you're not a child. You know what outlawry means. Talents should submit themselves, not run away. If these people are innocent, why have they fled?"

Jerek opened his mouth, but shut it again without responding. That was the kind of argument adults used when they weren't going to listen to you.

"Perhaps you should take your son inside, Lord Firoxi."

Jerek allowed the pressure of his father's hand on his shoulder to turn him and guide him toward the house. They stopped just inside the door, where his father turned to face him. Jerek stiffened before he saw the man's eyes were only clouded, not blazing. "Don't judge yourself harshly, son, you did the right thing. We can't believe everything these people tell us." His father shook him slightly, but at least his grip had loosened. Jerek would have a bruise as it was. "Orderly transfer of power, my horse's ass. This won't end here, Jerek, mark my words. We'll have to mind ourselves very carefully if we're to come out of this with our property and ourselves intact."

There was a smudge on the tile closest to the door. Jerek fixed his eyes on it. "Yes, Father."

Just then a woman started screaming, somewhere outside the house, and Jerek was glad that his father's grip had tightened again.

Ker's toe caught on an irregularity on the tunnel floor, and her own momentum carried her down. She threw up her hands to save her face, and the claw skittered off into the darkness ahead of her.

"You all right?" Tel and Ganni hooked their hands under her armpits and hauled her to her feet.

"I've lost the claw," she said, rubbing the graze on her left hand.

"Does it matter?"

"Who knows what's going to matter?"

Ker searched frantically as Tel held the glow stone for her. She'd just caught the gleam of something smoother than the rock floor and was reaching for the claw when a noise made them all stop and look around.

"Het! Het! Meeaou! Meeaou!"

The echoes came from everywhere. Tel scanned the space around them with narrowed eyes. "What is it?" His voice was hollow.

Ganni called into the surrounding darkness. "Anybody hurt?"

"Wait." Ker snatched up the claw and shoved it into the front of her tunic. "It's the griffin. He knows he's being herded, and it's frightening him." She clenched her jaw tight. It had sounded like a baby crying. A very large baby, but still . . .

"It doesn't sound very fierce, that's for sure," Tel added, echoing her thought.

"Doesn't it?" Ganni's tone was grim. "It's a baby yet, a chick like. But it's got no way to know we're trying to help it."

Ker bit her lower lip. What would happen if the griffin wouldn't communicate with her?

A sharp yell in the near distance got them all running, but they hadn't gone more than a couple of dozen spans when the light revealed a pair of Miners. One was the scar-faced woman, on her knees, cradling what was obviously a broken arm.

"I'm good, I'm good," she insisted, as they crowded around her. "It just nipped me with its beak, didn't break the skin. It's heading toward Face Nineteen. It's scared of us." She looked more worried about that than about her broken arm.

They left her being tended by her partner and ran on. This time Ker was careful where she placed her feet, though the bobbing light of the glow stone in Tel's hand wasn't too helpful.

"No! No!"

The words were clear enough, but the voice resonated in a

way that even the rock walls couldn't account for. The tunnel suddenly ended in a space that would have seemed larger, if it hadn't been full of a baby griffin.

The beast was as large as a bull, and almost as hefty. For all that, he was obviously a kitten. Or a chick. Both. Kerida shook her head. The feathers on his head and neck were still downy, though there were some longer true feathers as well, and his wings were well fledged. His lion's coat was the palest of golds and his paws seemed much too large.

Ker felt the hair stand up on the back of her neck. *Would he grow into those paws?* The beast was simultaneously the most terrifying and the most adorable thing she'd ever seen.

Tel had stopped just in front of her, facing the grifflet, net at the ready.

"Stop. Help. Stop." There was the explanation for the unusual resonance. It was the griffin speaking. He lowered his forequarters, tucking in his wings and turned his head to one side, as if intending to roll on the floor, so much like a cat about to ask for a belly rub that Ker stepped forward, hand outstretched, before she knew what she was doing. Tel barred her way with his free hand.

"Wait," she said, putting her hand on his arm. "It's trying to speak to us."

"It's just making sounds, like a mockingbird." Tel didn't let her pass.

"No. No. Speak. Speak." Again the griffin turned his head, this time lowering himself to the ground and tucking himself as far back against the wall as he could.

Tel glanced at Kerida as she inched away from him, his lips parted.

"Be so steady, Talent," growled Ganni. "Steady and sure."

Ker edged forward. "Are you speaking to us?"

"Speak! Out! Out!" He stood up, almost dancing, and his wings rose.

An arrow sprang out from behind her, and a curse, but it

shattered itself against the far wall to the beast's right. Both
Ker and the griffin had ducked, and both straightened slowly.

"Sorry, sorry," said a voice Ker didn't recognize.

"Hold still! Everyone!" She turned back to the griffin.
"Please. Sit." It was all she could do not to back away. Instead,
Ker patted the air with her hands, as if she was talking to a
dog. "Sit."

The griffin lowered himself once more to the ground, his
tail twitching back and forth. Had he responded to her request, or just to the movements of her hands? Ker swallowed,
stepped forward, holding out her right hand. "I'm going to
touch you, all right? Touch you, that's all."

"Kerida, no." Tel lunged for her sleeve but she managed to
stay out of his reach.

"I've got to, it's the only way I can Flash him." Ker kept her
eyes on the griffin. "You won't hurt me, will you?" She
stretched out her hand, hoping no one else could see her
trembling. At first, the griffin sat on his haunches and pulled
his head back as far as possible. Then, slowly, he moved his
head forward, just enough to sniff at Ker's fingertips. She felt
hot breath blow from his eagle's nostrils.

Finally he relaxed, his wings settling, and stretched out his
neck until his head was within her reach. Ker set her hand
down gently, and found the feathers unexpectedly warm,
downy and soft. *Paraste.*

Ker concentrated, trying to see the griffin not so much as a
living being, but as an extension of the claw she'd been carrying most of the morning.

"He doesn't have vocal cords like humans. But—" She held
up her hand and heard the murmurs behind her die away.
"He isn't just repeating the sounds, either, the way a mockingbird would. He's *choosing* the words." She looked back over
her shoulder. "He *is* speaking to us."

Ganni came closer, rubbing at his top lip with the fingers of his left hand. "Does he know of the Prophecy?" He pointed his sword, but he was only using it for emphasis, like a cook might use a knife to gesture with. "Will he—is he here to help us?"

"Help. Help. Yes. Food. Help. Food."

Now that she was standing so close, Ker could hear that each word was separated by an audible click.

"Wait." There should be some way to get a clearer sense of what the griffin wanted to say. She needed to communicate with him directly. Serinam, her old Tutor, had told them about Flashing the injured and sick, those who were unconscious or unable to speak. Like all Flashing, it involved the five questions, so she knew how it worked in theory . . .

This was part of what she was supposed to be able to do with people, but couldn't. Still, the griffin wasn't a person . . . wasn't the old bone of a tortured and murdered man. He was a newborn, scared and alone.

Tentatively, taking slow breaths to relax herself, Kerida felt for a deeper Flash. *Paraste*, she repeated, emphasizing that her blocks were down. At first, all she could feel was what she'd Flashed already, and then she became aware of a . . . resistance, a reluctance, as if she were trying to push herself against a current of water, or through a thick membrane, that turned hard and tough like the shell of an egg the more she pushed. She wondered if a block might feel this way, if you were Flashing it from the outside.

A chill trickle of fear ran down her spine, but she clenched her jaw and kept moving forward. *Who*, she thought. *Who are you? What are you? Tell me. Speak to me.*

Suddenly there was a dull tugging, a drifting feeling of nausea, and then her senses filled with light, and the resistance was gone. Lights, colors, flavors, odors—swirled over her until she floated on waves of brightness, nothing but space around her, like an open sky. The colors were everywhere, and came from everywhere, from inside her and, in particular, from the griffin.

<<Yes. Yes. Yes.>> She heard from far away. <<Now you. Your turn. You. What? Who? Why? How? Whenwhenwhen?>>

It was like flying in a dream, swooping on great bursts of air and light, like a kite on a windy day. A barrel in a maelstrom. A wall of water, thick and smothering, suddenly disappearing, leaving them free to soar. Dual images superimposed themselves. Ker realized this was how the griffin perceived things. Depths seemed deeper. Colors sharper. She saw herself, a being made entirely of streams of colors, some she had no name for. But then she saw that a shadow surrounded her like a mist of dark fog. Before she could become afraid, a wind came and blew the fog away.

"Are. You. All. Right? Kerida! Are. You. All. Right? Are. You. *Now*. Now? Not. Still. Then?"

Ker drew in a deep breath. What had happened to Tel's voice? Her lungs felt as if they'd been without air for days, but she felt lighter. She closed her hands, felt fur, and feathers. Then she knew. It was the griffin's voice.

Each of the others in the cavern with them was a concentration of colors and swirling, dancing light. Some were close to her, their auras actually touching, brushing hers. But were there more, many more, some much farther away?

People in the tunnels, her new awareness told her. And more beyond them—and beyond them, more still. The auras would go on forever, the colors—

Ker swallowed the panic that rose in her throat. *Terestre.* The world around her steadied, but the colors didn't fade.

Terestre, she said again, but nothing changed. <<Stop this!>> She knew she'd spoken aloud, but she could barely hear herself.

<<Why? It does not stop, it is always there. Why?>>

<<NO! I can't. Please.>>

<<Ah. I see. Curious. Here. Allow me.>> One of the griffin's unnameable colors separated from his aura, a broad ribbon

of light that reached toward her and wrapped itself around her like a warm shawl. The world steadied even more, the auras fading, and the light returning to normal.

She was still standing in the rock cavern, her hands on the griffin's back. Tel was still advancing in midstep toward her, with Ganni and the others behind him, their auras invisible again. As if nothing had happened.

Kerida swallowed and licked her lips. They had been terrifying when she'd thought she couldn't control them, but now that the auras were gone, everything seemed duller, less interesting. Was *this* what "Griffin Class" meant? Certainly, none of her Tutors had ever mentioned the auras. Was it because not everyone could see them? Ker started to smile.

"Thank. You. Oh. Thank. You. Kerida. Nast. Thank. You. I. Have. Remembered. Now. All. The. When. And. Where. And. Why. That. Came. Before. The. Who. *And.* The. What. I. Might. Never. Have. Remembered. Without. You."

There was still that slight click between each word, every one of them pronounced precisely, but the vocabulary had expanded, the griffin spoke faster.

"You're welcome, uh . . ." Ker dredged through the still jumbled Flashes . . . "Weimerk." That was the griffin's name. "What have you remembered?"

"Everything. The. World. And. The. Gifts. And. It. Is. Thanks. To. You. Without. My. Parents. I. Might. Never. Have. Known. I. Did. Not. Know. That. Talents. Had. The. Ability. To. Awaken. Me. Awaken. Us. Griffins." Weimerk looked around, eyes bright. Ker could almost believe he was smiling. "I. Know. How. To. Go. Home. Though—" He fixed her with one eye. "I. Could. Stay. Here."

Tel loomed up on Ker's free side, his brows drawn tightly together. "Ker, you're all right?"

Weimerk tilted his head to fix an eye on Tel. For a second Ker saw him the way the griffin saw him, the yellow, blue, and green swirls of light that formed him. Then it was just Tel again. His dirty face, tired and drawn with worry, his large hands. His pale eyes.

"She. Is. More. Than. 'All. Right. '" The griffin shook his head, his tail lashing like an angry cat's.

"Was I speaking to you?" Tel's eyes slanted sideways as he spoke.

"Show a little respect, soldier boy. This is a griffin." Ganni moved up to stand next to them. "Well, now, Weimerk, is it? There's nothing we'd like more than you staying, of course. Your coming is a sign to us, and a welcome one, that the Prophecy's time is here—"

"The. Prophecy?"

Ganni's eyes narrowed, and looks were exchanged among those gathered behind him. "You don't know the Prophecy?"

Weimerk cracked his wings. "Of. Course. I. Know. The. Prophecy.—I. Know. *Now*. I. Know. The. Who. And. The. What. And. The. Where. Until. The. When. Of. The. Last. Great. Gathering. After. The. When. Of. The. Gathering. I. Do. Not. Know."

Ker held out her hand. "What do you mean by 'know'?"

"It. Is. What. I. Remember. What. You. Have. Awakened. What. All. Griffins. Know. The. World. Until. The. Time. Of. The. Last. Great. Gathering."

"When—how long ago was that?" Ganni asked.

"I. Would. Have. No. Way. To. Know." Weimerk shrugged his wings. "The. Prophecy. You. Speak. Of. Was. Made. By. Griffins. At. The. Last. Great. Gathering. It. Was.—Oh! You. Believe. The. Prophecy. Is. About. *Me*. That. I. Am. The. Second. Sign! Yes. It. Could. Be. What. Fun. If. It. Is. So!"

"It's what we hope." The old man nodded and Ker saw the scarred woman nodding from the rear, her arm now in a sling.

"She *is* a Talent, and you *are* a griffin. So it seems the Prophecy speaks." Ganni looked like he didn't know whether to laugh or cry. Ker knew exactly what he felt. "But the fact is—"

"You. Cannot. Feed. Me?"

Ker was listening, but the voices seemed far away. She was suddenly light-headed, as if she'd had a glass too many of the sparkling cider her father used to have prepared for the winter feast. Everything around her was brighter, sharper. She felt light enough to float. She blinked and tried harder to concentrate.

"As it happens," Ganni was saying, "You've eaten some of our winter supplies already, and—"

Weimerk shook himself, the feathers around his eagle head standing out in a ruff until shaken back into place. Ker took a step back. He fixed one eye on her, and blinked.

"There. Is. Plenty. Of. Food. Outside," he said, speaking more to Ker than to Ganni. "More. Than. Enough. To. Restore. Your. Supplies. I. Should. Think."

Ganni came closer now, rubbing his fingers through his rough gray beard as he eyed Weimerk. "There's an exit we think is big enough for you. If you were thinking of obliging us, could you bring us, say, some cows, or sheep, or pigs. If you can bring us live ones, then two will do. If dead ones, three. Can you count?" The old man spread his hands in apology and backed up a step when Weimerk rattled his wings. "No offense. There's many can speak but have no head for figures."

"Three. Is. Not. A. Number. I. Have. Trouble. With," Weimerk said. "Three. Then. Two. Then. One. It. Is. The. Way. Of. Griffins." He bobbed his head.

Ker made a face. *Weimerk means the other eggs. The ones he's eaten.*

The griffin waggled its head as if exasperated. "So. The. Food. Question. Is. Attended. To. But. Something. More. Troubles. You."

"Not to say troubles, no. It's just . . ." Ganni scratched at his beard again. "The Prophecy didn't say you'd be so young. We were expecting someone who could give us advice, see?"

"Talents. Advised. By. Griffins? Of. Course. It. Has. Ever. Been. So. For. Tens. Of. Nest. Seasons." Ker staggered as Weimerk suddenly bumped her with the top of his head, as though he was nothing but a cat. She stroked the feathers between his eyes. "I. Remember."

He thinks we're all Talents. Ker exchanged a glance with Tel. She thought about how the arrow had jumped aside, missing Weimerk in the last moment, even though it had been heading straight for him. And Tel's wound, now nothing more than a scar. *Maybe he isn't entirely wrong.* Ker turned her attention to the old man.

Ganni watched her with narrowed eyes, one corner of his mouth twitching.

"I. Am. Hungry. Shall. I. Fetch. The. Food. Now?"

Weimerk insisted that Ker stay near him, so while Ganni walked ahead with Ennick, using the simple man's mapping skills, Ker and Tel stayed close to the griffin's side. The others, including the scar-faced woman, followed closely behind. The tunnels climbed steadily upward, heading toward the shaft the Miners thought was large enough for Weimerk. Before they'd gone very far, however, they reached an enormous cavern that was nothing more than a huge pit, the feeble flickers of the Miners' wristlets fading to nothing in the blackness.

"I don't remember Ennick mentioning this." Ker squinted. The place was at least twice the size of the great room at Questin.

"There's a way around," the simple man's voice boomed out. As if to illustrate his point, he set out along the right side of the pit.

Now that she knew where to look, Ker could see there was indeed a ledge, wide enough to walk on, leading around the edge of the hole.

"I shall fly across." Weimerk launched himself and in three

beats of his wings was across to the other side. Ennick waved and laughed, his eyes fixed on the griffin.

"Too bad Weimerk's not big enough to use as a ferry." Tel frowned at the ledge.

Ker grinned. "How can someone so tall be afraid of heights?"

"Yeah, very funny. Someone as tall as me doesn't always fit where the rest of you shorties can."

"Then we won't let you go first. Anapola! You lead the way, show soldier boy where to put his hands and feet. I'll go after you," Ganni said to Tel, "and Kerida can follow me." A woman with thick dark hair moved forward, looking Tel up and down as she squeezed past him to take the lead.

The ledge was wide enough at first, even for someone carrying packs, but as Ker half expected, it got narrower and narrower as they moved around the pit. Finally, a little more than halfway across, they could move ahead only by turning face-first to the wall, and stepping along sideways. Suddenly the darkness of the pit seemed darker.

"How far down does it go?" she asked out of the corner of her mouth.

"No one knows," Ganni answered the same way.

Like Ennick, Anapola had clearly gone this way before. She was quite a stretch in front of Tel, almost at the tunnel opening, where Weimerk waited, Ennick scratching him in the spot that qualified as "between the ears."

"Use the handholds," Anapola called back over her shoulder.

"Fine for you." From the sound, Tel spoke through clenched teeth. "You're half my size."

Just as Ker was bending her own knees to keep from tipping over backward with the weight of her pack, Tel yelped as his left foot missed the ledge entirely, and he slipped, hands scrabbling, over the edge.

Before Ker could call out, Ganni made a gesture with his left hand, his right one firm around a knob of rock. The old man's hand was held exactly as if it pressed Tel between the shoulder blades, and Tel fell no further, but began pulling himself up, feeling for hand- and toeholds, until he was once more standing on the ledge. He turned his head toward her, breathing hard and giving her a pointed look over Ganni's head.

Ker waited for him to say something, to ask what had happened, but all he did was stand, breathing heavily, his arms trembling. She opened her mouth to speak, when she saw the old man was looking at her as well. He moved his head from side to side. Just once. Ker nodded.

"Are you finished showing off?" was what she finally said. "Can we move along now?"

"Showing off. Yeah." Tel's voice was rough, but steady. "Remind me to tell you later how funny I think you are."

Once they were all safely in the far tunnel, Ker squeezed Tel's upper arm, and he patted her hand. They would talk about this, but they'd wait until they were far from here.

That's three, she thought, remembering an old saying of her mother's about looking for symptoms. First, the healing of Tel's wound. Then, controlling the movement of the arrow. And now, levitation, preventing Tel's fall. Three occurrences pointing in the same direction. None of them things Talents could do. All exactly the type of things Feelers could and did do, according to the old stories.

Ker shivered. Ganni and the others, the scar-faced woman, Anapola, even Ennick—there had been something similar in their auras. The colors she'd seen had been like her own, like Weimerk's. While she wasn't sure what that meant, she *was* sure it was nothing she needed to fear.

She took a deep breath and stepped back into place beside Weimerk.

They finally came to a wide shaft that was open to the cold, blue sky and a sharp, cutting wind. They were able to scramble up to the outer opening, but all Ker could see, her eyes slitted against the wind, was rock and snow. Now that they had come to "outside," Weimerk, paws shifting nervously, seemed in no hurry to leave. However, with Ker's hand on his shoulder, just above where the wings sprouted, Weimerk was brave enough to stretch his neck out of the opening of the shaft, pushing his beaked face into the wind. His eyes narrowed, but remained open. His beak clicked, as if he was tasting the air. His thick lion's tail lashed once, banging against Kerida's thigh.

He's never been outside, she realized. For all that he "remembered," Weimerk's egg had hatched in the mine.

"Are you sure about this?" she asked him.

"Yes," the griffin said. "I. Am. The. Second. Sign. I. Am. The. Wings. In. The. Sky. I. Am. Not. Afraid. Just. Tasting. And. Smelling."

Ker glanced at Ganni, and the old man shrugged and nodded at the same time.

"Someone'll be here waiting for you," he said, lifting his voice over the sound of rushing air. "Too much to hope you can bring a breeding pair, I suppose," he muttered to himself.

"Why?" Weimerk might have a bird's head, but he had the hearing of a cat. "Aside. From. Other. Things. They. Do. Not. Smell. The. Same."

"You can bring one of each?" The old man stepped closer to the griffin.

Weimerk put his head to one side, considering. "Yes," he said, finally. He looked outside again, blinking.

"It's all right." Kerida stroked Weimerk's flank. "You'll be fine." The griffin's fur was warm. He head-bumped her, knocking against her hip, and she took a step back to keep her balance.

Weimerk stuck his head out into the cold air again, this time taking a tentative step forward, claws out and curling on the edge of the rock face. Without warning, he tilted his head back, opened his beak, and shrieked.

The sound was a stabbing, bone-piercing pain. Covering ears did nothing. They knew the sound had stopped only because the intensity of the pain faded. Ker lowered her hands, shoulders still hunched.

"What—" Even now, Ker could barely hear herself speak; her ears were numb.

"I. Thought. Perhaps. If. My. Parents. Were. Near. . . ." He turned back and fixed his left eye on her. "*You.* Could. Come. With. Me," he said.

There was a silence so profound that Ker could hear everyone breathing. She hesitated, not sure exactly what she would say, or how she would say it. She felt the grip of Tel Cursar's long fingers above her left elbow.

"Thank you, Weimerk," she said. "But I don't think so. I don't think you're large enough to carry me."

"That. May. Be. So." The griffin bobbed his head. "I. Will. Come. Back. For. You. When. I. Am. Larger."

"I may not be here," she said.

"I. Will. Find. You." He turned back to Ganni. "Someone. Will. Await. Me. Here?"

"That's right. Day or night, until you get back."

"Very. Well. I. Am. Not. Afraid." This time when he turned away, Weimerk launched himself into the air.

This was nearer the opening than Tel Cursar was comfortable with, given that near miss in the mine shaft. He squinted against the cold wind, fingers itching to pull Kerida back from where she crouched even closer to the edge, watching the griffin until he was nothing more than a speck in the sky.

"Cuarel? You'll call the others?" Ganni rubbed his hands together, blowing on his fingers.

The scar-faced woman stepped nearer, wincing as her broken arm bumped against one of the others.

"Already have," she said. "Sala's on her way, and the rest of the small council with her."

Tel frowned. Kerida was still looking out of the opening. "Where does this leave us?" he asked, when it seemed that she wasn't going to turn around. "She's spoken with your griffin. Can we be on our way?"

At these words, Ker spun around, argument clear in every tense inch of her body. But when he raised his eyebrows at her, her shoulders lowered, and she nodded. She'd have been saying the same thing, if her encounter with the griffin hadn't turned her head.

If that was all it had done. Even now, there was a far-off look in her eye, and Ker was more than half turned toward the opening, as if part of her was already waiting for it to come back for her. He had to get her out now. They were both needed elsewhere, especially Kerida, and they'd better get out while they still could.

If they still could.

"You could stay," Ganni said. "You'd be welcome."

"We have our own commitments," he said into the silence. "We have reports to make, and warnings to carry." He pointed at the sky with his chin. "The griffin doesn't change that for *us*."

A sudden commotion in the background, and Larin squirmed her way between the waiting people, deftly avoiding the hands that reached for her. "I told you so." She ran to Ker and wrapped skinny arms around her waist, sticking out her tongue when she noticed Tel looking at her. "No one listens to me." Ker automatically laid her hand on the child's head.

"Peace." Sala threaded her way to the front, patting Cuarel on the shoulder as she passed her. She raised the hand that didn't have a spear in it and everyone quieted. Military training for certain, Tel thought. You couldn't get that crack of command in your voice without it. "Ennick, sweetheart, did you see the griffin? Is he happy?"

"He is. He was scared at first, but then Kerida talked to him—that's Kerida—and—Sala, you should have been here! He was this big, and his wings went out to here, and he talked and everything."

"That's good, Ennick, just fine. You can tell me more about it later, all right? After supper, when I'm off duty." She reached up to pat him on the shoulder. As tall as she was, the simple man was bigger. "That settles things for me, Ganni." She turned to take in the rest of the small council, who by now had gathered near. "Are we all in agreement? This is the Second Sign?"

Everyone on the small council nodded.

"This is wonderful," Norwil said, rubbing his hands through his close-cropped hair. "This'll show those other Clans which of us is more important." Sala rolled her eyes and shook her head, but she was smiling.

"I told you she was the one." Larin was swinging from Ennick's forearm.

"Yes, Larin, you did. You're very smart." Sala nodded. "What are your plans, Griffin Girl?"

"We need to go," Ker said.

Tel looked at her, relieved to hear her sounding so normal. She'd lost her wide-eyed stare and looked more and more like the girl who'd told him off about his wound. Tel rested his right hand on her shoulder. How could she be so calm? Was it her Talent training, or did it have something to do with the griffin? And while he was thinking about that, what *had* happened between them? Would he get the chance to find out?

"But won't they tell? The soldier at the least will." The pointing finger came from the deep-voiced Midon. Tel managed not to snarl.

"'They'll tell.'" The words were followed by a snort. "'Course they won't tell—who ever heard of such foolishness?"

This was an entirely new voice, clear, and thin, with just the hint of a crack in it. It reminded him of his grandmother, and Tel craned his neck to see where it was coming from. Ker nodded, her eyes narrowed. Whoever it was had to be in the shadows behind Larin, but he couldn't see anything back there.

"Ach, you're such children. You mustn't stop them and you can't. They won't tell about us, because we'll ask them not to, won't we?" There were some smiles among the larger group, though one or two looked puzzled until their neighbors whispered in their ears, whereupon they, too, smiled. "We're in the hour of prophecy—help them, don't hinder."

"You don't get a vote here," Midon said, his face and his voice sullen.

But the unseen speaker only laughed. "Boy, if you don't stop being such a fool, I'll tell your mother. Gods, it doesn't take a Seer to know why no woman will have you."

Most of the group looked down, or away, at this, but some smiled openly. Tel found himself doing the same. He saw Midon looking at him and smiled broader, shrugging one shoulder. Ker poked him, and he turned an innocent look in her direction.

"You're not helping," she whispered.

"Don't be so sure."

"Enough." Sala thumped the rock floor with her spear. "I have asked for confirmation, and received it. The Griffin Girl may go as she wishes, and her soldier with her, though we will ask them not to speak of us." Sala gave a short bow in the direction of the darkness behind the little girl.

"So then, Lizar, you and Marko wait here for the griffin. Amel, you and Borgan will escort our guests to the exit they need." Sala's eye fell on him, and her look made him stand up as straight as he could in the confined space. She turned to the old man. "You'll look after it, Ganni?"

"That I will."

The dark woman nodded and turned back to the group.

"This council meeting is dismissed. Thank you for your time and attention."

In almost less time than it took to dismiss them, the people who'd made up the council were gone, disappearing silently into the darkness, leaving only the two guides, Ganni and the other woman from the council, Hitterol. At the last minute, Midon turned to give them one final hard look, his lips pressed tight, shaking his head, before he, too, was gone.

"A lucky thing that old woman spoke for us," Ker said. "Who is she?"

Ganni smiled. "You saw her, did you?"

"Of course, I did." Ker glanced at Tel, a puzzled look on her face, before turning back to Ganni. "She was standing over there, with Larin."

"How about you, soldier boy, did you see her?"

Sudden exhaustion made Tel answer honestly. "I heard her speak, but I couldn't see anyone."

"But—" Ker shut up, her upper lip between her teeth. "Must have been the shadows," she said finally.

"Sure." Tel shrugged. What possible difference could it make now? The important thing was that they were going to be allowed to leave. "Will the rest of our gear be returned?"

"It's being carried to your exit now." Ganni fixed them both with his hard eyes. "You can't talk about us, do you understand?"

"Of course." Tel would have agreed to anything. Smiling, Hitterol took his hand and Ker's, and she waited until she was sure she also had their attention.

"I'm not certain you *do* understand," she said. Her voice was like music, soothing and soft. The silver strands in her faded red hair shone in the dim light. "Any mention of us, no matter how fleeting, and you endanger us all. That would be a poor return for our hospitality." She smiled. "To say nothing of what it might do to the Prophecy. You *can't* talk about us to anyone else. You must promise."

"We promise never to talk about you, don't we, Tel?"

Ker was serious. Tel paused. Keeping his promise would mean lying to his superiors—or at the very least leaving something out of his report. He took a deep breath and let it out slowly. Son and Daughter knew, he thought with an inner grin, it wouldn't be the first time.

"Sure, I promise. Who's going to believe us, anyway?"

THE tunnels were angling downward again, and cross
passages appeared more and more often, but it was obvious that both Ganni and Ennick knew exactly where they
were going. Tel was unusually quiet, so much so that Kerida
kept looking behind her to make sure he was still there. The
first few times he grinned, but gradually the grin turned to
something more like a grimace.

She shivered, wondering whether his aura might hold a
clue to how Tel felt—if she were brave enough to Flash it. She
missed the beauty of what she'd seen when in contact with
Weimerk, but a small part of her was relieved the colors were
gone.

"Here we are, then, youngsters." There was fatigue in Ganni's voice, though his eyes were as bright as those of Ennick,
grinning over the old man's head. Ganni stretched out a hand
and touched Ker's shoulder, putting his other hand on Tel's
arm. "We trust you to keep your promises." He wasn't exactly
asking.

On impulse, Ker covered the old man's hand with her own. "Will you be safe here? With the griffin?"

"Is anyone safe anywhere?" He patted her hand. "He's speaking to us, so all's well. Come back to us if you can, young ones."

Tel waited until they were a good few paces beyond the exit before he dropped his pack and wrapped his arms around her. Startled, Ker almost pulled away, but the comfortable warmth and nearness of him made her relax into his embrace.

"Kerida." She nodded and his arms tightened. "Those people are Feelers."

She nodded again.

"And there was a griffin."

"Yes, there was."

"I'm not going crazy."

"Well, I wouldn't go *that* far."

He barked out shaky laughter, his hands steady on her shoulders as he backed away. "Are we lucky to have escaped with our lives? Or have we allies we never expected?"

"A little of both, maybe," she said. "Thank the Mother we fit into this prophecy of theirs. Though we're not to tell anyone about it . . . or them," she added.

"Seriously, I'll say it again, I'm not sure anyone who wasn't here would believe us." He finally released her and picked up his pack. "What does it all mean, this prophecy business?"

"At the moment, it means they let us go," Ker said.

"And they'll help us in the future—or help *you*. They didn't seem to like me much."

Ker lifted her shoulders and let them fall. Ganni had healed Tel, and then saved his life. She cleared her throat, as a sudden need to cry swept through her. She took an unsteady breath. "I'd say something clever and reassuring, but I can't think of a thing."

"Now *that's* something to thank the Mother for." Tel looked around at the moonlight, his weak smile fading. "Shouldn't it be midafternoon? Or can Feelers manipulate that as well?"

"More likely they just keep to a different clock. And why not, since they don't have the sun?" She rubbed her forehead. "Dawn's not *that* far off." She tried to relax shoulders that kept creeping up. Suddenly, things seemed so *open* and *wide*. She looked at the sliver of moon that hung just above the horizon to the west and frowned. "How many times did we sleep?"

"What?"

"Look." She pointed upward. "Going by the waning of the moon, it's been three days since we entered the mines. I don't remember sleeping three times. More like once. No wonder I'm so exhausted."

"Not much rest in our immediate futures either," Tel said. "Three days." He looked up again, examining the placement of the moon and the stars. "We're a ways to the southwest from the road, even if this is the closest exit to it."

"What do you mean 'a ways'? We're in Bascat, aren't we? We've crossed the Serpents Teeth, haven't we?" She hitched her pack a bit higher, and took a deliberate step forward. They needed to be moving, not just to make up time, but to keep warm.

Tel, still looking up, nodded. "We're on the right side of the mountains, but I can't tell exactly how far we are from the road. At least a day, I'd imagine." He glanced at her. "And then, not far from Temlin Hall."

They'd each be going their own way then, and Ker wondered if Tel was feeling reluctant to leave her. She shook herself. That was about as useless a thought as she'd ever had.

Her experience with the griffin had been one of those breakthroughs her teachers at the Hall were always talking about, though none of them had ever mentioned the auroras of color and light. She wondered if she would know what Tel was feeling if she touched him now, the way she'd known with Weimerk? There was another useless thought.

"Are *you* going to include them in your report?" On the word "them" Tel had jerked his head back toward the entrance, as if he didn't want to say the word "Feeler" out loud again.

Ker shivered, and not from the cold. Luckily, Tel had stepped ahead of her and didn't see. She knew perfectly well she should tell the Senior Talent at Temlin about the Feelers. But she had an idea of how those hidebound bureaucrats would react to the news that there were Feelers in the Serpents Teeth—they might even decide the Feelers were a greater enemy than the Halians. And if she didn't report the Feelers, what could she say about the griffin, or their prophecy? She touched the front of her tunic, where the claw everyone else had forgotten about was still tucked safely away.

"I don't know," she said finally.

"Me either," Tel admitted. "Let's hope we think of something when the time comes." He straightened up. "Off that way, northeast. We should find the road easily enough."

"Do we want to?"

"Snow closed the pass, didn't it? It's not as if they can come through after us. And snow or no snow, the road will be easier going than cross-country."

That was true enough. "I know the road from the pass goes right by Temlin Hall, but that's all I do know."

"So I can see you safely there, at least. Oste's about a day or so farther along. The Mother knows the Luqs wouldn't be comfortable with the Battle Wings any closer to the Peninsula." Once again, there was a smile hovering in Tel's tone.

Ker nodded before glancing back over her shoulder at the mine entrance. "Should we get moving, then? We'd be able to get quite a bit farther along before the moon sets, and even after that, there's enough snow to keep things bright for walking."

Tel shook his head, mouth twisted to one side. "Anxious to get back to the comforts of your Hall, are you? I don't blame you." His face sobered quickly. "Though I don't envy you the news you have to bring them."

Ker rubbed at her forehead again, and swallowed. She hadn't thought about that. No, she'd managed to put that thought right out of her mind. Bad enough that she'd seen what she'd seen, and had to remember what she had to remember. Now she was going to have to tell it all to someone else, and bring down on them the same devastation she'd already suffered herself.

At least they'd believe her. At least she wouldn't have to go through what Tel Cursar and his mates had experienced. A touch on her shoulder startled her.

"Hey," Tel said. "Don't worry, we'll get there."

"I'm looking forward to it," she said. He drew down his brows, nodded, and set off between the trees. As she stepped out after him, Ker was surprised to find that what she'd said was actually a little bit true. "The sooner I can tell my superiors about the Halians, the better. Let older and wiser heads worry about what to do next," she said to Tel's back.

"I'm with you," Tel said. "That's what senior officers are for."

When the shouting started, Talian Pepin remembered his training and ran toward it, not away. It was the blond boy they had by the elbow, the tavern keeper and the large man with the broken nose who'd been eating in the common room. Talian bounced on his toes trying to see more, just like everyone else in the wide part of the street just outside the Pig and Acorn Tavern. They were shaking the blond boy hard enough that he couldn't have answered their questions if he'd wanted to.

"He was hanging around my table, I tell you," Broken Nose was shouting. "If he doesn't have my purse on him, it's because he's passed it off to a confederate."

"Then it's long gone, that's certain," the tavern man said. "We'll have him examined, is what we'll do, we'll—" He snapped his mouth shut and went red in the face. Several of those watching looked down, feet shuffling, and a few on the edge of the crowd melted away.

Tavern Man was murmuring to Broken Nose, and Talian edged his way closer. He didn't really know the blond boy, he'd seen the kid around, but he didn't belong to Old Goreot like Talian did. Still, the old lady would want to know what happened here.

"No, I won't let him go! He took my purse, I tell you, and I'll have it out of him one way or another." Broken Nose stabbed at Tavern Keeper with his thick finger. "How do I know *you're* not in with him yourself? It's *your* place I was robbed in."

Now Tavern Keeper stepped back, looking Broken Nose up and down with his lip curled in disgust. "Fine, then," he said. "We'll take the boy to the town hall, and see what they say. But I'll tell you right now, you won't be happy with it."

Talian melted away with the rest of the onlookers, bored now that it seemed there'd be no fighting. The two men were both right; the thief *had* passed the purse to a confederate, and it *was* long gone. It was just bad luck that the blond boy wasn't the thief. Bad luck for the boy, too, since there'd be no Talent who could clear him.

Talian shook his head as he walked away, careful to keep his expression neutral. Bad luck for everyone.

———

They found the road shortly after sunup. Though they'd been going north, and a little east, there was less snow here than there had been at the tunnel entrance.

"It's definitely warmer," Tel said, disregarding the way his breath fogged in the air. "I'm not even sure that the ground has frozen."

"Ground around here won't freeze until after Darknight," Ker said. "That's when the cold's really going to hit."

I can't believe we're talking about the weather, she thought.

Were they clinging to the normal, to balance what they'd been through? Still, she might be able to turn it to her advantage.

"So where you come from the ground should be frozen in Windmonth?" she said.

"I'm from Orrin Province," he said, over his shoulder.

"Oh." Ker frowned. Orrin was off to the east and north, she thought. "I didn't know they were admitting people from Orrin Province to the Wings." *And wasn't* that *a tactful thing to say*. A province normally had to be part of the Polity for three full generations before its people could be considered for citizenship.

"They aren't," Tell said. "But it's only my dad's from Orrin. He was a Lion's Wing auxiliary. My mother's a Lion, a Cohort Leader. So I can claim full citizenship on her side. She's from Andal Province."

That made more sense. Andal was actually part of the Peninsula, one of the original five provinces. It explained why a military career was open to Tel Cursar, and might even explain his rank. Only citizens could be in the Wings, though there were auxiliary units made up of non-citizens. In fact, that was often how citizenship was won early.

Now that they were on the road, Tel fell into the measured marching stride that all troops were trained in, regardless of rank. That pace, and the roads that made it possible, were what accounted for the Wings' uncanny speed, to say nothing of the Polity's rapid communications, since the roads were also used by Polity couriers wherever they ran. A road meant not only that she and Tel could make better time, but it relieved the strain on ankles and leg muscles that couldn't be avoided among the roots and rocks of the forest.

Ker staggered a bit at first, but she soon fell into old habits, and matched her stride to Tel's, keeping pace with him without even being aware of it. The steady monotony was helpful, in that it gave her time to think, and to prepare what she was going to say to the Senior at Temlin Hall. Temlin's Senior was a man, unusual, but not unheard of. Women in the Polity did tend to live longer than men, but it wasn't that kind of seniority alone that gave a Talent administrative rank.

She glanced at Tel Cursar. He'd have to come into the Hall, to resupply if nothing else. If he agreed to be examined, his testimony and evidence would add valuable detail, but . . . Ker took a half step and almost stumbled before resuming her pace.

"You can't be examined," she said. "The Feelers—"

"Would be exposed." He nodded his understanding. "What about you?"

"They'll believe me without examination, but if they want all the detail . . ." Suddenly Ker almost choked on an unexpected bark of laughter. Thanks to Barid, that kind of discovery wasn't something she needed to worry about. The block he'd taught her, the one that was to keep Inquisitor Luca's secrets safe, could now be used to keep the Feelers' secret as well. There was irony for you.

"I'll be all right," she told him. "All we have to do is stop them from examining you."

"Shouldn't be a problem." He shrugged. "They can't force me, and there's no senior officer to order it—well, what do we have here?" He stopped and peered at the road surface, pointing out a track. Roads were maintained by the Polity, but locals did use them, and there were always tracks crossing and meeting them along their routes. This one showed more use than any of the others they'd passed already.

"Does this look like a hoofprint to you?" Tel asked, squatting on his heels.

"Well, if it doesn't, this certainly looks like a horse dropping." Ker pointed to another spot on the road. Tel trotted over to take a closer look. Ker knew there were soldiers who could tell from the size, shape, and temperature of droppings how old they were and what the horse had eaten, though it was never something she herself had been called on to learn.

She scanned the road surface around them. The hard-packed gravel showed dirt from the track, maybe some marks where snow had taken longer to dry—

"Kerida."

She turned her attention back to where Tel still looked down on the horse dropping with a peculiar expression on his face. He glanced back up at her, and lifted his brows.

"Oh, no," she said, raising her hands and shaking her head. "You're joking, right? You can't mean it."

"Polity soldiers travel on foot," Tel pointed out. "And Polity cavalry travel in troops. This is a single rider. We need to know whether this is a courier, or a noble, or a farmer—or something else entirely. We need to know how safe it is for us to be on this road."

Ker huffed out her breath. He was right, of course. They'd been assuming they were safe in Bascat Province because the pass was snowed in, but the Halians had landed in more than one place in the Peninsula. What if they'd landed outside of it as well?

"It's not like it's fresh," he said as she still hesitated. "It's practically frozen." It helped that Tel wasn't smiling. If he had shown the least sign of laughter . . .

"Oh, sure. That makes *all* the difference. Stand away from it." Ker waited until he'd backed a few paces off and then crouched down next to the dropping. She made a face, clearing her throat. According to the stories the Tutors had told them, Full Talents were called on to Flash much worse things than days-old horse excrement.

Paraste. The first thing she Flashed was Tel's aura, three colors beautifully bright and clear, but not overwhelming—perhaps because there was only one of him, or perhaps because the griffin wasn't here as well. Ker took a breath and refocused.

"It was a Polity horse," she said. "But the rider—" She

frowned. "The rider was a Halian. The horse was heading back toward the pass. Two days ago."

"Blast. I thought you said the pass was closed." Somehow, even his aura seemed to be frowning. "Are there any more on the road?"

Ker straightened to her feet, stung by his tone. "How much do you think I can tell from one horse dropping?" Ker had a sudden image of Tel looking around for more droppings for her to Flash. "Or more than one, for that matter? There's a limited amount of information involved, and most of it's about the horse. I was lucky to get what I did."

"No, of course, well done." But Tel was looking up and down the road. It didn't take a Talent to see indecision in the way he was standing.

"We have to go on, Tel," she said. She bent and scrubbed her hand on the surface of the road, though she knew that wouldn't make it any cleaner.

"Then we should get off the road," he said. "It might take longer—what?"

Ker had frozen, her hand still on the gravel. She was Flashing the road itself.

"Tel." Her voice sounded far away. She looked up at him. He really was impossibly tall. "Tel, the Hall." She licked her lips. "Something's wrong." She turned away, but Tel grabbed her arm.

He scanned her face. "No running," he said. "A good steady double time. Kerida!" Her name was like a whip. "Are you listening? Double time. Nice and steady."

Ker took a deep breath and let it out slowly, though it didn't slow the beating of her heart. "All right." She nodded. "You lead." If the Hall actually connected to the road, she might have been able to Flash more. As it was . . .

They set off again, and Ker focused on the familiar rhythm of double-time pacing, tricking her mind into shutting down her thoughts. And it worked, until an odor drifted past her and she stopped dead, feet automatically falling into the correct stance.

Tel Cursar took several more steps before realizing she was no longer trotting behind him. He stopped, crouching slightly, hand on the hilt of his sword. Scanning the edges of the woods, he spoke without turning to look at her.

"What?" His voice was pitched not to carry.

"Did you smell that?" she said, her head up and her nostrils wide. "Something's burning."

Tel tilted his head back and sniffed. Ker had the horrible feeling she was going to giggle. To anyone looking at them, they must resemble a pair of dogs.

"Not burning," he said. *"Burned."*

Ker wasn't aware she'd started to run until she felt Tel's painful grip on her arm, holding her back. "Let me go," she said.

"Let you go where?" he said, his voice hard and cold as steel. "If that smell means what we fear it means, then running there won't help. We've got to go slow and easy, careful and measured."

Ker knew he was right. But she wanted to smack him anyway.

He must have read that in her face, but he also saw she was listening because he let go of her arm. She could still feel the pressure of his fingers. His voice wasn't the only steely thing about him. She straightened her pack and set off once more.

"It might not be as bad as you think," he said, catching up with her.

But of course it was. It was worse.

Tel had not let her run, but he did increase their speed until they were sprinting in triple time. The muscles in Ker's legs had only just begun to remind her how long it had been since she'd run anywhere at attack speed when the woods opened up to the right.

The Hall should have been easily visible from the road, yet it wasn't. For the first time in days Ker didn't feel the cold air, the chill of her fingers. She didn't feel anything.

Tel was poised to grab hold of her again, but there was nowhere for Ker to run. Temlin Hall had been considerably smaller than Questin, just a regional Hall, serving anywhere that the road reached on this side of the Teeth, whether farms, villages, or towns. It had housed at most twelve people, counting the Full Talents, who would have doubled as administrators, plus their clerks, servants, cooks, and hostlers. Unlike the military, Talents relied on horses to reach the people who needed the Rule of Law as quickly as possible.

But instead of the familiar two-story edifice made from stone and wood, with its central courtyard and its outlying buildings for storage and stable, there was nothing here but the utter and complete destruction that she had not waited to see at Questin.

Charred beams jutted up from piles of stone broken and cracked open. Walls had crumbled from the top as the fire had worked on the mortar. Everything was streaked with soot and ash, except where new snow had fallen—though, judging from the wet and the muck, snow had also fallen while the stones and debris were still warm enough to melt it.

"Careful." Tel had hold of her arm again. "Some of it's still smoldering."

"I don't feel any heat." There was something surprising in how ordinary her voice sounded.

"Just the same, don't touch anything." Tel released her. "And be careful of the cellar hole."

The cellar hole. Of course. That's why there didn't seem to be enough debris left for a whole building. Much of it must have collapsed into the cellar.

"I don't understand," Tel said from behind her. "These are useful buildings. Why burn them? They've even pulled the stones apart where they could. Why would anyone do this?"

"You were right." Ker's eyes hurt, and she realized she needed to blink. "Don't you see? You were right all along. They *are* targeting Halls on purpose. They're destroying the Law."

"How did they get here ahead of us?" Tel was focused on the destruction in front of them, as if he wished he could deny what his logic and training couldn't understand. Finally, he looked down at her. "The snow closed the pass," he said. "So how did they get here?"

Ker licked her lips. It wasn't an idle question. They needed to find out if they could. There was no one here to report to, but surely at Oste . . . She shucked her pack and rubbed her palms together.

"No." Tel held her shoulders from behind. "Don't do it, Kerida, don't. Not here. Just leave it."

She might have listened, but at that moment the breeze shifted and the quality of the burning smell changed from charred wood to something meatier. Ker swallowed, blinking away sudden tears, and hoping her stomach would settle. She clamped her hand over her mouth to stop the whimper she was afraid would escape. She wished she could do as Tel said and just leave it.

"We need to know," she said, lowering her hand when she could trust her voice. She turned to face him, glad that he still kept his hands on her, kept her steady. "Gather intelligence when you can. It's what any commander would say, you know that."

"Of course, but you're not . . ." Tel let his voice die away.

"Not a soldier." She gestured at the mess in front of them. "If the Halls are gone—" She shook her head. "That makes me a soldier again. It makes all of us soldiers." She clenched her jaw. Now, when she no longer wanted it, she would be a soldier again.

She saw comprehension in Tel's eyes. Until now they had clung to the belief that their world hadn't really changed, that somewhere, at the next Hall, over the next range of hills, they would find their world intact. What she saw in Tel's face was the realization that this hope was gone.

"Don't take long," he said finally.

"Yes, sir," she said, and was startled by his sour grin.

Kerida rubbed her hands dry on her thighs, looking around, trying not to see charred beams, blocks of stone, bits of melted glass and fractured tiles, but the item that would best fit her purpose, that would tell them the most. She blew on her fingers. She had to watch her footing; everything underfoot was a soggy, broken mess.

She spotted a squared block of stone, perhaps part of the chimney, and crouched down next to it. When she brushed tentatively at it with the edge of her hand, she could see it was undecorated, too rough to be wall tile, but too smooth to be a piece of the courtyard flagstone. *"Paraste,"* she said under her breath, placed her left hand on the least cracked part of the block, and found it pleasantly warm.

Nothing. Ker flexed her fingers and concentrated, tried not to be frightened by the fact that her quiet place, the place her mind needed to be for Flashing to begin, wasn't within her reach. For the first time in two years she found herself cursing the completeness of the block she'd been so happy, at first, to learn.

She slowed her breathing. Focused on her small room. The hangings on the wall made by her mother that shut out all drafts. The wide chair, with all its cushions, and the rug to cover her legs. A small table with one of her mother's precious books on it. The fire laid in the brazier. She could feel the rough warmth of the rug. Smell the apple wood waiting to be lit. *Paraste.*

"Ow!" She jerked her hand back, and hoped that Tel hadn't heard her. She'd felt the fire. The block had been burned, for the Mother's sake. She took another deep breath and tried again. The stone had been cut from a quarry not far from here, by a man named Dorwod; it had waited weeks for others to be cut, days being placed and mortared by Dorwod and his sons—

"Ker! What's taking so long?"

Startled, Ker almost fell over backward. "It's very old," she said, when her heart was no longer in her throat. "There's a lot to sift through." She blinked. Tel's aura had grown spiky.

"Can you tell when it was burned?"

"Four days ago." As usual, the answer popped into her head, and Ker sighed. No need to go on touching the object to learn all she wanted to know. That was a mistake she hadn't made since her first year of training.

"And how did they manage that? How did they manage to be here four days ago?"

Ker shook her head. "I'm afraid it doesn't work like that," she said. "The stone block can only know things about itself."

Tel looked down at the stone, a vertical line forming between his brows. "It *knows* things?"

Ker blew out a breath. There really wasn't any better way to put it. Just for a moment the air around the stone flickered, almost as if it had an aura of its own, or as if one lingered around it, if that was possible, something to do with how the burning had started . . . but the sensation faded before she could Flash anything more than the ghost of a spidery web of . . . red?

"Look around," she said finally. "See if there's anything that might have belonged to one of the Halians." She frowned. "Maybe something red."

Tel turned away and began to pick his way through the debris. Ker straightened and stood up, but didn't move at first, afraid of what she would see if she really started looking. Three years ago, she wouldn't have hesitated to search a battlefield just because there might be human remains about. She swallowed and set off on an angle from Tel. As a Full Talent she might have been asked to Flash bodies, to determine how they'd died. She couldn't afford to be squeamish now when a great deal more than a case of Law might be at stake.

As her shadow moved off to the right, Ker began to worry that she wasn't going to find anything quickly enough to do any good. They'd been here too long already, and someone was sure to come back and find them. Would anyone at this Hall have fought the Halians? Perhaps injured one enough that they'd had to take off tunic or shirt to have their injury dressed? Would anyone have left even a damaged piece of clothing behind in weather such as this?

Ker was so sure that the answers to these questions had to be "no," that it took her a moment to realize she was standing still, staring at a mark on the ground. A boot print. In the mud. Not hers. She glanced around, saw Tel off to her left. Not his either. Someone had been here after the fire. She squatted and placed her hand on the print.

"Tel," she called, straightening up again. "I've got it. Let's go," she said as he joined her and handed her the pack she'd discarded. "There was no snow in the pass when these people came through," she explained. "They must have been another Company, one that didn't stop at Questin Hall, but came straight along to the pass." She hesitated. "Nothing to do with the man I killed." She wrapped herself tighter into her cloak. With all this standing around she'd lost the warmth she'd generated running.

Tel was frowning. "Makes no sense. They should be consolidating their gains before they move on."

"The main force *is* still to the south." Ker shook her head. "This is maybe half a Company, about sixty men, being used like a scouting patrol. Large enough to deal with anything that isn't fully armed resistance, small enough to forage for itself and move quickly."

He tilted his head, examining her face. "There's something else, isn't there?"

Ker chewed on her lower lip before answering. "They came

here on purpose. They knew about Temlin before they got here. They may know where all the Halls are. But the important thing right now is that they're using the road."

Tel looked around. "From those rocks"—he pointed west—"we can ambush anyone who comes this way."

"If by 'anyone' you mean 'one.' I'm certain a single soldier and someone who's been doing combat drills with sticks should be able to take on a seasoned warrior, so long as the enemy comes along one at a time."

"You have a better idea?" From his tone, Tel wanted to kill someone—and soon. Ker knew just how he felt. But they couldn't stay here, whether the Halians returned or not. No shelter, nothing to eat . . . She looked up into the sky, no birds flying overhead.

"Can we get to Oste Camp without using the roads?"

"Well, we *can*." Frowning, Tel scanned their surroundings as if he was expecting the ruins to give him advice. "It won't be the fastest way, but it can be done." He glanced up at the sky, then back the way they'd come. "We'll have to follow the road for a bit, though." He began to lead the way back.

"Tel." He stopped, turning to face her. The words came surprisingly hard. "Maybe it's best that we don't tell anyone I'm a Talent." With a jerk of her head, she gestured behind her. "I'm not a coward, but . . ." She bit her lip. "Best we keep it to ourselves until we're sure it's safe."

Tel Cursar frowned, looked again at the destruction around them, and nodded. Shocked as she must be, Kerida was right.

Back on the road, he started them off at double time, needing to get Ker away from the destroyed Hall as quickly as possible. He was just as pleased to leave it behind himself, if he was honest. They hadn't gone much farther when Ker began to falter, and he brought them back to normal walking pace. Finally he spotted what he'd been looking for, a point where the trees grew thin, and he signaled a halt. Ker stuck her hands into her armpits and raised her eyebrows.

"The road runs north northeast from the pass," he said, pointing in front of them. "And then veers more to the west." He pointed to the right. "We'll be off the road if we head this way, without adding too much to the journey."

Ker nodded and glanced upward before responding. "What about leaving the road back there, where those rocks are." She pointed with her chin. "It would hide our trail."

Tel shook his head, trying not to frown at her. "If they have dogs—"

"They'd have to come along pretty quickly for our scents to last in this cold and damp. And that's if the dogs were looking specifically for us." She glanced upward again.

Tel felt a surge of irritation. "What do you keep looking for?"

"What? Nothing. I was just wondering where the griffin might be."

Tel bit down on the response that leaped to his tongue. *The griffin.* Whatever he might have said next went unspoken, as they both turned to look down the road in the direction they were headed.

"*Singing?*" How could there be singing?

"Off the road. *Now.*" Tel turned to run, and Ker followed him without hesitation. Later he realized that they'd left the road by way of the rocks. The nearby tree line was the only cover and they ran straight for it. With luck, their prints wouldn't be particularly visible in the rough terrain.

Tel strained to hear anything over the sound of his own pounding heart—was the singing closer?—but he kept most of his attention on his footing. Ker was close behind him, and as they neared the safety of the trees, Tel gestured to the right with chopping motions of his hand. She veered off, heading for what looked like a snow-covered rock. Apart, they'd make smaller targets and have a better chance to do some damage themselves.

Tel dove into a shadowy cleft under three trees, breathing more easily when he crawled farther in without dislodging any snow. He flattened himself as best he could, struggling to get out his sword, and hoping that Ker remembered she still had the crossbow. She was somewhere off to his left, though he couldn't hear or see her. He couldn't see anything else either. The singing *was* louder, however, though the tune wasn't familiar. He should recognize any of the Battle Wings' marching songs.

Which meant this wasn't one of the Battle Wings' marching songs.

You can't carry a tune to save your life, he told himself, wincing at the irony of the observation. Just now, saving his life was the point. Tel relaxed his grip on his sword.

The singing stopped raggedly, not sharp, like Polity soldiers when called to a halt. Tel inched over to his left, where the space left by a missing branch gave him a better view. There were seven people down on the road, all on foot. Five were Eagles, and carried packs. They weren't standing in formation, which was odd, but the other two were Bears. Almost laughing with relief, Tel backed out of his hiding space, careful not to stand up too soon and bring snow down on himself.

Of course, the Bears would be the ones running point, fore and behind, though they were a bit close to the main group to be useful. At that moment one of the Eagles lifted his left arm and scratched the back of his neck in a most familiar way. Tel grinned and leaped to his feet.

"Shorden! Shorden!"

The two Bears looked around. One of them called out and pointed, and Tel ran toward the road.

Kerida was tightening the last fastener on the crossbow when she heard Tel call out, and saw him heading for the road. The soldiers were all looking his way, but only the two in Bear Wing purple were moving out to meet him.

"Thank the gods." Ker's head sagged down onto her forearm as every muscle loosened. Finally, they weren't alone. Wherever these soldiers were headed, she and Tel could go with them. She slid over to her left, then froze.

Tel yelled "NO!" and sprang away from the purple tunics, running toward the road in the direction *away* from where she lay hidden. Startled into motion, Ker jerked the crossbow into position, but stopped with her fingers resting on the crank.

Tel must have seen something when he got closer to them, something that got him running, and if she got up now, even if she managed to shoot a couple of them with her crossbow before they reached Tel, all she'd accomplish was to be caught herself, making Tel's efforts to save her worthless.

She almost did it anyway. Anything not to be alone again. But if he got away, the Mother knew he wouldn't thank her for getting caught herself. She was still turning over options, trying not to feel like a coward, when the men who'd set off after Tel returned, dragging him between them.

Tel was on his feet, but his arms had been tied behind his back. Ker grimaced. They reached the waiting men—*all* men, Ker now realized, no women—and Tel was pushed to his knees. Her breath caught in her throat, and Ker cursed herself for not doing something, anything, in time to save him. She didn't want to look. Didn't want to watch as what happened to Cana at the Hall happened to Tel Cursar. She snaked forward a little more, feeling into the outer pocket of the pack for more crossbow quarrels.

But as she squirmed around, trying not to dislodge the quarrel already in the crossbow, Ker realized they were pulling Tel to his feet again, having fastened a rope around his neck. There was some arguing among the soldiers dressed as Eagles, but eventually these all shouldered their packs again and set off down the road once more. Ker waited, cold and getting colder, until she could no long hear the tramp of their feet. Then she came out from behind her rock.

"They'd have had me as well," she said aloud, needing to hear a friendly voice, even her own. It was true, but she didn't feel any better than she had when she'd left her teachers and friends to be slaughtered back in Questin.

This small group of invaders was heading back down the road, toward the burned-out Hall, toward the Pass. The day was fairly well advanced; they'd be stopping soon for the night. Before she knew it, Kerida was bending over her own pack. Maybe there hadn't been anything she could do except run, back at Questin Hall. But she wasn't going to run now.

"SHORDEN! Alken! What are you doing? Help me!"

Tel was shoved to his knees; with his elbows tied behind him, it was a struggle even to stay upright. He spat out blood and searched the faces of the Eagles watching him. For a moment he thought they were like the two in Bear colors who'd lured him out of hiding, Halians in Polity clothing. But these men weren't in disguise. He didn't know the others, but Shorden and Alken were two of the group who'd had to leave him behind in the cave when his wound got bad.

And here they stood, unarmed but free. "Hey! Don't you know me?"

But they did. Tel was sure of that. He'd seen people knocked on the head, dazed, momentarily unsure of where they were and who was speaking to them, but these two men had none of that look. They recognized him; that was clear.

They just didn't care about him.

The Halians said something in a language Tel didn't understand, and when the soldiers dressed in Eagle Wing green didn't respond right away, they cuffed and prodded at them, but not as though they were slaves or prisoners. More like they were stubborn, or a little slow. Two of them, thankfully two that Tel didn't know, helped hold him down while his hands were retied in front of him, a length of thong was looped around his neck, and he was hauled back to his feet.

"There's only the two of them," he said, looking around at the calm faces. "Why aren't you fighting them?"

It looked like he wasn't going to get an answer, but then Shorden said, "No point."

"What do you mean? Even if some of us got hurt, all of us would be free."

At this Shorden turned narrowed eyes on him. "What do you mean, 'free'? What do you mean 'all of us'? There's only you."

Tel's mouth was so dry he couldn't swallow. Shorden was genuinely puzzled. "There's six of us, counting me, and there's only the two of them. That's what I mean."

Shorden shook his head. "What're you talking about?"

One of the enemy, the one with a red hood thrown back over his purple tunic, not the one with the broken nose, said something to Shorden and laughed. Shorden tilted his head, looking puzzled, and Red Hood repeated what he'd said, slowly. Shorden hesitated, and then he laughed, too.

Tel looked around at Alken and the other burdened soldiers. Some of them were smiling. He hunched his shoulders against a chill that had nothing to do with the weather. Suddenly, he wished Kerida were with him, even if she wasn't very well trained at Flashing people yet. She might to able to figure out what was going on.

He clamped his teeth tighter shut. Imagine wishing the girl were here, instead of safe in some hidey-hole, or on her way down the road. After he'd done everything he could to give her the best chance of escape.

Red Hood said something to him, and when Tel didn't respond, Shorden spoke. "Get up," he said. "We're going."

For a moment Tel thought about resisting, and the impulse must have shown on his face because the noose around his neck tightened abruptly, cutting off his air and threatening to pull him off his knees. He nodded and swung himself up on legs growing numb from contact with the cold ground. Resistance was going to have to wait for a better moment.

Along the way, Tel tried several more times to engage Alken or Shorden in talk, but neither one paid him any further attention. Eventually, he gave up. The awkward, unsteady pace the Halians set was bad for the breathing, and made it difficult to talk. Or so he told himself. They'd only covered half the distance back to the burned-out remains of the Hall when they stopped. Red Hood and Bent Nose shoved and prodded the men dressed as Eagles—Tel couldn't bring himself to think of them any other way—to set up camp. Alken and one of the others dropped their packs and went to forage for wood, while Shorden and another set up a fire. The fifth, a thickset blond, began going through the packs, sorting out foodstuffs and blankets. The oddest thing was that, left to themselves, each of the men moved more and more slowly, finally stopping completely, until Red Hood or Bent Nose came over to nudge them again.

Even then they were sluggish, giving every action, no matter how commonplace, a fair amount of thought before they carried through. Once the fire was set up, Red Hood lit it, using the starter he'd taken from Tel's pouch.

Tel, himself, they left alone once they'd shoved him into a sitting position. No one seemed to want him to do anything but stay out of the way, and he wasn't sure how he felt about that. Would they feed him before the questioning began?

"Don't suppose you'll untie me and let me escape?" he said to the blond when the two enemy were out of earshot. The beefy man stopped what he was doing and appeared to think about it. Tel found himself starting to grin.

"No," the blond said finally, but as if he'd actually given it some thought. "There wouldn't be any point."

"Sure. Fine, then." Tel sat quietly after that, his own thoughts turned inward.

As it happened, they did feed him, a thin stew made from melted snow and dried fish. Tel was just happy they didn't offer him any travel cake, as they seemed to have plenty of those. He tried to be ready once the food was gone, but the questioning he had been expecting never came. Red Hood and Bent Nose didn't mistreat him, but they didn't pay him a lot of attention either, after leading him off to one side to relieve himself. When they doled out the blankets, they even tossed him one.

The men dressed as soldiers settled around the fire, each rolled up in his blanket, and appeared to fall asleep almost at once. Was this more of the strange magic that made them slow? Tel shook his head. Red Hood and Bent Nose played some version of flash-the-fingers that Tel was unfamiliar with, and as soon as it was over, Red Hood picked up his own blanket and Bent Nose moved out to the western edge of the camp, nearest the road, and just beyond the reach of the firelight.

Whoever and whatever they were, the invaders knew how to stand watch where the fire wouldn't interfere with their night vision, and where the sentry wouldn't be obvious to anyone who came upon the camp.

Tel lay on his side and tried to get comfortable. Even with his hands tied in front of him, the ground was too cold to make it easy to settle. He didn't expect to fall asleep, but all his training told him to rest while he could, just like it had told him to eat when he could. If Ganni were here, he thought, would the old man be able to lift him right out of the camp and away? Or was that a different skill from keeping Tel from falling?

Tel grinned. You had to be in a bad spot, if you were wishing for Feelers. Best not to think about it.

He didn't want to think about Kerida Nast either, but given his other options, he found it hard not to. Even the first time he'd seen her, in the kitchen at Questin Hall, he hadn't mistaken her for a servant, though he'd never dreamed she was a Talent. She was average height for a girl, which made her much shorter than he was, but a good size for a soldier. Dark brown hair pulled off a long oval face, a sharp nose, and the greenest eyes he'd ever seen. Greener even than a cat's.

He'd done what he could to make her safe—he still couldn't believe after all he'd seen in the Peninsula, that he'd been fool enough to run down to the road when he'd seen the Polity uniforms. At least he'd managed to draw them away before anyone thought to see if there were more like him in the trees. Kerida even had the better part of his pack, though his captors were the richer by his glow stone, his sword, and his fire starter.

He shifted again, prompting a break in the snoring of the nearest sleeper. Tel breathed silently through his open mouth, counting one-Cohort, two-Cohorts to help himself relax. No point in giving the others a grudge against him by keeping them awake.

Kerida tried to blow on her fingers without making any noise. Not that she thought anyone could hear her. The last time she'd heard snoring like this was when Donard the gardener's boy had fallen out of an apple tree and cracked his head. Because of the injury training she'd received in the military, Kerida had been one of the people assigned to sit by the sleeping boy, and make sure he woke up at measured intervals. Now it was as if the whole camp of men had head injuries, though they'd all been able to walk, and go about setting up camp.

Ker shivered. She was almost cold enough to wish herself near the fire. When she'd finally set off down the road after Tel and his captors, she'd found she wasn't as far behind them as she'd expected. The men were carrying heavy packs, and weren't using any kind of orderly march. Ker had been able to keep up with them easily, even though she'd had to keep off the road. She'd been fortunate that the ground, though not frozen, was firm. There had only been one marshy bit she'd had to detour around.

Even that had turned out luckily, since she'd found and climbed this tree, from which she'd been keeping an eye on the camp. She'd seen the men gathering wood, cooking and eating, and had watched them settle down for sleep, easily picking out Tel Cursar from his height. She didn't know whether to be surprised or relieved when it seemed only two of the enemy soldiers were going to keep watch. If the other men weren't prisoners—and Tel seemed to be the only one bound—why weren't more of them taking their turn?

Ker checked that her knife was secure, shifted the crossbow, and blew on her hands again. She knew that the cold could affect bows and bowstrings, but just couldn't remember whether it affected the mechanisms of crossbows. Her military training was too long ago, and she'd had to study so many other things since. Just learning to read and write took up a lot of time, concentration, and memory.

Her pack she'd left at the bottom of a birch tree, two pine trees farther from the road. She couldn't afford to have someone who came into the woods to relieve himself find it at the bottom of her tree. From here, she had the sentry silhouetted against the light of the fire, and all she had to do now was wait until the middle of the second watch. And not fall asleep herself.

The sentry was sitting where anyone who came creeping up on the camp in the dark wouldn't see him clearly. But to anyone who'd watched them set up, as she had, he was a clear target. Though if he kept turning to look at the fire, he'd have no night vision at all. Between that and the noise the sleepers were making, Kerida was fairly certain she could walk up behind him and stick a knife in his ribs before he even noticed she was there. Just like the man in the stable. She rubbed her suddenly sweaty palms on her breeches.

The sliver of moon had not moved any significant distance when the sentry got to his feet and prodded one of the sleeping forms with his toe. The watch seemed very short, but Ker knew that could work in her favor. Any soldier learned—and never forgot—that the body had natural rhythms, particularly when it came to sleep. Wake too soon, and you'd be groggy and fall asleep again easily. Either these two didn't know that, or the invaders' bodies worked at rhythms different from what Ker was used to.

Kerida blew on her fingers again, and brought the crossbow up to a ready position. She was farther away than she'd like to be, but her height in the tree would give her shot more distance. Still she waited, biting on the inside of her lip to stay alert. She couldn't wait long, not if this watch was as short as the first, but she had to wait long enough for the first sentry to fall well asleep, and this second one to begin to doze once more. There, didn't his head drop just a little?

Kerida breathed in, breathed out slowly, and let fly.

Without waiting to see where—or whether—she'd hit the guard, Ker set the butt of the bow on her breast bone and pulled the string back with both hands. She fit the new quarrel into place and took aim, only to see her target on his feet and staggering toward the fire. She was trying to get the sighting bead back on him, when one of the recumbent forms rolled over, knocking the man down. *Tel?*

Before she could relax, the sleeping sentry, a man in a red hood, came charging to his feet. Without pausing to aim, Ker again let fly. She was certain she'd missed, but before she could call out a warning to Tel, she froze. In coming to the aid of his mate, the invader in the red hood had stepped into the path of the flying quarrel, taking it square in the chest. Ker's breath burst out in a giggle. She couldn't have made that shot on purpose if she'd tried.

She came out of the tree in a controlled fall, grabbing at branches as she slid down, and ran for the camp, trying not to twist her cold, stiff ankles on the uneven ground as she went. Whoever had knocked down the first guard was on her side, and she needed to go and help.

The first guard was still down, tangled up in limbs long enough that they could only belong to Tel Cursar. As Ker reached them, Tel rolled on top, grinding the crossbow quarrel, high in the man's right shoulder, into the ground. The second man lay completely still, though Ker could see blood trickling out of his mouth, and his eyes moved toward her. As she watched, the human light in the man's eyes dulled, until there was only the flicker of the firelight left.

"Quick, quick, free my feet." Tel had a good grip on the living sentry, but was losing the wrestling match since his bound feet kept him from applying the leverage his longer limbs gave him. Ker drew her knife, but Tel was moving about so abruptly she had to be careful not to cut him instead of his bonds. Finally, she lay down on top of both of them and sawed at the strip of hide until it snapped.

Once his feet were free, Tel twisted his torso around and braced himself to put maximum pressure on the guard's chest, holding him pinned to the ground. "Don't just stand there," he growled.

Startled, Ker looked at the knife still in her hand and grimaced. She reversed it, and knocked the man on the head with the heavy hilt. She'd judged well, and she clenched her teeth against the crunching sound, but at least there was no blood.

"Watch it!" Tel jerked his own head back. "Why didn't you cut his throat?"

"And cut you by accident?" Ker said. "Stop complaining and hold out your hands."

As soon as his hands were free Tel snatched the knife from her and cut the sentry's throat. "Better to be sure," he said.

Ker nodded. The man had to die; she just hadn't wanted to do it. She frowned, realizing she could still hear snoring. None of the others around them had woken up.

"What's wrong with them?"

"What's wrong with *them*? What's wrong with *you*?"

"What?"

"What are you doing here? Why aren't you escaping? I only let myself get caught so you could get away."

The injustice of it almost left Ker speechless. Almost. "You *let* yourself get caught? Oh, I'm *sure* of it. You mean you deliberately left hiding, calling to the enemy and running around like a mad fool in order to help *me*? Here *I* thought it was because *you* mistook them for friends."

"You were supposed to get away." He spoke through clenched teeth.

"And go where? How? I'm no good cross-country, and you see what I'd likely run into going along the roads." She pointed at the guard's corpse with her chin.

Tel snorted. They were both on their knees. Yet even so, he towered over her. Their breath fogged around them. It might be a good idea for them both to calm down, Ker thought. She was trying to think of a soft way to say so when she noticed that the snoring *still* continued. She broke eye contact with Tel and looked around at the sleeping men.

"Is it just me, or does this strike you as unnatural?" She glanced back at Tel, to find him looking around as well. Ker began to breathe easier. She got to her feet and he followed.

"There's more to it than this," Tel said. "I know them—at least these two." He pointed. "They were with me at the cave, before they had to go on. But they didn't try to help me or try to get away. All the way along they seemed to be witless, like they were drugged."

Ker thought about her broken skull idea and nodded. "Might it be magic?"

Tel wrinkled up his nose. "A few days ago I'd have made

fun of you for asking that. But since the mines . . . What about Flashing them?"

Ker sucked in her breath and tucked her hands into her armpits. The very last thing she wanted to do was Flash these men. "I told you I'm not good with people," she said.

Tel came closer to her and put his hand on her shoulder. "It's all right if you can't," he said.

Ker breathed in through her nose. Somehow his sympathy made her reluctance feel like cowardice. "I'll try," she said, moving away from him. Maybe their auras would tell her something.

Still looking at her with narrowed eyes, Tel squatted by the nearest sleeping soldier and turned him over on his back. He opened the neck of the man's tunic, and his shirt, looping his identity plaque out of the way. "This one's Shorden, if knowing his name will help you."

"Who knows? It might." Ker's mind jumped from place to place and she had to take a couple of deep, slow breaths to steady herself. Tel hovered over her and finally she twisted her neck to look up at him. "Do you mind? I can't concentrate with you hanging over me."

"Sorry. I'll go search the corpses."

Ker watched him for a moment, but then she closed her eyes again, and this time she managed to reach her safe room right away. *Paraste.* She placed her hand on Shorden's chest. And there was his aura, but the colors, yellow, blue, and green, were muted and barely moving, fogged over with a red haze. She looked up at Tel. His colors—the same three—were rich ribbons of dancing light. Suddenly, she heard someone crying. As her training had taught her, she tried to follow the sound, but just as it seemed she was gaining on it, it faded abruptly and was gone. She swallowed, took a deep breath, and tried again, this time repeating the five questions in time to the beating of the man's heart, but nothing more came.

Frowning, she took a grip on his shirt, and was immediately smacked with information.

"These aren't his clothes," she said aloud. "Didn't you say his name is Shorden? This tunic belongs to someone named Sar Malward. I'm afraid she was killed, and her clothes given to this man." She reached over to one of the other sleeping forms. "This man's not wearing his own clothes either."

"Would you mind checking all of them?"

It didn't take Ker long to check all five sleepers, and two others were wearing the clothes of a dead woman. Of the three, two had been killed in battle, one after capture. Ker stored their names away against the day she could report to someone in authority.

"Do you suppose they're killing all the female soldiers?" she asked. Where was her sister Ester? She squeezed her eyes shut. This is why Talents stayed apart from the world. So that what they Flashed couldn't affect them personally.

"Let's not jump to conclusions." Tel's voice was brittle, and his grip on her shoulder was tight. "What about the enemy? Worth checking them, do you think?"

"Of course, it would be." Ker crouched down again, this time next to the man in the red hood. She picked up a blood-free corner of his tunic between her thumb and forefinger.

There was no point in saying that the Halian's clothes came from a soldier in the Bear Wing, Tel could see that much for himself. And she might just as well keep the man's name to herself as well. Whether Tel knew the officer or not, he didn't need bad news of that kind right now.

Kerida concentrated. Problem was, the clothes wouldn't tell her anything more about the Halian. "Did you take their weapons?"

"Here." Tel handed her two knives, one with a plain, leather-wrapped hilt, the other with a more intricate hilt of horn. "One from each of them. Keep the one you like."

"These two were on their way back through the pass," she said, sorting through the images. "They were separated from the main body, the ones with horses." She looked around them. "They had to follow on foot, because these men can't ride."

"What do you mean? Alken told me his father's a hostler."

"Well, he can't ride *now*." Ker noticed she still had hold of the dead man's knife and stuck it in her belt, rubbing her hands on her thighs, and muttering her closure word. "Maybe that's part of what's making them stupid."

"Why take them at all? Why not just kill them? What makes these five men so important?"

Ker shook her head. She wished she knew how to interpret the auras, and what the obscuring red mist meant. "Could they just need the manpower? Could it be as simple as that?"

There were dark circles under Tel's eyes. Suddenly he knelt next to the one he'd called Shorden. "Shorden! Come on, man, wake up."

Whether the man reacted to the authority in Tel's voice Ker couldn't be sure, but his eyes snapped open, and his hand reached for the weapon he wasn't wearing.

"Get up, soldier."

The man then made a face as if a fly had been bothering him and rolled over again, muttering something that sounded like "no point." Tel reached down again, but Ker took hold of his arm.

"I don't think we can wake them up," she said. "Not in any way that will do them or us any good. They *were* our people, but they aren't anymore."

Tel's face hardened and Ker licked her lips. *Don't say it*, she thought. *Please don't say it*. It was one thing to kill an obvious enemy, another entirely to kill sleeping men. She held her breath, steeling herself. If it had to be done . . .

"We'll leave them," Tel said finally, his voice a croak. Kerida breathed again. "We've no choice. We'll leave food and blankets—we couldn't carry all this away even if we wanted to." He gestured at the packs. "What about our things?"

"My pack's down there, just off the road," she said, pointing in the direction of her tree. "The rest I hid where we were when we first saw them."

Tel looked up at the sky. "Come on. We can get back there by daylight, and find a better place to hide. We'll try traveling by night for a while."

It took them four days traveling across country, using the stars when they could and Tel's sense of direction when they couldn't, to reach Oste Camp. Twice they'd caught glimpses of enemy patrols, both larger than the group they'd escaped. They'd spent only one night in comfort, with an outlying farmer whose holding was cut out of the deep forest. He'd had no news of the outside world since the snow had come, and neither Tel nor Ker had much enjoyed having to tell him what they knew.

"Oste seemed much closer to the pass before." Tel's voice showed the roughness of disuse. He'd been quieter since his escape from the false soldiers, and they'd had little energy and even less inclination to talk since they'd left the farmer.

"I'm sure it is, by road. But with our having to go round about . . ." Ker shrugged. Neither of them mentioned the fear in both of their minds—that the fort would be in the same state as Temlin Hall.

Administered by the Eagles, Oste Camp, in the northern foothills of the Serpents Teeth range, had at one time marked the border of the Peninsula, where the Polity had begun. But for generations since, it had been the main transit camp of the Battle Wings and the place any Battle Wing Faro had to wait for permission before crossing the Serpents Teeth and entering the Peninsula. Like all military camps throughout the Polity, Oste's main gate faced the road. Coming as they were through the surrounding woods, daybreak found them watching the approach to the rear gate.

"Blast." Tel's exhaustion leached any emotion out of his voice. "Something's up." The corners of his mouth and eyes drooped, and Ker resisted the impulse to reach over and pat his arm. "There should be Eagles on the walls, and all I can see are Bears—not that the color of anyone's tunic means much just now."

Ker squinted, but in the dim light, she couldn't see colors at all. However, what she did see worried her far more. The usual village that grew up around any fort, made up of tradespeople who made their living off the military, plus the families of those stationed here, was gone.

"Tel, the village—" she began.

"They've been under attack," he said. "They've had to pull the houses down."

Ker nodded. Of course. Anything that might give an attacker cover would have been removed. She only hoped there'd been time to get the villagers behind the walls.

"So the gates are closed," she said. Though she herself had never seen Oste, it looked familiar. All military forts were built along the same lines. Ker scrubbed at her mouth with the back of her hand. "What now?"

Tel was still frowning at the distant gate. "No cover for the enemy means no cover for us."

Ker nodded. The open fields between them and the safety of Oste's gate suddenly seemed twice as wide.

Tel stood up straighter and squared his shoulders. "Come on. Let's not waste any more time."

As soon as they stepped out of the forest, Ker saw activity on the wall. Though they were still some distance away, she could tell they'd been seen, and that their approach was being watched. She hesitated, scanning the sky above them. What with traveling at night, and mostly through forest, she hadn't seen a clear sky for quite a while.

"Son and Daughter, are you still looking for that griffin?"

Stung at the harshness of his tone, Ker spun to face him. "And what do you mean by that?"

"Never mind." Tel straightened his shoulders and stalked away, raising his hands to wave at the guards watching them. The sound of trumpets came softly through the morning air.

Ker straightened her own shoulders and lengthened her stride as Tel broke into a rough trot. They were both exhausted; whatever it was that was bothering Tel would have to wait.

Halfway across the field an arrow appeared suddenly from the nearby woods, sticking out of the ground at Ker's feet. She jumped to the left, as instinct and old training cut in; she changed direction, running faster, and then slower, and then faster again in as random a pattern as she could, to make it harder for the hidden archer to hit her.

Out of the corner of her eye she could see that Tel was doing the same thing. She dodged another arrow just in time to stumble over the rubble that marked the beginning of the demolished village.

"Halt! Identify yourselves!" The guard chosen for the gate post always had a good carrying voice.

Ker hesitated, but hauled herself up and kept moving when she saw that Tel's pace didn't falter. Picking her way across the debris of wooden walls and abandoned furniture, Ker expected an arrow between her shoulder blades at any moment, not relaxing even when she realized that she and Tel were out of range.

At last they were plastered against the fort wall, almost under the guard post that overlooked Oste's rear gate.

"Who are you? State your business."

Tel tilted his head back and took a deep breath. "Tel Cursar, Third Officer, Green Company, Carnelian Cohort, Bear Wing, asking leave to report." He gestured to Ker. "This is Kerida Nast, Talent Candidate, Questin Hall. Bringing information and asking for refuge."

Kerida's mouth fell open, and she missed what the gate guard said next. How could Tel just blurt out that she was a Talent, after what she'd said to him at Temlin Hall? They'd reached Oste, but they weren't inside yet. And what made him think it was safe to announce it to the whole countryside?

She squeezed her eyes shut. Bad enough how the soldiers were going to treat her. At best, she'd be seen as a useful tool, but she'd be ready to wager that "best" wasn't going to happen.

"Did you say a Talent?" The guard's tone had changed radically, however, sounding far warmer than it had a moment before. There were other voices, and then the sound of the gates moving.

"Why did you tell them?" It was hard to talk around the tightness in her throat.

"We may be lucky I did." His tone was tired, as if he'd been arguing this point with her for hours. "Did you hear him? Looks like they might not have let us in otherwise."

"That's supposed to make me feel better? You promised you wouldn't tell, that you'd wait until I said it was all right."

"Our Talents weren't with us Bears," he said. "What if the ones stationed here crossed into the Peninsula? Did it never occur to you that you might be the only one left?"

Ker opened her mouth and shut it again. No, it hadn't occurred to her. What had happened to the Talents that normally traveled with the Bear Wing? She scrubbed at her face with her filthy hands. So Tel had a reason to break his promise—a real reason, that the more sensible part of her brain recognized as a good reason. Tel was a soldier, and he had to put the needs of the Polity first. But he hadn't even discussed it with her. This was exactly the kind of treatment she feared—and hadn't expected from Tel. Under the blazing heat of anger, all she could feel was a hollow emptiness. She squeezed her eyes shut. "You're going to tell them everything, aren't you?" Because if he wasn't going to keep his promise to her, why would he keep his promise to the Feelers?

As usual, the gate had no person-sized door to give it a weak spot, and it took a few minutes longer for the guards to roll it to one side enough to let them through. They were met by three soldiers wearing the purple tunics of the Bear Wing. The man in front carried his short sword and wore a horsehair-trimmed helmet marking him as the commander of the Company which had wall duty today. Behind him stood two others, both armed with crossbows aimed directly at Ker and Tel.

"Thank you, Gate Commander." Against her will, Ker had to admire the calm in Tel's voice.

"You did say Carnelian Cohort, Third Officer?"

"Yes, Gate Commander. Tel Cursar."

The older man turned to Kerida. "And you, you're the Talent?"

"Not a Full Talent." Kerida cleared her throat. They might believe it was the dust of the road that roughened it. "I'm still a Candidate." It had been a long while since Kerida had spoken to a military commander, and suddenly she remembered she shouldn't volunteer information, just answer the questions.

The man nodded, and the crossbows were lowered. Maybe Tel had been right. Maybe they wouldn't have been let in if she hadn't been a Talent. "Leave your packs here," the commander said. "Follow me. This way please, Candidate Nast." He gestured to her as he turned to go, and Kerida found herself falling into step at his side while Tel walked behind them. It appeared she was going to be treated as a useful tool, at least by this man.

"Where are we going, Commander?" she asked. She heard Tel's quick intake of breath behind her, and smiled. The officer had treated her with the formal courtesy accorded a Talent, so her question wasn't the severe breach of discipline it would have been if she'd been a soldier. Even so, she was sure she'd never have had the nerve to ask if she hadn't been so angry with Tel.

"Fort Commandant's office, Candidate. It'll all be explained there."

Which was the nicest way any military officer had ever shut her up.

The Gate Commander escorted them up the short avenue that led from the rear gate, around the quarters usually assigned to visiting Wing Faros, and over to the administrative offices. Facing the square, two-story administrative block across a wider avenue were the buildings that housed senior officers, visiting officials, and guests—even royalty. As they went, they passed other soldiers who saluted the Gate Commander, but Ker thought the place quieter than she would have expected, given that close to three thousand people should have been living, eating, and drilling here.

Even if she'd wanted to speak to Tel, they were around the corner and into the administration building before she could think of anything to say. The anteroom had the usual desk, with the Fort Commandant's aide sitting behind it, getting to his feet as they came in the door. From the speed they were passed through to the inner office, it seemed that news of their arrival had preceded them.

Kerida didn't know what it was that made Tel hesitate halfway through coming to attention, until she saw the bearskin military cloak lying tossed over one of the chairs. The aide's harness, she now noticed, was also adorned by a strip of bear's skin.

So, this wasn't merely the Fort Commandant, this was the Faro of Bears. The woman lifted her stone-gray eyes from the paper she'd been studying, looking first at Tel Cursar, then at Kerida before she leaned back, rested her elbows on the arms of her chair, and entwined her fingers in front of her. She must have been about the age of Kerida's own mother, but she'd let her hair go to its natural gray, and cropped it short to accommodate the helm with its horsehair crest that hung on the wall behind her.

Kerida cleared her throat and tried not to lower her eyes or look away. She'd faced Matriarch, when she was being punished. This had to be easier.

"Welcome, Candidate Nast. I am Juria Sweetwater, Faro of Bears. Will you please sit, and I will speak with you in a moment." She turned back to Tel. "You are Tel Cursar, Third Officer, Green Company, Carnelian Cohort of Bears?"

"Yes, my Faro."

"And the rest of your Company? What can you tell me of them?"

Tel's faced stiffened, and Ker would have felt sympathetic if she was still his friend.

"My Faro? We were totally routed at the capital. We were in full retreat. There was only myself and a mixed squad of Eagles—from different Cohorts let alone different Companies—the Eagle's garrison at the capital was completely overwhelmed, my Faro, and those of us who escaped were sent to report here." Tel licked his lips, but before he could continue, the Faro interrupted.

"Sent to report here? Everyone?"

"Yes, my Faro."

Juria Sweetwater leaned forward, her forearm on the table, her hand a fist. "And the Luqs?"

Tel swallowed, and Ker fought the urge to reach out and touch him. "Our mission was not successful, my Faro. The Luqs is dead." This was followed by a silence so complete Ker's ears hurt.

"I will need to hear more about that. But tell me, Third Officer Cursar. How is it that with the pass closed, and the enemy roaming this valley in sufficient numbers to attack this fort twice, you and you alone of all my Bears have managed to return to me?"

Tel's mouth fell open, and this time Ker's sympathy prompted her to speak.

"We came through the mines, Faro Sweetwater."

"The mines?" The woman leaned back again. "I must hear more of this." She waved at the others in the room. "You people may return to your duties. Jak, fetch me my Laxtor immediately. See that we're not disturbed."

THE smell of roasted almonds was almost too much to bear. Jerek pushed the kitchen door open enough to slip in sideways. The large fragrant room looked deserted, except for the trays of almond cookies cooling on racks next to the courtyard door. Jerek was stuffing one into his mouth when a noise made him turn.

"No need to ask what you're up to, young man, as I can see you chewing." Antuni the cook came out of the storage room wiping his hands on a small towel. A tall, thin man, his thick hair had been gray as long as Jerek could remember. Antuni cast a cold eye over his trays. "I suppose I should be grateful you didn't take more." He hung the towel on a drying rack close to the stove before crossing his arms and looking Jerek up and down. "Enjoy them while you can. There'll be no more of my almond delights when I've gone to cook for the Salcias."

Jerek almost choked on his cookie. "What? When did this happen?"

The man shrugged. "They've been making me offers since your mother died."

"Sure." This was common gossip among the staff and servants. "But you've never taken any of them."

"The old lord's retiring, and his daughter, the Lady Ekian, will take his place as Lady of the holding."

Jerek paused to think. Ekian was the heir, she would have inherited anyway. So why—unless Lord Salcia thought she might not, if he waited too long. There were so many changes, now that the Halians were here. It was hard to know what might happen.

"And since the Salcias are a much larger family, and the Lady Ekian is known to entertain a great deal, why, where else would a cook of my talent and ambition go?"

That made sense. Or it would have if Antuni had ever shown any signs of ambition. "I'll miss you," he said, a little surprised to find how true it was. The cook was a familiar presence, but Antuni was more likely to chase him out of the kitchen with a well-thrown pot than to seat him down at the table with warm treats and hot chocolate.

"You'll miss my baking," the tall man pointed out, his lips twisted to one side.

"Then I'd better take advantage." Jerek scooped up a handful of warm cookies and fled, hearing the clatter of a wooden spoon hit the wall next to the kitchen door as he ran through it. Antuni *could* have been laughing.

Jerek walked around through the outer yard, chewing. The temperature had dropped overnight, though not dangerously so for the vines, and the morning sunlight glinted off the frost that still edged the cobblestones. The whole yard had been frosted earlier, when he'd gone out to check on his new horse, but the sun was burning the sparkle away.

Shoving the stolen cookies into the front of his tunic, Jerek let himself into the narrow corridor that led to the business rooms of the holding. Here were offices and workrooms for anything that had to be done indoors, from keeping accounts to distilling. The Factor's office was first, and Nessa liked almond cookies as much as he did. He hoped this morning's baking would sweeten his welcome. Nessa had been so busy since the morning their fencing lesson had been interrupted, that he'd hardly seen her at all.

Jerek stopped short in the doorway of Nessa's office, his tongue frozen in the act of licking a crumb from his lips. Her worktable had been moved from its spot under the window, and the cold sunlight now shone on the shrine table, where a strange man was setting up small redwood statues of the Mother, Daughter, and Son.

"Something?" The man moved the little red Son a fraction to the left before turning to Jerek with one fair eyebrow arched high.

"This is—where's Nessa?"

The stranger moved away from the gods' shrine and sat against the edge of the worktable, crossing his arms and looking at Jerek from underneath frowning brows. "And you are?"

Jerek felt his face grow hot. He became aware of the crumbs on the front of his tunic.

"I'm Jerek Firoxi," he said finally, his voice choosing that moment to crack. He resisted the urge to brush himself off.

The man straightened to his feet, and a warm smile transformed his face. "You're the young lord? A pleasure." He gave Jerek a bow that was exactly correct. Like Nessa, the man would have come from a long line of holding staff—professionals, only a step or two away from the minor nobility. "My name is Trien Petain, and I'm your father's new Factor."

Jerek coughed to clear the sudden obstruction in his throat. *My Factor,* is what he didn't say aloud. *I'm the lord here, not my father.* But he'd never actually had to tell anyone that before, and he felt awkward to say it now. Besides, there wasn't any real need. The other staff would soon let the new man know. If Jerek said something now, it would only embarrass them both.

"What—" Jerek cleared his throat again. "Where's Nessa?" This time his voice stayed low.

"Your father very kindly gave her the day to move her things from the Factor's rooms. You'll likely find her there. Unless you would like me to have her summoned?"

It wasn't this man's fault, Jerek reminded himself. Whatever had happened, this man hadn't done it. This was his father's doing.

"No. Thank you," he remembered to add. That was one of the courtesies he'd been taught. "That won't be necessary."

The man smiled again, and Jerek tried to smile back before turning away, placing his feet carefully one in front of the other. Once in the hall, Jerek slowed down even more, suddenly not trusting his balance in the dark hallway. He didn't run until he reached the stairs leading to the upper floor, and the rooms of the house staff. A shaft of light, bright and sharp as a blade, struck through the window slit high up in the stone wall at the end of the corridor, and showed that one of the doors stood open.

Nessa's quarters were just at the top of the stairs, and once again Jerek stopped in the open doorway, heart thumping. He'd been here before, of course, though not for a long while, he realized now. Not since his voice had started to change. Now Nessa met him in her office, or in some other part of the house. The layout of these rooms was simple. There was this small sitting room, with its window that gave onto the stable yard; a brazier table, two chairs, and a set of shelves. Of the other staff, only the house steward also had a private sitting room, and, like Nessa, a carpet on the floor. The door in the far wall that led to the bedchamber swung open, and Nessa herself appeared, holding a pair of boots in her hands.

It was only then that Jerek saw the pack sitting open on the table, and the saddlebags hanging over the back of the chair. The cold place in his chest that never went away grew larger.

"Ah," she said. "I would have found you. I wouldn't have left without saying goodbye."

Left? "What's happened?"

Nessa folded the boots and tucked them into the top of the pack. "Your father has hired a new Factor."

"But why? This is your place. Your father was my mother's Factor, and your grandmother before him." Jerek turned back to the door. "I'll fix this."

Nessa was across the room in time to grab him by the elbow. "Don't, Jerek, it's too late. Don't put yourself in jeopardy for me."

"But my father—"

"Is within his rights." Nessa tugged him over to the nearest chair and pushed him into it. She removed the saddlebags from the other and sat down herself. "He's your guardian. It's for him to make decisions about the property until you become of age."

And that wouldn't be until he was seventeen, after any chance that the Talent might make its appearance. Another four years. Where would Nessa be in four years?

Jerek pressed his lips together, feeling the corners of his mouth turn down. He blinked away the sudden stinging in his eyes, scanning the room for something—anything—to distract him. The real meaning of the pack and the saddlebags sank in. "You're leaving." Not just moving to other rooms. *Leaving*.

"Yes. I said so."

"But *why*? I mean, I know you won't be Factor anymore, but why do you have to leave?"

The look on Nessa's face was one Jerek had seen many times since his mother had died. He felt his own face harden. "Tell me," he said.

"I was not given the option to stay."

Jerek's head felt full of dust and cobwebs. "He can't dismiss you without cause. You must report him!" The enormity of the suggestion almost stopped him from continuing. "The Halls . . ." The words dried up in his throat.

"Yes. Exactly. The Halls. I went to Gaena last market day and asked the magistrate there what my rights were, and it appears I haven't many. Not anymore." Nessa took a deep breath. "I've decided not to stay and find out for certain," she said. "The magistrate's an old friend, with old friends of his own at Farama the Capital. His advice was not to take my case to the Law." She shrugged and looked sideways at her pack, hands gripping her knees. "Maybe if I was a holding lady, it would be worth the attempt. But when all's said and done, I'm just staff. So, I'm going while my clothing and my coin and my horse still belong to me."

Jerek pulled the almond cookies out of his pocket and placed them with care on the edge of the table. They were cold now. "Antuni is going as well," he said.

Nessa blinked and sat up straighter. "Really? He promised your mother he would never leave."

Jerek shrugged. "Where will you go?"

She leaned back in her chair and looked at him for what felt like a long time. "Do you remember old Bedeni Soria?"

Despite what Nessa had said, Jerek decided to speak to his father—if there was any chance at all, he had to take it. There had been times when his father *had* listened to him, and the older man had been in good spirits lately, since the soldiers and the Halian had visited.

Dern Firoxi was usually in a better humor after the midday meal, particularly if lamb had been served, but past experience had taught Jerek that if he waited, he might not say anything at all. It wasn't that he'd lose his nerve, exactly, it was just that, well, other things would interfere. He did wash his face and hands, however, before tapping on his father's partly open door. Had the door been closed, no one would have tapped on it. Not more than once.

Dern Firoxi glanced up from his desktop and smiled, picking up his cup of chocolate and taking a sip. "Finished looking after your horse, have you, son?"

"Yes, sir." Jerek studied his father's face. Sometimes the man liked to be called "sir," sometimes he liked to be called "father," and there was no way to tell which one it was going to be. "I've just come from Nessa."

"Did she ask you to speak to me?" Voice and face alike hardened and Jerek swallowed.

"No, Father. In fact, she asked me not to. I just thought—if there had been some kind of neglect, or some default, I could see having to replace her, but Nessa's a great Factor. You've always said so yourself."

Dern Firoxi's eyes glinted, and Jerek steeled himself, forcing his shoulders not to rise. Finally, the older man relaxed, the stiffness of his mouth replaced with a more calculating look. Jerek breathed easier.

"A default, well, that's what this is, in a manner of speaking. Nessa's default, but not her fault." His father smiled at what he evidently thought was a joke, and Jerek managed to return it. Dern Firoxi gestured at the stool near the bench he was sitting on, waiting until Jerek was seated before continuing. "You remember that visit we had? The military men and the Halian?" Jerek nodded, even though his father didn't wait for a response. "I had quite a talk with them after you went to bed." Here his father stopped, brows drawn down, as if he was considering what he should say. Jerek waited. He'd seen this look before, too. "I didn't want to worry you, but they made it plain how things are, now that the Halians have come. It's possible that everything we have could be taken from us— from you—if we're not very careful indeed."

"What? Why?" Shock gave Jerek courage to speak.

"Because your inheritance is through your mother. The Halians only recognize inheritance through the male line." His father raised his hand. "I asked about it, believe me. It's not as though the military officer didn't have the same reaction as I did, when he first heard of it." Dern frowned. "If you've been paying attention to your studies, you know that Farama has run into this kind of male-dominant social structure before—the Polnisitts for one—and we've managed, with patience and the Rule of Law, to bring them around to a different way of thinking."

Jerek *had* been paying attention to his tutors, but he knew better than to provide answers his father clearly wanted to provide himself. And he definitely knew better than to correct the man. It hadn't been only patience and the Law that had changed things for the Polnisitts. The Battle Wings had had a say in it as well. But his father was still talking.

"You might say the boot's on the other foot this time. Now it's our turn to adjust, and with patience, and the time they are giving us, we will. According to what the Halian Shekayrin said, no one currently inheriting from the female line will be disinherited, not even females. But for the next generation, it will have to change. So your daughter wouldn't inherit— first-born or not—but your son will."

Jerek nodded. That was all so far away—two years before he could even be betrothed, four years before he inherited and then—he shook the thought away. "So wouldn't Nessa inherit the Factorship from her father, then?"

"Ah, that's a little different." His father handed him his empty chocolate cup and waited for Jerek to go to the sideboard, fill it from the small clay jug sitting warm over a short candle, and come back before he continued. "First, the Factor's position is not an inheritance, it's a job. And it's a custom that we give family members first chance at it, not a law. Second, this isn't about Nessa, but about you."

"Me?"

"You. The Halian Shekayrin made it clear that they'd be watching people in your position, people who inherited from their mothers. You've got to be most careful, most scrupulous about the new rules. You can't be seen to flaunt them, even in the smallest way."

"But how . . ."

"No women in positions of authority, not even something like a Factorship. House Steward is apparently acceptable— just. But no position that would put a woman on a horse, or that would arm her."

So all this was being done, Nessa sent away, for his sake? Jerek's hands closed into fists. His father talked as though they were conquered. As though—

"But when the Battle Wings come—" The blow to the face came now, when he was no longer expecting it. The tears that popped into Jerek's eyes were as much his disappointment with himself for relaxing his guard as they were for the pain. He clenched his teeth to stifle any sound he might have made. That would only make things worse. As if from a great distance he saw his father's mug of chocolate on the floor, the dark liquid staining the muted browns and reds of the carpet.

"Can't you for once just listen? I'm trying to save you, you stupid, selfish boy. I'm trying to save *you*."

Jerek forced himself to look up, but not quite into his father's eyes, in case that might be taken as defiance. He nodded. "Yes, sir. Yes, Father," he whispered. A whisper didn't give much away. Showing shock or fear would only make things worse. Jerek had to be careful not to suggest in any way that his father had done anything wrong. He tried to straighten himself in his chair, racking his brain to think of some reason for leaving that his father would find acceptable. So they could pretend this hadn't happened. His father stared at him, the whites of his eyes showing all the way around, his nostrils flared. Jerek licked his lips.

Nessa was going. Antuni was going. Who would be next?

"Do you need to sit down, Cursar?"

The Faro's voice was sharp as the snap of a crossbow, and Kerida could well understand why the Faro had asked. Tel had gone white as a full moon and had actually swayed a bit to one side before righting himself again. He shook his head, but said nothing.

"We saw no other Bears, Faro," Ker put in when it was clear that Tel couldn't speak. "But we left five Eagles on the main road, near Temlin Hall. And I can give you five other names for the dead."

"Left them?"

"They'd been in enemy hands, Faro." Ker stopped. Tel had made an aborted movement with his left hand, as if he wanted to signal to her, but had thought better of it. "They didn't act normally at all, more like they'd been drugged somehow."

The Faro's eyes narrowed, pulling a scar near her left eyebrow into prominence. "You Flashed nothing more from them?"

Ker shrugged. "I'm still a Candidate, Faro. Right now I'm better with objects than people."

"I see."

"My Faro, if I may?" Tel cleared his throat. "Two of these Eagles escaped Farama the Capital with me, but you say no one else got here? Then these men must have been captured before they reached you." Tel closed his eyes. "So there may be others."

"There may." The Faro's tone could evaporate water. "What is *your* story, Candidate?"

Ker cleared her throat. Giving reports was common to soldiers and Talents alike. Her voice faltered when she began describing what she'd seen in the great room at Questin Hall, but before she could continue, the Faro had raised a finger.

"Wait. A man dressed in a blue tunic with a black cloak.

Chain armor over his head? We have seen such a one in the distance, but only in the distance."

The door opened, and a man stepped through, shutting it behind him. He barely glanced at them as he circled the room to stand at the Faro's elbow, but Ker was sure he'd be able to pick either of them out of a crowd if he ever saw them again. "You sent for me, my Faro?"

"You can finish your report later, Candidate Nast. This is my second-in-command, the Laxtor Surm Barlot. Surm, these youngsters have been through the mines."

Ker acknowledged the introduction with a slight bow of her head. Tel straightened and touched the muddied crest on his shoulder.

"Now that my Laxtor is here, tell us the details of your journey through the Serpents Teeth."

Tel froze with his lips parted. He closed them, opened his mouth again, and frowned. Ker gave him a hard look.

"Talent?"

Ker glanced automatically at the Faro before lowering her gaze to the tabletop.

"You can't tell me, can you? Either of you?"

Ker glanced up again. Surm Barlot the Laxtor was nodding at the Faro, who was neither surprised nor angry. "Sometimes," the Laxtor said, "when a person has been asked not to speak of a thing, they find they can write of it."

Faro Sweetwater smiled. "It would not surprise me. Tell me, Third Officer, can you write?"

"Yes, my Faro."

"Good. Candidate Nast." Ker braced herself. "Please take this opportunity to retire to the Talents' rooms to rest and recover from your ordeal. Report any needs to the duty officer."

Ker had known enough superiors of one kind or another to recognize orders when she heard them. "Certainly. Thank you," she said, exactly as she'd been expected to.

"This way, if you would, Candidate Nast." Surm Barlot

opened the door as Ker approached it and signaled to a young officer waiting in the outer office. "Kalter, if you would escort Candidate Nast to the Talents' quarters?"

Grinning, the younger man led Kerida outside and across the avenue, heading toward a building on the right, too plain to be guest quarters, but with more windows than the nearby barracks.

Tel had let her go without a glance—not that Ker had looked back herself. But as her escort paused at the blond-wood door of the third building, she began to wish she had. As furious as she was with him for so casually revealing her Talent, Ker hadn't expected to feel so alone without him. She wondered whether Tel was feeling the same way.

Then she wondered what he was going to write, and her anger flared up again. She slowed, stopped. The Kalter turned to look at her, eyebrows raised.

Tel hadn't said anything about the Feelers, but he'd clearly *tried* to. And the Faro apparently understood that he'd tried, but wasn't *able* to. And she'd found a way around that, or so it seemed. Ker hadn't said anything either, but then, she hadn't tried to. They'd been asked not to tell. *Could* she, if she *did* want to? She glanced at the Kalter, then looked away. She wasn't going to try telling him, not just to see if she could.

Ker's skin prickled, and she felt cold. The Feelers had done this to them. To protect themselves, surely, but the idea that someone had tampered with her in this way . . . She rubbed the outside of her arms.

"Candidate? Is something wrong?"

Ker took in a deep breath. What could explain her behavior? "Is there news of the Panther Wing?" she said finally.

Her dark-haired escort smiled at her. "They're at their post in Elvia, why?"

"My sister is Wing Faro, and I wondered—"

"Oh, you're *that* Nast, of course." His smile changed completely as he put out his hand for the military hand grip. "Jakmor Gulder, one of the Faro's Kalters. From Farama, originally, though my family's lands are in Andal Province." His smile was friendly. Ker nodded as she held his wrist. Faro's Kalters were usually appointed from old families—or rich ones—who wanted their sons to have some military experience before they took positions as Polity counselors, or advisers to the Luqs. "You don't need to worry. From all we've heard, your sister is well. We haven't heard from everyone, of course." Now he gave her a more sympathetic look.

"I was wondering, all things considered, whether I might not be more use to the Faro as a soldier than a Talent. I've had military training," she added, as Gulder tilted his head and raised an interrogatory eyebrow.

"Oh, I don't think that's the issue." Gulder turned back to the door and lifted the latch. He pushed the door open and stood to one side, letting her precede him into the tiny entry hall. There was no orderly sitting at the receiving table, and Gulder led her through to the inner door, which he opened without knocking. Across from the door of the small sitting room was a narrow window, shuttered against the cold, and another door leading to the inner courtyard. There was a brazier table near the right-hand wall, ready, but not lit. Four high-backed chairs were placed around it, each with its own rug neatly folded over the seat. A worktable with stools was set up nearer the window, the tabletop lightly clouded with dust. Here the wooden floors were covered with rugs. An arched doorway opened into a space from which two closed doors led into what Kerida assumed were the bedrooms.

Dust on the worktable. An unattended anteroom. Window shuttered in the middle of the morning. Lap rugs folded as if not in use. Ker's mouth felt strangely dry. There would be no help for her here. She became aware that someone was speaking to her, that she was sitting on a hard chair with a straight back, and that the Kalter was putting a cup into her hand and closing her fingers around it.

"Candidate? Kerida? Try to drink."

Ker's hand closed, and she lifted the cup to her mouth. The smell of the contents didn't register until she had taken a mouthful. Luckily, she didn't gasp until after she'd swallowed. Some kind of brandy. She made a face, and the cup was taken from her hand.

"Better? That's the second time you've almost fainted."

The Kalter leaned over her, peering into her face with a look of concern. She'd thought him older, but now she saw that the spray of white in his hair was due to some past injury. His face was nearly unlined, and he couldn't be much older than Tel Cursar. He'd opened the shutters, but if anything, more light only emphasized the neglect.

"The Talents were sent away," she croaked. "Tel said so."

Kalter Gulder drew up another chair and sat. Their knees were almost touching. "It's a political thing, like recalling ambassadors, or threatening to." He sounded almost apologetic. "It happens from time to time." He shrugged. "Just the Wings' way of making a point. Wasn't meant to last long at all. In fact, couriers asking for their return were sent weeks ago. We thought the lack of response was just the Halls' making a point of their own. Now we know better."

Ker sat up straight, taking a deep breath. "So that means I'm the only Talent you have." *And Tel Cursar was right.* She made a face.

"I'm afraid so." The man's eyebrows were lifted in the center. He had dark brown eyes. Big dark brown eyes.

"Kalter—"

"You'd better call me Jakmor, or Jak, if you like." He smiled. "You're from a military family, you know I'm not really in the chain of command, so we might as well be friends."

Jakmor got to his feet and set the cup of brandy down on the tabletop next to Ker. "But here, you've had a shock. If you feel up to it, I'll send over some food, and the cleaners."

Real cooked food would be a treat, but the idea of people

in here, crashing around and moving things when she needed to think . . . "Could I be alone? After the food, I mean," she hastily corrected. "I'd just as soon clean the rooms myself. It's a kind of meditation exercise," she added when Jakmor looked skeptical.

"As you like." He turned back from the door. "You're sure you'll be all right?"

Ker stood up, and nodded. She knew better than to try for a smile. "I'll be fine." *Someday. Eventually. Probably.*

"We can't spare an orderly for your door, but there's always someone in the watch room, if you need anything. I'll see about that food."

Ker waited until the door closed behind him before she sat back down, and lowered her face into her hands.

"Now, Third Officer, sit down here. Don't pretty up the narrative, just write quickly." Surm Barlot pulled out a chair at the end of the Faro's worktable, clearing away a hand of solitary Seasons.

Tel sat, wiping his palms on his trousers. "What—where should I begin?"

"Start at the part you can't say aloud."

Tel nodded, licked his lips and picked up the quill. He dipped the pen into the ink and tapped it, letting out the breath he was holding. He touched the nib to the surface of the paper. *There are Feelers in the Serpents Teeth*, he scratched out. "It works," he said, and his heart sank. Kerida would hate him even more now, but what could he do? This was his Faro. Besides, he told himself, it was obvious that he wasn't telling Juria Sweetwater anything she didn't already know.

He looked back at the paper. Really, once the main fact was shared, what more was there to say? He dashed out a few more lines, and handed the paper to his Faro.

"'There are Feelers in the Serpents Teeth,'" the Faro read

aloud. "'They have a prophecy that makes them believe they should give Kerida Nast whatever help she wants.'" The Faro glanced at Surm Barlot. "'There is also a young griffin who acts like she's his mother.' Well, it seems we're lucky she decided to come to us, if there is all this help that comes with her."

Tel couldn't be sure whether his Faro was being sarcastic. "She came with me because she wanted to warn the Talents in Temlin Hall about the Halians. After what we found there, she stayed with me." *And this is what she gets for it*. He shook himself. No point in thinking that way.

"Will she work with us?" It seemed to be Laxtor Barlot's job to ask the difficult questions.

Would she? Kerida could have stayed with the Feelers—the griffin had certainly wanted her to. She could even have turned back, once they'd seen the remains of Temlin Hall. She'd come on with him, knowing they were coming here, to Oste. "I believe so," he said. *I hope so*. If she didn't hate him too much, she might stay.

"Good. Normally, I would be telling you not to discuss this with anyone, but we have already established that you cannot." The Faro took the paper and tore it across twice before tossing the pieces into the brazier, which briefly blazed up.

"Yes, my Faro. But may I ask—"

"I will not tell you how it is I am not surprised, Third Officer. I'm afraid you must trust me."

"Of course, my Faro." Strange, but he felt comforted.

Ker had pulled all the linens off the three beds in the inner chambers and spread them out to air. She had the windows open, though the breeze was cold; the rooms needed to lose their shut-in smell. She looked around the sitting room, hands on hips.

"Maybe I shouldn't have been so quick to say I'd clean the place myself," she muttered. Not that the work was beneath her—Candidates at Questin were expected to keep their rooms clean—it was just that she couldn't find so much as a broom in the place. The knock at the door came as she was wondering which of the pillowcases was the oldest and therefore the best to use as a dusting cloth. She opened the door to find a girl about her own age staggering under a pile of bed, table, and bath linens, with a broom and dustpan tucked under one arm.

"Oooo, thanks, much appreciated. Wondered how I was going to manage the door, truth be told." The girl staggered in and made it by what must have been instinct to the table, where she almost overbalanced before dumping her load on the surface.

"Whew, that's better. Almost tripped on the outside step. Why are the storage rooms always so far from where things are needed? Can you answer me that?"

The girl who appeared from under all the supplies proved to be the minimum height for a soldier, with bright red hair, the whitest skin Ker had ever seen, and the bluest eyes. When she saw Ker staring at her, she sobered.

"Oh, sorry. I've never actually served a Talent before. I don't know the protocol. Am I allowed to speak to you?" But there was still a smile creeping around the corners of her eyes, and Ker found herself smiling back.

"Kind of difficult to get anything done if nobody spoke to us."

"Well, that's what *I* thought, truth be told. Here." The girl turned back to the pile of material on the table. "Fresh linens for the beds, though, between you and me, the ones you've got here are perfectly clean." Her hands deftly sorted out sheets and pillowcases, towels and washcloths, as she spoke. "Where are the others? Out spying around?" She glanced over her shoulder on the way to the bedchambers. "Oh, I guess I shouldn't have said that." This time she really did look serious.

"No, it's just me."

This stopped the girl in her tracks, and she turned back to

face Ker. "Just you?" She looked Ker up and down, her eyes narrowing. "Then I guess I'd better find you better clothes, and if you don't mind my saying so, first thing I'm going to organize is a bath."

Ker wasn't sure exactly how it was done, but the girl—"I'm Wynn Martan, Second Barrack, Blue Company, Pearl Cohort, Eagle Wing"—soon had two others bringing in hot water for the tub hiding behind what Ker had thought was a tapestry, the beds made, the place dusted, and the white shirt and red trousers and tunic of the Halls of Law laid out on one of the beds.

"That's a Full Talent's uniform," Ker pointed out. The bath had been incredible, the best one she'd had since childhood, but now all she had wrapped around her was a toweling robe several sizes too large.

"If you're the only Talent we've got, that makes you full enough for me. Besides, this is what the Badger sent, so this is what you've got."

"The Badger?"

"You know." Wynn gestured at her forehead. "Tall? Good-looking? Silver streak of hair? He's *that* Gulder, by the way. You know, his grandad was condemned for stealing with the old Faro of Wolves back in the dawn of time."

Ker sat down on the edge of the bed, considering. "He's not that tall, actually. And I think it's called embezzlement."

Wynn laughed. "I notice you don't say he's not good-looking?"

Pulling the robe more securely around her, Ker hoped she wasn't blushing. "*I* notice you're a lot more careful with your speech when there's other people around."

Wynn straightened the perfectly straight quilted cover on the bed farthest from the window. "Sure, well, protocol and discipline, right? Don't want to be put on report for being cheeky with the Talents, truth be told."

Ker laughed. "Figured out there's not much likelihood of that with me, have you?"

The girl bounced upright. "So do you want help dressing? Want me to do your hair?"

"What are you, a ladies' maid?"

"Not now, no. But I could have been."

Ker thought of meeting Tel Cursar in the kitchens, and what she'd said to him about being a kitchen serf. "And now?"

"Now I'm an archer." Wynn pulled up her left sleeve to show her leather bow guard. Archers got so they slept in them, Ker knew. "But when it isn't battle stations, I don't know much else—I can't train people, animals don't really like me, I'm not an armorer and I've no head for numbers and letters—so I'm a Boots." The girl sat down, tucking her right foot under her. "While I'm in camp, anyway."

Ker nodded. Soldiers often had specific camp duties which had nothing to do with their military usefulness.

"The Halians have been here—did the Faro tell you?" Wynn's voice had gone still and quiet, and her eyes were fixed on the toe of her left boot.

"You must have been surprised to see them."

"Surprised?" Wynn looked up from under her brows before letting her gaze fall back to the contemplation of her boot. "Surprised doesn't half cover it, truth be told. This isn't a fortress, for all the walls and gates." She looked up again. "There hasn't been an enemy at the gate since long before any of us were born."

"It's been much longer than that since any fighting was done in this province."

Wynn's grin faltered, and she let both feet slip to the floor. "We get the distress signal from the Peninsula, and we pass it on, and four Cohorts of Bears arrive. Faro Sweetwater keeps Ruby, and sends off Carnelian, Onyx, and Coral. Most of us Eagles go, too. Just the bare minimum of us stay to hold the fort against an attack no one ever thought would come. We almost let the invaders in. They were dressed like us." Wynn shook her head. "They *were* us."

Ker thought of the men on the road, dressed as Eagles and Bears, and nodded. "What happened?" she asked. "Why *weren't* they let in?"

"Would you believe they didn't know the password?"

Ker understood immediately what Wynn meant. Even though the Camp had never been under attack in living memory, the walls and gates *were* there, and the standing orders of a military fort would have been also. Passwords and signals would have to be exchanged, even here.

"And when they weren't let in?"

"They told us the Luqs was dead and that we should surrender, and when we didn't, they attacked." Wynn got to her feet and went to the window, where she straightened the rug on the window seat. Everything she said next she said with her back to Ker. "There were enough of us to hold the main positions, and we've lost very few. And the signal goes, smoke by day and fire by night. But you have to understand, the people attacking—some of them were our own people. Some of them had been stationed here."

So that was why the Faro hadn't asked more questions about the men she and Tel had left on the road. She already knew.

"But you held out," was what Ker said aloud.

Now Wynn turned back to face her, lowering herself to the seat. A shadow of the smiling girl who'd come into the room a few hours before settled on her face. "We held out," she said, the satisfaction plain in her voice. "We archers did our jobs, I can tell you." She nodded—short, sharp nods—and the sparkle came back fully into her eyes.

"Tell me about Faro Sweetwater."

Wynn shrugged. "Smart but cold. Tough, like all of them, but there's a distance you can feel, truth be told."

"Jakmor Gulder seems happy enough to be near her."

"Oooo, *Jakmor* is it?" The transformation back to the cheeky Boots was complete. The archer of the Pearl Cohort only existed in the uniform, and the crest on her left shoulder. "I didn't realize you and the Kalter were on such terms already! Fast mover. I like that in a person." Wynn sobered, but not much. "She values talent, does Faro Juria Sweetwater. When she finds it, she puts it to work, sometimes near her, if that's what she needs. Those that *are* near, well, it's like a family, they say, and then again it's not."

"How not?"

"They don't bicker." Wynn laughed. "Who knows of a family where there's no bickering? Her second, the Laxtor Surm Barlot, has been with her for ages, and they're like the mum and dad, and it's him you want to go to if it's cookies and hugs you need."

"Better to go to the cook," Ker said, with a grin of her own.

"Speaking of which, if there's nothing else just now, Talent Nast, I have duties elsewhere." She gave a mock salute and headed for the door.

"Wynn?" Ker waited until the girl turned back around. "Why did you stop being a ladies' maid?"

The girl's grin froze for an eye blink. "Truth be told, my auntie, who was to train me, changed her mind, and like I said, there's not that much I'm good at." She mimed pulling a bow, and winked. "What's a girl to do?"

Jak Gulder stepped out of the Faro's offices into the cold evening air, finally released from duty. He stretched his arms over his head and twisted from side to side. He'd stayed close the whole day, and he didn't know any more about what was going on than before the Talent and her soldier boy arrived. Though, now that he thought of it, the young woman herself might be a source of information if she was over her shock and ready for some sympathetic company.

He set off across the street but slowed as he approached the Talents' quarters. It looked as if someone else had the same thought. From the man's height, it had to be Tel Cursar. Well, what more natural? Though they hadn't seemed all that easy with each other when he'd last seen them, they *had* been traveling together for days. Just as Jak was about to call out, three soldiers came around the far corner of the Talents' quarters, barely slowing down when they saw Cursar at the door. Jak moved forward, hugging the wall as he got close enough to listen.

"You're the third officer from the Carnelian Cohort, aren't you? Just returned?" That was Second Officer Akimri of Yellow Company, a burly, fair-haired man quite a bit older than the Cursar boy. He was smiling at Tel as though they'd been friends their whole lives. "What news can you give us?"

The Cursar boy straightened. It was easy for him to look down on the other man. "None."

"Come now, you can tell us." This came from one of the other men, one Jak didn't recognize.

"Not according to my orders," Cursar said.

The Yellow Company officer held up his hand, silencing the other two. "I don't know how things are done in your Company, boy, but in ours, junior officers answer the questions of senior officers." His voice had been hard before, now it was cold.

Looked as if it was time to step in.

"You people have business with the Talent, have you?"

It was almost funny to see how they all froze in place, even Cursar, who certainly wasn't guilty of anything.

"No, Kalter. That is . . . no, sir." This was one of the soldiers he didn't know. In the field they might not be so ready to obey him, but here in camp a Kalter ranked more or less as a Cohort Leader.

"Then I suggest you be about your duties. This man has duties of his own." He waited until the others had turned away before adding, "Oh, and Second Officer Akimri?"

"Yes, sir?"

"No matter what Company you're in or Cohort, for that matter, Faro's orders take precedence."

"Yes, sir." All three men touched the crests on their left shoulders and were gone.

Jak turned to Tel, inwardly sighing. He could hardly grill the man himself, now that he'd stopped others from doing so. And the other men's actions put another, more unpleasant look to his coming to visit the Talent. "Well, Cursar, have you eaten yet?"

"No, Kalter."

"Come with me. If there's one thing the Wings have taught me, it's that everything looks better on a full stomach."

K ER had managed to pass the whole of yesterday and most of this morning without actually putting on any of the Talent's clothing. But the Faro was likely to want her, and Ker knew she couldn't show up in a dressing robe, no matter how splendid.

The Full Talent's white shirt, red tunic, and trousers were still laid out where Wynn had left them. Ker examined the white shirt closely without touching it. It was made of the best lawn, something her own mother would have chosen to wear, though her mother would have embroidered any such shirt on the cuffs and fronts in white thread with the panthers of the family crest. The trousers and half-sleeved tunic were made from a fine weave of linen and wool, but Ker hoped there was an equally fine cloak somewhere, since these wouldn't be all that warm for the current weather. Luckily, there were also leggings set out. Her own were too worn to even think about.

Ker was reaching out to feel the thickness of the tunic's

fabric when she stopped, her fingers hovering over the cloth. She *could* be a coward about it. She *could* put on shirt, tunic, and trousers without Flashing them. She wiped her palms off on the skirt of the robe. *Paraste.*

Ker picked up each piece separately, skipping quickly past the maker of the cloth, and the tailor of the clothing, both women from New Atenas Province. It was far more important that the clothing had all been worn by the same Talent, a woman much older than Ker, who had traveled with the Bear Wing almost all her professional life. A woman named . . . Celian. With another Talent she had a daughter, who had been sent to live with her father's people. Celian hadn't forgotten her, although it was forbidden. She'd died still wearing a pendant that they used to send back and forth between them. If her daughter wore it for even a week, and sent it back, Celian could Flash from it anything she needed to know.

"Good for you," Ker said, stroking the shirt. Celian had found a way to get around the rules imposed by the Halls of Law. Maybe all those years living with soldiers had given her a different view of the world. These articles of clothing had been in the laundry when Celian had been sent back to the Halls, and she hadn't bothered to take them with her, she'd been *that* sure she'd be coming back.

There had been five Talents posted with the Bear Wing. All of them had made it to Temlin Hall, but like everyone else there, Celian and her friends hadn't made it out again.

Terestre. There really wasn't anything more to know.

Ker massaged her temples, muttering a prayer to the Mother to hold these Talents in particular in her arms. She pulled the shirt on over her head and hugged herself, more to keep from taking it off again than because of the sudden chill that made the hairs on her back and arms stand up. She would wear Celian's shirt. She would remember the dead Talent with respect. She brushed the garment straight. It was a little long, but it wouldn't matter when it was tucked in. Ker sat down on the edge of the bed to pull the leggings on. She was turning up the cuffs on the trousers when a knock came at the door.

Tel. Ker had avoided thinking about him. Now she swallowed, brushing her hair back off her face with both hands.

"I'll be right there." She tugged on her boots and grabbed up the tunic.

He'd be coming to apologize, or at least give some better explanation for his actions. Maybe he'd done what he'd had to do, but that didn't change the way she felt, and her anger still smoldered. However, the hours alone had persuaded her that she'd listen to an apology if it was thorough enough. That much had changed for her. Maybe it was because, wearing Celian's clothes, she felt she knew something about how that woman would have handled the situation. Still, Ker yanked the tunic on over her head, thrusting her arms through the half-sleeves and pulling it straight. No need to forgive him *too* quickly. She fixed what she hoped was a cold smile on her face as she went to the door and pulled it open. Her smile faded.

"Well. So glad you're happy to see me." Jakmor Gulder stepped past her into the room and let her shut the door behind him.

"I'm sorry, Kalter. I was expecting Tel Cursar."

"You were?" Jakmor tilted his head to one side, and Ker wished she could be sure she wasn't blushing. "Ah, of course, I'd forgotten that you're still a Candidate. And *you've* forgotten that I'm Jak." He grinned. "Under normal circumstances, lower ranks don't associate with Talents."

Ker thought about Wynn and wished the girl was here with her. She would probably find Jak Gulder's teasing more enjoyable than Ker did. And there was something about what Jak had said that struck her as wrong.

"I would have thought that Talents chose their own associates."

"Ah. True." Jak leaned against the edge of the larger table, studying her with narrowed eyes. "What I meant was, if Talents want to talk with someone from the lower ranks, they go through their Company Commander or Cohort Leaders. Tel Cursar has neither, at the moment."

In other words, the Faro thinks she'll see if she can control who I speak to and when. Ker drummed her fingers against her thigh. The problem was, she didn't see what she could do about it. *And there's no point in arguing with Jakmor Gulder.* Juria Sweetwater seemed to be using Jak as the link between herself, Ker, and Tel Cursar. Was that because of some innate ability? Ker wondered. Did the Faro assume that because Ker was young, she could be swayed by a handsome face and a lock of attractively placed white hair? Ker's lips pulled back, but her smile felt grim.

"If you would come with me, the Faro Juria Sweetwater requires your counsel."

Jak's switch to formal speech told her this was an official summons. She stood. "Please lead the way, Kalter."

Ker's mouth hadn't felt this dry since she'd been summoned to Matriarch. It couldn't be much more than a month ago, but it seemed like another lifetime. Faro Sweetwater was seated behind her worktable, as if she hadn't moved since yesterday. The Faro didn't actually smile as she waved Ker to the chair at the end of the table to her left, but her face looked friendly at least. So did the face of Surm Barlot, seated at the far end of the table, on the Faro's right.

"Forgive my early summons, Talent Nast. You have eaten, and rested?"

"Yes, Faro."

"We are being joined by my Ruby Cohort Leader, Wilk Silvertrees, and the Eagle Camp Commandant, Mekner Rost. Before they arrive, can we agree to discuss your passage through the mines as simply that, a journey through the mines?"

"I—" Ker blinked and shut her mouth.

"I see." The Faro raised her hand, palm out. "Say no more—I beg your pardon, I could have phrased that better. So the inability to mention or discuss the Feelers in the Serpents Teeth applies to you as well."

"He told you?" She *knew* it.

"Only because I knew how to ask. Please do not be concerned; he will not tell anyone else. And before you can ask, *I* only knew how to ask him because I am myself privy to the Feelers' secret. Given what I already know, may I try asking you some questions?"

Ker closed her eyes. "Go ahead."

"Had you heard of this prophecy before?"

Ker's mouth opened in automatic response to the Faro's authoritative tone, but no words came out. She spread her hands.

"Ah, I see. I expect that *you* can write, Candidate?"

A tap at the door saved Ker from having to answer. Just as well, since she didn't know what her answer would have been. Ker laced her fingers together on the top of the table as two older men walked in.

As Surm Barlot performed the introductions, Ker studied each man in turn. Wilk Silvertrees was a big bear of a man, as tall as Tel Cursar and easily three times around. His hair was still thick, but almost completely gray, and cropped as short as the Faro's. Mekner Rost, the Camp Commandant, wore Eagle Wing green. A short bull of a man, thick through the shoulders, his face showing a dark stain of beard even though he was closely shaven. It was he who went to the side table under the window and poured wine, bringing the first cup to the Faro, and the last to Ker.

"Mother, Daughter, and Son, smile on our efforts, today and all days," the man said. Ker lifted her cup to her lips and took a ritual sip. She usually found wine too sour for her taste. The Faro, the Laxtor, and Wilk Silvertrees all lifted their glasses, but then allowed a few drops to fall to the floor rather than drinking.

Jossists, she thought. Not unusual in the Wings, but most weren't so strict about avoiding alcohol.

"The first order of business is to confirm the deaths of the Luqs and her family," the Faro said when the cups were back on the table. "We must know whether anyone of royal blood escaped or is in hiding, and if so, we must rescue them."

How are you planning on rescuing them, if they're in hiding? Ker knew better than to ask her question aloud. She knew why everyone was so concerned. Talents didn't spend all the time they were training learning how to use their gift. Since they might be assigned anywhere, there were lessons on behavior and manners, and in politics, history, and the law. The first Luqs, Jurianol the Unifier, had been Faro of what was now the Eagle Wing, and rose to the throne—or, as some said, created the throne under her—with the backing of both the military and the Halls of Law. Since then, custom and careful management had kept the throne more or less in the hands of her descendants. What would happen if there were no such person left? Who would the Wings follow? Ker shivered.

"I understood the pass was closed." Wilk Silvertrees' voice rumbled like a battle drum.

"We can send a small party through the mines, by the route Tel Cursar and Talent Nast used," the Faro said.

"I volunteer to lead the party," Silvertrees said.

The Faro looked up, her eyes sparkling. "I need you here, Cohort Leader. You are the only senior officer I have left." The man took a deep breath and nodded. Was he blushing?

"Talent Nast?"

Ker jerked her attention back to the Faro, her ears growing hot as she realized it wasn't the first time the woman had said her name.

"I asked if you had any way to help us with this question."

"I don't think so, Faro," she began, when her eye was caught by movement across the table. The Camp Commandant was turning a ring over and over on his index finger. Suddenly Ker was back in her seat next to Barid in Questin Hall, watching the Leader of the Bear Wing's Carnelian Cohort place a signet ring on the table in front of Matriarch.

Ker licked her lips. "Does anyone here have any keepsakes or tokens from the royal family?"

The Faro looked at Surm with eyebrows raised. The Laxtor leaned back in his chair, mouth twisted to one side. "Not that I've heard," he said. "And surely no one would keep silent about such a thing."

"Nevertheless, have your Company Commanders ask."

Mekner Rost immediately stood and went to the door, where he gave instructions to the orderly in the outer room. The Faro had turned back to Ker. "It's your thought that such an object would give you information about the royals?"

"I'm good with objects." Ker explained how Matriarch had Flashed Prince Hanlor's ring.

Juria's eyebrows drew down in a vee. "Ah, yes. I had forgotten about Jen Sha'na's ring."

"My Faro, your pardon." Everyone looked at Wilk Silvertrees. "Even if we lack for something that comes directly from the hands of any *present* member of the royal family, what of the standard?"

The Faro smiled. "If the tale is true, you mean?"

"What tale?" Ker knew what they were talking about. The standard of the Wing, mounted on a long straight pole of ash wood, decorated with honors, and carried wherever the Wing went. During battle, it marked where the Faro stood. "Even if some of the honors were presented by a royal, there wouldn't be enough personal connection for me to Flash what we need to know."

"Not the honors, the pole." Juria Sweetwater's smile broadened. "Tradition has it that the pole has never been broken, that it is still the original, dating to when the Bear Wing was first formed. There are stains on the pole supposed to be the blood of Rolian the Lawgiver, from when he was just the prince, not the heir, and was the standard-bearer for the Wing."

"He saved the standard," Surm Barlot said. "Even though he was injured, he managed to keep hold of it, and keep it out of enemy hands. The blood was never cleaned off."

Tradition has it, Ker thought. *Supposed to be.* "So at least in theory," she said, "I should be able to Flash the standard?"

"Exactly. Can you do it?"

Ker looked at the hopeful faces around her. Even sour Wilk Silvertrees managed to look less forbidding. "I can try."

"Allow me." Wilk Silvertrees stood up. "If you will follow me, Talent Nast, I can escort you to the shrine room."

"A moment, Cohort Leader. I have need of your counsel here. I believe Kalter Gulder is still outside; he may escort the Talent." The Faro turned to Ker. "If you would be so good?"

Ker found the door open and Jak Gulder at her elbow almost as soon as she'd stood up. So he *was* delegated to keep an eye on her.

The door was barely closed behind the Talent and her escort when Wilk Silvertrees turned to the Faro. "This could be a great opportunity for you, my Faro."

Juria Sweetwater looked at the grizzled man in front of her, his eyes, as so often, lit by a fire from within. "If I had any ambitions in that way, perhaps."

"If you don't, there are others who might." Typical of Surm, to be so practical. It wouldn't be the first time that the throne had been taken by the closest one with the most military backing—everyone knew old Jurianol, the first Luqs and Juria's namesake, had created the position, with her Battle

Wing behind her to convince others it was a good idea. That had been generations ago, but no Faro forgot it.

"Don't forget, anyone with ideas in that quarter would still need to deal with the Halians," Juria said.

"You would make a fine Luqs, my Faro. Better than many others, if it should come to that." Wilk looked at Surm and Mekner Rost, as if daring them to disagree.

Juria smiled and waved around the room. "What, and leave all this?"

"Sorry about this," Ker said, as they exited the Faro's offices. "I'm sure you have other duties."

"Escorting you *is* one of my duties."

"Would you be escorting me if I were Celian, or one of her colleagues?"

He didn't exactly stop, but there was a hesitation in his step. "You know their names?"

Did he know what a stupid question that was? Or was he playing some sort of game? He'd been the one who'd sent Wynn with these clothes.

"I *am* a Talent," she said finally. "I'm living in the same rooms they used." She gestured at herself. "I'm wearing their clothes. Did you think I wouldn't know anything about them?"

"You told the Faro you weren't very good with people." Was she imagining suspicion in his tone? Now that she was dressed as a Talent, would people treat her differently? The way Tel had in the kitchen when they first met?

"Not at Flashing them directly, no. But I can Flash information from the things they owned and touched. Isn't that why you want me to Flash the standard?"

Shouts erupted around the north corner of the stores building before Jak could answer, shouts, and the unmistakable sound of running feet.

"Wait here," Jak called over his shoulder as he rounded the corner, heading into the cleared yard in front of the building's main doors.

"Oh, *that's* likely." Ker set off after him. Was she a Talent, or wasn't she? She couldn't let him—or anyone else—think they could order her around.

Soldiers were running up the central avenue toward the main gate from all directions. She was right behind Jak as he reached the cluster of soldiers standing near the bottom of the stone steps leading up to the watchtower that guarded the right side of the gate. Some were looking upward, while others were watching the runner heading for the administrative barracks. Two of these were answering Jak's questions.

"Kerida."

At the touch on her elbow Ker spun around, fists raised, relaxing only when she saw it was Tel Cursar. She tilted her head back to get a good look at him and almost returned his smile until she remembered she was still angry with him.

"What do *you* want? Don't you know that the lower ranks aren't supposed to associate with Talents?" His smile faded so fast Ker felt ashamed. But not too ashamed to add, "Looking for something else to tell on me?"

His hand dropped from her arm as he licked his lips and swallowed nervously. "Look, I wish it didn't have to be this way. Maybe in a different time and place I could have held my tongue, but in this place, and at this time, what you and I want isn't particularly important."

Ker felt her face go hot, and her hands clenched. She *had* worked that out for herself, though she didn't relish being told so bluntly. She didn't relish having to be reminded where her loyalties should be. She took a deep breath through her nose. "You know, that was a good exit line. You should have spun around on your heel and gone stalking off. Now you've gone and wasted it."

Tel looked away, but his shoulders had relaxed. "The Faro

already knew about the . . . the *mines*," he murmured. "Not from me, she *already* knew."

"I figured that out for myself. Did she tell *you* how she knows about them?"

Tel shook his head.

"Typical. We're supposed to report all we know, but it's all right for them to have secrets."

Tel looked at her, the corners of his mouth turning up. Just for a moment, they were two ordinary soldiers, griping about officers.

"They've put me in the Talents' quarters," she said, even as she realized he must have known that. "What about you?"

Tel looked over his shoulder again. With his height, he had a good view of what was going on at the gate. The Camp Commandant had arrived and was mounting the steps.

Tel turned back to her. "They've got me in the couriers' room," he said, referring to the room kept ready for those mounted soldiers who carried messages for the military, and the Polity. It was the closest thing any camp had to guest quarters for non-officers.

"Makes sense," Ker said. And it did. Where else would they put someone who was a soldier, but wasn't part of any Company? Though Tel didn't seem very comfortable with the idea. "Do you know what they're going to do with you?"

His face stiffened. "No one's really had time to think about me yet." His left shoulder lifted and dropped.

Ker pushed her hands into her sleeves. "We can't talk here," she said. "Come to my rooms if you won't be missed."

Tel's lips parted but Ker never found out what he was going to say.

"Hey, Cursar! To me!"

The Camp Commandant's assistant waved Tel over to the tower. Ker started up the stairs with him, but Jak Gulder was there and stopped her.

"Much too dangerous for you, Talent. They look to be out of archery range, but we can't be too careful."

Ker bit back her response. Clearly, she hadn't *completely* considered what being the only available Talent meant.

"This way if you please, Talent Nast."

Ker gritted her teeth and turned. She wasn't moving from this spot until she found out what was going on. Even if they wouldn't let her up on the rampart, surely she was safe enough down here? But when Ker turned to see who'd spoken to her, she found Wynn Martan, her eyes sparkling a little too much for her very serious face.

"If you'd come with me, please, Talent." A waggle of the eyebrows convinced Ker to do just that.

"We can see more from over here anyway," Wynn confided in a near whisper as she led Ker to one of the smaller towers which flanked the main gate, positioned to allow archers to fire on anyone making a direct assault on it. Once up the ladder, Ker found someone had erected a useful, though probably nonregulation windbreak. Two young soldiers, one with a flat nose, the other with hair almost as red as Wynn's, grinned and made room for them both.

"What's the problem?" Wynn was asking.

"They're dressed wrong," Flatnose said. "Some are wearing Eagle colors, some Bear. Even if they were refugees from the same conflict, they'd line up with their own, surely, not stand all mixed up like that."

It took Ker a minute to see what he was talking about, but he was right. There were the purple tunics of Bears, with green tunics mixed in among them. And she wasn't so sure they *were* out of arrow range.

"Come closer and identify yourself, soldier!" Mekner Rost, the Camp Commandant, must have run here from his meeting with the Faro.

"I'm Palo Sixgrass. I was Red Company Commander in

the Carnelian Cohort of Bears," the man standing out in the field said. "I'm here on orders from the council to speak to the Laxtor."

"That's why they wanted your friend," Flatnose said. "If they're from the same Cohort, he should recognize the man."

"The Faro is coming herself to speak to you," Mekner Rost said.

"Is she now? Well, she can keep her speech to herself. I'll speak only to the Laxtor."

An almost audible growl floated over the soldiers on the wall, spreading to those on the ground as what the man had said was passed back. No one spoke in that tone about a Battle Wing's Faro and got away with it.

Glancing around, Ker saw that Juria Sweetwater had arrived at the bottom of the steps leading up to the ramparts. It was obvious she'd heard what the man had said, and Ker saw Surm Barlot the Laxtor listening to her, nodding, the smile on his face fixed as if he'd forgotten it was there. The Faro signaled to those higher on the steps, and the result of her instructions became clear when the next voice Ker heard was Tel's.

"Palo! Palo Sixgrass, it's Tel Cursar. Where's the Cohort Commander? Where's Jen Sha'na? Didn't she make it?"

"That you, Cursar? Didn't know you'd got away. Well, you might have waited and saved yourself the trouble. It's to save you all from the rule of women that we've come."

The murmur that swept over those listening was more puzzled now than offended. What did "rule of women" mean? Did he mean the Luqs?

A sudden chill settled on Ker's skin. Dead women's uniforms. But no women. Is that why they'd killed the Luqs? Because she was a woman? But hadn't they killed *all* the royals?

The man was still speaking.

"Do none of you understand?" There was a flicker of white teeth in the man's face as he smiled. "All the witches are gone. Beheaded and burned. We're all free now."

He went on talking, but Ker didn't hear anymore. She'd never heard the word "witches" before, but she knew what it meant. She knew who'd been beheaded and burned.

Witches meant Talents. She sat down, crouching below the edge of the parapet, even though the windbreak concealed her. Dimly, she realized that Wynn and her two friends were readying their bows. There was a new voice now, the voice of Surm Barlot. Ker blinked. The Faro was standing still as a statue at the bottom of the stairs, listening with a calm face as her Laxtor spoke. The Ruby Cohort Leader, Wilk Silvertrees, stood next to her, his face like a stone and his hand on his sword.

Ker turned as a man came pounding up the nearby stairs. He was calling as he came, and whether it was the man's own noise, or the pounding of her heart, it took Ker a minute to understand what he was yelling.

"There's one here! They've got a witch!"

They've got a witch. He meant *her.*

She wasn't aware she'd moved until a hand on her shoulder pushed her roughly down, and a bow spring *snapped!* above her head. The man hadn't quite reached the top of the stairs when the arrow caught him full in the throat, knocking him sideways. He slid off the narrow steps, sprouting three more arrows before he hit the ground.

"Anything?" That was Wynn, standing over her.

"Nothing. Looks like no one heard him." That was the third man, not Flatnose, the redhead. "Good shooting, Wynn."

Ker started breathing again.

"Really? I was aiming for his leg. Now we won't be able to question him."

There was a hardness in the young woman's voice that Ker had never heard before. She swallowed. She would have been expected to do the questioning. Suddenly she was even more happy the man was dead.

———

"You sure you want to get out here, lad?"

Luca Pa'narion surprised himself by smiling. He didn't run into many people old enough to call him "lad," and until lately even those had called him "sir." He swung his legs over the edge of the cart and lowered himself to the ground.

"I can manage from here," he said, brushing the hay off his pack as he reached it down. "Thank you again for the lift."

The farmer, a wizened old man with skin like a winter apple, studied Luca with narrowed eyes before looking away. "Have to see for yourself, is that it?"

"Something like that, yes." The old man wasn't going to go running to the nearest Halian. Luca wouldn't have climbed into the cart if he hadn't Flashed that much without even try-ing. Still, that was no reason to burden him with details.

"Never mind, lad. You're not the first who's come looking. I did the same myself. Not sure I would have believed it other-wise. I've been carting along this road for longer than you've been alive, since my dad's day. Well . . ." He shrugged and took up the slack in the reins. "The Hall road's not been kept clear, but you should have little trouble on foot." He hesitated, and let the reins go slack again. "It goes against my heart to leave you in this place."

Luca stood without saying a word. Finally, the old carter nodded. "I'll be along this way again in two or three hours, if you want a lift back."

"I may be here. Thank you again." Luca waited, watching the carter and his load of hay roll away. Whatever they might be thinking, or saying to passing strangers for that matter, people in the area around Questin Hall seemed to be going about their regular lives. It could have been much worse. Or so he kept telling himself.

At last the carter was far enough away that Luca felt com-fortable about leaving the road. If necessary, the old man would be able to say, quite truthfully, that he didn't see where Luca went. It had taken him longer to reach Questin than he'd planned, but the detours he'd taken to check the other safe houses for Talents in hiding had been necessary, as well as fruitful. There weren't as many still living as he'd hoped, but more, perhaps, than he'd expected.

In Windmonth the windows of the dormitories and attics of Questin should have been visible above the leafless maple trees planted between the Hall and the main road. After one look at the empty sky, Luca kept his eyes down, telling himself he needed to watch his footing.

As if he wouldn't be able to Flash where to put his feet.

It was every bit as bad as he'd expected—though he hadn't expected to feel this tightening in his chest, and this fog in front of his eyes. The Halians hadn't merely set fire to the place, they'd pulled down the ruins afterward. There was not one stone still resting on another. There was not one shard of wood whole enough to recognize its purpose. Not one piece of glass larger than the palm of his hand.

For the first time in weeks the weight of the guilt that never left him threatened to loosen his spine. He took a deep breath and rubbed his face with his hands. This was lunacy. If he couldn't Flash this place, to learn whatever there might be here to learn, he was no use to anyone, not even himself, and he should go back to the road and wait for the carter.

Luca squatted and pulled off his gloves. A moment later, he was on his knees, uncertain whether he was using his hands to Flash the remains around him, or to prop himself up. He didn't remember kneeling. Harvests might be taken in, markets still observe their days, hay carts might still wheel their way down country lanes, but there was no one left here. Luca Pa'narion was the only Senior Talent—certainly the only Inquisitor—left in the Peninsula. Such was the end result of all his work of the last year, looking for evidence to convince others of the conspiracy he'd uncovered.

It had started so simply, with a dead body who wasn't the person everyone in his town thought he was. And the gradually unraveling thread that had led to more suspicion and more investigation. And then all the meetings with that arrogant woman who might very well be the last Luqs of the Faraman Polity, unable to persuade her, after the oddities he'd discovered at Jobado, that the officers of the Eagle Wing should undergo a systematic examination. This—what he saw around him now—was the result of his failure.

Even if he had been successful, might he not be standing here alone, just the same? By the time his suspicions were aroused, it was likely already too late. The invasion had been much farther along in its planning and its execution than he and his fellow Inquisitors had been able to find out. He hadn't even known how wide the Halian network had been. He hadn't even known that Talents were at risk.

Luca rose to his feet, brushing snow off his knees. The old carter was right. He'd needed to see for himself that Questin was gone. And with it every scroll, every book, every artifact that had trained Talents for thousands of years. According to his Flash, a few of the boys and the younger men had been taken away living, though for some reason he could not tell exactly who. The rest were gone. Many of them not even Talents. No one's enemies. Killed out of fear—he could Flash that much. The Shekayrin hadn't bothered to use the jewel on everyone. Hadn't checked to see who were only household serfs and gardeners.

The Shekayrin . . . Luca took three paces to the left, and seven to his right. Here was where the Halian priest had stood. From this spot Luca could see faint red lines radiating outward, spreading over the rubble and debris. Allowing for the unevenness of the terrain, the lines seemed to form a faint web. This web, almost impossible to see, was the remnant of the mage's power.

Wiping off his face with the hem of his cloak, Luca left the ruin of the great hall, tramping around to where the outbuildings and stables had been. Even here the destruction was complete. The Halians had taken the horses, though they'd first had to round up the ones that had run off into the fields. Luca concentrated, breathing slowly and letting the Flash deepen. The horses hadn't broken down their corral out of fear, someone had let them out. His heart began to beat faster.

Someone had let the horses out. Someone had escaped.

He closed his eyes and walked into the field, past stable yard and pen, across ditch and through wheat field, his feet the only ones that had walked here since the horses had been rounded up. The person who'd managed to escape had gone this way, on horseback. Luca pushed his Flash deeper until he knew the names of the horses who'd been loose, milling about in the field. Until he could Flash how long the snow had fallen, and where the moisture that made up the flakes had come from. Until he could name the rider who had escaped.

Kerida Nast.

Kerida Nast alive and well and headed for the old mines.

Luca Pa'narion began to laugh.

11

66 **T**ALENT Nast." Juria Sweetwater's voice drifted upward in the cold air. Kerida looked around her. The Laxtor was just coming down the ladder. The confrontation with the squad of soldiers outside the walls was over. For now.

"Here, Faro." Ker made her way down the steps, edging around soldiers who made room for her. Many of these stood stiff with anger, lips showing white over clenched teeth. Someone steadied her, holding her elbow as she stepped off the last step. It felt like every eye was on her. She straightened her shoulders and lifted her chin.

Faro Sweetwater gestured at the corpse. "What can you tell me about this man?"

Ker looked around at interested faces. "Is there somewhere more private?" she said.

"Kalter Gulder, see that the Talent gets whatever she needs." The Faro looked around as if seeing the gathered soldiers for the first time. One steel-gray eyebrow lifted. "Is there a feast day I am not aware of?" Was it Ker's imagination, or was there actually a hint of laughter in the older woman's voice?

All around her, soldiers relaxed, some even grinning, as officers snapped orders. Many, officers and ranks alike, acknowledged the Faro with a touch to their crests—a salute normally not done inside a camp unless to acknowledge orders. Even Kerida felt a certain degree of tension leave her shoulders. By acting as if there was nothing out of the ordinary, the Faro had made everyone feel better.

"Will the infirmary serve for your examination, Talent Nast?"

Ker pulled her attention away from the Faro and turned to Jak Gulder. "That would be fine." She'd never actually done it, but in theory Flashing a dead body wasn't much different from Flashing clothing, or weapons, or any other inanimate object.

"I'll need someone to scribe for me," she said. Usually, there would be two Talents at an examination like this, one to Flash, and one to record. These officers would know that as well as she did.

"I would be pleased to do it," Jak Gulder said, holding out his hand as if he was partnering her for a dance.

"No, thank you, Kalter. You must have other duties. Tel Cursar hasn't anything else to do right now and since I know him better, he'll be less distracting." She smiled at Jak and waited to see if he would overrule her. As Talent, the choice was hers, and the man's response to this simple request would show her what her standing really was.

"As you say, Talent. Let Cursar know if you need anything else." Jak turned to Tel. "You heard her, Cursar, you're the Talent's shadow until you're told otherwise. Got it?"

"Yes, sir." Tel touched his crest.

The body was placed on a stretcher, and Ker and Tel followed as two of the ranks carried it to the infirmary building. They laid it out on the bed nearest the window. There was an oil lamp on a nearby table, its wick trimmed and a sparker waiting to light it, but for Flashing the amount of light was fine.

"We're in luck." Tel gestured at the empty room. "There's no one sick. And speaking of luck, did you notice that Kalter Jakmor Gulder isn't very happy with either of us at the moment?"

Ker lifted her eyebrows. "Well, I think that's unluckier for you than it is for me. I'm a Talent, remember?"

Tel cast his hands into the air. "So *now* it's all right you're a Talent? Does that mean I'm forgiven?"

Did it? Tel grinned like he was joking, but his pale eyes were dead serious. Ker studied him. He'd done what a soldier should do. He couldn't put her wishes before the needs of the whole Polity. He'd done what she would have done herself. Probably.

She wrinkled her nose. "I'm speaking to you, aren't I? You want more? You want me to thank you as well?"

Tel's grin widened, and his shoulders lowered just a fraction. "Not thank me, no. Just keep in mind that Gulder actually *can* make more trouble for me than he can for you. At least until I get a permanent assignment."

Ker shrugged, glancing up at Tel from the corner of her eye. "You've landed on your feet so far, haven't you? I'm sure you've got at least as many lives as a cat."

"Looks like I'm going to need them."

"What do you mean?" Ker shifted her eyes to the corpse. *Where would be the best place to touch it*?

"Weren't you listening, there at the gate?"

Ker turned to face him fully, her mouth gone suddenly dry. Certainly, she'd have to think about the madness she'd heard at the gate, and so would everyone else in camp for that matter, but . . . She eyed the body. She, at least, had a legitimate distraction.

"Tel, I stopped listening at the part about witches."

"Sure." He nodded, rubbing his face with his long-fingered hands. "I can see that. But he called on Surm Barlot to hand over the Faro and surrender the Wing. Said we had no legal authority to hold the fort against them. That they were the Polity now."

Fingers drumming against her thigh, Ker nodded. That was what the Faro had been afraid of. "Have they declared a Luqs?"

"Well . . ." Tel's brow furrowed. "Nothing was said about that."

Ker shut her eyes. "Sorry, I need to focus," she told Tel. "Examining a body for the first time is a big enough challenge without worrying about all that."

"Right." Tel moved a stool close to the bed for her and stood back, looking around the room. "I'm going for paper," he said. "There's not likely to be any in here. Light the lamp for me, would you?"

Of course. Tel would need light to write by, even if *she* could work in the dark. Ker moved the lamp to a good spot on a table nearer the bed. The wick caught right away. She dragged the stool even closer to the body and sat down, rotating her shoulders to relax the muscles.

In minutes Tel was back, holding up a thin sheaf of paper, a pen, and a small inkpot. "Duty officer had some," he said, settling down at the table. "Whenever you're ready."

She nodded again, and turned back to the body. Who, what, when, where, and why. She took in a deep breath, let it out slowly, and gripped the cooling right wrist. The skin was still warm. *Paraste.*

The sudden colors startled her almost into losing her hold on the wrist, but she relaxed as soon as she realized it was only her own aura, and Tel's, that she saw. Around the body was just a faint cloud of red. Nevertheless, her Flash was clearer and brighter than she'd ever experienced before. For the first time when touching a human, she didn't feel as though she were trying to swim in mud.

"His name was Markon Zahlia," she said. "He was a Second Officer in Yellow Company, Opal Cohort of the Eagle Wing. Born in Ariand. Served in the military since he was fifteen. Didn't rise higher because his reading wasn't very good. He was much better with figures, so long as he did them in his head."

"Ker."

"Yes, all right." This wasn't the kind of information the Faro was looking for. Ker touched the clothes with her other hand. The tunic and shirt were definitely his own, but . . .

"He's killed women," Ker said.

"Every soldier has." The lamp cast shadows on Tel's face that made his cheekbones stand out, and his eyes look golden.

Ker focused her own eyes back to the body.

"That isn't what I meant," she said. "This man killed his First Officer. He let people think she died in the fighting, but he did it and stepped into her place."

"No female soldiers." Tel's voice was like ice. "That's what you said."

"None at all."

"Your sister . . ."

Ker held up her free hand. She was *not* going to think about Ester. *She was not.* "Do you remember what I said about the soldier at the Hall? The one I killed? Remember I said it was like there had been some kind of event in his life that changed him?"

Tel shook himself. "I remember *now.*"

"The same thing's happened to this man. He's Markon Zahlia, but it's as if he's—" How could she describe it? She glanced over at Tel, his pen poised. How often had she seen clerks in the Hall, copying out documents. "As if he was a copy of himself. But with something added in . . . or left out."

Tel was frowning back at her. "Is that what you want me to write down?"

"I think you'd better. If something happens to me, someone else will want to know what I Flashed, in case they ever Flash anything similar."

"If something happens to you, there won't be anyone else to Flash anything similar."

That thought triggered something . . . something about the *when*, and the *where*.

"Listen, whatever happened to this man, it happened long before the invasion of the Peninsula." Ker looked at Tel, suddenly sure. "He was already one of the enemy before the enemy came."

"That's the difference that you're Flashing? That he became one of the enemy?"

"Part of it, yes. He didn't become someone else. He didn't stop being Markon Zahlia, and he didn't think of himself as one of the enemy. He thought he was still on the same side. Tel—" Her friend was missing the point. "Don't you see? He's been like this for years, not just since the Halians came."

Tel rubbed his hands over his face. "And the people we met on the road?"

Ker shook her head. "I didn't try Flashing anything from them directly, remember? Not like this. There's something I don't see clearly, something I don't understand." Frowning, she mentally set the two Flashings side by side; perhaps one would shed light on the other. "There's not many Shekayrin, not enough to 'purify' everyone who resists." Ker frowned. She shifted so she could look at Tel more directly, waiting until he lifted his pen from the paper and looked up. "This man was 'purified,' but the people we met on the road, they were only 'pacified.'"

"Huh. I'd say 'stupefied,' but I suppose it's much the same thing. I *said* it was like they were drugged."

Ker nodded. "In *that* state, they couldn't have done what this man was doing. They couldn't have come into the camp and spied on us. He's been spying and passing along information, but he's also been spreading tales and influencing others, turning them against their officers—"

Tel pointed the pen at her. "There was someone like that in Red Company, I remember. Never said anything treasonous, exactly, but made a lot of people think."

"Even you?"

Tel pressed his lips together before answering. "Even me, a little. But what was this one doing here? Now?"

Ker frowned. "He was to wait until they saw what kind of response we gave to the ones at the gate, and if it wasn't what they wanted, he was to let them in."

"So why didn't he wait?"

"Because of me. Because I was here." Ker wiped her hands on her knees. "A Talent. A witch."

"Can you tell us how long this man has been changed?"

Ker was sitting in the Faro's personal quarters. Her chair was comfortable, but she had to stop herself from fidgeting. She and Tel Cursar had reported to the Faro together, once she'd been sure she'd Flashed everything she could from the body, but Tel had been left standing at the door. Rank was still rank, no matter where they were. The Faro was never off duty, apparently, not even in her own bedroom. Ker eyed the Laxtor, Surm Barlot. Was he on duty here as well?

"It was more than three years ago, but less than five," Ker said. "That's as close as I can get."

Surm Barlot was nodding. "There've been rumors . . . an uptick of malcontents. An increase in feeling against the Halls. More in the Eagle Wing, perhaps, than in the Battle Wings— though that may have been wishful thinking on our part."

"There has been much transferring of personnel back and forth between the Eagles and the rest of us in the last three to five years." The Faro sounded thoughtful. "We thought we were maintaining order and discipline, by breaking up cliques and moving troublemakers. But if those we moved were like this one, we may have done ourselves greater harm than good."

They'd been transferring the enemy, Ker thought, nodding. Spreading them through the Wings. That's what Juria Sweetwater meant.

The Faro stopped drumming her fingers on the table and sat up straighter. "If nothing else, this explains much." She looked Surm Barlot in the eye. "Beginning with how we lost the Peninsula so quickly." Her eyes narrowed and she tilted her head toward Ker. "And the standard? Can you Flash it tonight?"

Ker hadn't felt tired until that moment, but now her shoulders sagged. "The morning would be better."

"Very well. Third Officer Cursar, you will escort the Talent back to her rooms, and fetch her to me at the first hour."

Ker slept badly, and woke up the next morning to find Wynn Martan frowning as she set down a breakfast tray and opened the window shutters in the Talents' sitting room. There was oatmeal with dried fruit cooked in it, and a cup of very watery kaff. The last time she'd had any decent kaff was the morning the enemy had come to the Hall. The morning of the day she'd killed her first person, though that was starting to feel further and further away.

Tel tapped on the outer door just as she was swallowing her last mouthful of oatmeal. Ker threw on her cloak and followed him out. They stepped into the square between the administrative buildings just as a red sun was clearing the edge of the mountains. The air was crisp and smelled of snow. The year was turning. A week ago it had been full light at first hour. There were people out and about, and it seemed that those who passed near slowed down to stare at her. Some touched their crests. Startled, Ker nodded in return.

When they reached her quarters, the Faro was already in

conference with her senior officers. No sign of breakfast. Surm Barlot was there, of course, as was Wilk Silvertrees and the Camp Commandant.

Surm Barlot smiled at her. "We've had a chance to read the notes taken by Tel Cursar, and we have questions, if you don't mind, Talent." Considering this was her job, Ker could hardly mind, but she felt oddly reassured by the courtesy.

"Can you tell us anything more about this change you Flashed in Markon Zahlia? There were people here who knew him, vouched for him." This was Wilk Silvertrees, with a current of antagonism in his voice that hadn't been there the day before.

"Do not forget, Cohort Leader, that he was killed while trying to give information to the enemy."

"I don't forget, my Faro."

Ker laced her fingers together. Everything she had to say was in the report. "All I could Flash was that a Halian, one of the Shekayrin, touched Markon Zahlia with a jewel, and the way he looked at things was changed. Refocused."

Faro Sweetwater glanced upward, her eyes sharp. "Which was it? Changed, or refocused?"

Ker breathed in through her nose. The Faro would have made an excellent tutor. "Refocused. His thinking wasn't completely different, more like he wasn't sure before, and now he was."

The Faro nodded. "Anything more on what this jewel is?"

Ker shut her eyes, concentrating. What had she seen, exactly?

"It's like a red crystal, about the size of an egg." She held out her hand as though she held something in the palm. "It's faceted, highly polished, and it seems to have light inside it, like diamonds do. Except . . . except I think this would have the light even in the dark."

"And you think this jewel is what effected this change? Or was it merely that Markon Zahlia thought so?"

"Markon knew nothing about it himself, Faro. That wouldn't stop my knowing what it did."

"But not *how*?"

"It has to do with the man who used it, the Shekayrin."

"Do you think it was the same man you saw at Questin? How many of them are there?"

Ker tilted her head to one side, raising her shoulders. "I've no idea. This one, though . . ." She shook her head slowly. "Not the same man I saw before, not exactly. Though I can't tell what the difference is."

"Can you tell us how many more there are like Markon Zahlia? Where they might be found, or how we might recognize them?"

"No, Faro, I'm sorry. He reported to—" Ker shook her head. "I'm sorry, I can describe him, but nothing more. It wasn't a military man, Faro. It was a merchant on Potters Street in Farama the Capital." Ker paused, but no one spoke. "As for finding more like Zahlia, well, the obvious answer won't help us much right now."

"Because you don't do people well, at least not live ones."

Ker thought about the red mist that had obscured the auras of the men on the road, and was the only residue of color around Markon Zahlia's corpse. She might not be able to Flash people as well as a Full Talent, but she could Flash auras without any problem, at least since the griffin.

"There might be a way," she said. "But I might have to Flash everyone individually."

"The soldiers won't like it," Surm Barlot said.

"They'll follow the Faro's orders, or I'll know the reason why." Wilk Silvertrees got to his feet.

"Just a moment, Cohort Leader." Juria Sweetwater's quiet tone stopped the man in mid-turn. "Vital as this is, we have another priority. I thank you for your counsel, Talent Nast. Third Officer Cursar, you will escort the Talent to the Standard room now and scribe for her."

*   *   *

Kerida blew on suddenly cold fingers. This kind of Flashing was much easier than what she'd already done with the corpse. It would be no different from Flashing the oldest scroll in the library, or that stone with the flakes broken out of its edge. Items that Questin Hall kept so that Candidates could hone their skills at Flashing objects with plenty of history.

"Things the Hall *used* to keep, anyway."

"What was that?"

Ker jumped. She was so focused on what she had to do she'd forgotten Tel was there.

"Questin Hall," she said. "We had old things for the Candidates to practice on." She described the old vellum scroll and the ancient stone. "It was a hand ax," she said. "A man with a name I can't pronounce made it by hammering away flakes of stone from the edge until it was the right shape. It's older than time—though that doesn't make any difference to the Flashing." At least not to the ones with the strongest Talent. Ker didn't want to say that aloud; it would sound like she was bragging.

"How do you mean?"

"You can get a sense of the time an object has been in existence, but to the thing itself, the time is always 'now.'"

Tel blew out his breath. "Well, it's probably still there," he said. "The stone," he added when she looked at him. "It's probably been in fires before, so it's probably still there."

Ker felt oddly better. "You're right."

The Standard of the Bear Wing rested in its special stand against the left wall as you entered. The Wing's images of the Mother, Daughter, and Son faced the door from the far wall. The Standard, and its honors, were always placed at the Mother's right hand. The Standard was only something old, Ker reminded herself, with plenty of history to access.

"The time of Luqs Rolian isn't nearly as far back as the stone ax," she said aloud.

"Easy stuff, then?"

Ker blew out her breath. "A Full Talent could just touch the thing and get the answer right away. I'll have to trace back through all the bearers to Rolian, and then forward again, tracking his blood to the present."

"Should we get started, then?" Tel gestured at his writing materials. This time his paper and pens had been supplied by the Faro's own scribe.

Kerida rubbed her hands together. It seemed that nothing was going to warm them. She took several calming breaths and reached out. *Paraste.*

This time it took her only a moment to shunt aside the information particular to the shaft itself—who made it, from what wood, where the tree had grown—and focus on the information she wanted to know. Right now, three people shared the job of Standard-bearer for the Wing. They were all still alive, and it was easy for Ker to push their images aside. Two of the previous bearers had retired from the military. The third one had died falling from a horse, and there were no others still living. Only three had been women—it was almost the only position in a Wing where actual strength was valued over skill.

There had been a time when the position of Wing Standard-bearer belonged only to someone from one of the old Shield families, like her own. And like that of Rolian Kestrel who, because of plague and an unexpected abdication, had become Rolian the First, the Lawgiver.

His hands and, according to Wing lore, his blood had touched this shaft.

"He was very young," Ker said. "Our age. And not very close to the Luqs' throne. Eighth or even ninth in line. He certainly didn't expect to become Luqs, didn't even want to be." Ker swallowed. "He was looking for a career in the military, but his father thought he'd get over it. His father was the Luqs' cousin, and he had Rolian given the standard-bearer's spot because he thought it was safe." Ker shared a grin with

Tel. Lots of people thought that. "He thought Rolian would see the horrors of military life and come running home again."

"And?"

"Rolian saw horrors all right, just not the ones his father expected. Rolian *loved* being on the march and the rough country and the camaraderie—even the food. His first battle was against the Felnids, and what he saw horrified him so much he pissed himself."

"You mean it's his piss on the shaft, not blood?"

Ker jerked upright, gasping. She'd completely forgotten Tel was here to scribe. "For the Daughter's sake, Tel, don't write that down." She was half laughing, but she meant it. "I can't be the only Talent who's ever touched this thing, and none of them have ever told, so we definitely can't."

"All right, but if it isn't his blood . . ."

"No, no, his blood's there as well." Ker shut her eyes again and tried to concentrate. Rolian's blood was on the shaft, all right. The question now was, could she find it anywhere else?

In his own time, the people between him and the throne had died, or abdicated. But the one who abdicated had no children—the real reason for the abdication, Ker saw. Huh. That was something that would have been known by the Inquisitors of the time, obviously, but by precious few others. It certainly wasn't something *she* was supposed to know, so she said nothing out loud.

"Rolian had three children," she said. "This is like studying history again. Except now I'm Flashing the names of *all* the royal children, not just the ones who inherited." She frowned as she followed the line of names down to the present Luqs, an only child. Her father had died young, just after she was born, and she'd inherited not from him, but from her grandfather, Fokter the Fourth. And then—

"Fokter had another child," Ker said aloud. "A son." She blinked and turned to look at Tel, letting go of the shaft. From the feel of her face, she was grinning.

"There was only the Luqs' father," Tel protested. "There wasn't anyone else."

"There was." Ker nodded. "When he was much older—too old, anyone would have thought, to father a child. With that young woman from the Worrin family, his last consort. The Luqs must have been fifteen or sixteen when the child was born."

"How could Fokter be sure the child was his?"

"Oh, come on, Tel! How is anyone sure? They go to the nearest Hall and they ask a Talent. If common everyday people do that, don't you think the Luqs would?"

"So the Halls knew?"

"The Inquisitors and Matriarchs knew, yes. But old Fokter decided not to muddy the waters around the Luqs' succession. You know how there's always someone who'd prefer the ruler to be a man." She thought of the scene at the gate and shivered. Was *that* what had happened in the Halians' country?

Tel shook his head. "The throne's hers by right—*was* hers by right, I mean, no matter what. This new child would have been her father's younger brother, so she'd still be before him in the succession."

"That's just politics, and you know it." Ker rubbed at her face. She was exhausted again. "He would have been someone the Wings could have rallied around, if they decided they didn't like the Luqs. He's her half-uncle, but he's of age to be her brother."

"And he's still alive?"

"And he's still alive."

It felt strange sitting at the same table with the Faro and her officers while there were soldiers—Tel Cursar among them—standing. Sitting with the Faro's council was the normal place for the Talent of a Battle Wing to be, but it still didn't feel right.

"Talent Nast." Ker jerked upright. How long had the Faro

been speaking to her? "Can you confirm the location of the remaining prince of the blood?"

A large map was unrolled on the tabletop in front of the Faro, and small silver map weights, shaped like bears in various poses, were placed on the corners. The older woman gestured Ker closer. Ker had never seen a map so big, and it took her a moment to orient herself. She started by tracing the Juadal River up from the coast to Farama the Capital and worked her way inland, following Polity roads through the pass in the Serpents Teeth to the fort where they stood.

If she could then focus on what she knew of the missing heir and translate it somehow into a spot on the map—her Tutor used to say, when she and the other pupils were having difficulties finding information, "This isn't a hunt, people. Don't chase the facts, let the knowledge rise in you. Trust it."

Trust it. Ker took a deep breath and, without further thought, put her finger down again. "Here," she said. "This is where the prince lives." If she was reading the map itself correctly, this was farmland tucked between the mountains and the plains of the western coast, about as far from the capital as you could get and still be in the Peninsula.

"Valden Plains, old land," the Faro said, nodding. "Where some of the first families came from. Thank you, Talent."

"Makes sense," Surm said, drumming his fingers on the map as Ker resumed her seat. "It's an area where no one would look twice at someone who has a resemblance to the royal family."

The Faro nodded and removed the weights, letting the map curl closed. "A small party will go," she said. Her eyes were focused on the tabletop, as if the map was still there. Wilk Silvertrees cleared his throat. "I have decided, Cohort Leader," she added.

"As my Faro, wishes. Of course." The older man bowed.

Ker looked down at her clasped hands. Did the Faro find Silvertrees' devotion as embarrassing as Ker did?

"We must penetrate into territory which is likely held by the enemy. A large force will only draw attention to itself." The Faro wasn't explaining herself to the Cohort Leader, Ker realized. She was speaking out of courtesy to those who hadn't been consulted at all, like Ker herself. "If I could send a large enough force to overcome the enemy—" She shrugged. "But that I cannot do, not until one of the other Wings joins us."

And was that likely to happen? Ker wondered. Obviously, the Bear Wing had been close enough to answer when the Eagles had sent distress signals. The Faro would have sent other messengers herself, before leaving her own position, and for that matter the signal fires here were still lit. But it could take weeks before another Wing could reach Oste Camp. They were spread throughout the Polity, a strategy which had always kept the peace and maintained the law, and it also kept ambitious Faros from rubbing up against each other. Only the Eagle Wing, with the Luqs herself as its Faro, was allowed in the Peninsula, and on occasion the Eagles' job had been to keep the others at bay.

There were some Wings which couldn't come to help them at all. Many were too far away, and if too many troops were pulled off the border forts and walls, the enemy from overseas wouldn't be their only worry. But the Faro was still speaking.

"Talent Nast," she said to Ker. "You are too valuable to spare, and yet you *must* be sent for the prince. Without him, the Wings will waste valuable time arguing among themselves instead of moving against the enemy. We need him—and quickly."

Ker swallowed and tried to nod. Some part of her had been expecting this. Who else would know whether the man they found was really the prince they were looking for?

"Jakmor Gulder will accompany you, Talent Nast."

Ker sat up straight, her jaw suddenly tight. Whoever went with her had to be someone of Commander rank or higher, which technically Jak was, being a Kalter, though that didn't put him in the chain of command.

Wilk Silvertrees cleared his throat, but stayed quiet. *He doesn't like this*, Ker thought. *I don't like it myself.*

Faro Sweetwater turned to Jak. "You are the highest ranking noble in the Wing, and as such the proper person to deal with a royal personage. I will, of course, choose seasoned veterans to accompany you."

"Thank you, my Faro." From the look on his face, Jak understood that this was intended as both reassurance and as a warning that he wasn't completely in charge. From the way he smiled, Ker saw he was actually quite content.

"A moment, please." Ker leaned forward. As a Talent she had some privileges, and choosing her own escort was one of them. Jak turned toward her, his eyebrows raised, but Ker kept her own eyes firmly fixed on the Faro. "I'd like to have two particular soldiers included in my escort."

"Reasonable. And they are?"

"Wynn Martan, the woman who is serving as Boots in the Talents' rooms. She's the one who shot Markon Zahlia. She acted immediately to protect me, and I'd feel better if she came along."

"If I may, my Faro," Jak interrupted. "As the enemy have difficulty dealing with women, and with female soldiers in particular, would another woman really be the right choice?"

"But—" Ker stopped when the Faro held up a finger.

"As the Talent was no doubt about to point out," she said dryly. "Societies which have difficulties dealing with women in authority usually also take a dim view of a woman traveling alone with a group of men."

"And if *I* may, Faro?" Ker waited until the older woman nodded at her. "Surely none of us will be dressed as soldiers?"

"A good point, Talent Nast. And who is the second person you wish to attend you?"

"Tel Cursar. I've traveled with him already," she added. "We're used to each other. We'll be going over some of the same terrain."

"He's very tall." Jak was shaking his head. "He'll attract attention."

"If anything, we'll look less like a group of military personnel if we're not all a similar regulation height." Ker turned back to the Faro. "There's a final point, Faro. How, exactly, do you expect us to get across the Serpents Teeth?"

The corners of Juria Sweetwater's mouth turned upward. "Oh, I expect you to use the same methods you did the last time."

"I'm sorry, Faro, but what about—" Ker stopped. Now, at least she could be sure that, just like Tel, she wasn't able to speak about the Feelers. Not even to refer to them in some indirect way.

"Kerida, what is it?" Jak frowned.

"Talent Nast is concerned for the security of the mine dwellers who aided her on her last passage through the mountain range," the Faro said. Ker pressed her lips together. How was it that Juria Sweetwater was able to talk about the Feelers? "You will be using the tunnels as their guests, and I would advise you to treat them as you would foreign allies."

"But who are these people," Wilk Silvertrees said. "Why have I never heard of them?"

"Few people have, Cohort Leader, and those only who had a need to know."

She's not actually lying, Ker thought, watching the stiff faces around the table. *And how do I know that?*

Ker shouldn't have been surprised at how quickly the Faro's orders were carried out. Stores were canvassed for civilian clothing, and—even more important—civilian weapons. The latter consisted of two staffs, three knives almost long enough to be swords, and two actual short swords which showed enough wear to pass as what they actually were, secondhand military issue. It wouldn't be unusual for farmers or traders to own such things, even if they weren't themselves former military.

In the last moment, Jak Gulder added a hunting bow, and three spears, sturdy and serviceable, in about the same condition as the swords.

"We'll be a hunting party," he said, though no one had questioned him. Jak himself hardly looked like a soldier at all, once he was out of his military tunic, and into the homespun shirt, earth-colored trousers, and short leather jerkin of a huntsman. His hair was a bit on the short side for fashion, though many professional people wore theirs as short. He could pass as just about anyone, when he remembered not to walk like he owned everything he could see.

They were all clothed fairly easily, except for Tel Cursar, whose height made it a challenge to find him civilian clothes out of their limited stores. He ended up having to wear his own boots and leggings, though trousers, tunic, and shirt were eventually found for him.

Scouts from the fort had reported traffic on the road, and there had continued to be encounters in the woods, though there was no sign of the small force that had asked for Oste's surrender. Rumor around the cook fires throughout the camp was that they were occupying Pudova, the closest Polity town. Nevertheless, Ker's group took advantage of a late moon to leave the fort, going quietly by the rear gate. They'd decided to travel as much as they could across country, more or less retracing the trail Ker and Tel had used to reach the camp. Ker was more than a little relieved by this. Keeping off the road meant they'd be avoiding enemy patrols, and it also meant she wouldn't have to pass the ruins of Temlin Hall again.

Ker quickly realized that Jak Gulder had been long enough with the Bears to become accustomed to the rough military life, and that he'd spent enough time actually hunting to know how to live off the land. In fact, the Kalter was treating their expedition as if they *were* a hunting group, professionals hired by villages—and even on occasion the military—to supply meat or deal with an unexpected predator. After the first morning, Ker was sure the man was secretly enjoying himself.

Though Jak was nominally in command, Wynn was the only soldier who had served less time than he had. Along with Tel Cursar, there was Nate Primo, a Second Officer in the Pearl Cohort of Eagles, and Fed Durk, a veteran Barrack leader in the Ruby Cohort of Bears. Jak listened to them both, and deferred to their advice, but in particular to Nate Primo. The officer began by offering an immediate suggestion.

"If I may, best if we don't use our ranks."

Jak was silent a long minute as he chewed this over. "Quite right, Nate," he said finally. "It's that kind of habit that could give us away."

"It would be all right for us to say 'sir' to you," Nate pointed out. "Someone has to lead, and you're obviously it." As professional hunters, they'd have some sort of hierarchy, someone who would literally call the shots, even if they were too informal to have ranks.

"In response, perhaps," Jak said. "But in addressing me, use Jak."

"Yes, sir," Wynn said. All the soldiers' grins were gone by the time Jak glanced around.

"Don't know why we're being so careful with our story," Wynn said to Ker after Jak had gone over it with them yet again. "I thought we'd be avoiding people."

"Sure," Tel agreed. "But what if we're unlucky? It's better to be ready with a story, not trying to come up with something at the last minute. Hunting's a good cover, it explains why we'd be traveling, and why we're armed."

They settled very quickly into a routine, with Nate and Fed taking turns at the front and rear positions. They acted as scouts, and also flushed out small game for Wynn's arrows, rabbits for the most part. It was, Ker realized, the kind of formation that any travelers would use when in an unfamiliar place.

It was on the second day that Fed Durk came back to say they'd reached the edge of some cleared land.

"That'll be the farmer we stopped at on our way to Oste," Ker said.

"You go, Tel," Jak said. "The rest of us will wait here, out of sight. See if they have news since you've been here, or if we can give them some."

Tel Cursar trotted along the edge of the forest holding's small field, his spear balanced on his shoulder, butt forward, in what he hoped was a nonthreatening manner. Hay stubble showed stiff and pale through what was left of the last snow fall. It was a pleasure to be alone at first, but soon he found himself feeling exposed. Somehow, the wind was colder out here in the open.

When they'd passed this way before, he and Ker had come and gone in the darkness, and this was the first clear view Tel had of the homestead. He'd seen plenty of holdings like this in Orrin, cut out of old forest. There was the small living quarters with its thick log walls, the cow shed butted up against one side, with low openings for the hens to come and go from the warm interior. It was early enough in the season that the two small hayricks behind the dwelling were barely touched.

He knew something was wrong as soon as he got within earshot of the buildings. He slowed and shifted his grip on the spear, turning it business end forward. Last time, he and Ker hadn't gotten this close before the household dogs had started up. Now there was nothing except the sound of his own footsteps, light and careful on the crust of snow. Tel stood still, turning his head slowly from side to side, trying to pick up any sound, any smell that could give him a clue as to what had gone wrong. Then he realized that the wood smoke he *should* have smelled wasn't there.

He shortened his grip on the spear and crept to the door.

Last time they'd called out, giving the people within a warning, but now he kept silent. He stretched out his free hand, stuck his fingers through the opening, and lifted the latch. The door swung open on its own.

The interior was a single room, with the hearth in the center built up out of good flat stones that had come out of the fields, mortared with mud and hardened clay. The fire was out, and judging from the coldness of the ashes, had been out at least two days.

Lack of a fire in this weather was enough to let Tel know that something serious had happened. A screen neatly woven of strips of leather and osiers marked off the bed of the farmer and her husband. Off to one side of the main room was his mother's bed, and that of the two children. There was the old lady's chair—the only one with arms—closest to the fire. Next to it the wife's chair, and three stools, all drawn up close to the edge of the hearth. All neat, all tidy. All empty.

He thought he was already prepared for the worst, but when he saw the small shrine to the household gods overturned and trampled, the white-painted image of the Mother completely smashed, his stomach sank. Like most people his age, Tel took his piety for granted. Maybe he'd feel differently about it when he was old enough to be the one making the observances, but until now he'd made his responses with the same carefree attitude he'd had since he was a child.

He squatted down and touched what was left of the Mother's statuette. The man at the gate had spoken of ending the rule of women.

He found them in the cow shed. Other than their cut throats, they'd had no violence done to them. Soldiers, then; not bandits or wild men. Tel squatted down next to the farmer and touched the man's shoulder. It was stiff and hard.

"This is going to smell really badly when the spring comes," he said. He was a little surprised that his voice sounded so normal; he didn't know if that was good or bad. He closed the cow shed door behind him and headed back for the forest. On the way he realized he might know the men who had done this.

Or at least, who they used to be.

Ker's face, when he got back and told them, was as white as he'd ever seen it, so white her eyes looked like smudges of charcoal.

"Talent Nast," Jak Gulder said. "Do you think—"

"No." Ker's voice was as tight as a noose. "I *don't* think." She took a deep breath and blinked rapidly. "There's nothing to be learned here."

ALMOST a week later they were squatting just to the east of the road, staring down at a map sketched in the dirt.

"Here's where we are," Jak was saying. "We could go around these hills to a valley that parallels this one." He looked around. "From there, we should be able to access the mine opening Tel and Kerida used."

"*Should* be isn't *will* be," Nate pointed out.

Jak nodded. "That's why I suggest we take the road instead. It's risky, but it's surer, and it will take a deal less time." Tel's discovery at the farm had given them all an increased sense of urgency.

Nate gave the deciding vote. "A few hours on the road, compared to a few days going around and maybe we can't get to the entrance after all? Not much of a choice, is it?"

And so they all thought, right up until the moment they heard the sound of hoofbeats and saw, ahead of them, a small group of mounted men.

"If we've seen them, they've seen us." Wynn said aloud what everyone was thinking, but no one wanted to hear.

"Spread out, slouch." Jak kept his voice from carrying. "Try to look less like soldiers."

Fortunately, they'd just been changing their order of march, so it was easy for them to look like a random group of people walking along the road. Ker saw Wynn glance at the bow Tel Cursar was carrying. The young woman was the best shot among them, but without any way to know how far this female prejudice went, Jak had decided not to risk having either woman carry obvious weapons on the road. Apart from the knife every adult in the Polity carried, they were unarmed.

"What should we do?"

"Keep walking," Jak said. "Innocent people wouldn't have reason to leave the road. It's all right to check your weapons, anyone would. When they get close enough, we'll do what the Wings expect any nonmilitary to do—get off the road and look respectful. They might go right past us."

Though, after what Tel had seen at the farm, no one expected that.

"If it comes to it, I'll do the talking."

Ker nodded and fell into step between Wynn and Tel. The group of soldiers, no more than half a Barrack, were trotting along in good, disciplined formation, not like the bunch she and Tel had run into on their way to the fort. When they got close enough Ker saw that, discipline or not, some wore the green tunics of Eagles, and others the purple of the Bears.

Tel stiffened abruptly, and Ker hissed at him. The last thing they needed was for him to stand up straight and have either the movement or his height draw any attention. Tel relaxed finally, slouching his shoulders a little more. Without his helmet or military tunic, and with his hair so long, Tel didn't look much like a soldier. But would it be enough to fool someone who had known him?

Jak was walking in front and, without signaling in any way, simply led them off into the ditch beside the road before the soldiers reached them. He continued leading them forward, raising his hand in a casual acknowledgment as the patrol drew even with them.

The soldiers gave them a couple of sideways glances as they went by. Ker was beginning to relax when the officer at the rear of the group did a double take as he passed Jak.

"Gulder? Jak Gulder? Is that you?" The man signaled to his Barrack, who slowed but kept moving.

Jak also stopped, but as they'd been told, the rest of them went past him before coming raggedly to a standstill, trying to look like people more interested in reaching their destination and their dinners than people bracing for a fight.

Though what they could do against half a Barrack of soldiers, Ker didn't know.

"Eoro Zalen? It can't be," Jak said. "Nobody's skinned you alive *yet*?" And he laughed, he actually laughed, as if he hadn't a care in the world. Ker, meanwhile, did her best to look bored and exhausted, exactly what young people would look like when oldsters were yammering.

The officer grinned and leaned out of his saddle to grasp Jak's offered wrist. "What are you doing here, you old wolf? Last I heard you were joining Bear Wing."

"There was talk of it, but you know my father; he changed his mind. I've been up here in Bascat hunting deer. Got caught by the snow."

The other man was nodding even before Jak had finished. "Your father will be finding things a bit more to his liking now, I imagine." He fixed Jak with a hard eye. "Where are you coming from, and what have you heard about doings in the Peninsula?"

Jak shrugged. "Plenty of rumors, that's certain. We're working our way back from Sontan Village. Thought we'd wait at the Hall until the pass clears."

Ker tensed, but if they'd really been away where Jak said they were, they wouldn't know about the Hall.

Eoro Zalen nodded, but still with the same hard look in his eye. "Don't bother stopping there," he said, raising his hand as if he thought Jak was going to interrupt him. "What if I was to tell you the Luqs is gone," he said. "Gone, and the rule of women with her. Especially those witches in the Halls."

"What?" Now Jak's voice had an edge to it as well, though Ker was impressed at how well he faked surprised outrage. "The Luqs is dead? What's happened?"

"Our brothers from across the sea is what's happened. You of all people must know the witches were never to be trusted, with their uncanny ways. They've been secretly running the country for ages, keeping us men down. We're going back to the old days, taking power for ourselves, and putting it into the hands of a council of men."

Ker tried hard to keep looking bored, as though she wasn't paying attention. Surely that wasn't right? Surely, even before Jurianol became the first Luqs, there had been both men and women on the council? And there'd been Talents and Halls for that matter.

"Have you news of my father? Has someone set themselves up in the Luqs' place?"

Again Ker tensed, but again, Jak had done the right thing. That was exactly the question a noble would have asked.

"Figures your father's son would be asking that." The other man laughed and gave Jak a knowing look. "There's been some trouble from ones who wouldn't put down their arms, but that's all getting sorted now."

"It could mean war," Jak said, in exactly the tone of a man who'd only this minute thought of it.

"It could. But it's not all that likely, not now. More and more are coming over to our side, once they understand what freedom is." He narrowed his eyes. "What about you? I'm sure there'd be a place for someone with your connections, now that the we've purged the Wings of women."

His face didn't change when he said it. That's what horrified Ker the most. The man said "purged the women" and his face never changed.

But Jak was shaking his head. "I don't see myself a soldier, Eoro," he said. "But with the Luqs and her pack of rats gone . . ." Jak smiled in a way that Ker hoped she'd never see again. "There may be some other way for a man of my 'connections' to serve the Polity." He let his voice die away before shaking his head slowly. "Too bad I'm stuck way over here. By the time I get home, my father will have my brother set up and I'll be out in the cold. I never had the luck."

"Not to worry." The other man snapped his fingers and his horse shifted. "The pass is open. We can thank our new friends for that, along with everything else they've done."

"You don't say? So where are you off to now?"

The other man shook his head. "You know better than that. Good luck, man, and if your father does set you up, don't forget your old friends!" With a final wave, the man turned away.

They stood in silence watching the man trot his horse to catch up with the rest of his troop.

"Easy now," Jak said. "Don't relax too quickly. We don't know who might be watching us."

"If the pass is open—" began Tel.

"We still can't use it," Jak said. "It's one thing to get away with our story with a ragtag group like this one, but at the pass they'll have real guards. With real questions."

———

Jerek left home before dawn, creeping down to the stable before anyone else was up. He'd lain awake most of the night, ideas and options chasing themselves 'round and 'round. Once he'd made up his mind, however, it was easier to leave than he'd expected. Though it had taken him most of the morning to reach the market town of Gaena, as the growling of his stomach reminded him, Jerek would be willing to wager he hadn't yet been missed. With Nessa gone, there'd been no one keeping a close eye on him.

Fogtail snuffled at the back of his neck, breath warm against his skin. The poor old boy wasn't up to the distance they'd come, but Jerek had been afraid to take his new horse. Not only was it more likely to be missed by the stable staff, but it was far more likely to be noticed once he left his own land. No one would look twice at a thirteen-year-old boy with a pony, but that same boy on the back of a good riding horse would be a different matter.

Looking around, it seemed Jerek was lucky with his timing. Despite the chill, the market was at its height, though the crowds' attention was not on the stalls and barrows with their cabbages, carrots, and turnips, braids of onions and garlic, nor the chickens and geese hung up by their feet. Rather, everyone—even the vendors—was looking at the far side of the square. Jerek wanted to work his way through the edges of the crowd to the armorers' stalls, but he knew he'd draw unwelcome attention if he wasn't curious about what everyone else was looking at.

A small procession was coming through the center of the crowd from the four-story gray stone building that formed the south side of the square. Six Polity soldiers on foot, in Eagle colors, swords out. They surrounded three people in civilian dress, two women in dirty but well-made clothes, one man in homespun. Behind the group came four more men, two of them Shekayrin. One of these was that same Shekayrin who'd come to Brightwing Holding, the other was a stranger. Jerek shifted until Fogtail was in front of him. Walking with the Halians was a fair-skinned man wearing a Cohort Leader's helmet, his military cloak thrown stylishly over one shoulder.

Behind these three came another soldier, but he wasn't formally cloaked like the others. His green tunic was crisp and clean, but the only weapon he carried was a large battle ax.

The Shekayrin and the Cohort Leader mounted the steps of the platform together, and waited for the buzzing of voices to stop. The Cohort Leader stepped forward.

"Citizens," he called out in a voice meant to carry over battlefields. "May I have your attention for the public announcements. Today is the last Thirdday of Snowmonth, in the ye—"

Jerek had begun to relax, hearing the familiar preamble, but when the Cohort Leader broke off without giving the current year of the Luqs' reign, he froze. Just as revealing, when he began again, the Cohort Leader made no mention of the Mother, Daughter, or Son.

"There have been seven counts of civil disobedience, for which three fines have been given, and one act of restitution."

It wasn't what he was saying so much as how the man said it that struck Jerek. He'd had a great deal of practice measuring tone, guessing feelings and attitude from it, even predicting behavior. The people around him weren't relaxing. They were waiting to hear about the final three counts of disobedience.

"The remaining three counts are of treason, and public punishment is required."

Treason? Jerek's hand tightened and Fogtail shifted. Treasonous behavior wasn't unheard of, but it usually involved public criticism of the Luqs or her policies, and even then, a Talent would be called in to determine just how serious it was. Without Talents to examine the accused—without a Luqs for that matter—just what did this mean?

At a signal from the Cohort Leader two of the soldiers escorting the prisoners carried a punishment block onto the platform and centered it. Jerek's heart skipped a beat. His father had never allowed him to attend a public flogging. He wasn't entirely sure he wanted to.

The older man was brought up onto the platform and

made to face the spectators. There was a puzzled frown on his face, as if he wasn't sure where he was.

"For the harboring of witches, Tay Kingfisher is sentenced to death." The man with the ax stepped forward.

The buzzing in Jerek's ears was so loud he missed what the Cohort Leader said as the unresisting prisoner was pushed to his knees and bent forward. Almost at the moment the man's cheek touched the wooden surface of the block, sunlight flashed on the ax as it fell. When it rose again, the metal was dull.

"Don't look away, boy. Shut your eyes if you have to, but don't look away." The gruff whisper had to belong to the hand clamped, viselike, on Jerek's shoulder. "He'll see it if you look away, Tattoo Face up there. He'll see it, and he'll know you don't approve. Don't give them reason to mark you down for a talking to."

Jerek gritted his teeth and kept facing toward the platform. He didn't shut his eyes completely, but he did lower his lids until all he really saw was his hands and their white-knuckled grip on Fogtail's saddle horn. He wished he was still short enough to hide his face in the pony's mane.

His stomach chose that moment to growl, reminding him how long it had been since the oatmeal cake he'd helped himself to as he was leaving his home. Jerek swallowed bile as his gorge rose. He never wanted to eat again.

The Cohort Leader was speaking again, but Jerek did his best not to hear anything more. Finally, the movement of the crowd signaled that the executions were over. Under cover of that general shuffle, he searched the faces of the people around him, but couldn't see anyone who matched the voice that had warned him. No one caught his eye or nodded at him. Even without looking directly, he could follow the progress of the Shekayrins' black cloaks as they passed through the crowd and reentered the gray stone building on the southern side of the square.

From where he stood now, Jerek could easily make out the wide double doors, half again the height of a tall man, which made up the entrance. The right-hand door was carved with the usual circle of laurel leaves, to show even those who couldn't read that this was the Polity building. On the left-hand door, where the griffin symbol of the Talents should have been, there was only deep scoring in the wood, the edges dark and sharp in the bright sun.

Now Jerek did close his eyes, trying not to think of *edges* and *sharpness*.

A man carrying a squealing piglet under his arm jostled him, and Jerek realized he'd been standing and staring for too long. No one else seemed to be looking at the doorway and its defaced symbol. *Don't give them reason to mark you down.*

"That's a nice pony. Is he yours? Are you selling him?"

Jerek almost dropped Fogtail's rein. He flushed, but the other boy didn't seem to notice. Fair-haired and blue-eyed, he was about the same age, Jerek thought, though a little taller, and a little skinnier. His clothes fit him well enough and looked like Jerek's own: plain, but of good, serviceable cloth. He was smiling, crooked teeth white against the remains of a summer tan, and Jerek's trembling subsided.

"Yes. I mean no. He's mine, but he's not for sale." Jerek blinked. It was hard to focus. His eyes still saw how the sun glinted on the ax as it fell. It had all seemed so clear. His father's guilt, the twisted wrongness of the new order. He glanced at the defaced emblem and swallowed. Standing alone and cold, it took an effort to remember that he'd thought he'd be better off here.

The taller boy was stroking Fogtail's neck. The pony ignored him. "I wish I had my own pony. Are you all right?" he added under his breath. Jerek looked at him sharply, but the boy's face showed only his admiration for the pony.

Jerek examined him more closely. The boy was wearing a cloth cap and a scarf wrapped twice around his neck, but he had no coat, just the tunic over his shirt. On his feet were shoes, not boots, and his hands were covered by woolen mittens, not leather gloves. And maybe the rest of the boy's clothes weren't quite as good as Jerek's after all. Jerek coughed. "I'm looking for a friend."

The boy grinned. "I'm Talian." He thrust out his free hand and Jerek took it.

"Jerek." He was careful not to give his full name.

Two blond eyebrows quirked upward over Talian's slightly bent nose. "Is your friend a town man? I've lived here my whole life. I might know him myself. Or they'd likely know in there." His eyes narrowed, Talian pointed his chin at the town hall.

Jerek shivered, and hoped the other boy would put it down to the cold. "It's a man named Bedeni Soria. Used to be a guard for the Firoxis." Best not to mention Nessa's name. Not yet.

"Old soldier like? Is it a private message? What I mean is . . ." This time he just moved his eyes toward the building. "What I mean is, you know what grown-ups can be like."

Jerek tried to return the other boy's knowing look. If there was one thing he knew, it was what grown-ups could be like. He lowered his eyes, and finally shrugged up one shoulder. Old soldier, Talian had said. That could be Soria. "You could say it was a private message. Sure."

"If it's the old guy I'm thinking of, I don't know him myself, but I think maybe my auntie does. Leastways, she knows most of the old soldiers in town, and I'm sure she'd be able to help you."

"Isn't your aunt a grown-up?"

Talian's lip curled and Jerek flushed. "Not *that* kind." He tucked his mittened hands into his armpits, shrugged, and looked away. "'Course, if you don't want my help . . ."

Jerek bit at the inside of his lip. He glanced back into the square. Someone there would know. If not the armorer, then someone else. But how many people would he have to ask before he found one who could help him? How long before people started to wonder who he was, and why he was here looking for an old retired soldier? What had seemed like a great idea when he was riding into town seemed dangerous now.

He squeezed his eyes shut. He had to trust someone. If he didn't, he might as well go home.

"Is your aunt's place far?"

Jak led them off the road as soon as the terrain allowed and made them pass by two perfect campsites. No one complained. They all wanted to put as much distance as possible between them and any more patrols. Just as Ker was beginning to think they'd be walking until dawn, Jak settled on a small clearing surrounded by tall pine trees, swept almost bare of needles by the wind.

"Don't bother," he said as Ker began to gather up rocks for a fire ring. "It's too open here for a fire."

Ker raised an eyebrow, but she didn't argue. Any fire they made in this place would be visible for some distance, which also meant that anyone coming after them would be just as visible. Right now, cold food and colder beds were a small price to pay for better security.

Lots were drawn for the first watch, and Fed and Wynn disappeared into the dark. By now Ker had stopped making even a token effort to be included, so she settled cross-legged next to Tel, holding a piece of travel cake she didn't really want. Strange, she thought, how they all sat in a circle, even though there wasn't a fire to sit around.

Jak cleared his throat and waited until he had their attention. "If the pass is open, the Faro needs to know. Right now she's assuming she only has to deal with the Halians already on this side of the Serpents Teeth."

Nate Primo blew air out of pursed lips. "Your friend seemed very certain."

Jak swung his eyes to the older man. "If we find the pass open, who would you send to report to the Faro?"

"I'd better go myself. I've the best chance."

"I don't doubt it." Jak's tone was respectful. "But I'm not so certain I can manage without you."

Ker wasn't sure what surprised her more, that the statement was true, or that Jak had actually said it aloud.

The officer took in a deep breath. "The decision's yours, of course. But consider, Tel Cursar and Fed Durk are two experienced soldiers, and Wynn Martan's one of the best archers I've seen. The Talent herself's military, if it comes to that."

Jak nodded, his gaze now turned inward. "We'll look at the pass in the morning. Then, if it's necessary, you'll go."

Tel Cursar wriggled back from the ridge of rock, gritting his teeth as a sharp stone scraped his left elbow. His hands, stomach, and the front of his thighs were numb with cold. He stayed low until he reached the others sheltered in the rocks.

"There's a clear path, maybe three spans wide. The ground actually looks dry." Tel wondered if he could convey the strangeness of what he'd seen. "There's snow, but it just stops at the road—sharp, like bread cut with a knife." He stifled the gesture he'd been about to make with his hand.

Jak nodded. "Confirmed, then. Nate, are you ready to go?"

"Anytime." Nate was squatting next to Ker now, a few flakes of new snow dusting down onto his dark hair and beard.

"Go swift, go cautious."

The man's teeth showed white against his beard. "I will. Jak? I'd like to give the Talent my plaque."

Ker's green eyes went round as saucers, and Tel supposed

his own face must look much the same. The other soldiers, even Jak Gulder, lifted a hand to touch where their own plaques hung under layers of shirt and tunic. Soldiers received their plaques on their first day of training. It marked their names, their Wings and Cohorts, and a soldier never removed his or her plaque during their service—which for many meant during their lifetimes.

"I figure you'll know where I am," Nate said to Ker. "You'll know when I get through with my message."

Or when he doesn't, Tel thought. From the look on everyone's face—even Nate's—they were all thinking that.

"Kerida?" Jak looked at Ker with one eyebrow raised.

There was a smudge of dirt on her left cheek, and a faraway look in her eyes. Another stray flake landed on her lashes, melted as she finally blinked. Ker's fingers were also resting where her own plaque would have been. Tel pressed his lips together. It hadn't occurred to him before this moment, but death *wasn't* the only way to lose your plaque.

"Nate Primo, it would be an honor." She took the small square of stamped tin, polished by years of contact with Nate's skin. She slipped the cord over her head, tucking the plaque into the front of her shirt.

"Closest Nate's plaque's come to a woman in weeks," Fed Durk murmured. Everyone laughed, grateful for the joke, but Tel noticed the blush that spread lightly over Ker's face, even though she laughed with the rest.

The forest changed again as the land started to climb. The closer they got to the mine entrance the more Ker wished she'd had a chance to speak to Tel about the Feelers. If only there was some way to alert them—but short of the griffin finding them on the march, Ker couldn't think of anything.

They were only a mile or two from where Ker estimated

the mine entrance to be when Fed Durk ran up from where he'd been watching the rear.

"Soldiers coming through the woods behind us," he said to Jak. "Maybe a Barrack."

Ker put her hand to her knife and wished there was time to unpack a sword. They'd have the high ground, but that wasn't enough to balance their odds.

"They see you?"

Fed shook his head.

"Dogs?" Jak said.

"No, but there's one of those Halian priests with them."

Ker coughed but couldn't loosen the cords of her throat.

"Triple time, everyone. Tel, you're in front. Ker, right behind him and don't lose sight of him. Wynn, keep her up. Fed, you're with me."

After a few minutes the snow that had been lightly falling on and off since they'd left the pass began coming down in earnest as the wind picked up, the flakes tiny and stinging like chips of ice. Ker kept her eyes focused on Tel Cursar's dark cloak. Where there were pines, there was some shelter. Often, however, the sharp crystals blinded her, and once low-lying branches whipped her face.

Ker ran until her breath came short and a sharp stitch knifed into her side. Her vision narrowed; all she could see was Tel Cursar moving like a shadow in front of her. At one point she became aware that others were running with them. Once she stumbled, and would have gone down, but a hand came out of nowhere, took a bruising grip above her elbow, and kept her on her feet. So she could run some more.

The next time she stumbled, Jak's voice came softly out of the gloom, calling for a halt.

"Rest for a count of one hundred," he said. The standard order.

Jak drew Tel aside with a gesture, but not so far away that Kerida couldn't hear them.

"Fed and I will try to draw them off," he said. "You go on. Don't stop until you reach the mine."

"We'll wait for you." Tel's tone didn't make it a question, but Jak answered anyway.

"No longer than morning," he ordered. "And then only if you're absolutely safe."

Ker wanted to protest, to tell them that she just couldn't go on . . . and then she remembered the Shekayrin and she pulled herself to her feet. She'd escaped the one at Questin; she was blasted if she'd let this one catch her now. Her blood thundered in her ears, until she couldn't hear her own footsteps, let alone any sounds of pursuit. Sweat dripped into her eyes and soaked the clothes clinging to her back.

At a sudden movement on her right, Ker clenched her jaw, stiffened the legs that wanted to fold under her, and forced her trembling hands to pull her long knife free. Someone took her arm, and she spun toward them, but it was Wynn.

"Sorry." Ker didn't have breath enough for more.

"Pretty good reflexes for someone who's not a soldier. Can you go on?"

She bared her teeth in a grin she knew the other girl couldn't see, not wasting breath on such a stupid question. She shrugged off Wynn's supporting hand, trying not to stagger as she set off once again.

Jak Gulder stood motionless within the shadow cast by three close-growing pines, breathing with his mouth wide open, holding his knife in one steady hand. With the other, he touched the spot where Fed's plaque now hung next to his own. They'd managed to draw the main force away from the Talent before Fed was caught and killed. By backtracking, Jak had killed three of them himself. He'd always been good at killing things. He'd have been happy to stay with the military permanently, if his father's ambitions had allowed it. He'd found Fed Durk lying under a bush, where the man had managed to drag himself. There'd been a body with him, so at least he'd accounted for one of them.

And here came another.

Jak let the enemy soldier pass by on the leeward side of the tree, then stepped silently into place behind him, his left hand on the man's chin, his knife hand at the man's throat.

Which was when he felt the noose drop down around his own neck.

"If you'd been a little older, you wouldn't have been caught by this trick." The noose jerked tighter, though not quite enough to stop his breath. "Now lower the knife, and let him go."

Jak spread his hands out wide, and the man he'd been holding dropped, first to his knees, then to his side. The dim light had kept the others from seeing the spray of blood, and the cold air from smelling it.

Jak laughed when they started cursing, kept laughing until a jerk on the rope cut off his air and pulled him to the ground.

They slapped him back to consciousness and kicked him to his feet, making him walk until they reached a fire, large and bright. They pushed him to the ground and bound him at wrist and elbows, knees and ankles. A cloth that tasted of the oil used to clean blades was shoved into his mouth and tied there. He could move his fingers and toes, so there was no fear of losing circulation although he didn't know whether that was a good sign. The clearing was a large one, and men on their feet moved around, some between him and the light, some on the far side, with others sitting down. Eleven. No, twelve. Must have started out with two Barracks. There were more packs on the ground than there were men in the clearing.

Jak flexed his limbs with caution, but there was no give to his bonds. There were no other prisoners within his line of sight. He swallowed with difficulty, grimacing at the taste in his mouth.

"I don't know why he's with them," one man nearby said.

"You'd think he'd have done with them of his own accord, after what they did to his grandfather."

Jak rolled his eyes. Not much doubt they were talking about him. He wasn't surprised by this reference to his grandfather. The story was well-enough known, and was behind the heat of his father's ambition to regain their status at court. He had his own memories of the old man, and his own ideas on whether he'd deserved his fate after the Halls of Law had discovered his embezzlement. What he felt about it was no one's business but his own.

Suddenly the soft murmurs of conversation died, all eyes turned in one direction, and those who were sitting down stood up. Jak twisted around as best he could. The black-cloaked man entering the clearing stopped to speak to one or two of the others as he came, but his goal was evidently Jak himself. He squatted on his heels and looked Jak over carefully. The Shekayrin's back was to the fire, and his face partly in shadow, making it hard for Jak to make out the dark tattoo traced around the left eye. The man gestured, and one of the two who'd been talking about Jak's granddad removed the gag. He coughed and swallowed roughly.

"Well, now." The accent was unfamiliar, but the voice melodious enough. "They tell me you are Jakmor Gulder, a nobleman's son. I am the Rose Shekayrin, Granion Pvat."

Jak said nothing. He'd hear the man out and then figure out what he needed to say to talk himself free.

"They say you have reason to hate the witches." When Jak stayed quiet, Granion Pvat searched his face, waiting. Finally, he smiled. "That's not so, is it? You have no love for them, but you have respect." He stood up, shaking his head. "Respect I cannot use, though a nobleman's son I can." He reached into a fold of his tunic and withdrew a dark red jewel, flat on one side, faceted on the other. Pvat gestured with his empty hand, and two of the others joined him.

"Hold him," he said.

Before Jak could react, one soldier had his head in a firm grip, while the other held down his legs. Granion Pvat knelt and placed the jewel between Jak's eyes.

Instinctively, Jak tried to pull away, to twist his head aside, but the two men held him with practiced hands. Pvat tilted his own head to one side, and his eyes narrowed, becoming as dark and red as the jewel itself. Jak renewed his struggle, but the way he was held, the way he was bound, made true resistance impossible.

"Don't be concerned," Pvat said. "There's no pain."

Jak felt an instant rush of cold, followed by a sudden heat on the skin between his eyes.

Ker was lying down, and there was something hard under her cheek. She'd fallen again! Her muscles convulsed as she tried to stand up, but a hand gripping her shoulder kept her down.

"Relax, we made it."

The echoes told Ker they'd reached the mine. She managed to roll herself up on one elbow, and looked around, squinting. Now she remembered. She'd sat down, and obviously she'd passed out as soon as she did. It was dark here in the tunnel, but she could make out the entrance, an irregular opening a couple of spans away. The snow had stopped falling, the sky must have cleared, and the resulting combination of moonlight and snow cover made the outside seem very bright.

A silhouette was suddenly outlined against this brightness, followed by the unmistakable "twang" of a bow string. "Got 'im."

Ker smiled at the satisfaction in the girl's voice.

"And that's them backing off." Tel squeezed Ker's shoulder.

"For how long?" Ker asked, using Tel's lower arm to pull herself up to a sitting position.

"Let's hope for a while. They must need rest as badly as we

do." Tel handed her a water pouch. Training made Ker take three small mouthfuls, barely more than sips, before resting the pouch on the ground.

No one said aloud that no matter how much rest the enemy needed, there were more of them, and they could take turns both watching and attacking. Being outnumbered was never a good thing.

"You can have more water," Tel said. "You know there's plenty in here." He glanced over her head, looking deeper into the tunnel.

Ker couldn't see his face. "Tel, what do you think—"

"You all right? Getting your breath back?" He waggled his eyebrows, shooting a glance at Wynn's silhouette near the opening.

Ker's eyes had adjusted enough to what light there was to almost make out Tel's features. "Sure." She wiped off her mouth with the back of her hand. "Any sign of them?" she said, tilting her head toward the tunnel. It felt almost strange that her breath had slowed to normal, that her heart had stopped banging in her chest. She rubbed the outside of her arms. Her sweat had dried, and she was noticing the cold.

"Not so far." Tel shrugged. "We'll hope Jak gets here before they do."

"That's not much of a plan."

"You have a better one? It's not as though we can tell him what to expect."

She found herself grinning back at him. "I can take a watch. One of you come rest."

"Here." Tel handed her a serving of travel cake, but Ker shook her head. Water she knew she needed, but her stomach rebelled at the idea of food.

"Eat something, and you can spell Wynn," Tel said. "We should get as much rest as we can while we're waiting for Jak."

Ker wrinkled her nose, but this time took the offered cake. "How long until morning?"

Tel shrugged. "Wynn and I have been talking. I'm inclined to give him a little longer than that."

Ker lifted her eyes from the piece of travel cake she was turning over in her fingers. "How much longer?"

Tel pressed his lips together without answering, his face hard.

"Whatever you and Wynn decide," Ker said finally. "I'm getting tired of leaving people behind."

"We'll wait until midmorning." Tel's nod was sharp as a blade.

Ker fingered the plaque she had around her neck. She knew where *Nate* was. If only she'd taken a token from each of them, she'd know exactly where Jak and Fed Durk were. They could be out there right now, unable to make out the entrance in the dark.

"What about showing a light at the opening," she said aloud, and explained her thinking.

"It's as much of a guide to the enemy as it would be for any of ours," Tel pointed out.

"But the enemy already know where the opening is," Ker said. "As long as we keep well back, they wouldn't be able to see us."

"Too much illumination . . ." Tel looked thoughtful. "No, you're right. The glow stone would serve as a signal, without lighting up so much of the ground that it couldn't be crossed safely. Yes." He got to his feet and rummaged in his pouch. "Wynn! Here, set this down as close to the center of the opening as you can, and come back out of the light."

"All quiet," the girl said as she rejoined them. "Might be a bit livelier with that light, though. We'll have to make sure it's our own people we're letting in. Easier if we just shot everyone." She grinned, and Ker grinned back.

"Here," she said, reaching out for the bow. "You rest for a bit. Both of you." But Tel shook his head.

"Two awake at all times," he said.

Wynn curled up in her military cloak, and her soft breathing showed how quickly she fell asleep. Another way, Ker thought, in which military and Hall training were similar. Without her own training, Ker wouldn't be able to drop off to sleep as Wynn just did. Her nerves jangled, her brain flickered with the images of trees, wet snow, fast-moving shadows. But she'd been taught a discipline for this at Questin. A Talent had to be rested at all times, for the best Flashes.

"Is Nate all right?" Tel's question startled Ker so much she almost dropped the bow. "I saw you touch his plaque. Is he . . . ?"

"He's fine," Ker said. "Almost halfway back, and no one's found him." She shifted back a little farther from the entrance. "I wish there was a way to use the glow stone without ruining our night vision," she murmured. "Though I bet you I can hit anyone who comes within the circle of light."

"No bet," Tel said. "I remember the rat."

"Do you think they'll come, Ganni and the others?"

"I don't know whether to hope they do, or hope they don't." Tel glanced at Wynn, but the girl was still asleep.

"I wish I knew for sure whether Jak and Fed were out there." Ker focused as well as she could on the outer edges of the circle of light, where the moonlight reflected off snow. People waited in the moonlight. It touched them, and it touched her, too. What if . . . *Paraste.*

Tel's blue, green, and yellow aura glowed softly beside her, so familiar now that she could ignore it easily. Wynn's was behind her, not close enough to distract. Ker focused her attention beyond the entrance. There *were* men out in the moonlight. Three men, whose auras had the same colors as Tel's and Wynn's. Blue, green, yellow. One off to the left, behind a ridge of rock, its rough edge softened by snow. Another was back in the trees. The third was on his stomach, crawling forward. Closer. Almost close enough. Ker lifted the bow, rocked forward onto her knees. Closer. Now.

A cry and the sound of cursing.

"What are you doing? That could have been Jak."

Ker turned her head. The green, yellow and blue of Tel's aura was brighter than the glow from the stone. "No, it wasn't," she said.

"You mean you can tell who they are without even seeing them? That's going to come in handy." Wynn was awake and watching her.

"You're supposed to be asleep."

"Who can sleep with all this excitement? Besides, I'm thinking."

"What are you thinking?"

"That whoever built this knew what they were doing." Wynn was peering upward, eyebrows drawn tight together. "Pull that glow stone in closer, will you? I want to look at the roof for a minute. Look at that cross-bracing." There was admiration in her tone.

"I thought you were a ladies' maid? What do you know about cross-bracing?"

Wynn grinned, still looking around the shaft. "Another one of my aunties. Apprenticed to a builder young, drew his plans and designs for him, swung a sledge when needed." Wynn drew down her brows. "I was apprenticed to her myself, until she fell from a tower. Then her builder wouldn't keep me."

"Hence the ladies' maid job?"

"Hence." Wynn's grin faded, and she stood up.

"What is it?"

Wynn was peering into the darkness behind the cross-bracing directly above them. "Looks like some kind of cables," she said, pointing. "But I can't see why they'd be needed."

Interested, Ker got to her feet, bow slack in her hand. She was still Flashing. "I guess there's one way to know for sure." She reached overhead, stretching to brush her fingers against the part of the rope harness nearest to hand.

She jerked her hand away immediately.

"What is it?" Wynn looked from the rope to Ker's face and back again.

"It's a deadfall." Kerida closed her hands into fists. "Pull on the rope, uh . . ." She peered around until she found the right spot. "There. Yank on that knot of rope and cord, and all this cross-bracing you like so much will come tumbling down."

"A booby trap?" Wynn moved down the shaft, peering upward as she moved away from the spot Ker was pointing to. "How far does it go?"

"Let's see." Ker followed Wynn away from the entrance, using her closing word as they went. The network of ropes and cords continued a full two spans farther down the tunnel.

"Does it mean what I think it means?" Ker asked.

"If you think it's a way to close the door behind us," Wynn said, "then, yes, it does."

The sun was rising on a clear, cold, crisp day, the snowfall of the night before sparkling with deceptive beauty. The trail of the man Ker had hit showed bloody against the white. Tel was leaning against the tunnel wall, far enough in that he couldn't be seen from the outside, close enough to the opening to give him as wide a view as possible.

"Still out there?"

Ker nodded. "Only two of them now. Either the one I hit died, or they've sent him away."

The corners of Tel's mouth lifted. His eyes never stopped scanning the scene outside. Suddenly, he stiffened to attention.

"Something's happening over to the west," he said. "It's a bad angle . . ." He edged forward, and Ker followed at his shoulder. She could see it also, a patch of dark green where snow had just fallen off low-hanging branches. But what had caused it?

"It's Jak!" she said. Tel grabbed her by the arm just in time to stop her from stepping outside.

"Wait," he said. "How is it he's just walking up to us?"

Jak stopped out of bow range, and stuck his thumbs in his belt. Ker had never seen him stand that way before. Was he trying to signal them?

"I can't see you," he called out. "But I know there must be someone there. Will you tell me who it is?"

"It's Tel Cursar," Tel said. "What's going on?"

"Well, what's going on, my dear Tel, is you're being given a chance." Jak smiled, and cold spread over Ker's whole body.

"A chance to what, exactly?"

"A chance to rid yourself of the witch."

13

COLD. Buzzing in her ears. A grin on Jak's face. All teeth. Wynn drawing in a breath that was half sob. Ker crept a little closer to the entrance. She tried to swallow, but her mouth was too dry.

"Is it Jak?" Wynn said in her ear.

"Not our Jak," Ker said, glad to look away from the man's smile. "He's like the ones at the gate."

Tel stood hunched and frowning, eyes squinting against the light reflecting off the snow. "What happened to you?" he called.

Jak's new smile faltered, but only for an instant, before reappearing. "They've cleansed my mind, Tel. Cleared it of all the dust and cobwebs and the dark shadow that the magic of the body creates."

"The magic of . . . ?"

"Of the body. The magic of the witches." Jak tapped himself on the chest. "What the witches do, my friend. Drawing on the narrow, dark magic that they have within them. Not

the true magic. The bright, wide magic of the mind and sky."
He shrugged, shaking his head and looking up, as if expecting
to see something that would confirm what he was saying.
"Only women use the magic of the body. Only witches."

"That's not—" Ker subsided when Wynn tugged at her.

"But there are men in the Halls as well as women." Tel was
thinking along the same lines.

Jak shook his head, his mouth twisted to one side, as if he
had bad news to share. "Tel, they're not stupid, the witches.
They know how to make things look good to cover up their
tracks. They let us think that men have magic of the body as
well, but you know they always travel with a woman. The
witches have been fooling us for years."

"We've lost him." Tel spoke out of the side of his mouth.

"Keep him talking," Wynn said.

Tel made an affirmative sign behind his back with his left
hand. "But the Halls are neutral," he said aloud. "The Talents
maintain the Rule of Law over the whole of the Polity."

"Listen to me, Tel. What they call the Rule of Law is nothing more than the rule of women. Think about it—they take
anyone who shows any Talent whether they want to go or not,
and we never see them again. Who knows what they really do
with those poor kids? What's that but tyranny?"

Ker licked her lips. She'd had similar thoughts herself,
once.

With a final squeeze on Ker's arm, Wynn turned away and
began picking her way down the tunnel, peering upward at
the ropes and bracing in the roof.

Jak was still talking. "What's the percentage of landowners
who are men? Council members? Top traders and merchants?
The women twist everything to keep us from thinking about
it, from examining it too closely. That's what the magic of the
body does." Jak sighed as if he was tired of talking about it.
"That's the world without balance, and that's why the witches
must be destroyed."

Tel shook his head, lips pressed tight. "I won't give you Kerida," he said finally. "Whatever you say."

Jak stepped forward and tilted his head, as if Tel had said something to him very quietly and he'd had to come closer to hear it. When he spoke, his voice was almost too low to hear. "Play along, you idiot. I've got them fooled."

Ker's heart leaped, and then she remembered Jak's smile. She knew a way to be sure, something she would never have tried before the griffin, but . . . *Paraste.*

Jak eased back to his original position, and raised his voice again. "Don't worry, the amnesty serves for your friends as well. The women won't be able to stay in the military, but they'll be safe enough. Sent back to their families or other work found for them."

As he spoke, Ker saw his aura as bands of color, spreading out from him, riding the air currents all the way to where she stood. Jak had the same three colors as Tel, but his looked pale, like a flame in sunlight. Worse, over all his colors lay a faint pattern of red webbing, like a spider's web, or the delicate nets of wire that had been all the rage as hair ornaments two years before.

"Tel, he's lying."

As she spoke, Tel took a step forward out of the shelter of the entrance. Alarmed, Ker grabbed hold of his sleeve. At the same moment a harsh scream froze them all in their places, and Ker looked up. A shape too big to be an eagle filled the sky with rippling auroras of color.

"Weimerk!"

As if he'd heard her, the griffin circled lower, coming in for a landing near Jak. He had definitely grown, and his aura was so bright, his feathers seemed limned in light.

Afterward, Ker remembered the next few minutes as if everything happened at once.

Jak spun toward the landing griffin, lifting the crossbow he'd been holding at his side.

Tel and Ker both took another step forward, crying out, "No!"

Jak jerked back toward them, eyes round, lips parted.

Ker heard the *twang* of the crossbow. Something punched her in the side, slamming her against the rock. She twisted, clutching at Tel, her knees giving under her.

The griffin screamed again, the sound filling every corner of her brain, shoving out all colors and all light. There was horror and fear in the sound. Strange that something which had eaten his nest mates should be so moved by someone else's pain.

"Tel?"

"I've got you. Breathe. Shallow! Take shallow breaths."

They were moving, and something blocked the light. Cold numbness spread through her side, and she couldn't see.

"Come on!" Now Wynn was with them, helping Tel walk her forward, the two of them supporting her under the arms. She heard thunder, like rapids off in the distance—felt a shiver under her feet. The rock around them rumbled, Wynn yelled something Ker couldn't make out, dust clogged the air, and something hard struck her on the shoulder. Wynn had activated the deadfall and collapsed the tunnel entrance. A sudden roar deafened them as the tunnel itself collapsed behind them, the impact bouncing them forward. Ker felt them stagger, but somehow they kept her moving.

"Ker! Kerida, come on!" That was Wynn's voice, Wynn's hands on her upper arms, tugging her forward. The sharp pain in her side felt like broken glass.

"Wait. Tel." Shallow breaths.

"He's right here, we're both here. How badly are you hurt? Can you move?"

A silly question, considering how much they'd moved her already. Though they'd had to, hadn't they, if they'd collapsed the tunnel?

The noise of skittering and clattering rock continued.

Something about the quality of the sound, and the feel of the air, told her that they were in a more open space. Her mouth felt full of dust, and she hoped that they still had their water. A light, at first faint, grew slowly stronger. The glow stone. And what an odd color it had.

Ker was still Flashing, but couldn't remember what to do about it. Dust floating in the air didn't obscure their auras. She wanted to cough, but something told her she shouldn't. There was a smear of dirt across Wynn's face. Wynn's very serious face.

"Ker? Kerida?"

Wynn was talking to her. "I'm all right," she said. "You can let me up."

Instead of answering, Wynn took Ker's right hand and moved it until it was touching something close under her left armpit. At first, her brain refused to accept the evidence of her fingers. Why could she feel the thick fletching of a cross-bow quarrel? Where was the rest of the shaft? As if asking made the Flash clearer, Ker knew. The shaft was inside her, all the way inside. The sharp edges of the point had found their way through the cage of her ribs, slicing through the lung and just nicking her heart, only the shaft itself now holding the hole closed. Ker tried not to breathe at all. Something warm trickled over her hand. Someone cursed, calling on Mother and Daughter. She was so cold. The only thing warm about her was her blood.

From the darkness came a rough, familiar voice.

"Let me look at that, child. Don't move now. I said don't move." Ganni's face, eyes narrowed. Where had he come from? His aura glowed, rippling bands of green, blue, yellow, purple, orange, and pink . "Looks worse than it is," he said to the shadow standing behind him. "Soldier boy, you're in my light."

"Give us a little room here, please." That was Tel. He really was impossibly tall, wasn't he? And so far away.

"Blasted griffin was right." This was a voice Ker didn't recognize. "Too bad he couldn't tell us sooner. She going to die?"

"Fix it. You fixed me." Tel's voice was shaking. Wynn said something, and Tel shushed her.

Ker's lips parted, but she was afraid to speak.

"Look at me, girl," came a growl close to her ear. "Keep your eyes on me."

Ker tried to do as she was asked. His aura still glowed, but Ganni's face was stained with shadow, and it was hard to focus.

"I can't see it, do you understand, my child?" There was fear and anger in his voice, and a current of despair flattened his aura. "I can't move skin and tissues I can't see."

Ker grabbed the old man's wrist as the world blurred. How could he not see when she could Flash his aura even with her eyes shut? Flash how his colors swirled, wrapping themselves around her. Five colors—no, six, with the deep pink she'd seen in no one else. How could he not see how the quarrel with its steel point lay alongside her heart, how her lung lost air with every shallow breath?

"Ah!"

Suddenly her breath stopped, there was a blossom of heat in her side, and it seemed as though her ribs would crack. Then—nothing. No pain. Just warmth spreading through her chest from where Ganni's hand pressed against her. Ker breathed again.

"I saw it," the old man murmured into her hair. "So clear as my own hand. I saw it, child. There," he said in a louder voice, lifting his head. "Told you it looked worse than it was." He held up the quarrel. It didn't seem to have anywhere near enough blood on it. "Does anyone have a spare shirt, or a tunic? Child's bled like a stuck pig."

"A pig would be more useful," said the unknown voice. Now Ker could tell it was a woman. The same colors as Ganni, but black instead of pink. "At least we could eat it."

"And what would Weimerk say to that, do you think?"

"Life was a lot simpler before the blasted griffin, that's what *I* think." Black, not pink. How strange. "She's back to us awfully quick, isn't she? *And* they've pulled down our tunnel."

"You unhappy, Cuarel?"

"Me? You know I'm always on your side, Ganni. But I can think of some who aren't."

Tel never thought, when Wynn was explaining how the dead-fall worked, that they'd be pulling it down with Jak Gulder on the outside. He counted the number of Feelers around them—or at least the ones he could see. He and Wynn still had their swords and knives, but almost everything else was buried under the debris of the collapsed tunnel. Three Feelers had stayed behind to dig out what they could, but Tel suspected it was more to rescue what food they'd carried, and less to get them their clothes and weapons. Outnumbered, certainly. Could they count on the same strange cooperation they'd had last time? What if—

"Did I see what I thought I saw?" Wynn looked back over her shoulder. "Was that a griffin?"

"Too bad he didn't come sooner." Tel shook his head. "As it is, we've managed to lose the Kalter, to say nothing about Fed Durk and Nate Primo."

"Which puts you in charge," Wynn said.

Tel clamped his mouth shut. He'd figured that one out for himself.

"We shouldn't complain about Weimerk. At least he told the others where to find us." Ker sounded so tired Tel lifted his hand to pat her on the shoulder. He let it fall without touching her, half smiling at the thought of what her reaction would be.

"And speaking of the others." Wynn stepped between them, lowering her voice. "One minute you're pale as a snowbank, your lips are turning blue, and you're dying. Next thing we know you're sitting up with a smile on your face, and the old guy's binding you up saying it's just a scratch." She frowned. "Though you're still pretty pale. Who are these people? *What* are these people?"

Ker looked up at Tel. "They're—" His throat closed and he shook his head. "They're allies, that's all I can tell you." With a tilt of his head, he indicated the people around them. "Faro Sweetwater knows about them."

"Uh-huh. And does Jak Gulder know about them, too, or am I the only one in the dark?" She glanced around. "No pun intended."

"No, he doesn't. With luck, he'll think we were killed when the mine entrance came down— Blast!" Tel stopped and grabbed Ker's sleeve. She looked up at him, and her face changed.

"Oh, Mother," she said. "He knows about the prince."

"Which means the enemy knows as well."

His heart still sinking, Tel resumed walking. "Which means we've got to get to the prince before them."

───────

The inn really wasn't far off, and sooner than he expected Jerek Firoxi was tying Fogtail to the ring outside the door and following his new friend in. At a signal from Talian, he lowered himself onto a nearby stool, leg muscles stinging from the sudden relief of not having to carry him anymore. He wondered if horses ever felt like this, or if having four legs spread the work out. He straightened his shoulders, lifted his chin, and looked around. He'd never been in an alehouse before.

The room was well set out, with the street door in the center of one wall and the serving counter to the left, next to a set of stairs. Another door in the far left corner, almost blocked by the counter, no doubt led to a rear yard. In the far wall, across from the street door, was a large fireplace, set with grates and hooks, for cooking in the old manner, though the fire was banked just now. The room had no windows, but the top halves of the doors opened to let in the day's light.

A square-built woman with a slightly underhung jaw and streaks of gray in her fair hair sat to one side of the room's longest table, with papers, pen, and ink spread in front of her. It was clear she knew they were there, but she didn't look up from her accounts until Talian was at her elbow. The boy murmured in his aunt's ear, his voice too low for Jerek to hear individual words. Suddenly, the woman was on her feet, her hand flashed out, and Talian was plucked upward, held just off the floor by a grip on his collar.

"You idiot!" the woman said from between clenched teeth. "You absolute fool. What were you using for brains? Alento! Watch the door!"

A noise and movement behind him pulled Jerek's head around, but before he could move, the square woman had grabbed him by the left arm, jerked him up off his stool, and started to shake him.

Jerek automatically froze at the sudden, unexpected attack, but the pain in his left arm was abruptly washed away by an unfamiliar heat. This was the kind of thing his father did, and maybe there was nothing he could do about his father, but there was something he could do now. He let himself fall heavily toward the woman and, remembering a trick Nessa had taught him, brought his right elbow up and plowed her in the stomach, at the same time twisting free of the now loosened grip.

Before he could run for the door, however, he was caught from behind, lifted, and thrown onto a short bench in the corner formed by the fireplace. A table was shoved up against his chest, bruising his ribs and wedging him against the stone.

The man who'd thrown him there was an older version of Talian, about five times bigger and with forearms the size of small hams.

The woman stopped coughing long enough to push the hair from her face. "By the Mother, who are you? And what do you want with Bedeni Soria? Speak up, boy, and don't lie to me, or it'll be the last thing you ever do."

If anything, Jerek's rage had been given fuel by pain and the tears he was trying to blink away before anyone saw them. That rage, and all the times he'd never been able to fight back, suddenly rose in his throat, nearly choking him.

"None of your business, you Motherless dog," he spit out, and for once his voice didn't crack. "My message is for Bedeni Soria and no one else, least of all you."

To Jerek's surprise, instead of lashing out, the innkeeper cocked her head and laughed until she finally resumed coughing. She wiped her eyes with the end of her sleeve.

"Well, you don't get that tone from somebody who's not a rich man's brat, that's one thing for sure." She turned to the giant. "Go back to the door, Alento. Tell anyone who comes we're closed and they can come back later—or not at all, for all I care." Shutting the top half of the street door cut off most of the light, but the room grew warmer. Without moving the table out, the square woman pulled up a stool and sat down.

"There now, young sir, or lord or whatever you might be. I had to make sure of you, can you see that? I had to make sure this light-headed nephew of mine wasn't bringing any black cloaks to my place. You know what I mean?"

Jerek nodded and sat straighter, a little flattered that the innkeeper had been frightened of him.

"Now then, there's plenty of people would like to get a message to Bed Soria. What if it's a message he'd rather not hear? Unless you tell me what it is, and who you are, nothing goes farther than this room—maybe not even you. Do I make myself clear?"

Jerek surprised himself by beginning to relax. Maybe this woman wasn't a bully after all—or not just a bully, he amended. If the innkeeper was being this careful of Bedeni Soria, maybe she'd be just as careful of the old man's friends. Among whom Jerek was about to place himself.

He risked a glance at the other boy, and saw fear in his face, but not, as he expected, residual fear of the innkeeper. No, Talian was afraid of Jerek himself. Afraid of what trouble, in these unsettled times, a stranger might bring. As for the woman, bully or not, there was surely a healthy line of fear under her aggressive caution. But also something stronger than her fear.

"I'm Jerek Firoxi—I mean Brightwing," he said finally. "Soria used to work for my mother, before he retired. He was one of our guards. It's not the old man himself I want," he added. "It's somebody who might be with him—or he might know where she is."

"'She,' is it?"

Jerek's ears grew hot and his tongue stumbled.

"While Soria was with us, he was good friends with our Factor's daughter, treated her like a daughter of his own. It's Nessa I'm looking for now."

"She's left your employ as well, then?"

"Yes. She . . . yes."

"Like to talk her into coming back, would you?"

"No." That came out more bluntly than Jerek had intended. "That is . . ." His throat closed. *I've run away.* That sounded childish and silly. "I've left home."

The innkeeper shook her head. "Are you sure? You said it was your mother's place, so is it yours now? Or have you older siblings?"

"No, but it's my father's place until I come of age. He decides what happens: who stays, and who goes." He might as well tell them the rest. "When the Halians came, they said that for now I'd keep my mother's land, but that my father could petition to have the land come to him."

Now the woman nodded. "You'd be right not to rely on anything the Halians can change, I'd say. Still, you'd be the first-born, you'd inherit even if your father remarried, just not so soon. As for the Halians . . . well, let me tell you, this is a bad time not to have a firm and obvious place to belong."

Jerek pressed his lips tighter.

"Well, never mind that. I can see you're someone who knows his own mind." The woman nodded and narrowed her eyes in thought. "I'm Goreot," she said, holding her hand out across the table. Jerek found himself taking it without hesitation. "Now that I know the way of things, I can get a message to Bed Soria. Mind, it may take a day or two. Old soldiers like him are being careful about who can find them. I can't send for him. You'll have to be content to wait for the right people to come in. Though that shouldn't be a problem, eh, Talian? Mostly, the right people *do* come in, don't they?"

Talian nodded, smiling at Jerek from where he leaned against the table still covered with papers. Goreot rose and shifted the small table, giving Jerek room to move.

"Are you hungry?" she said, gesturing toward a metal pot keeping warm to one side of the banked fire. "We can give you a bed here, and food if you have money to pay for it."

In some ways Goreot's establishment really was very little more than an alehouse. Everyone, including Jerek, slept on the second floor, but there were no other rooms for hire. Jerek had a bed of his own, but he shared the room with Talian and his huge brother, Alento. Fogtail was stashed away in one of the many small sheds and enclosures that formed a yard in back of the building, where Jerek himself spent most of the day in caring for the beast and teaching Talian how to ride.

A cook came in every morning, bringing bread from the baker on his way—again, not quite the usual thing for an ale-house. Jerek was asked to wait until the morning rush of

workers and others breaking their fast had been and gone before coming into the common room himself.

"Some of these folk haven't learned not to be curious," Goreot said. "Best not to draw any more attention than absolutely necessary."

No one minded if the cook saw him. The man might as
well have been mute for all the conversation Jerek ever heard
him make. And there were one or two others, regulars apparently, who could be trusted to ignore him.

Little as he was encouraged to linger, it didn't take Jerek
very long to realize that more went on in Goreot's alehouse
than the selling of food and drink. In the evenings, the tables
were filled with card players wagering on hands of Seasons.
In the late mornings, before the rush for the midday meal,
people came with items they were obviously trying to sell or
perhaps pawn. These visits often necessitated a trip to the
yard and sheds by Talian or one of the others. One afternoon
a horse, saddled and bridled and carrying full packs, waited
for two hours for a cloaked and hooded man to come and ride
him away, with neither words nor money exchanged.

On the morning of the fourth day, two guards came in just
as Jerek was coming down for his breakfast, and he stepped
back into the doorway of the room he shared with Talian. Goreot seemed not in the least put out, however.

"Has it been a whole week?" She poured them out a mug
of beer each, and Jerek watched her pass a small pouch to the
older of the two. Jerek sucked in his breath, everything suddenly becoming clear.

"It's a payoff," he said under his breath.

"Better not let *them* hear you say that." Talian came up beside him. "They like to think of it as a gift in appreciation of
their hard work." The other boy's smile didn't reach his eyes.

"I don't understand," Jerek murmured. Goreot's operation
was obviously well-established. "How did your aunt run an
illegal business with Talents all around you?"

Talian's eyes widened until he was the picture of innocence. "What illegal business? It's not illegal to lend people
money at interest. It's not illegal to help people move their
goods from place to place."

Jerek blinked and finally nodded. He'd never thought about
it, but why *would* Talents get involved, if no one ever com-
plained to the Law?

On the fifth morning Jerek was brushing Fogtail when Talian crept in, closing with care the old shutter that served as
the shed door. The boy looked paler than usual, though there
were two red spots high on his cheeks and marks that could
have been recent tears. Before Jerek could speak, Talian lifted
his finger to his lips.

"Listen," he said. "You've got to get away. Here, I've brought
your things."

Except for Fogtail's saddle and bridle, the rest of the gear
that Jerek had brought with him was now hanging from Talian's shoulder.

"What is it?" He kept his voice down to the low murmur
the other boy was using. "The Halians?"

The other boy shook his head slightly from side to side.
"Nothing like that. It's old Goreot. She's never waiting for Bedeni Soria. She sent for your father."

"What? Since when?"

"Since always, you chump. She never meant to help you
find Soria, she always meant to sell you back to your dad—
providing the price was right and you were wanted back."

Jerek's knees began to fold, and he caught himself on Fogtail's shoulder. He swallowed, tasting bile. "How long have
you known?"

Talian looked away. "Always. It was the plan right from the
start. I saw from your saddle and your clothes that you might
be worth something, so I brought you in."

Jerek blinked fiercely, gritting his teeth against tears of
anger and betrayal. How easy it had been. All they'd had to do

was pretend to distrust him, to be afraid of him. He'd been only too ready to convince them he could be trusted. All too ready to believe that they had to be what they seemed to be.

"So why are you telling me now?" he said, keeping his voice hard. "What's changed?"

"Goreot said she'd let *us* go, Alento and me. But now she says she's never said any such thing, and if we go, she'll send the guard after us as thieves and pledge breakers."

Jerek opened his mouth to protest that Goreot couldn't do that, that Talian could call for a Talent and the truth would come out. But he remembered where he was, and why, and closed his mouth again. There were no Talents anymore.

"You want to leave your aunt?" Jerek didn't bother pointing out that Talian had been ready to do to him what he was angry with Goreot for doing. If Talian wanted to escape, Jerek could see the beginnings of a plan.

"Yeah, like she's my aunt. When you're on the street, everyone's your auntie." With a sour grimace Talian glanced over his shoulder. "Our cut of selling you would bring enough to pay out our fostering, but if she's not gonna play fair by me, I'm not gonna play fair by her. Here's your stuff. Go now."

Before I change my mind. Talian didn't have to say the words aloud. Jerek could read them in the set of the boy's shoulders. He shoved Fogtail's brushes back into their pouch and grabbed up his saddle. "What will happen to you?" he asked. "You'd better come with me."

There was a flash in Talian's eye, and just for a moment Jerek thought the boy would say yes, but then the light faded. "Pony won't carry both of us," he said. "I'd only slow you down. And there's my brother." He shook his head, and Jerek could see how much it cost him. "Go out the back way, go left, away from the street. Head west as soon as you can and go to the woodcarver's square. You'll find your old soldier there."

So close? Biting down on his anger, Jerek wasted no further time, but hefted up Fogtail's saddle and swung it over the old pony's back. The beast shied, and snorted, as if to give his opinion of young boys who wanted rides on old ponies.

"Shhh, chah," Jerek murmured, rubbing Fogtail's nose. Talian had squeezed himself into the corner to help with the buckling of the bridle, when the shutter was thrown back, and Goreot's square body and smiling face appeared in the opening.

"There you are, boys. Going somewhere?"

Talian's face didn't change, but Jerek saw his hands tighten on Fogtail's bridle.

"Thought I'd give Talian a lesson with the saddle." Jerek couldn't tell whether his voice sounded normal or not.

Old Goreot's eyes shifted down and to the left, to where Jerek's pack had been next to the opening. Jerek held his breath, but Goreot's expression never changed. Jerek risked a glance of his own, found the corner empty. There was a chance, then, that Talian wouldn't get into much trouble. Especially if he could sneak Jerek's things back into his room.

"Come with me, boy, I've got something to show you." But Goreot didn't turn to lead the way. Rather, she stood and let Jerek sidle past her, and then followed him across the small yard and into the rear of the alehouse. It wasn't an unfriendly gesture in itself, but it meant he couldn't lag behind, or slip out the gate. He was being herded.

The taproom was dim after the sunlight outside, and it took a moment for Jerek's eyes to adjust completely. Not that he needed much light to recognize the silhouette in front of the other door. Or the sheepskin overcloak that wrapped the man's shoulders. No. Jerek knew who it was even before the man turned around. Talian's change of heart had come too late.

"Hello, son."

Exhaustion made Ker grateful to settle into the leather-covered seats on the council's dais. This time the cavern was empty, the darkness and the echoes making it feel all the larger. This time they were seated together, with the rock wall behind them, and a clear semicircular space between them and the Feelers' council.

The quiet, sullen man, Midon, was already there when Ganni brought them in. In minutes, Sala, the tall dark-skinned Speaker with the military bearing, joined them, leading a skipping Larin by the hand. The old woman wasn't with them. Norwil came in looking worried, his brow furrowed. Hitterol, the older, red-haired woman, rushed in last, wiping her hands on a long apron and glancing around as though she expected someone else.

They'd been given a chance to wash the dust off their faces, and to eat something, but Ker found that her eyes kept threatening to close, and her hand kept straying to her side. The wound felt like a bad bruise, or like that time she'd cracked a rib in training. But she knew she hadn't dreamed the feeling of the shaft touching her heart.

Wynn looked at her, laying her fingers on Ker's wrist, and Ker smiled, hoping that would reassure the young archer.

Sala cleared her throat and Ker's attention, along with that of everyone else, shifted to the Speaker. "There's a friend of yours missing, Griffin Girl, but we won't wait for him any longer."

Ker drew her eyebrows down in a vee. Did the woman mean Weimerk? Surely he couldn't fit through the tunnels to get here? But Sala was continuing.

"Not to say you are not most welcome, Griffin Girl, but none here expected to see you again so soon. Are we to take it your welcome at Hall and Wing was not as warm as you had hoped?"

Ker drew in a lungful of air, still a little surprised that she could. She straightened her shoulders. "No." She cleared her throat and tried again. "No, not at all. But Temlin Hall we found destroyed, the Talents murdered, and the buildings torched."

Ker took another deep breath, blinking her stubborn eyes open. She didn't want to be the one in charge, the one speaking, the one responsible. She looked again at the faces around her. Larin smiled and winked at her. Tel shifted so that the back of his right hand touched her knee. Wynn seemed to still have that irrepressible twinkle in her eye.

"There's a prince of the blood in the Peninsula." Ker laced her fingers together. "With the Luqs gone, the Wings— especially those who haven't encountered the Halians yet— may waste time sorting out a new leader and by the time they do that, it could be too late. But if we bring them the prince, they'll unite behind him."

Sala was nodding. Trust a soldier to see exactly what Ker was getting at.

They were supposed to help her, Ker thought. And Sala had called her "Griffin Girl." "Is there an exit we can use closer to the Valpen area?"

"The more important question is whether we should let her go." Norwil patted the air in front of him with his hands as Larin jumped to her feet, tiny fists on her hips. "Now hear me out, Larin." The child subsided but with her lip well curled. "She's fulfilled the Prophecy, hasn't she? We're talking to the griffin, aren't we? I wasn't happy about letting her go when we thought she was heading somewhere safe." He shook his head, but Ker felt her eyebrows rise. "But to let her go gallivanting off into territory we know is controlled by these Halians? And for what? To find some Polity prince? Let these others go if they must, but the Griffin Girl belongs here, with us. It's *our* Prophecy, isn't it?"

Hitterol looked thoughtful, and even Midon seemed about to nod in agreement.

Ker squeezed her eyes shut. She had to speak up, but her brain was working so slowly.

"Well, no, since you ask, Norwil, it isn't your Prophecy."

Ker spun around, shock bringing her halfway to her feet. *Impossible. This* was the friend Sala had meant? The last time she'd seen the tall, gaunt man picking his careful way through the empty cavern he'd been wearing the black tunic of the Inquisition. Now in homespun, with the sleeves of his tunic too short, Luca Pa'narion looked taller, and even thinner. He strode into the lighted area as if it was his own parlor. Ker shook herself. Now wasn't the time to wonder how and why the Inquisitor had appeared here and now.

"You started without me, Speaker for the Mines and Tunnels?" Somehow, coming from Luca's mouth, those words sounded more like a title than they had before.

Sala threw up her hands, a twisted grin on her face. "I sent for you, Inquisitor. How long were we to wait? Now explain yourself."

Luca gave the Speaker a short bow before turning to the others. "'Let all the peoples of the land awake and listen,'" he intoned, the music of his voice lifting the words. "'For the day of joining comes.'"

"'It comes near.'" All of the small council spoke in unison.

"That's the Prophecy. I believe. Isn't it, Larin?" Tilting his head, the Inquisitor swiveled his eyes toward the child.

"It is," she said, her voice suddenly deeper, as if to mimic his.

"All the peoples of the land, Norwil. Not only Feelers, not only Talents. Not even only the citizens of the Polity. It's everyone's Prophecy, Norwil. All of us."

Norwil threw up his hands. "I'm just saying she'd be safer in here with us, is all."

"I'm not so sure." Luca grabbed a chair from the edge of the platform and swung it into place between Sala and Ganni. Now that he was closer to the light, Ker could see how pale he was, how tired. "The Halians will be coming here, not for *you*, but for this. I was out searching for it when you sent for me."

Luca reached into his pouch and drew out a lump of red stone, like the ones she'd seen in Flashes, but uncut, without facets. She jerked back, and Tel took hold of her hand.

Ganni reached out, and Luca laid the jewel in the older man's palm. "Sure, I've seen this before, still in the rock. There are small veins of it, here and there."

"And some larger, which is where I found this one," Luca said. "You've seen one like it in use, haven't you, Kerida Nast?"

Ker nodded, shivering, glad of Tel's hand on hers, and of Wynn's warm presence at her side. "In Flashes. But they were faceted."

Luca took it back from Ganni. "This one isn't active. None of the old documents in the archives tell of how that's done. But I believe it's the basis for the mages' power."

Larin also reached out for the jewel, and Ker gasped in warning, but no one else protested. Larin eyed the gem on her palm from all sides, frowning intently, before closing her fist on it and shutting her eyes. When she opened them again, her pupils had expanded until there was no color in her eyes at all.

"The one comes," she said, and her voice was older somehow, plainer and more tough. "The time of light is upon us. We have seen the First Sign. The horses of the sea. The Second Sign shines on us. The wings of the sky. The griffin and the girl." She held up her closed fist. "The Third Sign comes. Blood and fire. Bones of the Griffin. The Third Sign must not pass us by." She turned her sightless eyes on Ker. "You must watch for the Third Sign, lest it kill us all."

She blinked, and her eyes were suddenly their normal clear brown. Now she spoke directly to Ker. "Grandmother told me there's no pleasure like the pleasure of being proved right. Mark those words, you'll never hear truer." The child's nose wrinkled up in a surprisingly adult expression. "Gods, griffins, and goats, people. Here's the jewel. So where's the prince? You're all a pack of fools. There's only one thing to do, and you all know it." She thrust the gem at Luca, and sat down again. "Has the grandmother been talking to herself all these years?"

"Did I hear right? *Feelers*? And Faro Sweetwater knows?" Wynn sat in one corner of the same sleeping alcove Ker and Tel had been given before. Cushions and rugs were still folded on the rock benches. Wynn tilted her head and looked at Tel with one eyebrow raised. "Well?"

Ker leaned back, letting her eyes fall shut. "We *couldn't* talk about them," she said. "I'm surprised we can even say this much." Neither she nor Tel much liked the idea that some kind of binding had been placed on them, but it was hard to keep feeling indignant.

"Great. Good. So they *are* Feelers, then?" Wynn slapped her hands down on her knees. "And this is a child's story." She squinted up at them. "And the man who turned up so timely?"

"I think I should speak for myself. Though Kerida knows me, she doesn't know how I happen to be here."

Ker automatically rose to her feet, with Tel and Wynn not far behind her. High Inquisitor Luca Pa'narion waved them down again. Tel settled next to her at one end of the sleeping bench, with Wynn at the other end.

"Well, Kerida Nast. I knew you were going to be important. I had no idea *how* important." Luca sat down cross-legged with his back to the curtain enclosing the alcove. "And to answer your question, Wynn Martan, archer of the Eagles, I followed Kerida here.

"As you know, my name is Luca Pa'narion, and I am—or I was—one of the Polity's High Inquisitors, stationed these last twenty years in the Peninsula. I was on the road when news of the Halians reached me." He shifted his eyes so he was looking directly at Ker. "Altogether luckily."

"Well, no disrespect, Inquisitor, but how is it you can talk about them?" Tel asked. "You and Faro Sweetwater. Everyone except me and Ker, is what it feels like." Ker bumped Tel with her shoulder, half in approval, and half in warning.

"Ah, you were bound, were you? I'm sure you've noticed it wearing off, now that you're back here. And you'll always be able to talk to each other about them. The block is only to keep you from mentioning them accidentally, and having questions to answer. What do you know of the history of the Feelers?"

Wynn inched closer to Kerida. "Everyone's heard of Feelers," she said. "They're a children's story, like I said. Aren't they?"

"They've become that," Luca said. "It seemed safest for people to simply stop believing in them."

"Safest for whom?" Ker said.

"Safest for everyone. That's what the Rule of Law is for, you know. At least when it was first conceived. Safety for everyone." Luca waited, and when it was obvious Ker had nothing further to say, he continued. "Feelers were once the partners and equals of Talents. Part of a larger group of what was called the Gifted, their Gifts detectable at about the same age, and by the same tests. There were Guilds, like the Hall schools, to train them."

Ker touched her side with cold fingers.

Luca's eyes narrowed as if he was looking back through the years to the time he spoke of. "Talents began to think of themselves as separate from those with other Gifts. Some say it was because we are the only ones who detect the Gifts in others, some that it was our early connection with the military and the Rule of Law." He shrugged. "In any case a schism formed between the two groups. One came to be called Talents, and the other, Feelers."

Luca suddenly sat up very straight, eyes narrowing as if he followed a new train of thought. He began to smile and then shook himself, looking around at them again, though the smile didn't fade completely. "I've just been struck by a little bit of irony."

"How so?" Tel's tone was cautious.

"'The time of joining comes,'" he quoted. "I'm thinking this invasion might mean the reuniting of the Gifts, when it was an uprising that broke them apart in the first place. It was a great-grandson of Jurianol, who tired of waiting for his father to die. A faction of Feelers supported the rebel, and were defeated with him. Because of *their* treason, Talents were able to turn the horrified monarch's heart against *all* Feelers."

"They were imprisoned here?"

"Oh, no. Worse than that. At first they were merely registered, and their activities regulated and controlled. It's from that era that most of the stories told about Feelers and their evil ways originate. Eventually, Rule of Law resulted in their being . . ." For the first time, Luca hesitated.

"Dampened." Ker felt chilled, as if a cold draft had come off the rock face behind her.

"Yes."

"But you're saying that *these* people are Feelers, aren't you?" Wynn looked from Luca to Ker and back.

Luca drew in a deep breath, nodding. "Not everyone—not every Talent even, agreed with the decree of outlawry. Some Feelers were helped to avoid the eventual roundup, some to escape if they were taken into custody. But the Polity was spreading, even then, and with it the Rule of Law, and the places for Feelers to hide are few."

Ker thought of Larin. "So new Feelers are born in these places?" How dreadful, she thought.

"Some are born here, yes. But the Gifts appear anywhere, as the Talent does, with every generation." He tapped himself on the sternum with his thumb. "That's where I come into this. People like myself, followers of those who disagreed, all those years ago—we save those we find, sending them to havens like this one. But we're few, those of us who know."

"Why?"

"It's illegal, my dear child. Haven't you been listening? Illegal to be a Feeler, or to aid them in any way. We'd be subject to the same penalties—or I should say penalty, since there is only one."

Dampening. This time Kerida didn't say it aloud.

"Only those of us who are powerful enough to hide our knowledge from the Inquisition can know of the secret." Luca's grin turned his face into a skull. "I won't tell who the others are, in case you're ever asked—I'm not the only Talent who was on the road when the Halians arrived."

"You thought I might become one of those powerful ones." Ker leaned forward, her elbows on her knees.

"You *are* one. How else could you have spoken with the griffin?"

Ker shook her head. "What if I hadn't believed you? Or hadn't wanted to help them?"

"You forget, I'm an Inquisitor, and Griffin Class myself. Do you think I could Flash you and not see the quality of person I had in my hands?"

Ker sat back, blinking. *Would* she have been willing to help Feelers, without knowing them first? She liked to think so.

On the other hand, she was getting pretty tired of everyone being so sure they knew her.

Wynn was shaking her head. "But how is it Faro Sweetwater knows? How is *she* protected from speaking of it to the wrong person?"

"Juria Sweetwater is a special case," Luca said. "Her aunt is a Feeler—not saved by me, and not here in the Serpents Teeth—and so Juria's known of their existence since she was a child. She can no more mention them accidentally nor refer to them casually than any of us."

"Her aunt. I suppose they're all someone's family, aren't they? They don't seem evil, truth to tell." Wynn's brow creased in thought. "Though appearances can by faked easy enough. My uncle Zavian didn't look like a killer."

"The fate of the Feelers is an old story." Luca was taking the jewel from his pouch once again. Even inactivated, it made Ker's skin crawl. "But there's one older still. From before the time of Jurianol, it's thought. Remarks in old texts, pieces of scrolls older still, speak of such things as this." Luca held it out again, flat in his palm. "People who used them, mines they were taken from."

Again the chill chased itself up Ker's spine. "Ganni said there are still veins of it here."

"Almost gone, but yes. This is one of the places to which the old scrolls referred. It's been forbidden for years to search here for precious metals. The whole of the Serpents Teeth is taboo—I suspect because it was known the jewels were found here. Then, those of us who helped the Feelers used the old stories and kept them alive for our own purposes." He fell silent, still studying the stone.

"What happens now?" Wynn asked.

Kerida swung an arm around the shorter girl's shoulder and hugged her. "Inquisitor Luca will go for the prince." She wondered if everyone could hear the relief in her voice.

Luca smiled a sorrowful smile. "Oh, no. Granted that either of us could Flash the prince and know him for who he is, I must go to Faro Sweetwater. There are other Wing Faros more powerful, more important politically, and we can't abandon her to pressures that could change her mind about supporting you. Your word on the existence of the prince might not have much weight with the Wings as a whole, but mine will." Could anyone be as confident as Luca sounded? "You'll go fetch the prince, and I'll go to Oste." He smiled.

*   *   *

Ker rubbed her eyes. Why couldn't she sleep? From the quality of their breathing, Tel and Wynn clearly could. Luca's dim silhouette was just visible in the opening of the alcove. He'd borrowed some of the luminescent vine the Feelers used, and wore it wrapped around his wrists and forehead as they did.

It felt as though the Inquisitor had been drifting in and out of her life forever, but she hadn't actually seen him since he'd taken her away from her sister Ester's tent. She'd often imagined what she'd say to him if she ever had the chance, but somehow, today, she wasn't reminded so much of the loss of her family, as of the security and safety of the Hall of Law. At this moment, Ker would have given anything to turn back the days, to wipe out the invasion. Right now, living as a Talent—and letting the Halls of Law hold everything in their iron hands—seemed a small price to pay if it meant everyone could be safe and alive.

As bad as she'd thought the Halls were, they weren't as bad as the Halians. They didn't kill anyone. *But they Dampen people.* Ker shivered, pushing that tiny voice to the back of her mind. She edged herself carefully out from under Tel's protective arm and crept over to Luca.

"Good," he murmured. "I was hoping for a chance to ask about the griffin. What was it like? Do you think I can meet him?"

Ker smiled, shaking her head. Luca sounded just like a child hoping to see jugglers at the market. "I've questions of my own, Inquisitor."

"Of course. After you."

Ker peered sideways at the older man. The light from the luminescent vine elongated his features. "Why aren't we Candidates told more, so we can be prepared when some new aspect of the Talent manifests?"

"You thinking of something in particular?"

"I'm thinking of the auras, in particular. If I'd known what to expect, it wouldn't have come as such a shock."

Luca went still. "What auras?" He turned to face her directly, gripping her arm just above the wrist. "Describe what you saw."

Ker blinked at him. "Let go of me. Sir."

The Inquisitor lifted his hand immediately. "Your pardon, please. It's just—can you explain?"

Now it was Ker's turn to stare at him. Was it possible he didn't know? "When I first met the griffin," she began. "He said I'd woken him up, and that he hadn't known Talents could do it. And then he said he'd do it for me as well." She wasn't sure she could make Luca understand the sensation of walking upstream against a current like a wall of water that suddenly wasn't there. "When he was finished, I could see that everyone around me, including the griffin himself, had an aura." She described how each person's aura was different, some with more or fewer colors. "I'm seeing patterns, though."

"How so?"

"Well, ordinary people like Tel and Wynn have three colors, and from what I can tell, the same three: green, blue, and yellow. The Feelers all have six colors. Five of them, the ordinary three plus purple and orange they all have in common. But the sixth color varies from Feeler to Feeler. I don't know what that means yet."

"This is amazing." Ker had never heard anyone sound so excited. "I ask you to trust and believe that I have never heard of such a thing. What about me? Do I have one?"

Paraste. "Yes. Oh!" Green, blue, and yellow, plus purple and orange, and then turquoise. "You have the same six colors I do. Wait—" She thought she'd seen a red mist, but it disappeared, as if her breath had blown it away. He also lacked the iridescent coppery tinge that she thought she'd seen in her own aura. Ker shook her head. "I've not seen turquoise among the Feelers. Would the Tutors at the Hall have known about the auras?"

He was shaking his head. "Inquisitors have full access to

all the archives; we're obliged to study them. I assure you there's no mention of this phenomenon."

"Weimerk seemed to think it was normal. When I asked him to stop it, he was surprised."

"But he didn't stop it?"

"No, he . . . cushioned it somehow, so I wasn't overwhelmed by it anymore." She squinted at the turquoise in Luca's aura. "I'd like to Flash more people, see if there are other patterns." She told him about the red mist she'd seen on the soldiers she and Tel had met on the road. "And Jak Gulder's aura had a kind of red net overlaying it."

"I know that red mist, I've seen it myself." Luca told her of his encounter with the Shekayrin, and how he'd used his special block to save himself. *Ah*, Ker thought, *that's where that residue of mist came from.*

Luca fell silent. His exhaustion was even deeper than her own, she realized. Kerida was suddenly struck with the depth of the man's loss. She'd only been a part of the Halls for a few short years. For Luca, it had been his whole life. No wonder he looked so thin and drawn. The relief that had left her blinking back tears when she'd seen him diminished just a little.

After a long time the Inquisitor spoke. "What a wonderful opportunity this would have been, if we weren't in danger of our lives."

"I'd love to see if Larin and old lady—Ara?—have the same colors in their auras."

He turned to look at her, head atilt. "You've seen the old woman?"

"When Tel and I came through the mines the first time and found the griffin. She persuaded the group who caught us to let us go."

"But you saw her?" Luca was looking at her intently. "You didn't just hear her speaking?"

"I saw her. But now that you mention it, Tel didn't see her.

I thought it must be something about the light. Or—" Ker sat up. "Is it a Gift? Can she make herself invisible?"

"Oh, it's more than that. I myself have never seen her. But it's not surprising. The woman's been dead since before I was born."

KER was one big bruise, with the sorest spot the place under her arm where the crossbow quarrel had pierced her side. She was trying to rub the sleep out of her eyes when Wynn stuck her head out from under the sleeping rugs on the ledge.

"It's too early to wake up." Despite her words, Wynn rolled off the sleeping ledge and stretched, pulling her knees to her chest one at a time.

"Who knows what time it is really?" Tel said, yawning as he pulled the cover off the glow stone.

"Please," a small voice piped from the darkness. Tel cursed and dimmed the stone again.

"If you please." A skinny boy with hair the color of a field mouse stepped around the curtain, almost dwarfed by the basket he carried. "The griffin said you're awake, so here's your breakfast." Ker's stomach suddenly rumbled and she stood up, pushing the hair out of her eyes. The boy set the basket down, bobbed his head at her, and disappeared into the dark.

"Don't keep us in suspense." Tel uncovered the glow stone again.

Ker folded back the cloth, revealing six eggs, brown-speckled and hardboiled. Likewise six rolls, still warm from the ovens, three mugs, and a stoppered jar of—

"Do I smell kaff?" Wynn pulled mugs and jar out of the basket and was pouring even before Ker had a chance to divvy out the eggs.

"What kind of eggs do you think these are?" Tel tied his hair back with a loose cord out of his pack.

"I don't care," Ker said. "I'm just happy it isn't more travel cake."

They were sweeping the last of the eggshells into the basket when Luca appeared. The Inquisitor had managed to shave sometime during the night, and even his clothing seemed less rumpled than it had the evening before. Ker grimaced, immediately conscious of the wrinkles and dirt on her own clothing, and the blood that had dried on top of them. And of how she smelled. Yesterday's face washing felt so long ago.

Luca grinned as if he knew her thoughts. "Good, you've eaten. Anyone else for the bath?"

A short time later, Ker was the cleanest she'd felt in days and was pulling on the clothes that had been left out for her. Fresh clothing had been found for Wynn as well, and even some items long enough for Tel, though the tunic needed more belting in than usual. Both he and Wynn combed and retied their hair into soldier's knots. Ker's own close-cropped Talents' haircut was growing out, but wasn't yet long enough to tie.

Luca brought them back to the meeting room where Sala was sitting, arms crossed, on the edge of the platform, talking to the older, scar-faced woman they'd often seen with Ganni, whose name Ker couldn't remember. Ganni himself looked up with a grin as they approached.

"Welcome to the day, Griffin Girl. We've determined which of the exits is closest to the Valpen region." Sala uncrossed her arms and braced her hands against the edge of the platform. "Alas, it isn't *very* close." She gestured at Norwil. "Some of the council wanted to limit our help to something in the way of weapons and provisions. What with the griffin, we're better stocked than usual." Luca opened his mouth, but Sala silenced him with a raised hand. "However, many of our traders, people who've been out on the surface and know how to manage, are volunteering to go with you."

"A few of us with each group," Ganni managed to cut in. The light in his eyes was enough to show he was one of the people who'd volunteered. Sala grinned and shrugged one shoulder.

"Without the use of roads and couriers, we're most in need of swift communications," Luca said. "Is there a Far-thinker among the volunteers?"

Wynn made some stifled noise, and Ker shivered in agreement. It was one thing to know that the Gifts from the stories were real, it was another to know that there were actually people who could read thoughts. As for traveling with such a person . . .

Tel must have been thinking along the same lines. "Someone who can push arrows and such aside, that would be a bigger help."

At that moment Ker found she had Nate Primo's plaque tight in her hand. He'd reached the Faro safely, that much she knew from Flashing it that morning. Was that similar to what a Far-thinker did? Or could the Feeler know other things, like where Jak Gulder was right now. They weren't the only ones who knew about the Valpen region.

"Too large a group might attract the wrong kind of attention," is what she said aloud. "Is there anyone who can do both? A, uh, Far-thinker and a . . ."

"A Mover," Ganni said. "'One person, one Gift' is the way of it, Griffin Girl."

Ker blew out a breath and sat back. The stories never mentioned that, but it might explain the different sixth color in the Feelers' auras.

"Kerida is right in saying that a smaller group attracts less attention," Luca said. "In our present circumstances, if we can only take one, then let it be a Far-thinker. At least we will be in close contact with one another."

"Truth to tell, I'm not keen on traveling with someone who can read my thoughts." Wynn spoke up for the first time. "Just saying," she added with a shrug.

"Full of silliness, these tales of yours." Ganni shook his head. "Far-thinkers can't read everybody's thoughts, child. We'd none of us like that any better than you. No, they only read the thoughts of other Far-thinkers." He turned to the women seated on the edge of the platform. "What do you think, Sala?"

Sala folded her arms again. "You'll need at least three. One of us for each group, and one to stay here."

"Volunteers," Norwil cut in. "Even the one who stays."

Sala rolled her eyes, though she was smiling. Then her eyes took on that unfocused stare Ker had seen once before. The hairs on Ker's arms lifted.

Sala was a Far-thinker? Ker's hands clenched tight. On a hunch, she said her opening word and, for the first time, examined another's aura on purpose. As she was beginning to expect, Sala's aura didn't look like Ganni's. Where the old man's had shown a deep pink, Sala's extra color was black. And so was that of the scar-faced woman next to her. Interesting.

Sala's focus returned to the people around her. "Cuarel and I will go. Dersay will remain in the Mines and Tunnels."

"When can you be ready?" Luca said.

"If Ganni can help with our packs," Sala said, "we shouldn't be long." She turned to Ker. "You go ahead. We will catch you up."

They were back in their sleeping alcove, packing their few remaining possessions along with the new clothing the Feelers had given them when Luca arrived.

"It's ridiculous for me to tell you all to be careful, Kerida, as if you wouldn't be. But that is the usual advice in these circumstances, so I give it."

"Yeah, well, you be careful, too." Ker's grin became a smile when Luca smiled back at her.

"This is new to you, but don't be shy of making use of your Far-thinker. Don't leave us wondering what's happening with you. Tell us, above all, as soon as you've secured the prince." Luca assessed her, head tilted to one side. He stood like that another long moment before raising his head. "Ah, here are your guides. Farewell, youngsters. May the Mother smile on you, the Daughter and Son walk with you, until we meet again."

Two unfamiliar Feelers appeared out of the darkness, their hands full. The first went straight to Luca, handing over a small pack, a waterskin, and a satchel. The second came to Ker. He unslung two small food satchels he'd had over his shoulder. Tel took up his larger pack and the one remaining sword, Ker and Wynn a satchel each.

Once Wynn had hefted her spear over her shoulder, the Feeler beckoned them to follow him into the tunnels, leading them away from the meeting cavern and the baths. He took them only a few dozen spans into the darkness, however, before he stopped.

"Head down this way," he said, gesturing at the more-or-less straight passage. "Sala will join you." He gave Ker a slight bow, turned on his heel, and left them.

"Great." Tel fumbled to pull out the glow stone before the Feeler's luminescent adornments faded completely from sight. "'Head down this way.' Wonderful." He held the stone higher, and peered into the darkness before turning back to

Ker, his mouth pressed tight and his brows drawn into a vee. "Can *you* find the way out?"

Ker gave him a hard look and didn't bother to answer.

Wynn shifted her pack and looked back in the direction they'd come. "What if Sala doesn't show?" She sounded as if she wouldn't exactly be sorry.

"I *could* get us out if I had to." Ker tried not to sound tired. "It would take longer, though. I might have to Flash every single tunnel and branching, to find the ones we wanted."

"Another thing, once we're out of here," Wynn asked, "will I be able to talk about the Feelers?"

"Can't talk about it." The voice wasn't Sala's. "Ganni says never talk about it."

Out of the darkness stepped the giant boy/man, Ennick. He squinted at the light, and Tel closed his hand over the glow stone.

"Ennick, why are you following us?" Ker's voice was gentle. She hoped he hadn't decided to come with them.

"Not following. Showing the way. Valley of Simcot Exit. Tunnel twenty-seven. Left at the fork. Third right, a left, a long march through tunnel one hundred and fourteen, a right, and a left. Past the wet rock. Careful along the ledge. Then the Valley of Simcot Exit." He smiled. "I brought my own food. Not following. Showing the way."

Kerida glanced at Tel, and he shrugged, nodding.

"Can we trust him?" Wynn said.

"Ennick doesn't get lost," he said proudly. "Not once, not ever."

"There's your answer," Ker said.

"Doesn't Sala know the way?"

"Not as well as Ennick does. Isn't that right?" The Far-thinker appeared at Ennick's elbow. She had a small pack of her own, with a cloak tucked in under the straps, a satchel that matched theirs, and another waterskin.

"I'm helping," Ennick said.

"That's right." Sala reached up to pat him on the shoulder. "No one knows the way as well as Ennick. Lead on, my boy. Lead on."

Ennick nodded, smiling, and they stood aside to let him walk in front. The tunnels here weren't wide enough for even Ker and Wynn to walk abreast, so Tel motioned to Wynn to take the lead position behind the two Feelers and took rearguard himself. They stopped once to sleep, after the "long march" and once to refill their waterskins when the tunnel opened into a chamber at the "wet rock" Ennick had spoken of. The chamber had a pool of crystal water, almost round, and as big as the span of Ker's arms. It must have been fed from a spring somewhere, though she couldn't see where it emptied. The water was cold enough to raise bumps on the skin, and numb the fingers.

"What about Weimerk? Will we see him?" Ker asked.

"Too big now," Ennick said, spreading his hands wide from where he crouched next to them as they finished closing the waterskins. "Can't come inside."

"He comes and he goes," Sala said. "Sometimes I can feel him." She tapped her forehead so Ker would know what she meant. "But not like I can feel Cuarel or the others."

"Ledge is next," Ennick said, as they all stood. "Now careful on the ledge. Hands free, everything else tied down. Be so very careful. I can't help you if you fall. Not like Ganni."

It took them well into the next day to reach the exit they'd been heading for. Once there, Ennick stopped well short of the opening, chewing on his thumb and shifting from foot to foot. Ker was as certain as if she'd Flashed it that he'd never been outside. He gave each of them a hug, and kissed them as if they all were brothers and sisters. Ker was happy to see that neither Wynn nor Tel held back.

This time the sun was shining as they stepped outside, and from the look of things it was late afternoon.

"Is it me"—Wynn was rubbing the outside of her arms—
"or are we a lot higher up than when we went in?"

Suddenly Ker was bowled over by a combination of sparkling feathers and damp fur.

"Oooof. Ah, Weimerk, there's a rock in my back."

The pressure immediately lifted and a single round eye examined her while two huge paws prodded at her. The griffin
focused first one eye and then the other on her face. "Are.
You. Well. Kerida? You. Do. Not. Smell. Like. Yourself."

Ker's ears burned hot. "Yeah, well, I've been cold and hungry and scared, and then scared and cold and hungry."

Weimerk tilted his head to one side and sat back on his
haunches. "Yes. That. Is. The. Approximate. Order."

"Um, Ker?" Wynn stood braced, holding the spear and
then, as if she realized what she was doing, grounding it. Sala
watched them all with a smile on her face.

Ker rolled upright. "Weimerk, you didn't say hello to Sala,
or to Tel Cursar and Wynn Martan."

"Ah. Human. Courtesies. I. Know. Of. Them. Of. Course.
Sala. We. Are. Well. Met. I. Felt. You. Coming. Tel. I. Have.
Seen. You. Already. Wynn. Martan. You. I. Am. Seeing. For.
The. First. Time. Kerida." The griffin turned back to her. "Are.
You. Staying. With. Me. Now. Or. Going?"

"Going, I'm afraid, Weimerk." Ker stood up and dusted
herself off. "We have to find a prince and bring him to safety."

"Of, Course. I. See. His. Thread. In. Your. Colors. You. Do.
Not. Have. The. Jewel."

Ker frowned. "Luca Pa'narion has one."

"Does. He?" Weimerk was smiling at her, though Ker
couldn't have said how she knew. "Interesting. I. Regret. I. Am.
Still. Not. Large. Enough. To. Fly. You. To. Your. Destination."

"You'd have to be big enough to fly all of us," Ker said.

Weimerk tilted his head the other way. "No. We. Are. Part.
Of. The. Prophecy. Kerida. Nast. You. And. I. And. Besides.

You. Awakened. Me. I. Cannot. Feel. About. Them. The. Way. I. Feel. About. You. It. Is. Impossible."

"Then it's a good thing you're not big enough."

"That. Is. A. Circular. Argument. But. I. Take. Your. Point. Shall. I. Accompany. Your. Group?"

"Well, thank you, but no." Ker tried to imagine how they could explain him away. "We're trying not to draw attention to ourselves."

The griffin nodded. "Will. You. Be. Going. Now?"

Ker picked up her pack. "That's right."

"I. Will. Welcome. You. Upon. Your. Return."

Ker glanced at her friends. Wynn's eyes were round as saucers, and she had her upper lip in her teeth. Tel just shrugged.

"We may not be coming back here," she told the griffin.

"Really? You. Imagined. There. Was. Some. Other. Way?"

Cuarel: I can't believe it's Mothering snowing again. What's with you?

Sala: Nothing here. Sky full of stars.

Dersay: I wish I could see a sky full of stars.

Cuarel: You had your chance. You could have traded places with either of us.

Sala: Not with me. I've got seniority.

Cuarel: Yes, we all know how much more experience you have with the outside than we do.

Dersay: Speak for yourself.

Sala grinned, safe in the knowledge that the Talent was asleep, the tall boy was on watch, and the little red-haired girl was turned the other way.

Dersay: I know you're smiling, I can feel it. Like an itch.

Sala: Can you feel me rolling my eyes?

Cuarel: You wouldn't have been able to travel with anyone but Luca, Dersay, and you know it. Right now I'd be

happy to make the switch. *Griffins,* **but I'm already stiff and sore. Luca says we'll be another three days at least.**
Sala: We could be at the prince before that.
Cuarel: If I'd known what was coming when you talked me into this, Sala, I'd have stayed away from that Mothering meeting. How are you holding up?
Sala: I've been in worse places. They've all had military training, at least, even the Talent, though hers is a while back. I don't have to teach them how to keep a good pace, or how to stay quiet in the woods, which is more to the point just now. And they don't expect me to wait on them hand and foot.

That's what she'd been doing when the Talent High Inquisitor had found her. Guiding official visitors through the newly sealed province of Ma'lakai while she recovered from a bad cut to her sword arm. She'd never had to learn whether the army would have taken her back, not once Luca had found her. Dersay wasn't completely right when she implied that Sala would rather be out than in. Belonging somewhere was a good thing.

Dersay: You're happier outside, Sala, even if you won't admit it. We can feel it in your thoughts, both of us.
Sala: Are you going to sleep anytime soon? Because I'd like to get some before my watch starts if it's all right with you two.
Cuarel: Fine, fine. Check in at sunrise.
Dersay: Wake me.

Sala resisted the urge to roll over. She wasn't going to find a more comfortable spot. At least those two chatterboxes had finally stopped talking to her.

Another two days walking had brought them to what the Griffin Girl said was the land of the man they were looking for.

"It's all so normal." The little redhead's voice was flat with more than simple exhaustion. "How is it possible that people are just going about their everyday lives with the Luqs dead and the Halians in the Polity?"

Sala looked at the others, but no one seemed about to respond. They'd twice seen the dead hanging at crossroads, and once a burned-out villa, but few other signs that an invasion had taken place. There'd been worse in Ma'lakai when the Wings first came in her grandfather's day. Or so she'd heard.

The Griffin Girl rubbed her face, and Sala grimaced. They certainly hadn't seen any Halls.

"Can you make out a name?" Tel Cursar was saying to the girl now.

"I'm trying to stay focused on the person we're looking for; that's hard enough." The girl was frowning as she said it.

"I'm impressed you can even find the place, never mind getting the land to tell you the name of the owner," the red-haired girl said. She smiled a sudden smile. "If it's this hard for you, won't it be even harder for Jak Gulder?"

A bark of laughter from Tel Cursar. "Let's hope so."

Sala held up her hand for silence.

"Sala?" The Griffin Girl was more comfortable with her than the other two, though Mother knew that, as a Talent, she should have been the most against them. "Sala, what is it?"

"I've lost Cuarel." All three youngsters froze, looking at her, and then at each other. Tel's hand went to where his sword should have been, if it weren't packed away with everything but their belt knives.

Dersay: What do you mean? She's right here.

Sala: I can't hear her.

Dersay: Wait. No, she says she can't hear you either.

Sala: Griffin dung! I guess we're not very "far" thinkers after all.

Dersay: Cuarel says could this mean there are more of us than we think, but they're too far away for us to hear them?

Sala could feel herself grinning. They'd have to send en-
voys to the other Clans, first chance they got. Just because
they hadn't heard anyone, didn't mean there was no one to
hear. In the meantime . . .

**Sala: We'll have to double our contacts. Dersay, you'll
have to relay.**

"It's all right," she said aloud, explaining in a few words
what had happened.

"Interesting," the Talent said. "So you didn't know that
your range had limits?" Her eyes narrowed, and Sala suddenly felt as if the girl could see through her.

"It *is* interesting." Tel Cursar gestured at the road. "But can
we talk about it as we go?"

"Nothing to talk about," Sala said as she set off in the lead,
Ker walking next to her.

A turn of the road brought them into view of a large villa. It
had the typical look of the central part of the Peninsula, owing
more to the architecture of Sala's homeland than anyone in the
Polity wanted to admit. A large, white, squared building with an
interior courtyard, and long narrow windows, the design intended to help with both the summer heat and the cooler winter
weather. The usual outbuildings gathered around the main one,
like chicks around a hen, likely stabling and storage for the
grapes and wine-making tools. There was no enclosing wall, but
then, it had been so long since war had come here, there probably wasn't a walled Holding in the whole of the Peninsula.

There was one odd feature to this place, however.

"I've never seen a tower like that on a private home." Sala
pointed ahead with her chin.

"Looks military, doesn't it?" Tel said. "A watchtower."

"There's someone in the upper window." The Griffin Girl
pointed.

Sala focused until she could see a shadow that seemed to
move behind the bars of the topmost window. A sudden men-
tal itch made her draw in her breath.

"Sala?"

"Nothing. It's—" She shook herself. "For a moment there I thought I could feel him, or as if he could feel me. But that's impossible."

"Why's that?" the little redhead said.

"No male Far-thinkers, that's why." Sala looked at the Griffin Girl. "Once or twice I thought I was getting something from you, but I put it down to the influence of the griffin."

"To Weimerk?"

"It's certain he woke something in you. And even if it wasn't obvious to anyone who looked, he keeps talking about it."

"But you're not getting anything from the boy in the window now?"

"No, I must have imagined it."

"Maybe." The girl kept looking ahead. "But then how did you know he's a boy?"

Jerek could see them only because the room at the top of the east tower was higher than the trees planted to shade the lower part of the house. He wasn't a prisoner, exactly. He ate his meals with his father in front of the people of the household, even though it must have been clear to them that he was being punished for running away. There were still a few familiar faces left among them, people who might have asked too many questions if they didn't see him every day.

The room at the top of the tower had originally been a study for his great-grandfather's wife. She'd been a military officer, though Jerek had found out that she hadn't been a Faro, as family legend had it, but a Wing Laxtor. Not that there was anything wrong with being second-in-command, at least, not in Jerek's mind. She'd spent most of her life in one military camp or another, so her husband had built her this square lookout tower to help her feel comfortable when she came home on leave.

The room was comfortable enough, now that a bed had been moved into it. Warm enough, since the chimney of the main fireplace went up the inner wall. You had to pass his own rooms, and his father's rooms, to reach it. The door could be bolted from the outside.

But it wasn't exactly a prison cell.

Four people were coming along the road down by the old olive tree. Jerek shifted until he sat where the bars curved out at the bottom of the window, forming a sturdy, if cold, window seat. The plant boxes that normally rested here in the summer months were down in the cellars.

That's all I need. More strangers.

He glanced down through the bars. He could see Trien Petain—he refused to think of the man as the Factor—walking from the barns to the door that led to Nessa's workroom. He cleared his throat and tossed his hair back out of his eyes. He wondered who *these* strangers would turn out to be.

As they got closer, he could see that one was quite tall, two shorter—almost the same height—and one very short indeed. For some reason the group made him think of an old children's story, a papa bear, a mama bear, and the two baby bears who got lost in the woods. Jerek relaxed. One wore the long tunic and cloak of a minor noble, and the others were dressed like upper staff, and all walked like they'd been on foot for a long time. Certainly not with the upright, striding posture of the Wing soldiers he'd seen in the last few weeks. There! One of them stumbled, and Jerek relaxed even further. He glanced over his shoulder. Was that a footstep on the stairs?

As if they'd seen him leaning in the window, the tall one raised his hand and waved. Jerek hesitated only a moment before waving back. The four of them stood a little straighter now, and walked toward the buildings a little faster.

Jerek squirmed out of the window, wondering whether his father would let him out to eat with the visitors.

Ker had seen activity as they walked up the road, but the space between the main house and the out buildings was empty now, as was the tower window. There were paving stones in front of the house, but the rest of the yard was nothing more than firmly packed dirt. Close to, the house was larger and more prosperous than it had looked from the rise. Along with glass in the windows, there were stone cornices under the eaves of the green-tiled roof, and metal-worked griffin heads on the ends of the water spouts.

One of the doors to the main house swung open as they approached it. A thickset, middle-aged man in suede trousers and a quilted vest over a plain cotton shirt came down the steps toward them.

"Morning," Ker said. "Good wishes to the land, good thoughts to the house." The man's eyes were unexpectedly dark, considering how fair he was. His smile didn't quite reach them.

"And to you," he replied, with the accent of the far west. "You've come to Firoxi Holding. I'm Trien Petain, the Factor. May I ask your business with us?"

"My name's Kerida Nast. And these are Tel Cursar, Wynn Martan, and Sala of Dez. We're on our way to my home, Nast Holding, in the Estremal. We'd appreciate shelter for the night. Or should we be asking your lord?"

The man's smile vanished and came back so quickly Ker almost missed the change. "Dern Firoxi would want me to welcome you. The holding is renowned for its hospitality."

"No offense meant," Ker said. "It's just, in these times . . ."

"None taken. Here's my lord Firoxi now."

This was it, the man himself. Ker looked for any sign of the Luqs' features in the man's face. He had the royal family's olive skin, sharp features, and slightly wavy dark hair, but then, she was olive-skinned and dark-haired herself, if it came to that. She'd even bet her nose was a little sharper than Firoxi's.

Was the boy in the upper window the prince's son? That would be good news, wouldn't it?

"My lord, this is Kerida Nast, and her party, Tel Cursar, Wynn Martan, and Sala of Dez."

"Looking for me?" The twinkle in his eye made his words a welcome.

"In a manner of speaking we are, Lord Firoxi." Ker cleared her throat as the man's smile broadened. "We've never met, but I've certainly seen your name on the lists of landowners. My family's holding is to the west, close to Meryta. You may have heard of our pigs." She glanced down at her clothes and shrugged. "I'm afraid my appearance doesn't recommend me, but the military took over my college, and I've been trying to get home." *Paraste*, she said to herself.

Some of the sunshine left the man's face even as he gestured a welcome and ushered them into the house through the main door. "The military, you say? If I could—that is, do you know which Wing?"

"I know I *should*." Ker pushed her hair back from her face. She didn't have to pretend to be exhausted. As rehearsed, Wynn slid her satchel to the stone floor of the entrance hall. "The main branch of my family is military." When planning, they'd thought they'd better stick as closely to the truth as they could. Firoxi would no doubt have the same family lists to check. "But my mother wanted me trained like herself, in the medical arts." She took a step forward, tripped on the satchel, and grabbed Dern Firoxi's forearm to steady herself—

And Flashed immediately, despite all those generations between him and King Rolian, that this was the man they were looking for.

"Here now, are you all right?" Dern Firoxi gripped her forearm and elbow, holding her upright.

"Yes, thank you."

Sala had rushed forward and had her by the other arm, while Wynn, with apologies, pulled the satchel into the clear.

"Yes," Ker said again, nodding at the Far-thinker, and getting the minutest of nods in return. "Sorry to be so clumsy."

"My own fault. I could tell by looking at you that you were tired, but I'm afraid I let my curiosity get the better of me. Here, Trien, show our guests to the baths and get them sorted into rooms."

Dern Firoxi's dining hall, while not huge, was obviously set up to accommodate the entire holding. By the time they'd had a chance to wash, most of the tables were full. The young boy they'd seen in the window was standing next to the prince.

"My son, Jerek," the prince said, gesturing for her to join them at the circular main table, placed in the center of the room in the old-fashioned way. The family and their guests would face each other as they ate, rather than sitting against a wall and looking out into the rest of the room.

There were places at a nearby table, but Dern Firoxi made it plain that he meant Tel, Wynn, and Sala to sit at the family table as well. "I hope you don't mind," he said to Tel, smiling. "But my son is hoping to question you about guard work. I think he wants to give up viniculture and go into the military."

The boy's eyes flicked to his father, to Tel, and back again. He smiled, but a muscle in his jaw moved, and Ker could swear he'd just gritted his teeth. He was old enough to be annoyed at what was clearly an attempt by his father to force him into socializing, but could there be something more serious going on? Ker resisted the urge to Flash. There'd be plenty of time to satisfy her curiosity when they were on the road back to the Mines and Tunnels.

Ker waited until the first course of a thick vegetable stew was being served and spoke to the prince under cover of his helping her to a serving. "Lord Firoxi."

"Dern, please." He finished ladling out his own serving and passed the tureen to Tel. "As you can see we're a bit informal here. My wife's doing, and I've kept it up since her death. I hope you're not made uncomfortable by it."

Ker wondered what he'd do if she said yes. "Not at all. We do much the same ourselves." That was because the only rank her family recognized was military rank, but she thought she'd keep that to herself. "I do have something I'd like to discuss with you privately, however."

Dern glanced at her, the quiver in his left eyebrow and the seriousness in his eyes the only signs that he found anything significant in her request. "Of course."

The rest of the meal passed in the discussion of everyday things. The boy, Jerek, didn't seem at all eager to ask Tel about being a guard. Tel tried to interest him with anecdotes about swordplay, but got quiet answers, the boy looking at his father frequently from under his brows. Finally, Tel got Wynn to tell stories about her numerous talented aunties, and the boy began to relax.

"You seemed a bit uncomfortable when I mentioned soldiers earlier," Ker said.

Dern kept his expression very bland, and leaned a little closer to her. "Since the . . ." The man hesitated long enough that Ker began to wonder if he was ever going to speak. Just as she was about to turn the subject, he continued. "Since what happened to the royals, you must be aware there's been quite a bit of unrest . . . chaos, you might almost say. The military seemed very unsettled, at least at first. And there were even rumors of them fighting among themselves—something, it appears, the Halians put an end to. You said your college has been closed, but you may not know that for the most part the Halians have left our social structures intact. Including the military where those have cooperated."

Here he paused and looked at her, his eyes level and steady, as if to ask her if she knew what he meant. She thought "surrender" might be a truer word than "cooperate," but she nodded. "For the most part," she agreed.

"Has there been any further news of the royal family?" Tel asked.

Dern frowned. "Are any of you students of history, or philosophy?"

They exchanged glances. Sala moved her head ever so slightly to the left and back again. It wouldn't have been noticeable to anyone who hadn't been sharing a camp with her for that last few days.

"Not really," Ker said, shrugging one shoulder. "Just what we learned in school, I expect. Jurianol the first Luqs, the expansion of the Polity beyond the Faraman Peninsula, that kind of thing."

"I used to be able to recite the whole line of Luqs, but I doubt I could do it now." Wynn smiled at the boy when she said this, and the smile he gave back to her was genuine. Much more so than the polite one from his father.

"Then you might not realize that the Halians could very well have been studying our own tactics and strategies."

Tel put down his knife very carefully. "How so?"

"Think about it. They've made hard strikes against the leaders: the Luqs and her family, the military, and the Halls. But the ordinary people, civil administrators, farmers and so on, they've left alone. And now, for all intents and purposes, day-to-day life for the common person is returning to normal. Trade continues, travel is barely restricted. A different person gives orders, perhaps—"

"Or a not so different person," Ker put in, thinking of Jak Gulder.

"Exactly. If there has been cooperation, many people have been confirmed in their positions. As a student of our own history, I can assure you that this is very much what the Polity has done. Smash the organized opposition, leave the citizens alone."

Ker thought she could see what Dern was getting at, and it didn't make her feel any better. After all, until the coming of the Halians, the Faraman Polity had been unstoppable.

"Take the matter of the royal family, for example. The succession isn't always a question of the next by blood—look at Gendriol, for example. She was only third in line but took her cousin's place when a better military ruler was needed back at the time of the second crisis with the then Ma'lakan Empire." Dern nodded at Sala. "Since then, the military have always formally accepted the proposed Ruler."

"But it's just a formality, isn't it? A ceremonial acclamation." Wynn looked from Ker to Dern Firoxi and back again.

"Oh, I assure you it's more than that," Dern went on. "Acclamation by the Wings is a necessary component of the Luqs' coronation. In default of a living heir, they might well feel that one of their own number should act as a second Jurianol and take the throne. Or, conversely, they could judge that cooperation with a group which intends to leave our society virtually intact is preferable to fighting it out among themselves. After all, by the time they got the succession settled, there might be nothing left to succeed to. No, it's possible we may never be rid of the Halians."

Ker frowned, as if she was considering these ideas for the first time. On the inside, she was smiling. All things considered, it was a lucky thing Dern Firoxi understood the problem so clearly. He'd said nothing about the Halls, though, and she was afraid to bring it up herself. For all she knew, it was something that no one spoke of.

The conversation passed to the differences inherent in growing olives for oil and grapes for wine until Dern finally called for the steward to make the oblation to the Mother, Son, and Daughter that signaled the end of the meal. The staff and servants wandered off, calling out good nights.

When the hall was almost empty, Dern gathered them up with a glance around the table as he stood. "We'll retire to my own sitting room," he said. "No reason to keep the servants up."

He led them through a heavy door into the interior patio of the house. There was a raised pool in the center, surrounded by stone benches carved to look like griffins alternating with lions. Dern cut across the space, leading them through a door identical with the one to the hall, but which opened directly onto a wide staircase that could only be in that square tower, Ker realized, on the east side of the house. The stairs led up to a broad landing, where yet another wooden door stood open to reveal a sitting room.

"Come, Jerek." Dern indicated the stairs leading upward with a nod. "It's an early day for you tomorrow."

The boy seemed inclined to linger, but he pulled himself up straight. "Of course, Father." He inclined his head to Ker. "Lady Nast, a pleasure to meet you." Ker found herself automatically bowing back. Jerek nodded at each of the others before turning and taking the stairs, his back straight, his hands in fists.

Ker blinked as, after a moment, Dern followed his son up the stairs. True, the boy hadn't said good night to his father, but was that enough to make the man chase after him? Obviously, they'd shown up in the middle of some kind of domestic entanglement, some disagreement between father and son that neither wanted to play out in front of strangers. They didn't have time for this, and she was thankful when Dern returned quickly, ushering them into his own apartments.

His private sitting room was spacious, but oddly empty of furniture for the owner of a holding as large as Firoxi's. The walls had been painted some time before with the scene of a vineyard in full growth, the mural spreading over even the window shutters so that the image was uninterrupted when the shutters were closed, as they were now. Even faded, the work was richly detailed and full of color.

Dern waved Ker onto the padded bench nearest what was

obviously his own chair before he sat down. Tel and Wynn took the other bench, and Sala stationed herself against the wall by the door. Dern watched them with a slight smile on his lips, waiting until they were sorted before turning to Ker. "Now, what is it we need to discuss?"

Ker dried her hands on her trousers.

"You mentioned the royals earlier," she began. "In a way, that's why we're here." She paused, but Firoxi only raised his eyebrows and waited for her to continue. "We haven't told you the complete truth. I am who I said I am, but we haven't come from any medical school. We're sent to you by the Faro of Bears."

"Sent to *me*?"

"We, that is the Faro, discovered that there *is* still a member of the royal family living, and as you pointed out yourself, the Wings would quickly rally around this person, and the resistance to the Halians would have a leader. We"—she nodded at her companions—"have been sent to find him, and bring him back to Oste Camp."

At first, there was no reaction. Not even the expression on Dern's face changed.

"You've been sent to find him." He leaned forward, as if he was about to come to his feet. "To *me*?"

Ker nodded. *Good. He's quick.* Not every royal was, the Mother knew.

The prince stood, and Tel tensed, but Dern only went to the sideboard, where he pulled the stopper from a glass decanter, releasing the smell of apple brandy into the room. He splashed two fingers of the amber liquid into a nearby glass and downed it in a single swallow before turning to face them.

"I assure you I'm telling the truth," Ker said. "Your father was the late Luqs' uncle. You are the heir. I'm sorry I don't have any other proof, but this is what we were told." There was no way Ker was going to tell the man what her real proof was.

Dern raised his hand, palm toward her. He coughed, cleared his throat, and tried again. "I believe you. Once, when I was a child, I overheard my parents quarreling. When I asked them, they told me I'd misheard, told me to forget about it, and I pretended I had. But frankly, what you've just said bears out what I heard." He took a deep breath, glanced at the sideboard again. Wynn stood, took his glass, and topped it up with the brandy. He thanked her with a smile that had the corners of his lips trembling. He took another mouthful, walked back to his chair, and set the glass down on the marble-topped table.

"I'm sorry," he said, looking down at his glass. "It's not every day you learn you have family you never knew about, and at the same time that all of them are gone." He took a deep breath, and Ker was relieved to see a kind of strength come over his face as his posture straightened.

"Please." Taking Ker's hand, he gestured the others closer to him, reaching out his hand to Sala, waiting until she was standing in the circle with the rest. "I want to thank you. For bringing me this news. For putting yourselves to such risk to do so. You will be rewarded, I assure you." He smiled around at them. "And now? What is the plan?"

Ker glanced at Tel. Behind him, Sala watched them, her mouth a thin line. "Can you be ready to ride by the morning?" she asked. "We've reason to think the Halians may come here looking for you, and we'd like to get you away."

"But, my dear, where can we go?" He didn't ask like someone who was afraid, but just like someone asking.

"To Oste," Tel put in before she could. "The loyal part of the Eagles went there, and the Bears are there as well. Signals have been sent, and other Wings are on their way. You are needed to lead them."

The small sound at the door was so gentle that even Sala only turned her head. Ker half expected to see a servant bringing kaff.

The figure in the doorway wasn't dressed like a servant. Ker tried to pull her hand out of Dern's, but he held it fast. Tel whirled around and put his hand to his belt, but his short sword was with his pack, in the rooms they'd been given. Guests don't sit down to supper armed.

Jakmor Gulder stepped, smiling, into the circle of light.

"Thank you, my lord, that was very well done."

WHEN they first left the mines, it had made Cuarel the Far-thinker smile to see her breath fog in the cold air, but the novelty had soon worn off. Now she only hoped the sound of their breathing wasn't going to give them away.

"Not yet." Luca Pa'narion's voice in her ear was nothing more than a thread of sound, as his hands tightened on her shoulders. If she were honest, Cuarel was glad of the respite forced on them by the Halian patrols. Even the skin of her face felt exhausted. And her feet might never be warm again.

"Now."

Obedient to the hand propelling her, Cuarel followed the Inquisitor from their hiding place in the shadow of a fallen tree, into the open field between the edge of the forest and the walls of Oste Camp. At least there wasn't any snow left on upper branches to fall and give them away.

The skin on her back crawled, and her shoulders crept up. She had to trust that Luca's Flashing continued accurate. They'd been dodging patrols ever since they'd come close enough to Oste to see its wall across the surrounding field of snow, broken and darkened here and there by footprints.

"Down!" Cuarel managed to obey more by tripping than from deliberate intent. She tried to breathe shallowly, noise-lessly, and stopped breathing altogether when suddenly the tramp of feet and the murmur of voices seemed only steps away.

"I tell you it's Messon took my good knife, I know he did."

"Don't tell me, tell the Barrack Leader." From the tone of voice this wasn't the first time the unseen man had com-plained.

Please, please, please. Mother please let them pass by, please, I'll never miss service again, I swear it. Cuarel squeezed her eyes tight.

Dersay: Cuarel? You all right?
Cuarel: Not now!

The soldiers' voices drifted off into the night, and Cuarel shivered.

"Wait. Not yet. Wait. Now, quickly."

Luca ran, and Cuarel stumbled after him, knees and ankles throbbing even after so short a rest. Every breath threatened to be the last her lungs could manage. Only the Inquisitor's fist in her sleeve kept her moving. Half blinded by exhaustion, she saw the wall barely in time to brace for impact.

"Don't move. Stay where you are."

Two breaths later Cuarel realized it hadn't been Luca speaking, but the guard at the top of the wall.

"Tell Faro Juria Sweetwater that Talent High Inquisitor Luca Pa'narion wishes to speak with her."

"Now, that's one nobody's tried yet," the voice from above said. "Don't suppose you have any proof?"

Luca released a breath, and Cuarel realized for the first time that the Inquisitor was just as exhausted as she was. "What if they don't let us in?" she asked.

"Patience, my dear." Luca patted her arm, and pitched his

voice upward. "If you would put both hands on the wall, young woman, I think I can accommodate you." There was a pause, and Luca placed his own palms on the mortared stone. "Not to worry, your partner can always kill us if he has to. Ah, thank you."

Though she strained her ears, Cuarel heard nothing.

"You are Farran Adriak, Second Officer, Green Company, Ruby Cohort of Bears. You have a healing arrow wound in your left thigh, and your last monthlies was three days ago."

"Hey, Farran? I think this guy's a Talent."

"Yeah, yeah. Come around to the gate, Inquisitor. Welcome to Oste."

They all had their knives out before Jak Gulder finished speaking, Sala pulling a second one she'd hidden only the Mother knew where. Belt knives were all they had, however, and Jak was no fool. He'd stepped to one side as soon as he cleared the doorway, allowing a soldier with a crossbow to stand in the opening, his weapon carefully aimed.

Tel shifted onto the balls of his feet, freezing when he saw the corridor outside filled with armed men.

Jak Gulder bowed. "Kerida, my dear, you look tired. Now, wouldn't it have been easier if you'd just come with me in the mountains? You'd have been able to travel in more comfort. You must have known we'd be coming straight here."

Ker curled her lip. "There was always the chance we'd get here before you." Ker hoped no one else heard the tremor in her voice. "If it comes to that, how *did* you find the place without me?"

"Ah, well, fortunately I have friends to help me." He swung his empty left hand at the soldiers behind him. "When you have men at your command, and a general area to search, it takes little time to find a landowner of the right age. But it appears you have new friends also." He smiled at Sala.

Ker kept sneering. Jak didn't know Sala was a Feeler. It was too late for Ker herself, but with luck they could hide what Sala was. The dark woman was standing well back, Wynn at her elbow, watching them with her eyes narrowed to slits.

But Sala *wasn't* watching them, Ker saw, she was Farthinking, letting the others know what had happened. For a moment Ker's heart lifted—then she realized that help couldn't possibly reach them in time to do any good, not even if a rescue party left the Mines and Tunnels immediately.

"I trust you'll deal gently with these young people, Gulder." Dern Firoxi hadn't moved from his chair. "I don't know why we waited. We might have avoided this entire business."

"With respect, sir, I needed the Nast girl's confirmation. She's the one who could identify you for certain."

"In what way?" Dern's eyes narrowed, and his nostrils flared.

Maybe it wouldn't be the ax. Maybe she could convince Jak to kill her himself. Ker felt horribly as if she was going to be sick.

Jak watched them, his eyes going from her to Tel, resting another moment on Sala and Wynn before returning to her. The flatness in his eyes was almost the worst thing about him.

Then he smiled.

"I'm afraid I don't know myself, my lord," he said, showing his teeth. "There are very few people privy to that knowledge."

"Can we not order her to tell?" Dern frowned. "Force her if need be?"

So much for dealing gently with us.

"I'm afraid that runs contrary to *my* orders, my lord."

Ker's heart skipped a beat. What orders? And from whom?

"It's late, sir," Jak was saying. "We must travel in the morning. You know your house and buildings best. Where can we safely store these people until we're ready to move them?"

Dern had pressed his lips together, as though he'd like to insist on the answers he wanted. At last his quiet smile appeared again. "The most secure place is just above us, though we will have to move my boy back to his own room for the night."

"Then if there's nothing else, my lord, we'll put these people away and let you get some rest."

In such close quarters, with armed men waiting on the landing, there was no chance to resist. Ker let one of the soldiers take her knife away, grimacing as another lifted his hand to strike Wynn when she didn't move fast enough.

"None of that, Hessik." Jak looked around the room. "Remember, all of you, that the Shekayrin wants these people, so we had best treat them with care."

And that answers one of my questions, Ker thought. And in the worst possible way.

Dern Firoxi led the way up the stairs, with Jak Gulder at his elbow. The four of them were kept separate as they climbed, each with their own guard. Ker's held her above the elbow in a painful grip that soon had her fingers growing numb.

When they reached the landing outside yet another thick wooden door banded with metal, Dern took a key the size of his hand out of an inner pocket and slotted it into the lock, turning it twice and pushing the door open. *That's* why he'd followed his son upstairs. Ker's hands tightened into fists. Not to say good night, but to lock the boy in.

The opening revealed a large single room with windows in every wall except the one with the door. Tel flicked his eyes toward the east window and looked back at her. She gave him the shadow of a nod. That would have been where the boy, Jerek, was looking out when they were coming up the lane. How long had the kid been locked up?

Even though he'd fallen into the habit of staying up and dressed until he was sure his father had gone to bed, Jerek hadn't expected the man at his door tonight. On the one hand, he'd been drinking, but on the other, there were guests, and that usually put his father on his best behavior. But here he was, and the guests as well, along with the man who'd come with a Barrack of soldiers a few days before, though Jerek hadn't seen him since. Only when they were in the room did he see the guests were in custody. He took a step back, but his calves were already against the hearthstone of the fireplace.

"Come, Jerek," his father said. "This room is needed for the prisoners."

"Prisoners?" These had been honored guests just an hour ago, given rooms of their own, fed at the family table. Jerek's mouth was suddenly dry. It was happening again.

"Come, don't dawdle."

Jerek looked from his father to the faces of the men behind him. To the smile of the well-dressed man who was obviously in charge of the soldiers. Halian soldiers. He looked particularly at Wynn Martan, who'd been so nice to him at supper, and the dark-haired Kerida Nast, who looked so much like his mother.

Maybe he hadn't admitted it, even to himself, but Jerek knew that things had been steadily worsening since his mother's death. Dern hadn't been a bad man, exactly, but his anger, always there, was closer to the surface now. Since the Halians had come, Jerek had seen an even darker side in his father. Dern hadn't come to fetch him from old Goreot because he loved him and wanted him home. Dern had only come because he needed Jerek, at least until he successfully petitioned to have the Brightwing Holding transferred to his own name.

These people, these "prisoners," they were just more tools his father was willing to use to gain some advantage he hadn't bothered to tell Jerek about. Then he'd throw them away. Just like he'd throw Jerek away. What difference whether it was now, or sometime in the future?

Jerek released the breath he hadn't known he was holding,

and edged behind the central table. "No," he said. "I'm not going."

"Don't be ridiculous. Get over here now. These are dangerous people wanted by the military."

"I don't care what they've done. I care about what *you've* done. I won't be a part of it. Not anymore. I'm staying right here." He swallowed. "I'd rather stay with them than go with you."

"Shall I have my men bring him, my lord?"

His father hesitated, and Jerek tensed, gripping the edge of the table. He'd resist, he told himself. He'd resist.

The officer turned to Jerek and smiled a little sadly, as if he'd read his thoughts. "Come now, young sir. You don't know what you're refusing. Your father is prince of the Faraman Polity, and we're here to escort you both to Farama the Capital. If something should happen to your father, which the Son forbid, you'd be able to carry on the royal line."

Jerek saw his father stiffen out of the corner of his eye. So, apparently, did the officer.

"My lord?" he said, turning toward the other man.

"I had not thought . . ." Dern's brow was furrowed, and Jerek steeled himself as his father straightened his shoulders and took a deep breath. "I would not mislead you, Lord Gulder," he finally said. "You have come to me as the nearest blood to the royal family, and if it is blood that is important, then I must tell you that this child has none of mine."

Jerek heard a great roaring in his ears, and his hands no longer felt the table. He opened his mouth to protest, and tears actually sprang to his eyes. How could his father—*why* would he say such a thing? Then he shut his mouth again. Well, what did it matter? He'd known this day was coming, he just hadn't expected to be discarded as soon as this.

"You haven't mentioned this before, my lord." Though Gulder's voice was mild, his smile was gone.

"It was of no consequence when he was just to inherit his

mother's land," Dern said. "But we're not speaking of a vineyard now. This is a matter of the Polity . . ."

"Of course. If you're quite sure you don't want him with
us?" Gulder looked at Jerek, and the boy realized that the man
was leaving it up to him. That they would take him if he
wanted to go, that this man, at least, was also shocked by
Dern Firoxi's willingness to leave Jerek behind, and was letting Jerek decide what to do about it. "Lord Firoxi?" he said
and, again, it was clear that he was talking to Jerek.

Jerek swallowed, the buzzing still in his ears. "It's Brightwing," he said. "Jerek Brightwing is my legal name, and this
is Brightwing Holding. I won't go with him."

"But you understand I cannot leave you with these people?"

"Very well." Jerek licked his lips. "You will be gone in the
morning?"

"As early as possible, my lord." The man caught Dern
Firoxi's eye and motioned toward the door, waiting until the
older man was on his way before turning back to bow again
to Jerek. "If you would?"

As the boy passed close to her, Ker reached out and touched
him on the shoulder. "Good luck, Lord Brightwing."

He stopped to look at her. "And to you," he said, before
walking out of the room.

With the door still open after the exit of the young lord, Jak
Gulder pointed at Tel Cursar. "Bring him."

Tel threw himself to one side, but he had no chance against
the men who leaped forward to obey Jak Gulder's orders.

"Give it up, Cursar. I have no intention of leaving you here
with these women."

As they dragged him from the room, Tel looked back over
the shoulders of the men who held him, and found Kerida
with his eyes. She pressed her lips together and nodded. The
door slammed shut, followed by the sound of the lock.

Ker ran forward and placed her palms flat against the wood. "They're taking him all the way down, out of the tower." She struck the door with her fist, struggling to control her face.

"And Dern seemed like such a nice man when we got here," Wynn said from behind her. Ker took a deep breath and turned to face her friends. Sala sat on the edge of the table, one leg swinging, her arms folded. Wynn shrugged one shoulder. "We'll get him back," she said.

Ker nodded, grateful for the words, though she didn't believe them herself. Taking a deep breath, she looked around the room. There was a bed, still neatly made, but clearly the room was normally part office, part storage room. A worktable sat near the south window, with a few books, a set of writing implements, and an oil lamp. Several rugs had been taken from a pile against the inner wall, and laid across the tiled floor. The window, larger than it had looked from down below, was barred.

"What a way to find out your dad's not your dad." Sala shook her head in disgust. "Did you see the boy's face? He had no idea."

Ker licked her lips. *Refocus*. Regardless of how she might feel, Tel was not their priority at the moment. "That's because it's not true."

Wynn stared with wide eyes. "You touched him, just at the end there, you touched him."

"You're sure?" Sala tilted her head to one side.

"It's a simple question," Ker said. "And I'm better at Flashing people since the griffin." But she wouldn't tell them what she'd seen in the boy's aura. Seven colors, more than Talents *or* Feelers—six was the most she'd seen in anyone except Weimerk himself. *Keep your mouth shut*, she told herself. One problem at a time. "Anyway, he's definitely Dern's son."

"So maybe—" Wynn sounded hopeful. "Maybe the dad's being forced, and he knows he can't save himself, but he wants his boy to be safe from the . . . from *them*."

Ker and Sala exchanged looks. "Sure, maybe," the older woman said.

"Because don't you see?" Wynn held up a finger, frowned at it, and lowered it again. "This changes everything."

Ker nodded, answering the other girl's grin with one of her own. "We don't need Dern Firoxi," she said. "Not if we have Jerek Brightwing. We get him to the Wings, they acclaim him as Luqs, and the fight against the Halians can begin."

Ker looked at Sala, and the Far-thinker winked at her and nodded. Clearly, the news had been passed along to the Mines and Tunnels, and from there it would reach the Faro of Bears. "All we have to do now is get out of this room, persuade the boy to come with us, find Tel, and get back to the Serpents Teeth," she said.

"Is that all?"

"Sit down. Make yourself comfortable."

"*That's* likely." Tel glanced around. From the quality of the furniture, this was a much nicer guest room than they'd been given.

Jak finished lighting the lamp and turned, smiling. "Let's find out, shall we?" A flaw in the wick made the flame flicker, sending shadows dancing across his face. Jak turned his smile to the guard at Tel's elbow. "That's fine, Pella, thank you."

The thickset man lifted bristling eyebrows. Though he seemed slow, Tel had met lots like him, and wasn't fooled. "You sure, sir? He's on the big side."

"I'm sure." Jak nodded, still smiling. "You think Cursar's going to knock me on the head and go out the window?" He tilted his head to one side and peered at Tel through his lashes. "*That's* not very likely, though I suppose it's possible. If it makes you feel better . . ." Jak circled the centrally placed table to reach a settee against the window wall of the room. He rummaged through several packs and saddlebags, and finally pulled a sword out of a hard leather sheath. It was an officer's weapon, longer than the regular soldier's blade.

"Put him there," Jak said, indicating with the point of his sword a low stool close to the fireplace. "With his long legs, it will cost him considerable effort to stand up from there, giving me ample chance to stick him with this."

The guard's grin widened. "You know your business best, sir. Still, we won't be far." He hauled Tel's arm up a little more, sheer bulk and strength making up for the leverage he lost due to Tel's height, and moved him into position near the stool. Off balance, and unable to twist out of the way, Tel had no choice but to sit down. The stool would have been a good height for Kerida to sit comfortably, which meant that Tel's knees reached somewhere around his armpits. It was true, by the time he could lever himself to his feet, Jak would have plenty of time to kill him.

The guard executed a crisp and proper salute, gave Tel a surprisingly friendly grin, and left the room.

"I'm happy to have this chance to speak to you again, away from your friend Kerida Nast."

"You're not going to call her a witch this time?"

Jak leaned back against the edge of the table, tapping his foot with the sword. "I'll tell you something. It doesn't matter what I call her. We have the prince of the blood. Such as he is." Jak's teeth flashed again in the flickering light of the oil lamp. "Soldiers are quite practical, as you'll have noticed yourself. Now that we have Firoxi, the other Wings will fall into line."

"After you kill all the female officers and ranks, you mean."

Jak sobered. "Those who refuse to be retired, or retrained, yes, most likely. I won't lie to you. The Halians don't believe in arming women." He shrugged. "You can see for yourself what it led to here. Though that was more the witches' doing than anything else, you know. Our women would have been perfectly normal if it hadn't been for the Halls."

All Tel could do was shake his head. This wasn't the Jak Gulder who'd been leading them until they reached the mines. "You really believe that?" he said finally.

"I do, in fact." Jak shrugged again. "But does that matter? Now? You think our friend Pella cares one way or another? He's a practical man, and his practical sense is telling him he should stand with the winning side."

Tel pressed his lips together against the sneer he could feel coming. He knew lots of practical men like this Pella. For soldiers like him, the military was a job like any other, where the smart ones followed the rules and did what the officers told them to do—and kept a sharp eye out for opportunities. No mage would be needed to change them.

"What about you, Tel Cursar? What does your practical sense tell you?"

"Kerida isn't a witch," Tel said before he knew he meant to.

Jak nodded. "That's a shame, it really is. Poor kid gets caught up and warped by the witches until she's in too far to save. That's a real shame. But hers isn't the only life that's been ruined by the witches. What about all the others they've wronged?"

"What others?" Even as he spoke, Tel knew it was a mistake to engage with the other man. Not that Jak needed any encouragement to talk.

"Though not everyone feels this way, I think the witches could have been wonderfully useful tools, if they'd only submitted themselves. I don't know how far back the turning point was, when they started their campaign against men. How did they become so powerful? They're useful, but so are horses and dogs, and we don't put them in charge. We don't put them in the best tents and give them better food than the men who are doing the dangerous work, do we? Haven't you ever wondered why the Talented should get better treatment than the rest of us?"

Again, Tel pressed his lips together. This wasn't the first

time he'd heard opinions of this kind—though not usually expressed so bluntly. Mother! He'd made a few remarks that way himself. But many of those who made this kind of complaint were women. It had always been soldiers against Talents. They were something to complain about, like over-strict officers or late pay.

"Why should I care about this?" he finally asked. "Why am I here?"

"You're here because I like you."

"You *like* me?" Tel couldn't have been more astonished if a dog had spoken to him.

The other man tilted his head to one side again, smiling, swinging his sword. "I don't expect you to understand. You see, you have something I always wanted."

"*I* do? And that would make you like me?"

"I know." Jak nodded. "Seems contrary to human nature, doesn't it?" He shrugged. "But there it is. I've always wanted a real military career—maybe be a Faro one day—something for which my family made me unsuited, and for which your family made you perfect. I'm well aware that I could easily dislike you for that. I've disliked others, if it comes to it. But I like you." He spread his hands.

"And *that's* why I'm here?" Tel shifted his feet, but the new position was no better than the old. He still couldn't stand up quickly.

"Here in this room, yes. Right now, yes. I wanted to give you an opportunity."

Tel shook his head. This was unbelievable. "I'm just a soldier."

"And so will I be, now." Jak's sword stopped swinging, and he leaned forward. "With a soldier's future. I can be a Faro now, and you could be my Laxtor. What do you think of that?"

Tel bit down on the inside of his cheek to keep from laughing aloud. Only a rich man's son thought you could become a Faro just by wanting it. For a minute he considered going along with Jak, telling him that, yes, he'd been persuaded. A dead hero did no one any good. He could fight from within, maybe learn something valuable and then escape. But if he could think of it, they could. And it would mean standing by and letting Kerida Nast die. To say nothing of Sala.

"Your face changed just then."

"What does it matter what I think," Tel said. "Can't they just change me the way they've changed you?" Jak's smile faded. "I'm not important enough, am I? After all, you're Jak Gulder, son of an important family, a political family. I'm nobody, a third officer of a mid-level Company. No special Halian magic's going to be wasted on me, no matter how much you like me." Now Tel did laugh. With nothing to tempt him, his choice was easier. "No," he said, and then cleared his throat. "No. I won't join you. No, I won't betray my friends. Just . . . no."

"She really has a hold on you, that witch, doesn't she?" Jak's tone was flat. He got to his feet, smoothly avoiding Tel on his way to the door. "Pella? You can take him away. But put him in a kitchen storeroom or somewhere, would you? Keep him away from the others." He turned back to Tel. "I'll give you some time away from her to think. You know what will happen to her. Maybe you'll feel differently then. I urge you to come to your senses. I hope you do."

It wasn't so much that everyone was asleep, as it was that Jerek knew all the secret and quiet ways to move through the house he'd grown up in. Even the two soldiers on watch in the dining hall never noticed him as he crept around the shadowy corners, hugging walls until he could let himself into the central courtyard through one of the large windows that was supposed to be locked at this time of year. Jerek knew every loose tile and floorboard, where to place his feet to make the least possible noise.

Not that experience in moving soundlessly through the

house was the only thing keeping him from being caught. Jerek's ears burned at the thought of how readily everyone believed that he was satisfied with the turn of events. Content to let people be imprisoned, so long as he was left to enjoy his property in peace. But that all worked to his advantage now. They'd allowed him back in his own rooms, and once settled there, no one paid any further attention to him. Even now, if he was caught sneaking into the tower, he was planning to say he needed to talk to his father.

For that reason, once he entered the tower itself, he ran up the stairs as he usually would, without trying for stealth. The only thing he wouldn't be able to explain was the key to the winepress room, weighing heavily in his tunic pocket. Jerek was reasonably sure that he was the only one left in the household who knew this same key would open great-grandmother's study. He knew for a fact that his father was unaware of it.

When he reached the heavy door of the old study, he knelt and put his eye to the keyhole.

"Kerida."

At Sala's whisper, Ker lifted her head up off her folded arms. The Feeler tilted her head toward the door. Ker held her finger to her lips and got to her feet, circling around the table and approaching the door from the side. Wynn rolled off the bed onto her feet, and she and Sala both came closer. Ker lifted her left hand to hold them in place, and reaching over to set the palm of her right hand on the door. This was no different from Flashing where the enemy soldiers were from the mine entrance. *Paraste*.

"It's the boy," she said. His aura was visible even through the door. As she spoke, the key clicked into the lock. The mechanism tumbled smoothly, with very little noise. Of course, if the boy had been confined here for any length of time, someone would have oiled the lock. The door swung open just as quietly, and Jerek slipped in.

"How did you know it was me?"

"The same way I know that your father's lying, and that you really are his son."

Suddenly pale, the boy flicked his eyes at the others before returning them to her. "You're a Talent?"

"And you're quick, that's good."

"Do they know?" His struck his forehead with his palm. "Of course, they do. Then you've got to get out of here; they'll kill you."

Ker tried to keep her face impassive. "Jerek, you know we came looking for the prince. We need the prince, desperately, to unite the Battle Wings."

"So they'll fight the Halians and not argue among themselves as to which Faro should take the throne. I've read my history," he said. A little color had returned to his face, but his eyes were in constant motion, flicking from Ker to Sala to Wynn and back again.

"You're a prince yourself, and next to your father, the most important person to the Polity . . ." Ker let her voice die away. How to put it? That the only reason Dern could have for claiming the boy wasn't his son was to raise his own value.

But Jerek guessed what she was so reluctant to say.

"That's what that man was saying, Lord Gulder. If I were only a stepson, I could be left behind. With a son, my father would be only half as important. They might use me, if they found him stubborn. That's why I have to go with you. To make sure the Halians can't use me." He looked at each of them again, but this time his eyes were steady. "You have to take me with you."

"Exactly what we were hoping to do. Can we get out the way you got in?" Ker went to the door.

The boy shook his head. "The house is full of soldiers. You wouldn't make it. I thought we'd use the window. The bars are on hinges. They're meant to open to let in big pieces of furniture."

Ker turned to Sala, but the older woman was shaking her head. "There's no rope on the pulley, and from what I could see in daylight, you'd have to be a monkey to find good enough finger- and toeholds in that wall."

"I was thinking of making a rope out of all these stored sheets and things." Jerek's tone was diffident, as if unsure how grown-ups would receive his suggestions.

"I'll do it while you plan," Wynn said, turning toward the chests standing against the inner wall next to the entry door. "I've got no head for strategy."

Ker turned back to Sala, who was still at the window, gauging the distance. "What do you think?"

"Might work," the older woman said. "None of us is any great heavyweight."

"Too bad we don't have Ganni here," Ker said. Somehow the tower looked taller than it had a moment before.

"Right now I'd settle for Ennick," Sala said. "He could probably climb down with all four of us on his back."

Ker nodded, frowning. "Assuming we get out, we've got blankets and even some extra clothing among the stores here, but what will we do for food and weapons?"

Jerek looked up from where he was helping Wynn look through chests. "As for food, the cook sleeps next to the kitchen, and he's a light sleeper. I'm afraid your packs and weapons have been taken by the soldiers, but there are tools and such in the stable storeroom. And Folet the stableman keeps his old sword and his hunting bows there as well. I can shoot," he added.

Sala nodded. "If we see a chance to take them, we should, though food might be a larger problem. Best if we don't split up."

"Agreed. Nothing is as important as getting away before the Shekayrin gets here." Again, Sala nodded, but not as if she were in complete agreement. "Remember the jewel Luca showed us?" Ker said. "Sala, you haven't seen what they can do. Wynn and I have."

"Then I'll take it seriously."

"Jerek, come show us the layout of the buildings."

Using items on the small table, Jerek created a model of the outbuildings, showing where the stables and other sheds were in relationship to the main house.

"We could go this way." He drew a line on the tabletop with his finger. "Once we're past the grapevines, we're into the trees that border the mill brook." He looked up. "It's not a lot of cover, but it's something."

"Well thought out." Sala patted the boy on the shoulder. "Tell us, young one, are there horses enough for the four of us?"

"Five of us," Ker said. "We can't leave without Tel."

"Wherever he is," Wynn said. Ker looked at Jerek, but the boy shook his head.

"I can Flash where he is, and there's no Shekayrin here," Ker pointed out. "We know that he's not changed."

"Perhaps so," Sala said. "But breaking him out? If it was just ourselves, I'd say let's chance it, but . . ."

"I know, I know." Ker rubbed at the tightness around her eyes. "We've got the prince to think of." She looked up at the older woman.

Sala grimaced. "We can't go looking for him. Agreed?"

Ker flexed her fingers; even her skin felt tight. "Agreed," she said finally. She turned her face away and went back to studying the model that Jerek had made them. Of course, she agreed. She had to. There were more important things at stake than one person. Tel would be the first to say so. She stuck her trembling hands into her armpits. Let them think she was cold.

"We need at least three horses, and even then, traveling across country, horses may not be the smart way to go."

Jerek frowned. "Wouldn't they be faster?"

"Hear, hear." Wynn looked up from her knotting. "Anything rather than another seven charming days cross-country at marching pace."

"Horses have to be fed, watered, rested," Ker pointed out. "We can eat on the march, providing we find food. They can't. Riding is less tiring than walking, but faster?" She twisted her lips to one side as she shook her head. "Depends on who's doing the walking."

"If it comes to that, we won't be able to keep up a marching pace ourselves, if we have to stay off the roads and hunt as we go," Wynn pointed out.

"Wait, though." Ker thought a moment longer. "If we take the horses for part of the way, we'll get a head start, and we'll prevent them from being able to follow us immediately."

Wynn smiled. "And we'll let them go when we can't feed them."

"If we go cross-country, as the crow flies, that in itself buys us time, right?" Jerek looked from one to the other.

Sala was shaking her head, but not as though she disagreed. "I'd have to see the stars, check where we are, exactly, with respect to the mine." She looked at Ker through narrowed eyes. "Unless you could tell us which way to go."

"Me? On a good day, with the Daughter's help, I can tell my right from my left, but north from east?" Ker shook her head.

"Really? You can't touch the ground and Flash our direction?"

Ker blinked, and felt her cheeks grow hot. She hadn't thought of that. Talents were used to find lost children, and lost objects, even to locate water for new wells, to say nothing of precious metals and other valuables hidden by earth or sea. Finding a *place*? That's what roads were for.

"Why not," she said finally. "Wynn, how's that rope coming along?"

"Ready as soon as you are. Thank you, my Faro," she said as Jerek handed her a cord he'd rolled from a strip of torn sheet. Wynn looked up when the silence continued. "What? The Luqs is the Faro of Eagles, and he's the Luqs, and I'm an Eagle."

Sala: Dersay, wake up!
Dersay: Go away, it can't be morning yet.
Sala: May griffins eat you and crap you out in tiny pellets. DERSAY! Open your eyes and sit up.
Dersay: What can you possibly need to tell me *now*? You've found the prince, the Halians have found the prince, you're locked up. We already know and people are coming to help you. Let me sleep, I've got mushroom duty in the morning.
Sala: Never mind mushrooms, we're escaping now. She could feel the other woman snapping alert and sitting up.
Dersay: You clever girl. How long will it take you to get back?
Sala: There's more. We don't have the prince, but we have his son.

WITHOUT Jerek, crossing to the stables in the overcast and moonless night would have been considerably more difficult. To say nothing of the dogs who came, snuffling and wagging tails, as they approached the dark corner of the stable. Wynn helped Jerek slide the heavy door across as silently as they could. Ker had Flashed they were alone in the courtyard, but that didn't stop sound from carrying.

Once inside the building, Jerek struck the lamp, placing it where it couldn't be seen from the outside. Ker grinned. It seemed this wasn't the first nocturnal adventure in the boy's life. A tall gray horse stuck his curious nose over the low wall of his stall, blinking sleepily.

"Where are the weapons, boy?" Sala hefted a splitting ax she'd found by the door.

"Through here." Jerek plucked a stub of candle from a basket under the lamp, lit it, and led the Feeler down the central space between the stalls to an enclosed area built into the rear

wall of the stable. Ker beckoned Wynn over to the stall holding the curious gray.

"Get this fellow out and get him saddled," she said. "And
I'll see what else we've got." Of the two other horses near the
door, one looked more like a packhorse than a lord's mount,
but Kerida thought it would do just fine. Beyond them, however, were three more riding horses, all showing military
marks on their shoulders.

"My pony's in there as well." Jerek appeared at her elbow,
still carrying the candle.

"I don't think we'll be able to take him," Ker said. The boy's
eyebrows lifted, then he nodded, his lips set in a line.

"That gray can carry Sala, you can take the roan, Wynn
that big-eared fellow, and I'll take this nice chestnut."

"These three aren't ours," Jerek said.

Ker shrugged. "I imagine they explain how Jak Gulder got
here."

"More mounts than we need." Sala reappeared out of the
darkness. She handed Wynn an elderly but well-kept ash bow,
with a quiver holding half a dozen arrows. An equally worn
but serviceable sword she kept for herself.

"And we're taking the extra ones with us, remember, to
slow down pursuit," Ker said.

Small as she was, Wynn needed no help clambering up
onto her horse, and Jerek was up on the roan in an eyeblink.
Ker mounted the chestnut, and took up the leads of the extra
horses. Sala wrapped the gray's rein around her forearm, and
positioned herself at the lamp, ready to pinch out the wick.

"Don't move, any of you, until you see the door is well
open."

The light went out, and Ker heard Sala moving the door
aside on its wooden rollers. In moments she could make out
the paler darkness of the opening, blocked only slightly as
Wynn rode through with Jerek after her. Ker followed, clucking

softly to the two horses she was leading. Sala would bring up the rear. Wynn led them left, heading toward the road. Shod hooves clicked on the cobblestones, and Ker gritted her teeth.

Suddenly Sala's horse screamed and reared, slipping and bringing them both down. The courtyard, empty only a moment before, filled with men. Ker dodged a staff swinging at her head more by instinct than cunning and, shouting at Wynn and Jerek to go, urged her own horse forward. She was immediately blocked by two men with staves, and a third man with a sword. She ducked again, pulled her horse's head to the left, and felt it start to go down.

She twisted just enough to land on her shoulder instead of her elbow, but not enough to get herself out from under the horse. Fortunately, it scrambled to its feet without stepping on her, though she was left lying completely winded. Arms raised to protect her head from flying feet and hooves, she'd just managed to suck in some air when the end of a staff swung past her face and she grabbed it, pulling and jerking it sideways at the same time.

Before she could use it, however, she was kicked from behind, and a shard of agony knifed through her back as her vision darkened. She lost hold of the staff, but managed to push herself to her hands and knees. Where was Sala, or Wynn? She was completely turned around, and raising her head to look only got her a view of boots, leather-covered legs and the swinging ends of staffs. Blinking didn't clear her eyes, and Ker was afraid to shake her head.

She tried to grab another staff as it passed by her, but only succeeded in losing what little balance she had left and hitting the ground with her face. She stayed down, and took a couple of deep breaths. She was pushing herself again to her knees, looking around for Jerek, and didn't see the bootheel that caught her in the temple.

*   *   *

The next thing Ker knew, someone was pressing a cool, wet cloth to the side of her face. It hurt and felt good at the same time. She was lying on something hard, and there was the smell of fresh straw, dried blood, and something less pleasant. The water moistening her lips didn't do much for the metallic taste of blood in the back of her throat. She opened her eyes, a light stabbed at them, and she closed them again.

"Kerida? How do you feel?"

Sala. The Feeler. They were still together, then. And alive.

Ker cleared her throat and gasped at a stab of pain in her side. "My head's banging like a gong, and I think my ribs are cracked. Other than that, I feel wonderful." She managed to push the words out between lips that felt thick as pillows. The left side of her face was stiff and painful. She probed her teeth with her tongue. A little loose, but she didn't think she'd lose any.

"Jerek?" she said. She'd ask about Wynn in a minute.

"He's right here." That *was* Wynn.

Ker squinted. The girl's right eye was blackened and swollen shut, her lower lip was split. Oddly, however, her nose looked straighter than it had before.

As if she knew what Ker was thinking, Wynn grinned, wincing as she put her fingers to her split lip. "You don't look so good yourself," she said, the words slurring a little.

"You're supposed to say, 'You should see the other guy,'" Ker said.

Wynn covered her mouth and waved her hand. "Don't make me laugh."

Ker squinted against the early morning light. They weren't back in the tower room. They'd been closed into the large box stall that had held the packhorse and the pony. The wooden half-door was closed, but the main doors of the stable were open, letting in light and cold, fresh air. The straw she was lying in was fresh, but the stall hadn't been cleaned out before the fresh straw was thrown in. That accounted for the smells.

Ker gasped as a muscle in her back seized, panted as Wynn

jabbed in her thumbs to loosen it. Jerek, a bruise forming on his cheek, stood over in the other corner rubbing an elbow as if he didn't know he was doing it. Ker swallowed, blinked, and swallowed again, as her stomach twisted. "Jerek," she said, and stopped, unsure what she had intended to say.

"I'm all right," he said, his face like stone.

"Good." She made her tone brisk. "Any sign of Tel?"

"Nothing," Sala said, "and no one's answering questions."

Ker lifted her head and raised a finger to quiet them.

"What questions would those be?" said a voice from above their heads. Jak Gulder, leaning with his forearms on the top of the stall boardings, smiled down at them.

Ker struggled to her feet, gritting her teeth against the pain in her side. She wasn't going to let Jak look down on her. "Where's Tel Cursar? What have you done with him?"

"I'm keeping him a safe distance from you, my dear." Jak's smile broadened. "And speaking of keeping things, it doesn't seem that His Highness' home is a very good place to keep prisoners, so you and your companions will be getting a chance to ride those horses after all, though I don't think we'll be taking you where you meant to go."

For a while all they'd heard was the sounds of horses being led out into the yard, the jingling of harness, and the voices of the men. Jerek heard the packhorse's familiar snort as she was led into the sunlight. She was all right once outside, but she'd never liked the idea of leaving the stable. Finally, foot-steps approached the stall they were in.

Jerek got to his feet, holding himself as stiffly as possible, so Kerida wouldn't see him trembling. As if she read his thoughts, she moved closer and put an arm around his shoulder. "It'll be all right," she said. "You'll see." Her mouth smiled, but her eyes were grim.

Jerek hoped his nod was convincing, but his neck was awfully stiff.

Bolts were thrown, and Jerek started. Ker's arm tightened, holding him back. A thickset man with a thin upper lip stood in the open doorway, with two of his father's new men behind him.

"You'll come with me if you please," the soldier said. Jerek knew that tone. That was the tone of a grown-up who wasn't going to stand for any nonsense.

Ker released him, after giving him a final squeeze. "Not like we have much choice," she muttered as they followed the man out of the stables and into the sun-brightened courtyard. Four other men closed in around them as they emerged. The horses were ready, and Fogtail had been saddled along with them. It looked like he was going to be riding him after all.

Jerek stroked the pony's nose, but didn't trust himself to speak, not even when the old beast nudged him hard enough to make him take a step back.

"Up you get, boy." This was the other soldier, the taller, bearded one. He and Thinlip must have come last night with Jak Gulder.

When Jerek didn't move right away, Tallbeard sighed and reached for him with the hand that wasn't holding his sword. Jerek drew away, swinging himself up into Fogtail's saddle before the man could touch him. When he leaned forward for the reins, however, Tallbeard was before him, tossing them to Thinlip, who was already mounted.

One of his father's new men, the blond with the silver rings threaded through the edges of his ears, was watching, and when Jerek looked at him, he smirked. Jerek turned away in time to see two crossbowmen just lowering their weapons and coming forward to their own mounts.

"So much for trying to grab the horses and escape," Ker said aloud.

"It would be touch and go who the bowmen might have hit, the way they've got us all bunched up." Sala looked around her with eyebrows raised, and Wynn snickered. Jerek felt his spirits lighten.

Once everyone was mounted, Jak Gulder came around to take a survey of them all. He smiled down at Jerek from the back of his chestnut horse, glanced over at Ker, and back again. "I can see how you could be carried away with the adventure of it all, Lord Brightwing," he said. "I shouldn't, but I'm willing to leave you here with your people."

Jerek looked beyond the circle of horses and guards. The man who had been his father was talking to the man in the silver earrings; he wasn't even looking this way. Of the few staff who had come out to see them off, there was only one familiar face. Even if he didn't understand how important it was to the Polity that he reach the Battle Wings, he was sure he didn't want to stay here.

"None of these are my people," he said finally.

The day was crisp, but warm enough, now that the sun was well up. Ker was painfully stiff, and from the way her jaw felt, she hoped they'd be given something soft to eat. At least her breathing was better, and she thought her cracked ribs might be only bruised after all. Her headache was beginning to clear in the fresh air.

Though she'd been looking for him since they'd been let out of the stables, it wasn't until they reached the main road that Ker finally saw Tel, riding next to Jak, just in front of Dern Firoxi and the attendants the new prince had brought with him from the holding. No women, but by now that didn't surprise her.

When Tel turned to look back, the movement caught her eye. She knew the moment he'd seen her from the way he held still, chin lifted. Then he turned to face front, without looking back again. He'd looked around only to find her. Ker realized she was smiling and brought her face under control.

Jak held them to such a good pace that Ker hoped the horses knew the road. Her feet had been firmly tied to her stirrups, her hands to the pommel of the saddle. If the horse went down, she'd go down with it. The reins were held by the man riding just half a horse length in front of her. Even with her hands tied, if she'd had hold of them, she could have escaped.

She glanced aside to where Jerek rode, his back straight, his knees and heels tucked in. He looked ready to be examined by his riding instructor, despite the bouncing of the pony as it tried to keep up the pace. A guard held Jerek's reins, too, though the boy didn't seem to be bound in any way. No one really thought he'd run off. As she was coming to expect, within moments of her fixing her eyes on him, the boy turned to look at her, his dark eyes, wide and clear, finding hers with no trouble. He pressed his lips together and gave her a little nod, though she didn't know whether he was trying to reassure her, or himself. She Flashed, and all seven colors of his aura shone bright and true.

He'd been quieter, and more calm than Kerida had expected a thirteen-year-old to be, and didn't seem to be thinking of his father all that much. Ker's own father, Elidon Nast, retired Faro of Panthers, had been away for most of her life, present only in letters and messages from soldiers on horseback. But somehow she'd always felt that she knew where he was, what he was doing. That he was thinking of her, and her brother and sisters. Now that she considered it, she felt it still.

Jerek didn't look like he felt that way, even though his father was within sight.

It was soon clear to everyone that Jerek's pony couldn't keep up. The column halted, and Jak Gulder rode back himself to see what the difficulty was.

"He's old." Jerek's voice cracked and he hesitated before he began again. "He can't keep up this pace, it'll kill him."

Gulder nodded. "Dismount, and get up behind Pella." He jerked his head toward Thinlip.

Jerek dismounted, but slowly. "It's not just my weight," he said. "Fogtail can't keep up. We'll have to slow down."

"That is exactly what we won't do," Jak said. "If he can't keep up, he'll have to be left."

Jerek, teeth clenched, tried to pull the reins from Thinlip's hands.

"We'll tie him to that tree," the man said with an accent much like Tel's. "I'll see someone comes back for him, or I'll do it myself."

Jerek looked the man in the eye long enough that Ker expected Jak to speak again. Finally, stone-faced, the boy nodded and accepted the soldier's offered hand, swinging up behind him. There were clear streaks in the dirt on Jerek's face. He hadn't cried for his father.

"Gaena," Jerek called over his shoulder as they approached the town gates, answering a question Ker hadn't asked. She nodded at the boy's back. It looked to be the sizable market town they'd so carefully skirted on their way to Brightwing Holding. It had taken only an hour to reach the place once they'd left the pony behind.

Such a large group, mounted, would normally have drawn a fair amount of attention, but the few people they passed on the streets studiously avoided looking at them. Except for one youngster who boldly followed them with round, innocent eyes. He let them pass without doing more than staring, but there was another such boy at the next sizable crossroads, and the one after that. Jerek turned his head to stare at that last one, a skinny blond, who lifted his chin at Jerek, and followed them all with his eyes.

It wasn't long until they were in the main market square, empty on this particular day. Jak Gulder led them directly across to the administration building on the south side of the square, where he dismounted immediately. With an escort of three soldiers, he led both Dern Firoxi and Tel Cursar through the open left side of the wide double doors. On the closed right leaf was carved the Polity's circle of laurel.

As she waited her turn to be released from her bonds, Ker took note of the streets and alleys that opened into the square before turning her attention back to the building. Like military camps, these administrative buildings were set up in much the same way throughout the Polity, and for much the same reason. From here disputes would be settled, taxes collected, and food distributed in bad times.

And prisoners would be held, suspects confined, until their cases were brought to justice and the Halls of Law.

Ker refrained from kicking the man who was freeing her and taking off down the street. With the archers still mounted she wouldn't get far, though she might have tried it if it hadn't been for her friends. She had a clear idea of what was going to happen to her when she was brought before the Shekayrin. And if she didn't, the defaced griffin symbol on the left door would have told her. The wood had been deeply scored, as though with an ax, though the edges of the cuts already showed weathering.

Somewhere in this building there would have been a Talent's office—maybe even a small suite of rooms, if the area overseen by this town was large enough. For a moment Ker wished she could remember the regional maps she was supposed to have memorized, back in Questin Hall. Somewhere in this building the Talents would have sat, writing reports, keeping records of disputes investigated, facts verified. Guilt confirmed, and innocence vindicated.

An office like that one might have been in her own future, before the Halians came.

It wasn't a private office they were taken to now, however, but one of the semipublic rooms on the ground floor, a place where people would take their petitions or wait for appointments. The braziers were lit, and the room was noticeably warmer than the corridor. Thinlip knocked and entered; beyond him in the room Ker saw Tel Cursar, his back against the far wall, and her heart lifted. Then she saw the shrine, with only the single figure of the Son placed on it. What had happened to the Mother and Daughter?

Tel caught her eyes and swung his to the left; Ker glanced over. To the right as they entered was the clerk's long worktable, backing on windows whose shutters were open, allowing the early afternoon light to enter through cloudy glass panes. Dern Firoxi was there, sitting at the far end of the long table, as if he'd called a meeting. Jerek made a soft, abrupt sound and stiffened.

It was only then Ker saw the man sitting with his hip propped on the edge of the table, negligently swinging one foot as he waited for them. He was dressed in a blue tunic, and a black cloak lay tossed across a chair. He was wearing a mail shirt under his tunic; she could see where he'd pushed the hood and lining back off his long, bony face. His short hair stood up in dark brown tufts. When he looked up from the roll of heavy paper he was studying, she saw that a sunflower had been tattooed around his left eye, simple, stylized, matching the badge on the front of his tunic.

Suddenly Ker smelled smoke, saw a man in a black cloak signaling, the ax rising and falling, her own throat closing over a scream. She felt pressure just above the elbow, where Sala's hand gripped her, holding her up as her legs turned to jelly. The Flash of the slaughter in the Hall was over so quickly—and this man *wasn't* the same person, her fear had deceived her—maybe no one but Sala had noticed anything.

Except for Tel. His hands had formed into fists, and even across the room she could see how his lips had tightened.

"Lord Shekayrin, these are the prisoners, as you requested." Jak was standing near Tel, not quite at attention. "Wynn Martan, an archer of the Eagle Wing." His voice was dismissive, and Wynn wrinkled her nose. Jak gestured at Ker. "And this is the one I told you of." He fell silent as the Halian lifted his hand, index finger extended.

"Are *all* these men necessary?" he said. His voice was rough, but had a hint of humor in it. "The prisoners are unarmed and bound, are they not? You three—" He waggled his finger at the guards. "You may wait outside the door. See that we are not disturbed."

Ker realized this was the first time she'd ever heard any of the Halians speak. His accent was strange, though he spoke Faraman fluently. *Paraste.* Since her meeting with the griffin, it was becoming second nature for Ker to Flash people. Now she saw yellow, blue, and green, plus purple, and finally a strange webbing of red, not superimposed on his aura, as she'd seen it in Jak's, but growing from within it, like the trunk and branches of a tree within the canopy of leaves.

The Shekayrin looked directly at her, his eyes narrowing. As the guards cleared the room, he straightened to his feet and approached her, examining her closely from head to toe. Ker hastily thought her closing word.

"She doesn't look very dangerous, does she?" His long face was made squarer by a spade-cut beard that emphasized his bony cheeks and forehead. His skin was remarkably smooth.

"She hasn't been dangerous that I've seen," Jak said. "Of course, she's still a Candidate, so that might make a difference."

The man nodded and spoke without moving his eyes from Ker's face. "And this last person?"

"A Ma'lakan," Jak said. "She acts like a soldier, but I believe they found her in the mines of the Serpents Teeth."

"The Serpents Teeth." The Shekayrin swung away from Ker and approached Sala. "Have you seen anything like this?"

He produced from an unseen pocket a jewel, the same deep red as the one Luca had shown them in the mines, but this one faceted. The shade of red, Ker saw, matched the tattoo on his face and the crest on his tunic.

Ker felt a shudder rising through her and stiffened, clenching her teeth. She couldn't be sure without Flashing him again, but the pattern of the jewel's facets looked to be similar to the webbing she'd seen in his aura. Every hair on her body felt as if it was standing up, and nausea clutched at the back of her throat. Luca's jewel had been inert, pretty, but a stone like any other. This one was the jewel as she'd Flashed it, active, and somehow alive. She felt a sudden warmth between her breasts flare up and die away. When she raised her bound hands to investigate, she felt the familiar shape of the griffin's claw she'd been carrying next to her skin so long she'd forgotten it.

She lowered her hands, linking her fingers together. Instinct told her she needed to disguise her reactions, to hide that she knew what she was looking at.

Sala raised her eyes from the jewel in the Shekayrin's hand and looked at him the sour way a teacher looks at a pupil who will bring her nothing but disappointment. Just as the man opened his mouth to ask again, Sala looked away, her eyes focused on the wall behind him, her face a mask.

"No hurry." He pocketed the jewel and turned to take them all in at once. "My name is Peklin Svann. I am the Sunflower Shekayrin recently placed in charge of this district," he said. "You may think of me as having the same authority as one of your military governors."

Ker swallowed. A Polity military governor was answerable only to the Luqs. That meant he had the authority of life and death.

"We will not be needing the boy," he said to Jak. "One of the men at the door may take him away for now."

Jerek looked between her and the Shekayrin. "I'd rather stay."

Svann made a shooing gesture with the back of his hand as he settled himself again on the edge of the table. Jaw tight, Jerek left with his chin up, not waiting to be dragged like a child.

Once he was out of the room Peklin Svann pointed at Tel.

"Now, Gulder. You say there is some reason you have kept this young man separated from the others?" Svann smiled again, and Ker was surprised to see genuine feeling in it. His teeth were good.

"Further contamination with the witch was my first concern, of course," Jak said. "But I think it would be worth your while to jewel him, Lord Svann."

Wynn made an abrupt movement, like a horse shying from a fly, but the only sign that Tel was shaken was the slow closing of his left fist. Ker was ready to swear she herself hadn't moved a muscle—but her intertwined fingers suddenly hurt.

The Halian made a face. "'Jewel' is not a verb, Gulder. Nor is every stubborn Faraman soldier's life worth preserving. Tell me why this one's is."

"His long association with the young witch, if nothing else, can give us insight into their way of life, and their thinking."

"If you can tell me what any woman's thinking, ever, you're a better man than I." Tel's tone made Ker stifle a grin.

Svann barked a short laugh, looking between Jak and Tel as if he were attending a stage play. "A good answer. I like it."

"He's lived with the witch," Jak persisted, "and he's been through the mines of the Serpents Teeth. Twice."

"Jak's just upset because they wouldn't let *him* in." Tel shrugged.

Peklin Svann nodded, one foot beginning to swing. "Possible. But I find myself inclined to Gulder's way of thinking. My lord," Svann addressed Dern. "May I have you escorted to your suite? I fear this grows tedious for you."

"I suppose it does." Dern took his time getting to his feet. *Doesn't want it to look as though he's just been ordered out*, Ker thought. She hoped her smile looked just as nasty as she felt.

"What about Jerek," she said to Dern Firoxi's back. "What about your son?"

Dern looked back into the room from the doorway. "Stepson," he said, as the door closed.

Jewel in his closed fist, the Shekayrin made a beckoning gesture and Tel jerked forward, walking with dragging feet to the chair placed close to the table. Once seated, he struggled as if to rise, but though nothing tied him down, it was clear he couldn't stand. His head didn't turn, but his eyes swiveled to meet Ker's, and Ker shivered. She stepped forward, hands outstretched, but Sala hauled her back. Wynn had her hands clamped over her mouth.

Jak came around to confront Kerida. "Don't worry, witch. He'll be free of you soon."

Ker bared her teeth, and deliberately spat on the floor, as close to him as she could get.

Oblivious, Svann stood, idly blowing on the jewel, polishing it on the front of his tunic as he approached Tel.

Tel stopped struggling and looked the man in the face.

Svann gave a short nod, as if of approval, before reaching down and placing the flat side of the jewel against Tel's forehead. Wynn, her eyes shut, tucked her head into the hollow of Sala's shoulder, both women hunched up as if bracing for a blow. Ker was glad that Jerek had been sent away.

At first she saw no change. Then Tel's eyes opened wide—wide enough that she could see the whites all around. *Paraste*, she said, and instantly the room was filled with a kaleidoscope of colors. She concentrated, her hands in fists, and her teeth clenched. There! There was Tel's aura, splashy and vibrant as always. Svann's colors, steadier, less chaotic, became more distinct as well. Ker had already seen how yellow, blue, and green were common to all people, while Feelers and Talents had two additional colors, purple and orange. Now she realized that while Svann's aura had purple in it, like any Talent or Feeler, it lacked orange, showing only the dominant network of red.

Tel cried out and Ker found herself pushing against a barrier she could not see, her own aura lashing out to the colors just beyond her grasp. She clenched her teeth against the cry that wanted to escape her throat.

Tel's eyes were open again, his face contorted, the muscles and sinews of his neck standing out. The arms of the chair creaked under his grip. The colors of his aura twisted and contorted like living ropes. Their brightness was fading, and Ker feared the worst, but the movement subsided and Tel relaxed. Not all at once, but gradually, first his limbs, then his shoulders, his neck, his face, and finally his eyes stopped staring, and his eyelids fluttered, and he blinked.

Tel's colors swirled more slowly, steadied, passing through the jewel and back again, though the stone never changed from its solid red. The green and the yellow and the blue, strongly showing, pulled a thread of red with them, that folded back and forth, forming a familiar pattern, thrown like a net over Tel's aura.

Terestre. There was nothing more Ker wanted to Flash.

"Would you like some water?" Tel licked his lips and nodded. The Shekayrin turned to the table for the cup and pitcher, poured, and offered the cup to Tel, watching him with narrowed eyes.

Tel took the offered cup and drank from it, and all the time his eyes stayed on Svann's tattooed face. Tel looked relaxed now, in a way Ker hadn't seen since they'd first met in the kitchen at Questin. She raised her bound hands and pressed them to her mouth.

"Sit quiet and relax, Tel Cursar. You'll feel yourself again in a moment."

Tel looked at her then, and Ker's heart stopped. He had the same familiar twinkle in his eye, and she leaned toward him, hoping that he had managed somehow to trick the Halian. But his changed aura was no trick. He knew her, but she wasn't anyone important to him anymore. If anything, in fact, his look was measuring, calculating, distrustful. After what felt like forever he turned his eyes toward Sala, and an icy hand squeezed Ker's heart. Tel pointed with a long index finger.

"That one, she's a Feeler."

Ker was still on her feet. She hadn't fainted. The taste of blood in her mouth meant she'd bitten her lower lip. Jak Gulder, his sword now in his hand, had moved to isolate Sala, and Ker found she was standing with her arms around Wynn.

Svann propped himself back on the edge of the worktable and twirled his forefinger at Tel. "Tell me."

Ker did her best not to listen, but Tel hadn't got very far into his explanation of their encounter with the Feelers in the mine when Svann held up his hand, stopping Tel abruptly. "I know of these. They are witches. A different type, perhaps, but witches nonetheless."

"The stories say Feelers and Talents are traditional enemies." Jak's eyes flicked between Svann and Sala.

The Shekayrin stroked his beard with thumb and index finger. "Interesting. They were allies long ago, or so *our* histories tell us."

"Can we use the Feelers against the witches? If half what the stories say about their Gifts is true—"

Svann shook his head. "There can be no common cause with those who use the magic of the body." He turned back to Tel. "What are their numbers?"

"We only saw a few, sir," Tel said. "But *she* must know." He pointed at Sala with his chin. "They said she's a Far-thinker. I don't know about that, but she's head of their council."

Svann indicated the chair, and Jak herded Sala into it with the point of his sword. "Will you tell me your numbers?" he asked once she was seated.

Sala did not react at all. It was as if Svann hadn't spoken. The Feeler had the Far-thinking look, and Ker hoped she was communicating with Dersay. Maybe there was something the other Feelers could do, even at this distance. Maybe Weimerk was out there somewhere, and could help them somehow.

"Your numbers?"

Sala took in a deep breath through her nose and let it out again. Her eyebrows up, her lids low, the Far-thinker was the very image of a polite but bored person coming to the end of her patience.

If the Shekayrin was annoyed, he didn't show it. He took out the red jewel again, and the minutest smile flickered over Sala's lips before her face returned to its impassive mask. Murmuring something Ker couldn't hear, the Shekayrin placed the jewel on Sala's forehead. Though her insides crawled, Ker lifted her arms from around Wynn. They had to be ready to take advantage of any opening that might occur while Svann was distracted. The Far-thinker would be the first to tell her to grab any chance to get away, even if it meant leaving Sala herself behind. Ker tensed, ready to bolt for the door. As if he'd been watching her, Tel placed himself in front of it.

Both Feeler and Shekayrin were still as statues, Sala with her face turned upward, her hands gripping the arms of the chair. She was shorter than Tel, and her head pressed against the chair, prevented from tilting any farther back. Svann stood over her, a look of mild curiosity on his face, exactly like what Ker had often seen on the face of her Hall teachers, when they waited for one of the students to complete some classroom task. Polite, nonjudging, patient. He touched the jewel to Sala's forehead.

Ker took a deep breath. *Paraste*. The room filled with color once more.

Red lines—red must be the mark of the Shekayrin— reached toward Sala, and her aura moved to enclose her in a loose sphere of pulsing color through which Ker could only dimly Flash her. The sphere solidified further as the red lines continued to probe and stab, finally forming into an opaque multicolored orb with Sala at its center.

Ker's heart rose as she saw Svann's red begin to withdraw, unable to penetrate Sala's shield. But her satisfaction quickly died. The strands of red reformed into a net, and became thicker, completely enveloping the orb that sheltered Sala. Before Ker could finish taking a breath, the net contracted, and the orb of Sala's aura shattered into a thousand pieces.

Ker threw up her arms to shield her face from the flying shards of color only she could see.

The red net sank through Sala's skin, and suddenly every muscle in her body contracted. The sinews and tendons in her neck and face stood out in rigid relief, so clearly that the Feeler looked flayed. There was a dull cracking sound, and a bend appeared in Sala's right arm between elbow and wrist as the paired bones broke.

"Stop!" Ker's throat hurt. Svann grunted and pulled the jewel back from Sala's forehead. She had stopped Flashing, so Ker could never be sure, afterward, of what she saw next. A flicker of bewilderment, underlined with just a touch of concern, passing across the Shekayrin's face, before the cool mask of scholarly interest fell over his features once again.

Ker knew before he stepped back from the chair that Sala was gone.

THREE people came running to fetch him when Dersay started screaming. It didn't take Ganni long to realize that she wasn't going to stop by herself, and he sent for Hitterol Mind-healer, and for little Larin. The girl was close—when was she ever anything but close when she was needed?—but Dersay's voice had worn away into a thin whisper by the time he and Hitterol managed, between them, to knock the Far-thinker senseless.

"Did you mark anything, Hitterol, while you were in there?"

The Mind-healer wiped her face with both hands. "There's no finesse to what I did, Ganni. It was all I could do to make her sleep."

"What about you, child? Anything to see?"

Larin squatted to one side, the knuckle of her right index finger in her mouth. She lowered her hand. "Nothing but the screaming, Grandfather. It's screaming all the way down."

Ganni didn't ask what Larin meant by that. He didn't want

to know. By this time others had arrived with a stretcher, and he helped them by lifting Dersay onto it himself. He might have lifted her all the way into the infirmary, if it wasn't for the discourtesy of it.

"Go with them, Hitterol, do what you can. Send for me when she wakes up." He raised his eyebrows to Larin in a question.

The child nodded, her eyes impossibly wide and knowing. "Oh, she'll wake up all right," she said. "Now that the scream-ing's stopped."

Cuarel dropped the scraper she was using into the basin, spat-tering the oil she'd scraped from her skin on the polished wood countertop and the tiled floor of the bathhouse. "Luca! Luca, come here!"

Luca gently laid his own scraper down. "I'm right here, for griffin's sake. What is it?"

"It's Dersay. She says she's lost Sala." Cuarel's hands hung limp at her sides. Luca handed her his own towel.

"What do you mean? Have they been moved too far away?" He understood that even the Far-thinkers themselves were only now learning how distance affected their Gift.

"No. Sala's *gone*."

Luca steadied himself, gripping the edge of the stone sink. He'd found Sala himself, and brought her here from Ma'lakai. He licked his lips. "The others?" Was the young prince lost to them also? And Kerida Nast?

Cuarel shook her head. "I don't know." She made no move to wipe away the tears running down her cheeks, or even to wipe the oil off her hands on the towel Luca had handed her. Her face was whiter than Luca had ever seen it. White even for a person who had spent three-quarters of her life underground.

"Come." Luca took her by the elbow and led her into the warming room. There he wrapped her in one of the robes hanging over the braziers and sat her down in a cushioned wicker chair. The tears ran more freely, but at least Cuarel had stopped shivering.

"What *can* you tell me?"

Cuarel pulled the robe closer around her. "All Dersay remembers is the jewel. A red jewel, like the one you showed us." She looked up, her eyes seeming now to actually take him in. "Just the red jewel, and nothing more. Dersay said that Sala pushed her away. Shut her out. That if Sala hadn't, she'd have been gone herself. Dersay would." Cuarel swallowed and took in a shaky breath. "Dersay says that Hitterol Mind-healer, says she or Larin can get more, but everyone's afraid to let them try."

Luca sat down in the chair across from her. He had never felt old in his life until this past autumn. Now he was beginning to wonder if any of them would see the spring.

———

"Take this away." The Shekayrin waited until Sala's body had been removed, along with the chair she'd been sitting in, before turning his blue eyes to Kerida.

"Sit." Svann pulled out another chair and set it down to the left of the worktable. He turned to Wynn. "And you, to that corner and stay there."

Ker was aware she and Wynn were still holding hands only when Jak Gulder loosened her fingers and pulled her away from the other girl. Her wrists hurt where she'd strained against her bonds. She couldn't be sure which one of them made the half-swallowed sobbing sound. She couldn't take her eyes from the spot where Sala's chair had been. The new chair, her chair, was only a few feet away.

Ker pulled back, but there was nothing to dig her heels into, no leverage she could use to twist away from Jak. Thank the Mother it wasn't Tel holding her. Thank the Daughter even the sight of him was blocked by Peklin Svann's blue tunic.

Ker told herself it was only because she was so tired that she finally sat down. Now she could see Tel, but after the first glance she kept her eyes turned away. Seeing the change in Jak had been bad enough. She couldn't stand the disinterest on Tel's face. How could she ever have thought that Tel wasn't her friend? Now that it was gone, Ker realized she'd seen friendship in his face every day.

She folded her hands on her lap and focused on the bruises. So long as she kept looking down, she'd see nothing else to upset her.

"Tel Cursar," Svann said. "You will remain. It may be that you know of something more pertaining to my inquiry. But you are forbidden to speak of anything you see here." He held up the jewel in his fist. "Do you understand?"

"Yes, sir."

Svann lowered his hand and turned to Jak Gulder.

"Yes, sir."

Ker closed her eyes. She wouldn't give him any opening. Wouldn't ask any questions, wouldn't make any remarks— nothing. She would stand mute. She wouldn't even look up.

She looked up.

She braced herself as the jewel came closer, determined to keep her eyes open, like Sala, but in the last minute Ker took the coward's way and shut them. She couldn't push away that image of the Far-thinker, the cords of muscle, the skull beneath the skin. Then she squared her shoulders. She would use the image, not push it away. Remember it, and along with it, Sala's fierceness, and her strength.

"I call on the Mother." Wynn's voice, from behind Ker's left shoulder, began to whisper the morning prayer and the familiar rhythms strengthened her even more.

She felt the cool touch of the stone on her forehead, making the skin between her eyebrows twitch. She hissed in her breath and then . . . nothing.

Then auras Flashed, blinding in their brightness. She hadn't used her trigger word, and yet she was surrounded by the swirling mass of colors as if the jewel had awakened them, green, yellow, turquoise, orange, blue, purple, and red—some her own, some Svann's. His central red pattern grew darker, sending out feelers toward her.

Ker's instinct was to wrap her aura around her in a protective shield, as Sala had done, but she forced herself to think. The Feeler's strategy had worked against her. What had Luca Pa'narion said? He'd used his block as a shifting and obscuring barrier to hide behind. Not as a solid shield. The Inquisitor had been able to resist the interrogation by jewel, even though he didn't know about the auras, didn't see the colors and couldn't use them. If she could use her own block in the same way, surely her awareness of the auras would help?

Ker wove a swift net of her own. Green joined blue, purple melded with yellow, turquoise with orange; all dusted over with the coppery sheen she'd seen nowhere else. The Shekayrin's red lines glowed brighter, reaching for her.

Ker held her ground and pushed back, but gently, softly, as if moving in a dance. Letting the red threads through a little here, holding them back a little there, not allowing, and yet not provoking them to form a fixed and dangerous pattern. She had no sense of time passing, no way to know how long she'd been holding against the jewel's attack, when suddenly she was alone again, the Flashing stopped. Slumping to one side, Ker kept her eyes closed, hoping that Svann might think she'd fainted. In the heavy silence she could hear Wynn breathing. Finally, curiosity got the better of her, and Ker cracked open her eyes.

The Shekayrin was watching her with a calm face. The warmth and humor she'd seen in his eyes was back now. And maybe something else. Maybe a touch of wariness.

"Interesting," he said. "You are not a sealed witch," he said. "You could have opened to me, if you had chosen to. You *use* the magic of the body, but you haven't been sealed to the

Mother. The books have always been unclear on what that meant, precisely, but I know now."

"I told you, she's just a Candidate," Tel said from the door. "She hasn't finished her training."

Ker pressed her lips together. His voice was the same—and yet so different. She hadn't known how it would tear at her heart to hear him speak against her.

"Interesting," Svann said again. He drew another chair up in front of her and sat down. He took her hands in his, and for a moment simply held them, his fingers as square and bony as his face. Finally, he pulled apart the knots that bound her and tossed the cords to the floor. Ker eyed the space between them.

"You are thinking if you attack me ferociously enough I would have to kill you," he said, so calmly he could be advising her on what to choose for dinner. "But you have forgotten your friends here." He tilted his head toward Tel and Jak. Without taking his eyes from hers, he raised his voice. "What would you do if this witch attacked me, Tel Cursar?"

"Kill her." The answer came swift and sure.

"You see? And he is not even armed. By the way"—Svann smiled—"you may arm yourself from the chest back there."

Out of the corner of her eye Ker watched Tel circle around the table.

"There has not been any great opportunity to examine an unsealed witch," Svann said.

Ker licked her lips. "You'd have had lots of chances if you hadn't killed everyone at Questin Hall," she said. "Most of the people there were only Candidates like me."

"I was not there, believe me." And somehow, she did. "The Poppy Shekayrin are often too quick to act—though you mustn't tell them I said so. They examined some—of the boys at least. But apparently it was not possible to save them, sealed or not. They had been contaminated by the magic of the body. Perhaps if one of us Sunflowers were there, the results would have been different. But there you are." He shrugged. "The opportunity for gathering knowledge about witches and their craft was wasted, something I hope to rectify with you."

He turned his head, aiming his smile at Tel. All the while they'd been talking over the clatter of Tel rummaging in the chest behind the worktable, lifting out swords and rejecting them one after another. It seemed he'd finally found one that would do.

"Found everything all right?" Svann asked.

"My own's a better length if I can get that one back," Tel said. "But this'll do for now, sir."

Svann nodded. "Good. Will you stand by the door?"

Tel gave a salute and circled round again, this time passing behind the Shekayrin. Ker's leg muscles tensed, but she forced herself to relax. That *would* have been the moment to move, if Tel had been faking. If he hadn't let Sala die. Evidently, her muscles hadn't caught up with her brain.

It didn't help that Svann was again smiling at her, exactly as if he knew what she'd been thinking.

"Why should I help you at all?"

He lifted his shoulders and let them drop. "Because I will kill you if you do not?"

Suddenly Ker felt very calm. She'd often heard her grandmother—and her father for that matter—say things like "a soldier walks toward death." Everyone is going to die, her gran used to say, but the smart soldier knows it, and faces it squarely all the time. It was suddenly very clear to Ker what that meant.

"Not good enough," she said to Svann. "You're going to kill me anyway, so why should I help you first?"

Svann leaned back, slapping his knees. "You give even better answers than Tel Cursar. I like you. I like you a great deal." He rubbed his fingers through his beard. "Let me see. What can I give you to persuade you to cooperate, if I cannot give you your life?" His eyes shifted from hers and came back. "What about the life of your friend over there in the corner?"

Ker swallowed. "Explain."

"This is what I mean." The humor left his face, but not the warmth. "Your friend stays alive so long as you cooperate with me, answer my questions, and submit to my experiments."

"And afterward?"

Svann lifted his hands and let them fall again. "Why should we think about that now?" he said.

Ker tilted her head to one side. She might be prepared to die, and Wynn, as a soldier, might feel the same. But so long as one of them stayed alive, they still had a chance to escape with Jerek.

"And Jerek," she said. "Wynn and Jerek both."

His right eyebrow quirked upward. "Of course, your friend here, and the stepson, both."

Ker pressed her lips together. He was agreeing too quickly. There was something here she wasn't seeing— "And you leave them alone meanwhile." The words almost tripped over themselves she was in such a rush to get them out. "No using that jewel on them."

Now he smiled again, the humor back in his face. "They stay alive, and I will not use the soul stone on them. Very good. *Very* good. I can see that I'm going to enjoy our association a great deal." He started to get up and then seemed to change his mind. "It is well past the hour to eat," he said. "And I have other demands on my time. Why do we not resume our discussion later in the day?"

Jerek was waiting for them in a room clearly intended for guests of minor status: couriers, perhaps, or even traveling Talents. He held himself erect and stiff until the door was closed on them before flinging himself into Ker's arms, and almost as abruptly pushing free of her, to step back blinking fiercely.

"Sala?" he said, looking from one to the other. Wynn looked away. Ker shook her head.

Jerek's face stiffened, and Ker looked away from the signs of earlier tears marking the dirt on the boy's face. There were two beds in the room, a couple of chairs, and a round table to eat at, though the brazier underneath it was empty and cold. Their captors probably thought giving prisoners fire was a bad idea. The window was big enough for any of them to crawl through, if it wasn't for the bars. The lock on the outside of the door was obviously a recent addition, but Ker knew they were lucky. This building would also have actual cells in it.

It was long past the midday meal, but they were brought lamb turnovers, stewed onions, and tasty—if coarse—bread. All things they could eat without using knives. Ker helped Wynn shift the table over to the end of the nearest bed, so they could all sit down. Plates and food were passed in silence.

"Could I have done anything differently?" Ker said finally.

Wynn wrinkled her nose. "I don't see what, truth to tell. This way, we're at least alive and in our right minds." The other girl's voice was firm and confident, but Ker couldn't help noticing that Wynn wasn't actually eating any of the turnover she'd so thoroughly broken into bite-sized pieces.

Ker reached for the basket of bread. "At the risk of being obvious, we have to get out of here."

"The sooner the better." Wynn indicated Jerek with a shift of her eyes. The boy's mouth was full, and all he did when he saw her looking at him was raise his shoulders. "We're urgently needed elsewhere."

Ker ripped the heel of the bread off the loaf, tore off a still smaller piece and popped it into her mouth. The Peninsula—never mind the rest of the Polity—had no chance against the

Halians if they didn't get Jerek to the Wings. She forced herself to chew slowly, seeing herself in the kitchen back at Questin Hall, frantically putting together a pack of supplies, grabbing up the kitchen knife. Saw herself in the stables, the spray of blood across the horse's head and neck as she cut the Halian's throat. At least this time, there was no question that they had to leave Tel behind.

"So we'll have to escape." Jerek said this so quietly Ker almost didn't hear him. He raised his head, looking from Ker to Wynn and back again. He shrugged and helped himself to another turnover. Ker wished she had the boy's appetite. "While we're still alive, we can work something out. If we're dead . . ."

"Well." Wynn looked around as though there were other people in the room. "No arguing with that, is there?" She picked up a sliver of pastry and put it in her mouth, following it with a sip of water.

Ker grinned, but she wasn't smiling inside. She hadn't been thinking very far ahead. Maybe it was time she started.

"We're all hostages for each other, aren't we?" she said. She had hold of the tail of an idea, but she needed to pull the thing closer. Wynn paused with her cup of water halfway to her mouth, and Ker continued. "You stay alive because I cooperate. If you escape, I wouldn't need to cooperate anymore."

"You want *us* to escape?"

"No. I mean yes, I want us *all* to escape." *Even Tel*, she didn't say aloud. *If I can figure out how to change him back.* "But it's like a prisoner of war giving a word-bond," she said. "They promise not to try to escape," she explained when it looked like Jerek was about to ask. "And in return they can get the run of the camp, or the precincts of the prison, that kind of thing. I've given my word-bond in promising to cooperate, and instead of a measure of freedom, I get your lives in return." She pulled the dish of stewed onion closer and spooned one out onto her plate. "The two of you could give your word-bonds in the more traditional sense."

Wynn shook her head. "Obviously, you mean us to break our words, so I don't see why we should give them in the first place."

"It'll get you the freedom of the camp, right? You could fetch your own food—"

"Keep our own quarters clean, go more or less where we'd like so long as we don't try to escape, but how does that *help us*?"

Ker looked from one to the other. "My movements will be closely watched, so it's up to you to prepare what we'll need."

Wynn had leaned back far enough in her chair that she was balancing it on its back legs, eyes focused on the middle distance. "I've a feeling the room-cleaning, food-fetching approach is the way to go." She let her chair down with a thump and put her elbows on the table as she leaned in. "Without our own brazier, we can't cook, so someone will have to carry our food in from the kitchens, and the dirty dishes and night jars out. I can easily see the guards letting us do that work ourselves."

"Especially as it's likely to be happening while I'm with the Shekayrin, and his attention is elsewhere." Ker also leaned forward, made sure both of them were looking at her, and lowered her voice still further. "With access to the kitchens, you'll be able to steal food, and likely find weapons as well."

"Weapons?" Jerek said. "Who keeps weapons in the kitchen?"

"You'd be surprised," Wynn said. "The odds are good that kitchen knives and cleavers have killed as many people as swords and axes." The younger woman stuffed another large piece of lamb turnover into her mouth, chewing and swallowing before turning to Ker. "This might work, but what about you? What will you be doing?"

"Other than staying alive, you mean?" Ker shook her head at Wynn's apology. "I'll Flash whenever I can, whenever it's safe to. If these buildings have any secret passages, I'll find out, and if there are any doors routinely left unlocked, where the patrols go . . ."

Wynn was nodding, her eyes narrowed. "Jerek's obviously harmless. We can ask if he can go out for supplies or—"

"No." Ker startled even herself with the force in her voice. "We don't want him to come back to us changed. We can't trust Svann." *Any more than he can trust us.*

Wynn's face crinkled in horror, but Jerek only frowned. They'd described to him what had happened to Tel, not to frighten the boy, but because the only explanation for Tel's absence was the true one.

"Does it hurt?" he asked now.

"It looked like it did while it was happening," Ker said. "Afterward, Tel seemed to be all right."

"Except he doesn't love you anymore," the boy said.

Ker blinked. "Jerek, Tel didn't love me—"

"Of course, he loved you." Wynn shrugged one shoulder. "What? Not our fault you never saw it." She turned to Jerek. "You're young to pick up on something like that."

Jerek shrugged in turn.

Ker put down the spoonful of onion she was holding and pushed herself back from the table. "Just when I thought things couldn't get worse."

"Ker, I'm so sorry, it never occurred to me you wouldn't know." Wynn got up and started around the table, stopping only when Ker put up her hand, palm out.

"It's a shock, that's all." *I should have known and I'm not going to think about it, not now.* Not ever. "Nothing to be done about it, in any case. What we should do—"

Sounds at the door stopped her. Bolts were shot, and the door opened. It was Tel. Kerida's heart began to thump, loud and fast. How could she not have seen it? *That's* what was missing in his face. When she contrasted the indifferent glance he gave her now to the way he used to look at her, how could she not have seen what he'd felt?

"The Shekayrin wants you," was all he said.

"Now?" A cold hand squeezed her heart. When he'd said "later" she'd thought she had more time. Ker thought about asking to finish her meal, then got to her feet. There was no way of knowing at this stage exactly what Peklin Svann considered "cooperation." Testing boundaries had to be done carefully. Jerek had risen to his feet, and she patted him on the shoulder.

"It'll be all right," she said. "See you when I get back." She glanced at Wynn and was reassured by the girl's nod.

Tel waved her to get in front of him, but before she could ask how she was supposed to know where they were going she saw the thickset guard with the thin upper lip in the hall, waiting to lead the way.

"Did you go back for the pony?" she asked.

At least she'd startled a smile out of him. "As it happens, I did."

"Good. Jerek will be happy when I tell him. Thank you."

Ker expected to return to the room she'd already seen, but Tel and the thickset man led her up a flight of stairs and along the gallery toward the rear of the building. The fountain in the interior courtyard had been stopped for the winter, and dried leaves had accumulated in the basin. The thickset man stopped in front of the third door on the right, just before the gallery turned the corner, and knocked before opening it.

Ker hesitated on the threshold. After leaving space enough for the door to swing open, someone had layered carpets and rugs over the rest of the floor, several deep. Peklin Svann was just closing the shutters, and judging from the amount of glass in the windows, this must have been the magistrate's own private quarters—unless those had been given to Dern Firoxi. Not one, but two braziers were glowing.

Svann turned from the window. He'd pulled his mail hood up over his head, and was wearing his black cloak. Along with his blue tunic, he wore loose trousers tucked into short boots, and cut in a riding style. What looked at first glance like spurs were in fact some kind of leather ornamentation, as if he didn't ride anymore, but wanted people to think he did. Likewise the gloves he was pulling off were the right size and shape for riding gloves, but not made from heavy enough leather.

He's cold. So Halia must be warmer than the Peninsula in winter. That wasn't *so* strange; even within the Polity itself there were warmer places. But this particular region was considered temperate, not cold, even at this time of year. Not like the province of Bascat, on the other side of the Serpents Teeth, where grapes wouldn't grow. Even Questin was farther north than Gaena.

But Svann hadn't been at Questin Hall.

A fist between the shoulder blades shoved Ker into the room, where she almost tripped on the edge of the piled carpets.

"That will do. Thank you." Svann stirred one of the braziers. From behind her came the sounds of the door closing and the rustle of cloth. Svann finally replaced the brazier's slotted cover and turned toward her. Ker braced herself, but his eyes shifted immediately beyond her. He frowned.

"When I say 'that will do,'" he said, "it means 'you may go.'"

"Sir? Yes, sir." Tel's voice, but in no tone she'd ever heard before, not even when he was talking to the Faro. She wondered what she'd Flash from him now. Though she had some idea. She remembered the shifted personality she'd Flashed from the helm and ax of the man she'd killed. Or the body at the camp. It would be Tel, but a Tel whose aura was laid over by a network of red lines. Her teeth closed on her lower lip. Not the Tel she'd known.

Ker turned in time to catch the look of worry on the face of the other guard as he closed the door. Her mouth suddenly went dry, and she spun around to face the Shekayrin. That *couldn't* be why she was here—but this *was* a bedroom, not the office they'd been questioned in. As her fists clenched and her jaw tightened, she made herself look away from the bed.

Ker tried to take a slow breath. This was the time to plan, not panic. Whatever happened, whatever the Shekayrin did to her, her job was to live through it. To escape. Come back and kill him later if need be. But first keep her eye on the goal. How many times had she been given that advice during her military training? And at Questin, for that matter, though the goals had been so very different.

Something of what she felt must have shown on her face. Svann stood looking at her with his head tilted to one side, his eyebrows drawn together. Then the puzzlement cleared from his expression, and he laughed.

"No, no," he said, waving his hands in the air. "Nothing like that. Though, now that I think on it, it makes an excellent cover story should I need one." He gestured at the round table between the two braziers. "I chose this room for its warmth, not because it has a bed in it. Still, very few know you for a witch, and if the rank and file think I am bedding you, I shall let them go on thinking so." He looked at her more closely, and frowned. "I am serious, I have no interest in you sexually. Now if it was your little friend—Wynn, was that her name?" He got a faraway look in his eye.

"You want my cooperation," Ker reminded him.

"I do. And even though I only promised to keep them alive, I will honor the spirit of the agreement, and not just the letter. I shall keep them *safe* and alive. So." He pointed again to the chair. "Sit down." He turned away, searching the top of the clothes press.

Ker forced her knees to unlock and made her way stiffly across the carpets to the table. The two chairs were identical, wooden, with carved arms and thick, embroidered seats. She sat squarely, placed both feet flat on the floor, and let her hands rest on her thighs.

Svann left the clothes press and approached her, carrying a small glass bottle in his hand. It was no more than the length of Ker's index finger, delicately faceted like the jewel, and the same red color. Svann tipped the tapered mouth of the bottle to the web of skin between the thumb and forefinger of his left hand, tipping out a minute dab of red dust. It was the dust that gave the glass its color.

Svann sniffed the dust up off the back of his hand, and stood still, head tilted back and eyes closed. "I would prefer not to tie you to the chair," he said, without opening his eyes, "but I will if I must." He set the bottle down on his side of the table. He looked taller, now that she was sitting down, though nowhere near as tall as Tel.

"You won't have to," she said, and cleared her throat.

"Good." He blinked, and picked up the remaining chair, moving it closer to her before he sat down. He was close enough to touch her, and Ker tensed again. He took no notice, but pulled the jewel out of a fold in his sash and set it on the table between them.

"First, tell me what it is you have concealed in the bosom of your tunic."

Ker shot another look at the jewel, and Svann laughed, bringing his hands down lightly on his knees. "No, no. It's not magic, I assure you. It's only that I've seen you touch the place several times, even when your hands were bound."

A buzzing had started in her ears. Ker swallowed, but the buzzing didn't stop. She reached into the front of her shirt, drew out the griffin's claw, and set it in Svann's outstretched hand. It was like giving away a piece of herself.

"What is it?"

Ker opened her mouth to lie, but remembered in time that Tel knew what the claw was. She had to assume he would betray her.

"It's a griffin's claw," she said. "I found it in the mines." Not quite a lie.

"A griffin's claw? In the mines?" He turned it over in his hands, watching how the light reflected from the claw's surface. Finally, he set it down on the table, close to the jewel.

Ker tensed, waiting for the next question.

"Tell me about your training," was what he said.

She let her breath out slowly. "I never completed it."

He turned his left palm up, a small smile curving his lips. "Tell me what you can."

Ker swallowed. *It doesn't matter what I tell him*, she reasoned. Without the Talent itself, all the training and instruction in the world wouldn't be useful.

"If I could know how much you know already," she started again.

"Nothing. I know exactly nothing. The magic of the body is not a permitted study—though that may very well be because we have no one in whom to study it. You represent a unique opportunity, my dear Kerida. An unsealed witch! I expect to learn a great deal from you."

Not a permitted study. Ker fastened on those words. He'd said that if the guards believed he was bedding her, it would make a good cover story. And he'd told Tel and Jak not to speak of her. Now that all made sense.

He'd only need a cover story if he was hiding something. Something that could get him into trouble if other Halians learned of it. Too bad she couldn't see any way this knowledge could help her. He obviously didn't expect her to be able to tell anyone. She took a deep breath. Staying alive long enough to escape depended on her keeping him interested.

"I'll have to start at the beginning, then," she said. "We call it the Talent. Inquisitors—very powerful Talents who have finished their training and have experience in this—start testing children at the age of ten, and go on testing them until they're fifteen. After that, the Talent doesn't develop."

———

"The Inquisitor's on his way." Surm Barlot laid the stores list on the table in front of Juria Sweetwater and sat down.

Juria stared for a moment at the single sheet, and massaged her eyebrows with the tips of her scarred fingers. "Wonderful."

"I thought you liked Luca Pa'narion?"

"I *do* like him—did I ever tell you he taught me to throw knives? I was six. My brother was mad with jealousy."

"What is it, then?"

Juria leaned back in her chair. "I don't like what he reminds me of. When my father asked me to keep this precious family secret, I was"—she shrugged—"sixteen? He thought I'd take over the farm."

"But you chose a soldier's life and left the cows and the cheese making to your brother." Surm laid his hand on his heart, grinning. "For which I and thousands of others thank you."

"And I wish I could have left the secret of my aunt among the Feelers to him as well. Who knew that oath would be such a burden—the Mother knows I never thought I'd become Faro of Bears. I look back now and wonder why I agreed."

Surm rolled his eyes upward. "Are you serious? A dangerous secret? What young person would have said no to the chance of being part of such a weighty conspiracy?"

Juria looked at him sideways. "Does it give you a headache?"

"What?"

"Having all the answers."

Surm laughed and rose to his feet, coming to stand behind her, and dug his thumbs into the muscle at the top of her shoulders.

Sighing, Juria let her head hang down. "Are there any new rumors?"

"Let's see. The Luqs is still alive and has fled to Juristand, where she's either gathering forces to come rescue us, or she's drunk. The Faro of Lions is coming over from Ma'lakai to rescue us, or he's behind all this because he wants to be Luqs himself, or—"

"Or he's drunk. Nothing about the prince?"

"Not from the ranks. Not that I've heard."

And he would have heard. That was what a good Laxtor did, and Surm was the best.

They both looked up at the murmur of voices in the anteroom, and Surm was seated with his list in front of him by the time the door swung open and Luca Pa'narion came in, closely followed by Cuarel the Feeler. The woman was never far from him, and Juria couldn't blame her.

The Inquisitor sat down at the far end of the table, in the customary seat for Talents. Was he Flashing, Juria wondered, and decided she was too tired to be bothered if he was. She scrubbed her face with her hands and sat up straight.

"Any further news?" she asked.

Luca shook his head. "Nor are we likely to get any, at this point."

Surm tilted his head to one side. "The odds aren't good. They may not know what they have, but the boy's a prisoner. Given the opportunity, free children grow older. Prisoners so often don't." His voice died away.

Years of close association made it easy for Juria to know what Surm was thinking. They were as good as prisoners themselves, trapped in Oste Camp. It might be her Bears who grew no older. She realized she was rubbing at her left wrist and drew her hand away, picking up the cup of kaff long gone cold in front of her. The old injury only bothered her if snow was coming, and the thought of more snow was bringing on the mother of all headaches.

"In the meantime, our stores are running low," Surm announced. "Everything," he added before he could be asked. "Food, weapons—we've even had to put a stop to the signal fire, to conserve the fuel for cooking and warmth. We're already on half rations of water, and we'll have to cut that, unless it snows again. This fort was never intended to withstand a siege."

At least there hadn't been any night raids since Luca Pa'narion came. He could Flash where enemy soldiers were, targeting them for Juria's archers. He hadn't come soon enough to save the arm of Mekner Rost, the Camp Commander, lost in the final raid before the Talent's arrival.

Juria raised her eyebrows at Luca when the duty officer tapped at the door. He was closest, and there were no aides or lower ranks in the room. "If you would?"

Before he could move, the woman Cuarel rose to her feet and opened the door, stepping aside to allow the officer entry. He had another soldier with him.

The Duty Officer correctly ignored everyone else in the room and addressed himself to the Faro. "I've got Nate Primo here, my Faro. Second Officer, Pearl Cohort of Eagles. You'll recall—"

"He's the one who came with the news of the open pass," Juria said, nodding. "Of course. You have some other news for us now, Pearl Second?"

"I hope so, Faro." Nate touched the crest on his left shoulder, and stood at attention on the right-hand side of the table, where empty chairs allowed him to both see and be seen. At a signal from Surm, he stood at parade rest, his thumbs hooked in the belt of his tunic.

"Speak, Pearl Second."

"Thank you, Faro." The man shot a glance at Luca. "I've only just learned that one of the Talents is of Inquisitor rank, Faro, and it occurred to me—that is . . ." The man hesitated, and a little color crept to his cheeks above his beard. "Faro, I gave my plaque to Kerida—the young Talent, I mean—so in case anything happened to me, she would know. Or she'd know that I made it here, if you follow me. Faro," he added.

"I do follow. A little unorthodox, perhaps, but understandable. I do not see any great punishment coming to you."

"No, Faro, and that's not why I'm here." The man looked at Luca again. "I thought—I don't know how these things work, exactly, but I thought, seeing that Ker—Talent Nast, I mean—seeing that she has my plaque, Talent Pa'narion here, being an Inquisitor, might be able to find her through me. Through the plaque, like."

There was silence in the room. Luca tilted his head to one side.

"Can this be done, Inquisitor?"

The older man lifted his eyebrows. "Soldiers' plaques *are* so much a part of them . . . well, there's a simple way to find out." Luca got to his feet and approached the soldier who now turned toward him, opening the collar of his tunic.

"Nate Primo, is it? Well, relax, Nate. You won't feel a thing."

The man nodded and lifted his chin. Luca placed his hand at the base of the man's throat, thumb to one side, fingers to the other.

"The plaque is in Gaena," he said immediately. "And Kerida is with it. She is frightened, but her spirits are good. So," he said, fixing his eyes on Juria. "Closer to us than she was, but likely still a prisoner."

"Precisely," Juria agreed. "Thank you, Pearl Second, and you also, Duty Officer. I would say take an extra ration of beer, but we're a bit short at the moment, so I'm afraid I'll have to owe it to you."

The man smiled. "I know you're good for it, Faro." Touching his crest again, he followed the duty officer out.

"Is the prince with her? Is he safe?" Juria asked once the door was closed.

Luca shook his head. "That I can't be sure of. If she were touching him, perhaps I could tell, but frankly, I was surprised to get as much as I did."

"I'd say that if the prince weren't with her, and in that sense safe, her spirits would be less good," Surm suggested.

Luca leaned forward, hands gripping the edge of the table, a new light in his eyes. "We must rescue them. If I took Nate Primo with me, a small expedition—"

"And how do you propose we do that, Talent Inquisitor? We cannot even rescue ourselves." Juria wished she could erase the bitterness from her voice.

A storm gathered on the older man's face, but before he could speak, the Feeler cleared her throat.

"Your pardon," she said. Her voice was rough, as though she had been crying. "We don't need to go ourselves. I will tell my people where the Griffin Girl is being held, and *they* can send a party to rescue her."

The skin crawled on Juria's back, even as she recognized the military usefulness of the Feeler's ability. "Of course," she managed to say. "Please do so."

A flurry of noise and the duty officer was back in the room without knocking. "My Faro, a strength of soldiers has been sighted to the northeast. Looks like a full Cohort."

Juria kept the hope rising in her heart from showing on her face. "Ours?"

"My Faro," the man said nervously. "How could we be sure?"

"Faro Sweetwater." Luca Pa'narion, smiling now, tapped the tabletop with his fingers. "I Flash a sleek beast dropping from the branches of trees onto its enemies below."

"Panthers." Juria got to her feet, sore wrist and headache forgotten. "Officer, call to quarters. They may need our help to reach us."

"My Faro, it shall be done."

Tel Cursar whistled as he rubbed another dollop of grease into the stiff edge of his weapons harness. The polish on his sword and dagger had come up nicely—what a relief to get back his own weapons. Sure, his dagger was a little more worn than regulations would normally allow, but a sword the right length for him wasn't easy to come by. He flexed the harness. A little more work on that last strap and it would be ready when he went on duty at the ninth watch.

"It doesn't bother you that the Shekayrin has your girl?"

"Hmmm?" Tel looked up. A full Barrack normally shared this dormitory room, though at the moment only he and Pella Dursto were in it. Pella was a fair, thickset man, with an upper lip that fairly cried out for a mustache to hide its thinness. Tel had found the first day or so of this new posting difficult. There weren't so very many Bears in the Peninsula, and none had come here with the Shekayrin, so doing his watches with the friendly Pella Dursto had been a real help.

The older man looked up from the cards laid out on the bench in front of him. "Your girl, what was her name? The dark-haired one who was with the prince's stepson. You know what everyone is saying, don't you?"

Light began to dawn. He knew about the rumors that the Shekayrin was bedding the witch—knew about them and didn't contradict them. "Better they should think he's making her his concubine than that she's a . . ." Tel's voice dried up. He wasn't to speak of that. *Better not even to think about it.*

"I've seen that look before. Never you mind, boy. If there's something you can't talk about, so be it. I was only wondering if there was something between the young woman and yourself."

Tel made a face. "'Course not." And if there was, Tel thought, if they *had* been friends, that was likely *her* doing, to make him more useful to her. That was all. "We were just traveling together."

Pella slapped Tel on the shoulder. "If you say so."

Frowning, Tel watched as Pella turned back to his game. Tel was beginning to understand not everyone even here in this building had received the benefit of the jewel. The older man hadn't, that he knew for certain. "Pella, tell me the truth. Do *you* think the witches should still be in charge?"

"No, of course not." Pella answered quickly, but his voice was firm with conviction. "I mean, no one in the military ever thought they should have the power they did. The Luqs favored them, so what could be done? Taking down the Halls was good. Gives us a clean starting point." He pursed up his lips. "There is one thing, though, that makes me wonder."

Tel nodded, turning the pot of grease over in his hands. *Why am I staring at this? What's so important about a pot of grease?* Shrugging, he fastened the lid and set the almost empty pot back into his pouch. "What one thing?"

"Well, break up the Halls, sure. I've always been of the opinion that the Talents should be under the control of the Wings. Anyone can see the logic there. But killing them all, when they could have been useful?" Pella shook his head.

Tel stood and picked up his harness. "Winter Inquisitor on Summer Luqs," he pointed out. "There are useful drugs, too," he added. "But in the wrong hands, they're poison. If the witches can't be controlled, they have to be killed. Look what was happening here in the Polity with the witches running free."

"I don't mean anything by it." Pella shifted a column of cards and looked up. "The Talents—I mean the witches—fine, they had to be stopped. But how does some of the rest of it follow? It seems that women aren't citizens anymore. Can't serve in the military, can't be in city government."

Tel paused in buckling on his harness, and turned to look at the other man. Pella Dursto was frowning, his eyes narrowed in thought. "There's bound to be some rough spots while everyone gets used to the new order," Tel pointed out. "Things will soon settle down again, especially now that the prince has been found."

Pella rubbed at his chin, frowning down at his cards. "I

wish I had your optimism, boy. It's difficult for a man to keep his footing at times like these—even a man like me. And the fact is, Shel Darwin was a good commander."

"I'm sure she was."

The voice came from the open doorway of the barrack room, and both Tel and Pella stood as Jak Gulder came in.

"No offense meant, Kalter," the older man said.

"And none taken, at least not by me. Please, resume what you were doing." He sat down on the next bench, just like he was one of them. Though Tel had been about to leave, he sat down again as Jak Gulder began to speak.

"Most of the Halian officers won't understand that there were many women serving—and many are still serving, I suppose—who were worthy of command. It's just that they don't think about women that way. Personally, I think we'll see women in the military again, maybe even as commanders, once things settle down, and we can be sure we have all the witches." The Kalter drew up his knee and hooked an arm around it. Tel relaxed. He felt a degree of comfort in Jak Gulder's presence that he couldn't exactly explain, except that he knew the Kalter had expressed a personal interest in his, Tel's, advancement. As a Kalter, an administrative assistant to a Faro, that might not have meant very much, but now that Gulder was the aide to the Sunflower Shekayrin, things could very well be different.

"From what I understand, it's very rare for women to be in positions of command among the Halians—why, they don't even inherit or own property in their own names—but you see that property ownership here remains unchanged. No one is challenging any woman's right. With the military it's a different thing, as we've all noticed. Armed women are something so unheard of for them that, along with the threat of witches, they feel they just can't take any chances. A man might withstand the power of a witch, but a woman apparently can't, and that's not something we could ever have known. Any soldier

who surrenders her arms is free to go, and only those who refuse are punished."

Jak Gulder fell silent, and Tel's mouth dried. He'd heard
some rumors of just what that punishment could entail.

"Still, witches don't go armed—never have, not even the
men," Pella said.

"Well, *we* know that, but why should the Halians believe
it? And why wouldn't the witches start to arm themselves
now, things being as they are?" Tel pointed out. He started to
say that Kerida could fight, that she'd been trained. But it appeared he couldn't even say her name aloud.

Jak was examining the other man with his head tilted to
one side. "I'm right in thinking that you don't know the stone,
Pella Dursto?"

"I don't, sir, no. There was no need for it, if you see my
meaning."

"I do, but perhaps you can explain to Tel Cursar."

Tel shifted his feet. It was one thing for the two of them to
talk in private, quite another for Pella to explain himself in
front of an officer.

"No need to waste the jewel on me," the old soldier admitted. "What does it matter to me who gives the order, so long
as our food and our pay turn up on time?"

Tel relaxed. This was familiar territory to anyone who'd
served in the military for any length of time. There were
plenty like Pella, who simply followed orders, and left it to
others to work out what those orders should be. Those who
"did their work and returned to camp" as the saying was. Tel
looked up to find Jak Gulder watching him, a look of understanding on his face. Tel gave the other man a minute nod.
Like Jak, he preferred to be on the giving end of orders.

Pella scrubbed at the graying stubble on his chin. "What I
said before was true. I'm not fond of the Talents and the way
they gave themselves airs." He looked around at them.
"Though I'd be lying if I pretended I won't play the safe cards,

whenever I can. And I can be trusted to know where the safe cards are."

"And do you think we're holding them?"

"Well, now, that depends on who you think of as 'we,' doesn't it?" Pella grinned. "We here, we in the military, we're all right. And there's probably plenty among the civilians that think the same way as me. So long as the price of wine and eggs don't change much, and taxes don't go up, they won't much care who sits on the throne."

Pella fell silent, and Tel realized both men were looking at him. He straightened up and cleared his throat. "I heard two of the others talking, and they were saying that Gendia had been sacked and burned. That there'd been some sort of resistance there." He looked at Jak Gulder.

"That's right, there was. The people there refused to accept the authority of the Daisy Shekayrin. I think you'll find, though, that we'll see less of that happening now that we have the prince."

"But if there's more resistance than we know of—" Tel stopped when Jak smiled.

"It won't matter," Jak said. "Do you know what the Halians call their armies? 'Blades of Grass.' Not because of their weapons, but because of their numbers. If we need them, the Sky Emperor will send more. As long as we have a foothold anywhere in Farama, whether here in the Peninsula or elsewhere, we'll win."

Blades of Grass. That had a nice, comforting sound to it, Tel thought.

G ANNI rested his chin on his clasped hands. He wished
  that people's spirits could be lifted as easily as the people
themselves. But he'd wished that before. Sala's death was a
hard weight for the community of Feelers to carry. Soldier
and guide, she had brought a sense of the wider world with
her when she came to the Mines and Tunnels. People listened
to her—and no one was listening just now.

Ganni raised his hand. "Who will go with me to Gaena?" It
wasn't the first time he'd asked.

"Are you insane?" Midon thrust his hands through his hair,
his gesture drawing everyone's eyes to that end of the table.
"After what happened to Sala, do you expect *anyone* to volunteer?"

Everyone was nodding, even Hitterol who never agreed
with her brother. It seemed his pessimism was spreading. "It's
hard to know what to do." Hitterol's normally rounded tones
were pitched unpleasantly high.

"The Prophecy asks us—"

"What good is the Prophecy if no one is left to see it fulfilled?" Midon leaned forward to continue his point, only to be interrupted in turn.

"Idiots." Ara's old woman's voice came from the empty chair Larin stood next to. The child grinned. "Grandmother Ara means, did you think there was no danger? She means, you're all acting like cowards because Sala's been killed." When Larin interpreted for the old woman, she took on some of Ara's voice and manner. "Did you think this would be like a walk to the well?"

Norwil slapped his hand down on his knee. "Ara's right. We knew the Prophecy brought danger with it, if not here and now, then later, when we reveal ourselves. I say we ask for volunteers, before the Springs and Pools Clan get involved and push us to one side."

"We haven't heard from Dersay. Surely her opinion has the most weight." Again, Midon sounded more reasonable than Ganni liked. Probably thought Dersay would take his part. This was her first council meeting. Until now, it had been Sala in the Far-thinker's seat.

"You can't know." She glanced at the empty chair next to Larin. "Not even Ara. None of you can know what it's like to be touched by the jewel. Sala showed me." She picked up the cup in front of her, took a sip, and carefully set it down again. Only Ganni knew the cup didn't contain water.

"Cuarel and I have talked this over, and the griffin, too. Oh, yes." She looked around at the startled faces. "Oh, yes, he's in this as well. It should be Cuarel sitting in this chair, I know that." She took another deliberate swallow, setting the wooden cup down as though it was the most delicate crystal.

Midon opened his mouth, and Dersay shot him a look that would have curdled milk. "I'm telling you, I felt the jewel, I know what it can do. I know what it is." She looked around the table, her voice gathering strength. "The Griffin Girl was right. The Halians won't stop at Talents, they'll come after us.

They'll come here for the stone, but they'll deal with all of us exactly as they did with Sala." Dersay tapped herself on the chest. "They don't see any difference between us and the Talents. The Prophecy is our only hope, and the Prophecy tells us to make common cause with them.

"You want to make sure Sala's death means something? Kill the people who did this to her. And if that means saving the prince, and getting the mothering armies to stand behind him and push these people and their griffin's blood jewels into the sea where they came from—then let's do that."

Dersay's voice had not risen, her tone hadn't changed at all, but Ganni felt his own heart beat faster, and from the look of the others around the table—even Midon—they felt the same.

"I'll go," he said. "I've the most experience of the outside. Let me choose a few to go with me, and I'll bring the prince back."

"You'll have to take me, Ganni." Dersay held up her hand when he began to speak. "This time I have to. How else are you going to know what the griffin wants to tell us? He can't be always landing to speak with you."

Ganni nodded, not even bothering to listen to the raised voices around him. Some were undoubtedly volunteering, either themselves or others from their Gift guilds, but let them talk. He already knew who he'd want with him. Just now he found something else more interesting. Something Dersay had said about the stone, and about griffins' blood, that he was sure echoed the Prophecy.

Kerida pressed her clasped hands tightly between her knees. Her tongue felt swollen, and her eyelids made of sandpaper. She left them closed. What was the old rule of three her training instructor used to yell at them? Three minutes without air; three days without water; three weeks without food.

Which one was it this time? In her first session with Svann, the Shekayrin had conducted tests very like those the Hall did to establish a baseline for a Candidate's Talent. They'd be given an object and asked to Flash its primary nature—what it was made of, for example—and then its secondary nature, its age, or ownership. From the results of these tests a Candidate's development could be measured. With Svann, she'd been careful to be as accurate as possible, matching what she said to what the man knew about each object. He'd been satisfied with her cooperation, even accepting it when she told him she couldn't yet Flash humans very well—which was true, she thought, in the traditional sense. What the auras told her had nothing to do with that. Ker was very careful not to mention the auras, and she was sure the Shekayrin didn't know she was holding anything back.

Once he'd established his baseline measurements, Svann had made her go three days without sleep, making Wynn and Jerek responsible for keeping her awake, before testing her again. The results had been the same; she'd been just as accurate. Now he was testing what would happen if she were deprived of water. Lack of food would be next.

But was this the second or third day without water?

<<Can you hear me?>>

Ker would have wept with relief, if she'd had any moisture to spare. She was not alone. Svann was with her, so it must be the third day. Testing day. All she had to do was answer his questions, and he'd give her some water. She tried to focus.

"I am putting something in your hands." Odd. Svann had sounded different a moment ago. She felt fingers, warm and strong, take hold of her wrists. As soon as they were free from the vise of her knees, her hands began to tremble again. "It's all right," Svann said. "I've got you."

Again the feeling of relief.

Svann turned her hands over and put something between them, holding them closed over the object when it seemed that she wouldn't be able to do it herself. "It's all right," he said again. "Take your time."

How can I take my time? The sooner she was done, the faster she'd get some water. *Paraste.* Suddenly she Flashed, not on the arm ring she was holding, but on Svann himself. A Flash as strong as anything she'd gotten from the griffin. He *was* worried, and he spoke out of genuine concern for her, and not just for his experiments. Surprise overwhelmed the Flash completely for a second or two, before she once again became aware of the arm ring.

<<Can you get outside?>>

There it was again, echoing in her head. "What did you say?"

"I did not speak." That was Svann. He was farther away. Not in her head at all. "Concentrate, Kerida."

She swallowed, and tightened her grip on the arm ring.

<<I will come for you if you are outside.>>

It was enough to make her weep. The voice in her head was surrounded by bands of colors, hundreds of them. Was she starting to hallucinate? Whose voice was she imagining?

<<You do not imagine me. I am Weimerk.>>

Oh, Mother, it sounded like him. It did. Ker felt herself falling forward, and then a strong grip on her shoulders that could only be Svann's hands. Of course, it wasn't the Halian speaking. She could tell that now.

"I can't leave my friends," she said, unsure whether she spoke aloud.

"Of course not." *That* was Svann. His hands gave her shoulders a gentle squeeze. "Tell me about the object, and all this can be over." He was trying not to show how worried he was.

<<Very well. But know I can come for you.>>

The presence, the echo that was sound and space and colors, was suddenly gone from her head, but Ker could still feel Svann's hands on her shoulders. That meant—it *must* mean—that she'd really heard Weimerk. That somehow the griffin had been able to Far-think to her, as though she were a Feeler. What was it she'd said to him?

"I won't leave my friends."

"Of course not, my dear. Of course not."

She was no longer Flashing Svann. He must have let her go. She ran a dry tongue over drier lips and focused on the arm ring, stiffening her shoulders. Right now, she needed water more than anything else, and this was the way to get it.

"This is made of silver, and it's very old. It was your father's," she said. "Nevlin Svann was his name. He wasn't a Shekayrin, but his father, your grandfather, was, and this arm ring was his as well. Before that it was *his* mother's, your great-grandmother. It's from her the magefire comes—" The arm ring was snatched from her hands.

"That can't be." The words were bitten off.

Kerida said nothing. Her mouth was just too dry.

"The thirst is affecting your Flashing." He'd started using her term for it.

Ker squeezed her eyes shut. "Your father always wore this on his left forearm; he used to turn it when he was thinking." She shook her head. "I either Flash, or I don't. I don't get some of it right and some of it wrong." A beginner might get confused, especially when generations were involved, but it had never happened to Kerida. "Your great-grandmother was a mage."

A sudden sharp pain on the side of her face and she was on the floor. Somehow she managed to raise her hands in time to land on her elbows and not on her nose. Svann seized her right arm in a grip that felt like a blacksmith's vise and dragged her upright. He shook her until her teeth snapped together and thrust her back into her chair before striding to the door and flinging it open.

"You! Fetch me—" His silence was abrupt. "No. Find Tel Cursar, tell *him* to fetch Wynn Martan. At once."

He slammed the door shut and turned back to Kerida, his

cloak swinging behind him like a black flag. When he was close enough, he grabbed her by the hair on the top of her head and lifted her until she was balancing on her toes.

"There is no chance." He shook her. "Do you hear me? No chance in this world there was a witch in my family! There is not a single taint of body magic in me. None!" He had the jewel clutched in his fist, and now shook it under her nose. "There is only the magic of the stone."

"But—" Kerida gasped, tears starting from her eyes. She would have nodded if Svann's hand in her hair didn't prevent it. She clung to his wrist with both hands, trying to relieve the agony that burned in her scalp.

And she Flashed on him again. And this time she Flashed on the jewel as well.

The stone was as old as the world and as hard as time. It had an aura like a living thing, but the colors were Svann's. And the facets, somehow they were his as well. She hadn't seen that before. The pattern was the jewel's, but it was his as well. Each had formed the other.

The stone was still connected to the earth it came from, and drew upon the slow magic of the mountains and the rock, the roots of the world. She saw how Svann was connected through the jewel to all these things, like an insect on the leaf of a tree is connected to the soil touched by the tree's roots.

"You are the jewel," she said, and saw his eyes widen as he heard her. The pain on her head eased as he lowered her to the floor.

A knock stopped whatever he might have said next. Svann went to the door himself, opening it only a few inches until he saw who was there, then swinging it wide to allow Tel Cursar to enter with Wynn.

Svann took Wynn by the shoulder and pulled her to face Ker.

"Their safety depends on your cooperation," Svann said.

"That is our bargain." He transferred his grip to Wynn's wrist, and before anyone could guess what he meant to do, he had twisted two of her fingers out of place. Mercifully, the sound of the joints dislocating was covered by Wynn's yelp.

With Wynn still hanging from his fist, Svann turned his stony gaze to Kerida.

"You will not lie to me again," he said.

Kerida parted her lips, but her throat closed tight.

Svann lifted Wynn's wrist again.

"No!" It was only a croak but Svann paused, swiveling his eyes to meet hers. "I won't! I won't."

Svann lowered his hand, though he still kept his grip on Wynn's wrist. "The next time I will not merely break the joints of her hands. And there is still the boy."

Kerida tasted bile in the back of her throat. It was only a couple of fingers, she told herself. Wynn would still be able to use a bow. Probably.

"Take her away." Svann shoved Wynn at Tel and turned away before seeing whether or not he caught her.

"Hold still. Breathe!" Tel eased Wynn down until she was sitting on the floor, her back against the wall. Fortunately, there was a tapestry on each side of the door, giving the injured girl some padding against the cold stone.

"Long, slow breaths." Tel squatted down next to the girl. "Don't faint."

"What happened?" Pella's voice from over his shoulder was quiet.

"Nothing." Tel made sure he had Wynn's attention as he spoke. "She fell and hurt her hand against the edge of a table."

Her lips were drawn back from clenched teeth, but the girl nodded. She understood. She knew the witch would be in worse trouble, if everyone found out what she was. And if it came to that, there was no way to explain what had really happened without mentioning the witch—and *that* Tel himself couldn't do.

"It's just a couple of dislocated fingers," Tel said. He was speaking both to Wynn and to his partner. He kept his voice calm and gentle. This wasn't the poor girl's fault. This was just another thing the witch had to answer for. "We've all had worse in training." He pulled his personal knife from his belt. The hilt was narrow and rounded, closely wrapped with tiny strips of leather. "Pella, hold her shoulder and upper arm."

Pella squatted down close against the wall. He wrapped one of his meaty hands around Wynn's shoulder and took a firm grip on her elbow with the other. He caught Tel's eye and nodded.

"Here, put this between your teeth." Tel waited until Wynn had her teeth clamped on the hilt of his knife. "Ready?" Pella nodded again and Wynn shut her eyes.

"On three. One." He saw the muscle in Wynn's jaw tighten. "Two." She was holding her breath. Without saying "three," Tel pulled and twisted first one finger and then the other.

"I thought you said on three," Pella grunted. He'd switched his grip to wrap his arm around the girl's shoulders.

"So did she." Tel watched Wynn's eyelids flutter down, and the knife drop to the floor. "You watch here, I'll get her back to their rooms." Without waiting for an answer, he scooped up his knife and resheathed it. Then he lifted the fainting girl in his arms and set off down the corridor.

Jerek was on his way back from the kitchen, where he'd managed to put three travel cakes into the front of his tunic, along with a double handful of dried plums. Wynn had sneaked a knife the night before, but they still needed a way to carry water. Jerek thought he might persuade Cook to let him have one of the old skin water bags, hanging disused in a storeroom, for a football. The gruff old man made the kitchen serfs jump, but he seemed to like Jerek, often patting him on the shoulder, and setting aside tasty bits for him. He and Wynn had soon figured out they got better food if Jerek fetched it.

He slowed as he turned the corner into the corridor leading to their room. Their door was open. Ker was with the Shekayrin this morning, and Wynn would never leave the door open. Anything out of the ordinary could be dangerous—that's what they'd told him. He crept closer, releasing his breath when he heard the murmur of Wynn's voice, and then Tel Cursar's. He knew that Tel had been changed somehow by the Shekayrin, but that bothered the women more than it bothered him. Here was a chance to judge for himself.

Jerek hesitated when they both turned to look at him. Suddenly, he was sure the travel cakes were making a huge bulge under his tunic.

As if he understood, Tel smiled at him, shaking his head. "There's never enough to eat, is there? Tell you what, cut me in on your swag and I won't tell on you." The tall man had stepped to one side as he spoke, blocking Jerek's view of Wynn, but she moved so he could see her again. He forgot all about the stolen food when he saw Wynn's bandaged hand. He pushed forward.

"What did you do to her?"

"It's all right, Jerek." Wynn put her good arm around him. "He didn't do anything." Just the same, the look Wynn shot the man was full of disapproval. "He's the one who bandaged me up."

"The Shekayrin." Jerek had to force his teeth to unclench. "He hurt you."

"It wasn't really the Shekayrin." Tel put his hand on Jerek's shoulder. "It was the other girl. She disobeyed him. She knew what could happen if she did that." Wynn's arm tightened around Jerek, and Tel lifted his hand. "But you don't have to be afraid, Jerek. You don't even have to stay here, with the w—" Here Tel coughed and cleared his throat. "With the women. You could bunk with me."

Jerek searched Tel's face. He could see it now, the change. He could also see the man meant well. "No. Thank you." He swallowed, but asking was the only way to know. "Why don't you love her anymore?"

Tel's face went blank, then clouded over, his pale brows almost meeting above his spit-gray eyes. "I never loved her. She's . . ." His voice faded away. "You know what she is," he said finally. He didn't sound very sure of himself, though. And he'd known right away who Jerek had meant.

"But you used to love her. Before the Shekayrin touched you with his jewel." Jerek angled to stand between Wynn and Tel. "I could tell, just watching you at dinner that night. And Wynn says . . ."

"Jerek," Wynn said in his ear.

"I'm asking," he told her. "I want to know. The old stories say true love is more powerful than any magic."

Tel's face cleared, and his smile spread as he straightened to his feet. "Well, there you are, then. Obviously, I didn't truly love her. That must have been her—well, you know what it must have been—keeping me sweet so I'd help her. Luckily, your stepfather saw through her, or we could have ended up only the Son knows where."

"Yes. My stepfather. Of course." Jerek closed his mouth.

Tel nodded and patted Jerek again. "Don't worry." He looked over Jerek's head at Wynn. "She won't let anything bad happen to you, now that she knows not to trifle with the Shekayrin."

Jerek watched Tel Cursar leave without closing the door. "Kerida, you ass," he said under his breath as anger boiled through him. "Her name's Kerida."

———

"Ker, really, it's all right." Wynn's face was still pale, except for the dark purple smudges under her eyes.

"How did he know you were lying?" Jerek sat with his shoulder pressed against Wynn, as if he'd been there for a long time.

"I *wasn't* lying. But I'll have to in future." Kerida wrung out a fresh cloth in the basin of cool water, and used it to replace the one wrapped around Wynn's hand. Tel's bandages had done nothing to help the swelling.

"But what was he so mad about?"

Ker shook her head, shooting a glance over her shoulder at the door.

"Keep your voice down if you have to, but I think *I* at least deserve to know, all things considered." Wynn winced. "You couldn't have known what would happen. Come on, tell us."

Ker frowned, but Wynn just lifted her eyebrows. The swelling in her hand was going down, thanks to the application of cold water. Better still would be herbs to help with Wynn's pain, but it wasn't likely the kitchen staff would give them such things.

"Well?"

Ker placed the cloth back into the bowl and set it to one side. She'd been slowly rehydrating herself since Svann had released her, but it took all her willpower not to empty the bowl down her throat.

"I said he'd got his magic from his great-grandmother." She frowned. "It's like they think there's two kinds of magic, one for men and one for women, and the women's magic is bad. So if what I said was true, if he got his magic from his great-grandmother, it would be like he carried some kind of disease."

"And *is* there a difference?" Jerek looked from Ker to Wynn and back again.

"No, there isn't," Wynn said. "Lots of men are Talented,

everyone knows it, even if those stupid jewels seem to make people forget."

"I don't think it's as simple as that." Ker drummed her fingers on her thigh as ideas formed and reformed. "The Feelers' Gifts don't seem to work the same way the Talent does; it looks like men and women *do* have different ones. The Far-thinkers are all women, for one thing, and the ones who can move and lift things all seem to be men."

"Both men and women get Gifts, though?" Jerek was frowning, eyes narrowed in thought.

Ker nodded. "But if the Halians think that women's magic is bad . . ." Was that one of the reasons they'd killed everyone at the Halls? There was something else bothering her. Something about how the jewel Flashed . . . She shook her head. "But Svann's great-grandmother had a jewel of her own. Her magic wasn't any different from his." Ker sat back on her heels. "How soon can you travel with that hand?"

Wynn leaned forward, grinning. "Never mind the hand. Jerek and I are ready to go tonight."

The boy gave a short nod, and reached into his tunic. "I got more food," he said. "Enough for when we get outside."

"Outside." Suddenly Ker remembered the voice of the griffin in her head. "Wait. Let me try something." She shut her eyes and took two long, slow breaths. *Paraste.*

Are you there? she thought, as loudly and as clearly as she could imagine. *Weimerk, can you hear me?* She reached for that feeling of a vast echoing space that had marked Weimerk's presence before.

Or had seemed to. Maybe she'd been hallucinating after all.

"Ker, are you all right?"

She opened her eyes and took one of the travel cakes from Jerek's hands. "Just something I wanted to try." She wouldn't tell them, she decided. Why get their hopes up? "According to what I've Flashed from the corridors, the guard shift changes at the midwatch, and then not again until dawn." She grinned. "The two men who patrol this section of the building tonight are the rigid, orders-are-orders types, and they'll stick strictly to the schedule of rounds."

"Making them easy to avoid." Jerek smiled in a way that made Ker wonder just who and what he had practice avoiding in the past.

"Exactly," she agreed, looking around for something to draw on before finding a dusty spot on the floor. She squatted down and roughly sketched their part of the building in the dust. "Here's where we'll have to watch for them. Here, and again here." She looked up. "The real problem will be the guard at the door."

Wynn smiled. "He's only here when you are, and Jerek and I have an idea about that."

The sound of the door opening brought Ker groggily awake. She'd been taking her turn to nap while Wynn kept watch, and had only been asleep long enough to wake up completely disoriented. She blinked, rubbing at her eyes.

"Come with me, girl," the guard said to her from the doorway. In the torchlight flickering from the corridor, Ker recognized Pella, the thickset man. As he waited for her, he glanced with raised eyebrows at Wynn, sitting at the table, lamp turned low. Wynn shrugged in answer to his unspoken question, and he nodded. Of course, Ker thought. He'd been there to help Tel when Wynn had been injured. Ker slipped past him into the corridor, and he closed the door.

"No use in you hanging about," he told the guard on their door. "I'll mind her." The man sketched a salute before jogging off in the other direction.

"He's never asked for me this late before." Depending on

how long Svann kept her, they might have to put off their escape until tomorrow. Always supposing that this summons, coming when they were only hours away from running, was just a coincidence.

"I don't know what it was you did that made him so angry before, but if I could make a suggestion, don't do it again," Pella said as they turned into the corridor leading to Svann's quarters.

"I'll do my very best," she said. Ker wanted badly to ask the man about Tel, but what would be the point? Her lower lip between her teeth, she glanced sideways. Did Pella even know what was really going on? He seemed friendly, in a gruff way, but how far would that friendliness go if he knew she was a Talent? She'd never imagined that a day would come when she'd look at ordinary people—even soldiers—with fear.

"Quiet watch," she said as they reached Svann's door.

He froze, his hand raised to knock. His eyes narrowed before he answered. "Quiet watch."

Somehow comforted by the familiar exchange, Kerida took a deep breath and squared her shoulders as Pella opened the door. She walked through, and heard it close behind her.

Only embers glowed in the braziers. Svann would have to put on more fuel if he expected to keep them burning through the night. The window shutters were closed now, and for the first time Ker saw their inner surfaces were painted with a floral motif that picked up the colors from the wall hangings. Someone had gone to a great deal of trouble to make this room comfortable and welcoming.

Kerida hoped whoever it had been was still alive.

Svann was standing in front of the dying fire, one arm braced on the table, looking at the little crystal flask he was tipping back and forth in his hand. Kerida stayed where she was, close to the door. She wanted to show him she wasn't afraid, but she just couldn't take that first step forward.

They held their places for so long, Ker wondered whether

Svann had forgotten about her. Finally, without straightening or lowering the tiny flask, Svann turned his head toward her.

"I need to say . . ." He cleared his throat and now he did straighten. He seemed smaller somehow, and Ker realized she was seeing him for the first time in only his shirt and trousers. No mail shirt, no tunic. "What I did was not scholarly."

An apology? Kerida pressed her lips together. Was the Shekayrin drunk?

He crossed the rugs toward her, moving with his usual casual grace. All right, maybe not drunk. But *something* was changed about him. He still had the small flask of red dust in his hand. He'd used it before in the way people used drugs. Now it looked as though there was less dust in the flask than there had been.

With her back against the door, Ker was unable to back away. She stiffened, but all Svann did when he got close enough was lean forward and peer into her face, squinting as if she wasn't in focus.

"Logic tells me that if you are afraid, you will not give me true answers. You will give me the answers you believe I hope to hear." If Svann *had* been drinking, Ker would guess that he'd reached the speak-slowly-and-clearly stage. "In the future I will not punish your friends, but you must speak the truth. Are we in agreement?"

Kerida pressed her lips together, suppressing a shrug.

"You wish to say something. Speak without fear, only truthfully."

Ker took a deep breath in through her nose. "You already agreed to keep my friends alive and safe if I cooperated. Then you hurt Wynn this morning. How is what you're telling me now any different? How are you to be trusted now?"

Svann narrowed his eyes at the flask before turning away to set it down on the table next to the lamp. "I cannot read you." He was still looking at the flask of dust, but he spoke as if answering her question. "I cannot read whether you tell me the truth." He swiveled his head toward her. His blue eyes glittered, and he gave her a smile that invited her to smile with him. "*I* must trust *you*."

Ker wrinkled her nose, but she nodded. If the Shekayrin used the jewels the same way her people used the Talent—you didn't need to trust someone when all you had to do was touch them and know for certain. For maybe the first time since he'd become a Shekayrin, Svann couldn't rely on the jewel for certainty.

"Maybe we have to trust each other," she said.

Svann took a deep breath and let it out slowly, gesturing at the chair she normally used. Ker lowered herself to the front edge of the seat as Svann pulled up a chair to face her. He now had the jewel in his fingers, and he studied it the way he'd studied the flask of dust.

"We Sunflower Shekayrin are scholars. We seek only truth, and the truth should not frighten me. Did you tell me the truth this morning? I promise on the soul stone I will take no reprisal. Only tell me."

Well. Ker gripped the arms of her chair. At first, all she could see was the shape of Wynn's hand as Tel carried her out of the room.

"We have to trust each other," she said finally. "Wynn and Jerek stay safe and alive if I cooperate. I've let you keep me without water and without sleep. Then the first time I say something you don't want to hear, you hurt Wynn."

He nodded. "Yet we must trust each other. How?"

"You say you can't read me." She nodded toward the jewel he held in his hand. "But I *can* Flash *you*. Then I'd *know*. And—" She shrugged. "If I truly have no reason to fear you, I'd have no reason to lie to you."

His lips pressed tightly together, and Ker knew he was afraid. Was he too afraid, or would his scholarly curiosity make him brave enough to chance it?

"I'd know," she repeated. "Beyond all doubt, I'd know. And your research could continue," she added.

"You would see the whole truth of me?"

"I'm not sure about the whole truth." Something compelled Ker to be open. "I know I can get a single answer to a single question, but how much more?" She shook her head. "That I'm not sure of."

He shot a glance at the flask of dust, but as she finished speaking, he was nodding. His eyes swiveled to meet hers. The whites seemed to be stained a little pink. He smiled again, and again Ker wondered if he were drunk—or whether the red dust *was* some kind of drug.

"The soul stone will protect me." Ker thought Svann was talking to himself. "The magic of the body *cannot* harm me. Therefore I will let you do this."

Ker cleared her throat and rubbed her hands dry on the front of her trousers. There was no way she could object to his holding onto the jewel. She got to her feet and stood over him, gesturing at his neck. Svann undid the three offset buttons of his Halian shirt, and pulled the embroidered collar open. She'd never noticed it before, but the threads were the same color as the shirt, exactly the kind of embroidery her mother liked.

Swallowing, Ker placed her hand on the base of his throat. Svann's skin was warmer than she'd expected, and smoother. *Paraste.*

The red structure in the center of Svann's aura was clear and dominant; the yellow, blue, green, and purple, spiky. She Flashed his fear, and his feeling that as a scholar he couldn't let his fear hold him back. Ker focused, and saw the answer she was looking for. He'd meant what he said. He wouldn't punish her if she said something he didn't like.

"I told you the truth," she breathed.

<<Do you speak to me?>> There it was again, Weimerk's voice in her head. She tried to answer it the same way. <<Weimerk? We're going to escape. We'll be outside soon.>>

<<Good. I will come for you.>>

<<No! Only watch over us.>>

<<Very well.>> The griffin's presence faded away.

Svann sucked in his breath. "What? Who was that?"

Ker opened her eyes, but his were still squeezed tight, the hand holding the jewel in a fist.

"Where did it go?" His aura vibrated, the colors shivering, dashing wildly from side to side.

Ker put her free hand on his shoulder. His distress was so real. Suddenly, she remembered what it was like to Flash the griffin for the first time. "It's all right, try to relax." Using the colors she and Svann had in common—and avoiding the red of the jewel—Ker tried to ease some of the spikiness and distress she could see in Svann's aura, smoothing his colors with her own.

Ker wasn't sure exactly what happened next or how she did it. Some of the colors had begun to move between Svann and the jewel, and her own had joined them, and the Flash she got then was so fierce that at first she could take nothing else in. Abruptly Ker was washed over with a whole pattern of light and color, streaked through with red. It was beautiful, and bright and warm. The webways of the jewel's facets were, she realized, an organization of spells and castings that enabled Svann to use the stone. Somehow, he and the stone together had made the web, created the facets. Fascinated, Ker focused her concentration, trying to Flash more. Curious, half laughing, she could see where the pattern began, and how it formed itself.

Suddenly, she couldn't breathe. Svann had her by the throat. His eyes sparkled, and his mouth pressed to a thin line, face taut and fierce. The fear she'd sensed before had risen up, turning all within him a deep red. He shifted his grip until he had her by the chin, lifted his free hand, and pressed the jewel against her forehead. Somehow he'd sensed that she was Flashing the jewel through him, and the thought horrified him.

Panic rose in the back of her throat, as she felt herself being pulled closer and closer to the red. She shifted her focus and, drawing her block around her like a cloak, she took hold of the roots of his pattern and tore them loose. The web flashed gold—for an instant—and disappeared.

And then Ker was down, pinned by Svann's weight, her left leg twisted painfully under her. Without the jewel's net, he'd gone down like a puppet cut from its strings. Ker struggled to get out from under him. *Terestre.*

Gritting her teeth, Ker was finally able to wriggle her upper body free, giving herself the leverage to roll Svann away and pull her legs out from under him. She felt for the pulse under his jaw and sighed in relief when she found it, rapid but strong. Though why she should be relieved was more than she could say. Surely, she'd be better off if the man was dead?

As she got to her feet, Ker spotted the jewel lying a short distance from Svann's hand. She scooped it up, the movement awakening new bruises. It felt unexpectedly cold. The facets were still there; the stone had not gone smooth again, like the one Luca had shown them in the mines. She glanced at where Svann lay on the floor, and then at the door. Nothing. No sign of the guard. They'd been quieter than she'd thought. She looked back down at Svann.

Ker knew she should kill him. He was one of the people murdering Talents, even if he wasn't the same man she'd seen at Questin Hall. He would have killed her fast enough if she'd been a Full Talent and he hadn't been able to use her for his studies. He'd killed Sala, though perhaps he hadn't been trying to.

Look what he'd done to Wynn.

She searched his belt, but found nothing beyond an empty pouch. The table, mantel, and sideboard yielded the same results. There was no edged weapon in the room. Ker chewed on her lower lip, eyes scanning her surroundings rapidly. And nothing heavy enough to crush a man's skull. She squeezed her eyes shut.

She had to get out. She had no way of knowing how long Svann would be unconscious, but she had to take advantage of it, to get Wynn and Jerek away. She still had the jewel. Maybe there was some way to turn it to her advantage as well. If she could get it to work for her, use what she knew of it—

Tel. It had seemed, just before Svann had panicked, that she'd Flashed something . . . if she could do more with the webway of spells than simply shut it off . . .

Pursing her lips in a silent whistle, she let the jewel sit flat on her palm. *Paraste.*

There. The structure of the jewel—the facets, the light and the colors—still there. But different. The red more golden now, the webways smaller. Only by stiff concentration could she see the patterns forming and reforming. There weren't an infinite number, as it had seemed at first, but only seven, or perhaps nine. She saw how she could allow her aura to mix with that of the jewel, but she also saw that she didn't need to. She could stay off to one side, take the webs into her own hands, make the jewel work.

She placed the jewel on Svann's forehead and tried Flashing through it. She saw that he slept deeply, like a man with a head injury. He'd sleep for hours. She saw the mechanism of that sleep. At least, she hoped she did. She slipped the jewel into the pocket of her tunic and, grabbing Svann by the ankles, braced herself to drag him out of the line of sight of the door.

Finally, she pushed her hair back from her face, pulled her tunic straight, patted the pocket where the jewel sat, and let herself out into the corridor.

"You're all right, then? Made it up with him, have you?"

"In a manner of speaking." Ker forced what she hoped was a normal smile on her lips.

Pella's eyes narrowed, and Ker thought he was going to question her further, but he nodded and gestured for her to precede him down the corridor.

When they arrived at her own door, she let Pella open it. As he was stepping back to let her walk through, she stumbled and he caught her by the elbow. She turned toward him as if she was trying to get her balance. Luckily, it wasn't Tel; he would have been too tall to try this trick on.

"You've got something on your face." She reached up as she spoke, and he was so sure of her he didn't even notice she had something in her hand until she had touched him with the jewel.

For the second time in an hour a man fell forward into Ker's arms, but this time Wynn was there to help her drag him into their room and lay him out on the floor.

"What did you do?" Wynn ran her hands over him looking for a wound—and helping herself to his weapons as she went. "Is he dead?"

"I hope he's just asleep. I'm hoping I *didn't* kill him." Ker shivered, laying her fingers on the pulse in his neck. "Quick, tie him up. I've got no idea how long this will last."

"How did you . . ." Jerek's question died away as Ker held up the jewel.

"We go *now*," she said. "Before anyone comes looking for this one." She tapped Pella on the chest. It would most likely be Tel himself, she realized.

"Great. Now we have weapons." Wynn held up the man's sword.

Ker knelt across from her friend and began to strip off Pella's uniform tunic. "And a disguise that will get us through the first awkward moments."

Wynn grinned. "At the least, it'll buy us time for you to use your magical stone." Her face changed. "Oh, Kerida, what about Tel? Can you use it on him?"

Ker's stomach clenched. Now that she'd actually used the jewel, she wasn't sure. It was one thing to put someone to sleep—but if she did make Tel sleep, wouldn't she then be able to . . . Her eye fell on Jerek. He was tying one of the pillow-cases into a carry bag.

"If it was just you and me, I'd risk it. But think." She nodded at Jerek. "Every minute we spend looking for Tel is a minute in which we can get caught. And then, what if I couldn't
change him? We'd lose all hope of escape. We can't risk that.
Not now." But there was a hollow inside her that her words
left empty.

19

JURIA Sweetwater examined the woman sitting across from her with interest. This would be the sister, or rather the half-sister, of the young Talent, Kerida Nast. Generally speaking, Battle Wings weren't something you could inherit, but Tonia Nast was the third generation of her family to be Faro of Panthers. There were older Wings, and older Faros for that matter, but this woman was one of the most well-respected military leaders in the Polity. The kind of person who could make someone Luqs. Or become Luqs herself, for that matter.

So which option brought the Panther to the seat on the other side of the round table, in the room Juria had begun to think of as her own? The Inquisitor Luca Pa'narion sat at her left. The chair to her right was empty, and Juria felt the absence of her Laxtor, Surm Barlot, though he was missing for the best of reasons, finding a den for her newly arrived Bears, the Ruby, Pearl, and Onyx Cohorts that the Faro of Panthers had brought to her.

"You say that no one has approached you since your surrender was demanded?"

"Not directly, no." Juria spread her hands wide and lowered them again to the table. "Smaller attacks—especially at night—increased, but there was no final ultimatum."

"Unless they thought you'd been given one already," Faro Nast suggested.

Juria nodded. "Since then, we've learned that the Halians are headquartered in Pudova."

Faro Nast signaled to one of her two aides with a lifted finger. "Have you numbers?"

"Now that your people have dealt with the squads in the forest, there are barely two hundred Halians in Pudova," the Inquisitor said.

Faro Nast turned to her aide. "Jade Cohort Leader will take three companies. Report to the Laxtor when they've taken the town."

"Your people will need to be careful of the twisted ones," Juria said. "The ones the Halians—"

"We're aware of the Halians' activities in that regard, Faro, thank you. We still have our own Talents with us, though none are of Inquisitor Pa'narion's rank."

Juria pressed her lips together, inclining her head. All things considered, she didn't mind giving the other Faro a report, but she wasn't sure she liked the woman's tone, with its implication that her Bears had somehow fallen short of Battle Wing standards. But Faro Nast's next words cleared that feeling away.

"I'm amazed you were able to hold out as long as you have, with only the two companies of Bears you kept with you," she said, shaking her head. "Oste isn't even a real fortress, for the Mother's sake. I'm going to put you and your people in for a commendation."

"If there's anyone left to award it to us," Juria said. "And speaking of such things, when do the rest of your Panthers arrive?"

"I'm afraid they won't be arriving."

"I don't follow." A point of ice grew in her chest. Juria was afraid she followed all too well.

Faro Nast laced her fingers together. "Now that you have your engineers to refit this place, and the area's been cleared of Halians, one Wing—or most of it—will be enough to hold this fort and keep the pass secure."

Juria leaned back in her seat, taking a deep breath in through her nose. The whole point of building Oste in its present location had been to make sure it *couldn't* easily be used to seal the pass against the Peninsula—no Luqs had wanted to be besieged or boxed in by land in that fashion.

Of course, no one had foreseen the present need to do exactly that.

"Let me understand you. We all know Oste is not close enough to the pass to be a truly effective deterrent." Juria waited, but Faro Nast said nothing. "You have just finished telling me it is only by the direct intervention of the Mother that I have been able to hold the fort itself in the face of the Halian invasion, and now you tell me I am expected to continue doing so?"

"No one's suggesting that it'll be easy. But it *could* be done." Tonia Nast leaned forward, propping herself with her elbows on the tabletop. "As things are now, you should be able to hold the pass with regular patrols."

"And while I am here, impersonating a cork in a bottle, what are the other Wings doing?" Juria didn't bother to hide how she felt.

"Right now the Polity's strength gathers in Juristand," Faro Nast said, "and we will coordinate operations against the Halian Empire from there."

"Juristand." Juria hesitated, unsure what she could say

without offending the other Faro. Juristand was an administration center second only to Farama the Capital itself, and what Tonia Nast was suggesting certainly made sense from a purely administrative point of view, but the city was at the eastern edge of the Mid Sea, and the implications . . . .

"You are going to choose a new Luqs. And in the meantime, you intend to abandon the Peninsula." She was almost daring the other woman to deny it.

Tonia Nast sighed, as if she didn't want to be the one who spoke the next words. "You know what our standard orders are when an area has been overrun. From what intelligence we can gather, that is the case with the Peninsula. There is no military post of Eagles left—and precious few Eagles. You know what that means."

Of course, Juria knew. It was just that the Polity had spread out *from* Farama. The Peninsula itself—safe behind mountain ranges and rugged sea coasts—had never been attacked, let alone overrun.

"Halians have also put ashore at Lebsos and Maglas, and they gained a foothold in Cantoli before any Wing could mobilize fast enough." It was as if the Faro of Panthers had read her thoughts. "The Halians are seafarers and that's been our downfall. Even if we could navigate at this season, we have no ships large enough to transport the number of troops we would need to retake Farama by force. Things are stable for now, but if we mount an expedition to regain the Peninsula?" The other woman shrugged.

"But what about the prince? It's not just the Peninsula. You are talking about abandoning the true Luqs of Farama. The person from whom we derive our authority."

"Do you suggest rather that we 'abandon,' to use your word, *all* the other citizens of the Polity—for many of whom, let me remind you, the Peninsula is very little more than the place they send their taxes? And for what? By your own report, Dern Firoxi has gone over to the enemy and must be considered a traitor to us, and to the Polity. The child, his son, is in their hands—though, granted, they don't know what they have. He could be put to death at any moment, undoing our every purpose."

Juria clenched her teeth.

Tonia Nast turned a hand palm up. "Again, according to your own reports, these Halians want some red stone that apparently exists in the Serpents Teeth range. Let them occupy themselves there, while we prepare strategies for the future— and yes, that may well include choosing a new Luqs. Let us strengthen our hold on the rest of the Polity. The Peninsula is a great loss, but our loyalty must be to the whole, not to a part, however rich in history and tradition."

Juria glanced at the Inquisitor. His face was hard, his eyes narrowed, as if he saw something Juria didn't see. Or maybe she saw it, but just could not believe it.

"The destruction of the Halls—" she began.

"Should we endanger the rest of the Polity in what can only be an act of revenge? And how many more of the innocent in the Peninsula will die? I respect the Talented, I always have, but sending the Wings into the Peninsula won't bring any of them back. I'm sorry to interrupt you, Faro, but what's done is done."

"And your sister?" Juria felt she was grasping at straws.

"Cohort Leader Ester Nast is missing in action. A possible fate for any soldier."

"I believe the Faro of Bears spoke of your other sister, Kerida Nast." Luca Pa'narion's dry words fell into a moment of silence.

The Faro of Panthers turned to face him. "By your own rules, Inquisitor Pa'narion, Kerida Nast is no longer my sister." She turned back to Juria. "Have you any questions?"

"Is there any point in my asking about relief or reinforcements?"

"I can leave two cohorts of my Panthers here, to bring you

to full strength, if you wish it. In which case, you may be sure that I, for one, would be taking a close interest in what passes here."

Which might mean anything, Juria thought. Best to speak carefully. "I will consider your offer, Faro of Panthers. But I must be clear, by what authority do you direct me? I am Faro of Bears, and you are not in yourself senior to me."

Tonia Nast jerked her thumb at the door and her remaining aide scrambled to leave the room. She waited until the door was shut before leaning forward again. "I'll speak plainly, Juria. I speak with the authority of the Battle Wings. In the absence of the Luqs, or any other supreme commander, this has been decided by majority vote of Faros." She sighed again and abruptly became more human. "Though how long this consensus will last, your guess is as good as mine. You're quite right, Juria, I can't compel you to stay. But I hope you'll agree to."

"That is why you brought me my people."

Tonia leaned back, drumming the fingers of her left hand on the arm of her chair, her eyes slanted to the right. "It's what I would have wanted done for me," she said finally, raising her eyes.

Juria felt the directness of the other woman's gaze, and understood. A Faro with no Wing was just a soldier. A Faro *with* a Wing to back her—or him—was a person who could act as she saw fit.

Faro Nast might be informing Juria of the decisions made by the majority of Faros, but in bringing her Bears to her, Tonia Nast was giving Juria the chance to decide for herself. She wished she knew the other woman well enough to know whether this act of support was also a hint to what Nast herself wanted. She'd reported the will of the Wings, but not what her own vote had been.

"I must take Inquisitor Pa'narion with me, but I will leave two of my Talents with you."

Luca's face went completely still. "You certainly have no jurisdiction over *me*."

"I'm sorry, Inquisitor, but I must insist. The shortage of Talents is dire. And, with the fall of the Peninsula, those remaining are without guidance and leadership. You may be the highest ranking Talent left in the Polity, and you *will* allow us to ensure your safety." She pushed her chair back and stood. "I'm sorry, I really am. I wouldn't be in your boots for anything."

Juria waited until the door closed behind her. "Well. That was interesting." A sudden need for movement brought her to her feet. She yanked open the door. The orderly—a Bear—in the outer room was still standing from the passage of the Faro of Panthers. "Jess, I need the Laxtor." She noticed Cuarel standing off to one side, and jerked her head at the room behind her. The Feeler woman sprang forward and went immediately to stand beside Luca.

Juria wrinkled her nose, but she wasn't annoyed with the Gifted. "What do you suppose the Panther really wants me to do?"

Luca looked up from his clasped hands. "You assume she has an agenda?"

"I assume *I'd* have one, if it were me bringing another Faro the better part of her strength. But does she want me to help the young prince, or does she want me to destroy the Bears trying?"

"Or does she want you in her debt when she makes a move for the throne herself?"

Juria choked off a laugh. "She wouldn't be the first."

"Uh, Luca? Luca, we have to go." Cuarel shot Juria an apologetic twist of a smile.

"That's what the Faro of Panthers was just telling us." Luca frowned. "She wants me with her."

"No, we can't. Weimerk says his girl's escaping. We're needed."

Luca Pa'narion got to his feet. "Well, Faro, you'll have to
excuse me." He didn't need to tell her he had no intention of
going with the Panthers. And he wasn't about to tell her where
he *was* planning to go. But Juria thought she could guess.

And that guess gave her an idea.

She took a deep breath. "A moment, Inquisitor. These
mines. How many people will they hold?"

———

The worst moment came not, as Ker had feared, inside the
building, but once they were out in the streets. Inside, she'd
been able to Flash where everyone was, though not *who* they
were—something for which she thanked Mother and Daughter. If she'd Flashed Tel, she didn't know what she might have
been tempted to do.

Flashing kept them out of everyone's way until they'd
reached the kitchen, empty except for the scullery serf, rolled
in a rug and snoring on the hearth in front of the banked fire.
From the smell of him, he'd been into the cooking brandy,
and they didn't need to be as quiet as they were. Ker was just
relieved they didn't have to do anything to him. She hesitated
with her hand on the door latch.

"Someone out there?" Wynn's breath was warm on her
cheek.

Ker shook her head and lifted the latch, letting in the
cooler outside air. Not the time to tell Wynn that this wasn't
her first kitchen escape. At least she wasn't alone this time.

They scrambled over the courtyard wall with the help of a
convenient handcart and hurried to put some distance between them and the administration building. They hadn't
gone far, just turned two corners into an alley Jerek pointed
out to them, when Ker swallowed, leaning with one hand on
the frosty stone wall.

"What?"

"I can't go on Flashing." Her tongue felt too big for her

mouth. "I'm getting too much information." A cat had stalked and eaten a mouse in this alley two hours before. The cat had been very pleased with itself and the mouse had been nothing more than a bright point of fear. On the other side of the wall was a . . . "If I was better trained, I could put up only a partial block, but I'm just not strong enough." She was exhausting herself. Why hadn't she done the blasted exercises her Tutors kept scolding her about?

Wynn put her hand on Ker's shoulder. "We're outside now, so we should be all right. There's never a large city watch."

Jerek was shaking his head. "Not before, but according to what I heard, there's at least a Barrack now."

Ker swallowed again. It couldn't be helped. *Terestre*. There, her stomach unknotted.

"Nothing to worry about," Wynn was saying to Jerek. "The day we can't avoid a few guards is the day I resign from the military and give up my plans to be a Faro."

"You want to be a Faro?" the boy asked.

"Do I *look* crazy?"

Ker smiled in spite of herself.

After that, they stuck as much as they could to the smaller alleys and laneways at the backs of houses, though at one point they'd had to cross one of the broader streets. At the worst moment, a guard pair entered the street at the far end.

"Do they see us?" Jerek asked.

"If we see them, it's likely they see us," Ker said. "Don't run."

Sure enough, the pair turned to walk toward them, calling out the challenge.

"Crap." The odds were very slim that these guards wouldn't recognize them. "I'll take the one on the left." Wynn nodded.

"Give them the password," Jerek whispered. "Owl tail feather." The boy looked from Ker to Wynn and back again. "It's tonight's password."

Wynn immediately tilted her chin up, and in a surprisingly deep voice called out, "Owl tail feather!"

The two approaching men halted. For a moment they stood still, and Ker's heart pounded. Then the one on the left raised his spear in salute, and the guards turned and continued their patrol in the direction they'd been headed in the first place.

Ker waited another heartbeat before herding the others into the next alley.

"Lucky they didn't catch us in here," Wynn said. "They'd have asked questions for sure, password or no password."

"How did you know what the password was?" Ker asked Jerek.

"I was in the hallway when the commander gave it out."

"That was lucky."

"At least you didn't have to use the jewel." Jerek rubbed his nose.

"Don't even joke about it," Wynn said, patting him on the shoulder.

"Who was joking?"

Ker grinned again, and pointed up the alley. Before they could move, another voice spoke out of the shadows.

"Now what jewel would this be, my dears?"

Ker shoved Jerek behind her, and pulled the rolling pin free from her belt. She took a step forward, the man's eyes shifted toward a movement to the side, and Ker's swing connected the rolling pin to his head with a hollow "thok." He grunted and Wynn eased him to the ground.

"Nice distraction." Ker swallowed.

"Someone's running away," Jerek whispered.

"Let them go," Ker said. "Whoever it is doesn't want the attention of the watch any more than we do. Check him for weapons," she added to Wynn.

"Teach your grandmother." Wynn had turned the man over and was patting him down. She paused when Jerek made a soft noise. "What is it?"

"I think I know him," the boy said, squatting down by Wynn's side. "His name is—was?"

"Is," Ker said. "I only knocked him on the head."

"Is then. His name's Danler. He works for an old woman named Goreot. Part of a gang."

"Criminals?"

Jerek shrugged. "They didn't seem to think so."

"Are they against the Halians? Would they help us?"

The boy thought, brows furrowed, before shaking his head. "She'd want to be paid somehow."

Ker nodded. "Drag him into the shadows, then," she said. "He'll have a chance to avoid the watch. No point in making an enemy of him."

———

Svann took a third deep breath, let it out even more slowly than the first two, and this time succeeded in opening his left fist, and revealing the vial of dust. Three doses, perhaps, taken carefully. That would buy him time. Another deep breath, and he managed to put the tiny glass container down on the table-top next to the griffin's claw he'd taken from the witch. Running out of dust did not come close to the catastrophe that was losing the soul stone. He had perhaps a week before the possibility of exposure to anyone who mattered. Everyone else he could take care of. So long as he regained the stone.

He reached for the vial again . . . and again drew his hand away. This time he stood up from the table and went to the window, resolutely putting from his mind what would happen to him if the other Shekayrin found out he had lost his stone— or, of even greater importance, *how* he had lost it.

Experimenting with a Talent. He could have justified that, could *still* justify it, with the information he had learned about how the magic of the body worked. Physical trials seemed to have no effect. The onset was with puberty, as the Mage

Edmard Pevelen had once theorized. But did that mean, for example, that if puberty was delayed, or otherwise stopped, would the magic of the body disappear? Would castration and spaying have any effect?

If he got the soul stone back before the others found out how he lost it, his experiments could continue. The girl—the witch—could live. If not, she would die, and he would be ruined.

A knock at the door. Svann returned to the table and placed the vial of dust in his tunic pocket, where the stone should be. The vial was a little smaller, but at the moment the weight was comparable, and he found it soothing. When he was sure his clothes were straight and that his face betrayed nothing, he spoke. "Enter."

Jakmor Gulder. Svann felt his lips tighten and forced himself to relax. It was unjust to think of this man as the beginning of his troubles.

"My lord." Gulder bowed low, but without obsequiousness.

"You have something, Gulder?" Svann leaned back against the edge of the table and crossed his arms.

"I believe I do, sir." The other man gestured at the doorway and Tel Cursar stepped through. Svann straightened to his feet again. If his troubles had started with anyone, it was with *this* young man.

"Why should I not have you killed?" he said to him. "You, Gulder! Tell me why I should not kill your boy?"

"Because he's still useful. Aren't you, Cursar?"

"My lord." Tel Cursar did not wait for permission to speak. "I know where they're going, sir."

The tightness in his chest easing, Svann sat down on the table edge again. "Go on."

The younger man came a few steps closer. "They'll be going to the mines, moving roundabout, traveling at night. We can take a direct route. We can get there ahead of them."

"Ahead of them." Svann would have his soul stone back.

And he would also have the girl. He could continue his research.

And there was something else. Something he had not let himself think about until now. She had been able to use the stone. That was clear, both from his own experience, and from the testimony of the soldier, Pella. What if he were able to use the stone to cleanse her? Was it possible for a woman to have the true magic? Would she be willing to give up the magic of the body, for the cleaner, purer, true magic of the stone? Was that what his great-grandmother had? There were histories that spoke of such things. There were orders of Shekayrin, the Marigold, the Crocus, and the Flax, which no longer had members, and in the scrolls they were spoken of in the feminine case . . . He blinked.

"The witch must be recovered," he said. "She has much more to tell me, before her usefulness is done." Another thought intruded. "*Where* did you say she is headed?"

"To the mines of the Serpents Teeth, my lord," Jak Gulder said.

The mines? Svann felt his spirits rise. His hand felt into his tunic pocket and closed on the vial of dust. He would go to the source of the soul stone, and perhaps he would bring back more than just his own.

20

"WHERE did you get that knife, woman?"

Dersay almost dropped the knife in question, and the rabbit she was skinning with it. She hadn't been paying attention at all. She'd been trying to see through the eyes of the owl who was sitting at the top of the tree, the way the griffin was teaching her.

She looked up, a little shocked at how close the strange uniformed man was. This would be a soldier, then. Her heart beat faster.

<<Why didn't you warn me?>> she asked, but the griffin gave no answer. So he wasn't near enough to help her. She looked down at her knife again. The man wasn't coming any closer, but one man in uniform usually meant more. Where were Ganni and Anapola?

"It's my belt knife." It wasn't until after she'd spoken that Dersay realized she maybe shouldn't have answered the strange man. Here in the outer world the more natural thing would be to answer with a question. "Why?" she asked now, hoping it wasn't too late.

"Women aren't supposed to go armed." The man came closer and squatted down on the other side of the small fire, holding his hands out toward the warmth.

Dersay hoped the soldier couldn't see her trembling. Ganni had said it was important to show no fear, to act as though they saw nothing unusual. Two days ago, Dersay wouldn't have imagined herself capable of acting calm, let alone of speaking with an outsider, but passing through that small village where the people knew Ganni had helped. One of the oddest things was that they seemed quite ordinary, just like the UnGifted of the Mines and Tunnels.

Ganni had laughed at her, or maybe with her, when she'd told him that.

"I'm not armed," she said to the soldier finally. Was she acting naturally enough? "It's just my belt knife. I'm not a soldier or a guard or anything."

Another man stepped out of the trees. "What's all this, Bernal?"

The man across from her straightened to his feet. "Just a woman cooking, Barrack Leader."

"Does 'just a woman cooking' need three packs?" The Barrack Leader jerked his head toward the packs Ganni and Anapola had dumped when they'd left her here by the fire to go looking for signs of the Griffin Girl.

<<If you can hear me, get the others to come back.>> But the griffin still didn't answer. He'd been so much help, getting her over the horizon sickness when she'd first seen how the sky went on and on without stopping. Where was he now?

<<Coming.>>

She could tell Weimerk was far away. His range for Farthinking was much greater than hers, or Cuarel's. Still, she felt better, knowing that he could hear her now.

"Are you simple, woman? I asked you a question."

Dersay realized the Barrack Leader had been talking to her while she'd been listening for Weimerk. "I'm sorry?" she said, blinking and trying to look as much like Ennick as she could. She knew what the man meant by "simple." Simple was good. Simple wasn't a danger.

"I said put the knife down, and tell us where your friends are."

Dersay put the rabbit carcass down on a clean patch of snow and laid the knife down next to it. She looked back up at the Barrack Leader and smiled as widely as she could.

"Where are the others?" the man asked again, slowly. A badly whistled tune made both soldiers turn and look over her head into the pine trees.

Ganni. She couldn't read his thoughts, but she could tell who it was.

"Evening, gentlemen," the old man said. He came right up next to Dersay and squatted down, laying an armload of deadwood on the ground. He was no longer carrying his sword, but his small ax hung from its loop on the back of his belt. "We haven't much, but you're welcome to share our meal."

"Travel's restricted. What are you doing here?"

Dersay marveled at how puzzled Ganni managed to look. She only wished she could control her face that well. But then, he'd had a lot more practice.

"We're small traders," Ganni said. He waved at the packs. "We've always traveled this route."

"Through the forest? Who're you trading with? Bears?"

Ganni grinned, as though he appreciated the joke. To Dersay, the man hadn't sounded as though he were joking.

"Well, with respect, Commander, the road's not so very safe as it once was." Ganni did indeed sound respectful. "And frankly, the food in the forest is cheaper than what we'll find elsewhere."

The new man nodded before jerking his head at Dersay. "And you've got your permit for her?"

"Sir?"

"Women aren't allowed to travel without a permit."

"Oh, but I didn't think that meant my own daughter, sir." Ganni recovered quickly. No one would have suspected he'd never heard about these permits before. "I can't leave her behind, you see how she is." So Ganni had also picked up on her playing simple.

"You'll have to come with us." The officer turned toward the first soldier. "Check those packs, and bring them along."

"But, sir." Ganni lifted his hands, was starting to turn them palms upward, when both soldiers suddenly grew arrows, one out of his chest, the other from the left eye.

"That's the last of them," Anapola said, stepping out of the trees behind Dersay. "Why didn't those stupid villagers tell us about these permits?" she asked. "What do we do now?"

Ganni began kicking snow and dirt over the small fire. "We'll have to go."

"Which way?"

Dersay waited, rabbit and knife back in her hands, to hear what Ganni would say. They'd been hovering around the spot where the Griffin Girl and her friends would most likely be leaving the road to turn toward the mine entrance. Always supposing they were using the road at all. But before Ganni could answer. . .

<<Dersay.>>

"Wait," she said aloud. "It's the griffin."

<<You must go east. Hurry.>>

She thrust her knife back into her belt and the rabbit into the food pouch. She could finish later. "The griffin's found her," she told the others. "We're to go east. Now."

———

The next patrol they saw in time to dodge without having to use the password. After that they were out of the city, and once in the country, Ker, Jerek, and Wynn traveled as much as they could at night, sleeping under hayricks or in the occasional outbuilding during the day. The few patrols they saw in the distance didn't appear to be combing the countryside at all, and Ker guessed that Svann was keeping the loss of the jewel to himself.

Which meant one thing. He thought he knew where he could get it back. He thought he knew where they were going.

It was the morning of their fourth day out from Gaena, and Jerek had fallen asleep in a disused lambing shed they'd found. Now that they were once again in the foothills of the Serpents Teeth, there were fewer farmers' fields and more pasture land.

"You think Svann could find us if he still had the jewel?" Wynn murmured.

Ker touched the spot where the jewel rested, held next to her skin where Weimerk's claw had been. "No," she said, keeping her voice equally low. "But I don't think he has to." She moved her hand away from the jewel. She was so exhausted, she sometimes couldn't tell if she were Flashing.

"You mean, because he has Tel, he knows where we're going." It wasn't really a question.

Ker wished the other girl would stop bringing up Tel. "That's right." She wriggled, trying to find a softer spot on the ground.

"So what do we do? Can we get there before them?"

"You mean the way we got to Dern Firoxi before Jak did?"

"So what, then?" Wynn sat up.

"I only know the two entrances to the mines," Ker said, turning to face the other girl. "I think we can be sure that Tel and his new friends will be waiting for us at the one we came out of."

"So where's the other one?"

"In the Rija Vale, past Questin."

Wynn blew out her breath. "That's a long way. Can we get there?"

Ker shivered, but not from the cold. "I don't know. I think we may have to try." Her muscles still trembled and twitched when she tried to relax, still recovering from the Shekayrin's experiments. Could she walk all the way to Questin from here? "Rest now," she said. "We'll decide in the morning."

She was just drifting off when she felt a familiar sense of space and color.

<<Kerida, do you hear me?>>

Ker's jerk caused Wynn to murmur. "Weimerk?" Ker spoke into the space she felt in her mind.

<<Go west. North and west. Find Ganni.>>

Ganni? If anyone knew of a different entrance, the old man would. Still . . . <<Now? We've been walking all night.>>

<<Go now. Sleep later.>>

Ker drew in a deep lungful of air and massaged a sudden cramp in her thigh. "Wynn, Jerek, wake up. The griffin wants us to move."

"You are sure she will come this way?"

Tel turned from watching the other men probing the rough folds of the rock face for the mine entrance, but the Sunflower Shekayrin wasn't looking at him. Tel kept his expression subordinate-smooth just the same.

"Yes, sir. She has to; this is the entrance she knows."

"And we are here before her?" Though Svann's voice was still beautifully smooth and controlled, his clothes were beginning to look loose, and his beard hadn't been trimmed or even combed in days.

"Yes, sir. That is, there's no sign of her. Perhaps you could . . ." Tel's voice died away as Svann's gaze focused on him. The man's grip on the little glass vial whitened the knuckles of his left hand. Tel was sure he hadn't let go of it for at least the last day.

And he kept patting the griffin's claw in the front of his tunic, just the way Kerida—no, he wasn't going to think about the witch that way. Pella, standing on the Shekayrin's other side, cleared his throat as Jak Gulder approached them from the rock face. Svann had brought only two Barracks' worth of men with him, and Jak had been directing half of them in the search for the mine entrance.

"We've found it, my lord. Well hidden, just as Cursar told us."

"Good. Very good." Svann coughed into the fist holding the vial. "We have no way to know from which direction the girl will approach. Suggestions?"

"If I may, Lord Shekayrin." Jak spoke up when it became clear no one else was going to. "We divide into three groups, two scout along each of the likely approaches, watching for the Nast girl. The third group stations themselves within the mine entrance itself, in case the girl and her friends somehow get past us."

For the first time in days, Peklin Svann smiled. "Yes. I agree. Cursar, you are familiar with the place. Take five men with you and wait within the mine. Gulder, assign the others."

"And you, sir? The mine might be the safer place."

"Perhaps so. But I will remain outside. I may be able to help narrow the search, as the girl nears us."

He can feel the stone, Tel thought. Svann wouldn't say so aloud, since the loss of the jewel wasn't common knowledge among the other men—and might never be if they could get it back. But if the Shekayrin could feel the soul stone's presence, their task just became much simpler. She wouldn't know it, but the witch would be walking into a trap.

Kerida frowned, looking upward through the bare branches of the thicket they were hiding in. <<Weimerk?>>

<<Close.>>

"What's up there?" Jerek whispered.

"The griffin," she said, smiling and patting his shoulder when he blinked at her open-mouthed. "I can feel him up there, I just can't see him."

"What about the others? Are they anywhere near?" Wynn looked over with interest.

"They're right here." Ker rolled to her knees and crawled out into the open as shadows moved outside the thicket. Jerek and Wynn scrambled after her, the boy drawing himself up to his full height as soon as he was out.

"Ganni." Kerida stepped back from hugging the old man to nod at the women behind him. Both were dark-haired, one armed with sword and bow, and another, older and smaller, smiling shyly from behind the first. Ker drew Jerek forward with an arm around his shoulders.

"Here he is, Ganni. This is Jerek Brightwing, Prince of Farama." The boy looked up at her and smiled before stepping forward.

A bigger smile spread over the old man's face, and his eyes lit up as he reached out. Without hesitation, Jerek grasped his hand.

"You know what we are, young lord? You're not afraid?" Ganni had his head tilted to one side, his eyes narrowed, though they still sparkled deep within.

Jerek straightened his shoulders. "I know," he said. "And I'm happy to meet you."

Ganni nodded. Still holding Jerek's hand, he sank down to one knee.

"You are so very welcome among us, my lord. So welcome as the sun in Seedmonth." Then the old man did something Ker had only heard about in stories. Still kneeling, he touched the back of Jerek's fingers to his wrinkled forehead. The boy's face flushed red before turning pale again.

Ganni stood and gestured the other two women forward.

"Here are Dersay Far-thinker and Anapola, also dwellers in the Mines and Tunnels, here to find and guide you, my lord." The women only bowed their heads, however, though Anapola gave him a sloppy salute.

"It's where you're going to guide us that worries me just now, Ganni." In as few words as possible, Ker told the old man what had happened to Tel, and why they expected Svann and his people to be waiting for them.

"I'm so very sorry to learn this of your soldier, my dear. So very sorry. He was a fine man."

Ker clenched her jaw as Ganni patted her on the shoulder. "And might be again one day, Ganni, but right now I'm more concerned about what we're going to do. We wondered about using the Rija Vale entrance near Questin, but is there another one closer?"

Ganni shook his head, his lips pressed into a line. "Simcot Exit was always the closest, my dear, that's why you used it in the first place. Closer than Questin?" He scratched at his unshaven chin. "Nothing that's any easier to get to, I'm very much afraid."

"That's the point, isn't it," Wynn said. "I mean, I've no head for strategy, truth to tell, but even I can see we increase our chances of being caught by *someone* if we walk all the way to Questin, even if we avoid our own particular Sunflower Shekayrin."

"Better the evil we know," Jerek said, glancing around as they all looked at him to continue. "It's something our Factor used to say. You're better able to deal with the things you already understand."

"Oh, we've all heard the saying, lad—I should say, my lord prince," Ganni said. "But I'm not sure—"

"Svann doesn't have his jewel," Ker said. She thought she could see where Jerek was going, all right. "In that sense, he's the safest Shekayrin we could meet. We don't know how many men he'll have with him, but I know someone who can tell us." She looked up. <<Weimerk, are you listening?>>

Dersay, the Far-thinker, looked up, smiling.

<<I hear you, Kerida Nast. I can come for you now.>>

<<Can you go to the Simcot Exit instead, tell us if there are men there, and how many?>>

<<I would rather take you away, Kerida. I can carry you to the Plum Tree Exit easily and you will avoid all danger.>>

Ker's heart lifted. <<All of us? One at a time,>> she added, when the griffin didn't answer right away.

<<No. I carry only you. It is the pattern of the Prophecy.>>

Though the griffin's thoughts had no tone, exactly, Ker knew there was no point in questioning him. <<Then will you check—>>

<<Yes. Yes. The Simcot Exit. It is not what I wish, but since you ask, I will do it.>>

Four days later they followed Ganni along a narrow path at the edge of a small ravine. They'd left the foothills behind, using the smaller paths only the Feelers knew. This wasn't the way Ker and Wynn had come when they'd left the entrance; if anything, it was even more bleak and deserted. It was nearly the end of Icemonth, and the ground at this elevation was hard with the cold.

"Shouldn't there be more snow?" Jerek, looking around at the rocks and frozen vegetation, sounded disappointed.

"True, young lord. It's late for snow in this part of the Teeth." Ganni pointed to where tiny drifts had caught in the lee of nearby rocks. "See how little there's been."

"No snow in the mountains means maybe a drought next summer." Everyone, even the two Feeler women, looked at Jerek in surprise. He was still frowning at the bare ground around them. "Winter rain and snow at elevation," he added, as though speaking to himself, or reciting a lesson. "That's what farmers need."

Ker exchanged a glance with Ganni. It wasn't how a soldier—or even a Talent—would think. But maybe it *was* the way a Luqs should.

The old Feeler nodded. "Not a thing we know so very much about, farming," he said. "Not so much as we'd like, in any case." He passed Jerek the waterskin.

"I guess not." Jerek took a sip and passed it along. "No farms underground."

"We've got mushrooms." It was the first time Anapola, the armed Feeler, had spoken. "And there's the upper slope valleys—though that's more animals . . ." Her voice died away and her face stiffened as she realized everyone was looking at her.

"I'll be glad to get inside," Ker said into the silence. "If only to get out of this wind." She rubbed at her upper arms, looking up again into the cloudless sky.

"Can you hear him all the time?" Dersay's voice had a tiny hint of jealousy in it.

"No," Ker said. "I think it's only when he wants me to, or when I'm particularly tired or—" She frowned, remembering Svann's room. "Or in pain."

"So all the time, in this last while," Dersay said. "I can see how tired you are, just looking at you."

Ker shrugged. Her feet felt like lead. It was such a relief to let Ganni, Dersay, and Anapola take charge. Jerek, his shoulders slumped, walked just in front of her, watching the ground at his feet, and Wynn hadn't said a word since their last stop. Ganni was leading them through a narrow defile that Weimerk had reported as free of enemy soldiers. There must be hundreds of such paths through the mountains, she thought, though not all would lead to a mine entrance.

"Here now." Ganni waved Ker forward. "This should be

close enough, girl. The entrance is beyond those rocks on the right. What say you? Flash anything untoward?"

Ker rubbed her face with chilled hands. There was nothing here in this tiny ravine but ground made uneven with rock and hummocks of frozen vegetation, boulders and folds of rock angling up the steep mountainside above them.

This was no different from the many times she'd already Flashed the area around them, checking for the enemy. It was just that her brain felt full of sand. *Paraste.*

"There's the two groups waiting in the southeast and eastern paths, just as Weimerk said. But I can't Flash the ones he thinks are in the mines."

"He *thinks*?"

<<Tell them the auras are uncertain. The blood and the bone change the shapes of the lives within.>>

Ker relayed the griffin's thought. "I think he means the veining of the jewels."

"That's as may be, child, but we can't wait on that certainty. What of the entrance itself?"

"There are three people standing near it," Ker said. She took a deep breath. "One of them is Svann."

"So we stick with the plan, then?"

Ker looked at the faces around her. "Do we know our places? Jerek, stay behind Wynn and Dersay, and head straight for the entrance, no matter what else happens. Anapola, you and I between them and Ganni—"

"And me in front. Yes, child, we know. Must I be careful not to hurt them?"

"Not at all," she said, returning the old man's grin. If Tel had been one of those waiting at the entrance she might have answered differently, but she hadn't Flashed him there. "Watch your footing, people. We don't need any twisted ankles."

They moved out of cover quickly, following Ganni, bearing straight for the entrance. Even if the soldiers between them and their goal had been faster to react, Ker doubted it would have made any difference against the Feeler. Ganni gestured as he ran, and men were flung bodily away. Others scattered, and the way was open.

As they dashed forward, however, arrows grew from the ground at their feet and soldiers came trotting from between the stunted trees. They hadn't been so close when she'd Flashed them; they must have been moving toward the entrance all along. More arrows flew from behind a tumbled outcrop of boulders, but these Ganni managed to flick away before any came close. Still, they had to move faster, or they could be overwhelmed. <<Now,>> she thought.

She was backing toward the entrance, sword up, with Anapola at her elbow just as iron fingers grabbed her from behind.

"Where is it? Give it to me." Svann's fingers dug into her arms as he shook her.

"My lord! My lord!" The fear in the voice penetrated even Svann's desperation and, without relaxing his hold on her, he looked away, and then up. A moment later, a piercing shriek made *everyone* look up.

Dersay began to laugh. Anapola took advantage of the momentary distraction to slice at the soldier who'd been threatening her, knocking his sword aside and impaling him on her own.

A voice calling out in an unknown tongue told Ker one of the others was a Halian. The man lifted an oddly shaped bow, shorter than Ker had ever seen, and with too many curves. He shot, but the arrow swerved wide.

<<I am here.>>

<<About time.>>

The sunlight struck a rainbow of color from the griffin's wings, and for a moment the beauty of it stopped Ker's breath. Then the Halian soldier shot again, and now another archer joined him. For a moment the griffin hung in the air, then he folded his wings and plummeted directly at them, hind feet tucked under his belly, forepaws stretched out, claws extended.

The Halian and the second archer stood their ground, but the other men ran. Ker twisted out of Svann's suddenly slack hands and ran to Jerek. Wynn was next to Anapola now, and Dersay had gone to Ganni.

The Halian, grim-faced, lower lip caught between his teeth, dropped his bow and drew out his short sword, standing with his knees slightly bent. He stepped forward, swinging his blade, but Weimerk batted the sword out of the man's hand and snatched him up, wings beating, lifting him into the air. As his powerful forepaws held him, Weimerk closed his eagle's beak on the man's head, while the claws of his back feet tore open the man's torso, spilling steaming entrails to the cold ground. Weimerk landed and screamed again, tail lashing, one enormous paw on the Halian officer's body.

"Into the shaft now," Ganni was yelling. "Quickly."

"Weimerk!" Ker yelled.

"I. See. You." A flash of color, a half curl of wing and Weimerk was lifted enough to allow him to swoop at the enemy, claws and beak ready to tear.

<<Stay safe, my own one.>> The griffin's voice echoed in her head.

"Are we all here?" she said as she allowed Anapola to pull her further inside.

"Did I see Jak Gulder out there?" Wynn was bent over, trying to catch her breath.

Ker just shook her head, her own exhaustion suddenly robbing her of the strength to speak. They were inside. They were safe. She leaned against the cold stone wall of the tunnel. She grinned at Jerek and got a shaky smile back. Their plan had worked.

Ganni, his attention still focused outside, spoke over his

shoulder. "Do you go on, you youngsters. Weimerk is still with us, and Anapola and I can hold this doorway until others can come. Dersay—"

"I can't, Ganni, I can't go with them. Please."

"That's fine, girl, you've done well. Can you find your own way in, Kerida?"

Her stomach heaved at the thought of more Flashing. "I think so, yes. Between us, Wynn and I can find the way."

"Good, then. Here." He slipped the wristlet off his left wrist and pushed it over her hand. "Do you go now."

Just as Ker remembered, the tunnel led straight for more than a hundred paces before it began to veer.

"The first intersection should be coming up." Wynn called from her position as rear guard. They were both doing their best to remember the route Ennick had brought them by, though in reverse. Ker wanted to put off as long as possible the effort that more Flashing would require.

"And here it is," Ker said, as her fingers found an edge. Jerek was right behind her, still holding on to her belt. The wristlet gave her barely enough light not to bump into things, nothing like Tel's glow stone.

"Really?" Wynn sounded hollow, but Ker knew that was an effect of the darkness, and the stone walls. "I remember it as farther away."

"Easy to check." Ker tried to sound confident, and not worn to the bone. "Here, Jerek, take my hand, I need a bit more slack. There should be three tunnels opening off to the left, and I may have to Flash all of them."

"Where's Ennick when we need him?" Ker could hear the smile in Wynn's voice, though she knew the soldier had to be just as tired as she was herself.

"Just what I was thinking." With Jerek's hand firmly in her

right, Ker shuffled forward. "Kneeling now." She placed her left hand on the floor of the tunnel. *Paraste.*

Immediately, the darkness was filled with the bright and somehow soothing colors of Wynn's and Jerek's auras. Ker clenched her teeth and mentally pushed them to one side, focusing on the tunnel floor. "Not this one." She heard Jerek give a kind of hiccupping sigh and squeezed his hand.

Inching around again to the left, Ker found and Flashed on the second tunnel. "Here we go. This is it." While it didn't have an aura like a person, Ker found she could Flash much more of the tunnel than she'd once been able to. She could feel it stretch out in front of them, every twist, every turn, almost every mark left by hammer or chisel—and something else. Some*one* else.

"What is it?" Wynn's question startled her, and the girl's aura swirled around Ker's head.

"I think . . ." Ker refocused her attention. She was definitely Flashing people, someone familiar. Perhaps the Feelers were—*Tel!* Ker jerked to her feet and pushed the others back toward the first opening. Perhaps because she was inside, or perhaps because she wasn't affected by the presence of the jewel's ore, she was able to Flash more detail than the griffin could. "Down this way! Now!"

Flashing to see the way, Ker again took the lead, pulling Jerek behind her and trusting that Wynn was following. Their auras were spiky now, but Ker easily distinguished the shape of the tunnel. All too soon, however, the light of a glow stone came crowding up behind them.

The tunnel turned a little farther along, and if they could reach it before Tel and his men, and if they were careful not to go too far—Ker's right foot came down on nothing at all. She twisted, pushing Jerek away from her, instinctively wrenching herself around. But momentum was against her, and she was already too far over to save herself. Frantic, she clutched at the edge as she slipped down, nails breaking as she pushed her fingers into a crack she felt barely in time.

There was just enough light to show her how close Jerek and Wynn had come to following her over.

"Jerek, back away!" The boy was trying for a grip on her wrist, but he wouldn't be able to keep her from falling. She would only pull him down after her.

"Help! Help us!" Jerek's voice cracked with horror.

Wynn, her hands on his shoulders, was pulling him back, even as he tried to lean farther forward, still reaching out. Ker scrabbled with her feet against the wall, trying to get some purchase. She had the one good grip with her right hand, but unless she found some other prop, she was going down.

"Jerek, hush, or they'll find us."

The light brightened, and Wynn and Jerek were thrust out of the way. A tall, familiar silhouette came between the edge and the light.

"Give me your hand."

Ker knew the voice, and her heart lifted despite herself.

She licked her lips. "Tel," she began, as he reached down for her wrist.

"Come." Was she imagining it, or was there a quiver in his voice? "You don't have to die. The Shekayrin will protect you."

The Shekayrin. She should have known. "Yeah? And who's protecting him?" Her throat closed, and the tears in her eyes weren't all from the brightness of the glow stones. Part of her must have hoped that Tel was here for her. She was such a fool. A cramp shot through her arm, and she gritted her teeth against the pain. Tel was only here because Svann had sent him.

But that meant he was here *only* for her, and the jewel. Not Jerek or Wynn. Without her, the others might yet be safe. She could buy them time, until the Feelers found them. The tips of Tel's long fingers brushed her wrist.

Ker gritted her teeth, and pushed free.

"How can the archers miss that thing? It's as big as a house." Jak Gulder barred Svann's way with an arm across his chest. He had allowed Gulder to push him behind a narrow jutting of rock, but he had no intention of going any farther away.

"The archers are not missing," he pointed out. Jak Gulder glanced at him with narrowed eyes. "Do you not see it? The missiles slow as they approach him, and fall away. There is something there, something in the quality of the air that surrounds him—almost like a heat haze." That was the closest he could come to describing it. He tried to take a step closer, but Gulder held him back by the sleeve.

"It's too dangerous, my lord. Let me call the men back. The girl's gone inside, and Tel Cursar will get her. If the beast thinks we've gone, it will fly away."

"It may not. It is a griffin." But perhaps that meant nothing to this man. Likely, it meant nothing to any of these people. Svann clutched at the claw he carried in the breast of his tunic. For a moment, he thought he saw colors in the air around the sacred animal.

"That's right, my lord." An arrow shot from the mine entrance struck the rock near them and Svann allowed Gulder to pull him back into safety. "Let me call the men, my lord."

"Fine, fine." Svann ducked his head, trying to catch the griffin's eye. Gulder whistled two piercing notes.

"The soldiers withdraw." Anapola gestured with her chin, lowering her bow.

"Don't stand down quite yet, my young one. Be so wary and so careful until the griffin tells us different."

The younger woman nodded, wincing as Weimerk tossed a torn-off arm into the air. "I wish he wasn't enjoying himself so much."

Ganni patted her on the shoulder. "Don't be so sure that he is." He looked into the dimness behind them. "Dersay—"

"I know, Ganni, I know. I've told them already to come for the Griffin Girl. Give me a minute. It would have been better if someone had been here waiting for us."

Ganni grunted. Of course, that would have been better, but where were they going to get the people to guard every entrance? Even if they could find enough for that, there were too few Far-thinkers. They'd never needed to guard entrances before. The Serpents Teeth had been forbidden for so long, people no longer even thought about hunting or exploring in the range. That unspoken taboo, along with the "stay-away" feelings that strong Mind-healers like Hitterol could give a place had always been enough—

"Ganni!" Dersay grabbed his arm. "Griffin says his girl has fallen down the Octagon Shaft."

Ganni's heart grew cold. Anapola slapped him on the shoulder.

"Go! We'll hold here."

When Tel Cursar cried out, Jerek lunged forward, pushing against the circle of Wynn's arms, just in time to see Ker's face disappear into the darkness. Tel stuck out his arm like a railing, as if he thought Jerek and Wynn might go over as well. Jerek whirled to face him, fists raised in the way Nessa had shown him, and got in two solid blows on the kneeling man's face before his hands were restrained from behind.

"You let her fall!"

"I didn't—Jerek, listen. I didn't let her fall; she wouldn't give me her hand. I couldn't save her."

Jerek's breath was ragged in his throat. For a moment he saw what he thought was real remorse in Tel's face. The man wiped his mouth with the back of his hand. "I couldn't save her." Tel's brows drew together. "I'll have to answer to the Shekayrin for that."

Jerek pulled forward again, but the hands on his shoulders held him fast, and eventually the rumbling in his ear stopped being noise and started being words.

"She did this for us, my Faro, don't throw it away. Our friends will come for us. Hold your cards hidden, and we can still win. We'll win for her."

Jerek swallowed. Wynn was right. He was Jerek Bright-wing now. Prince of Farama. Faro of Eagles. He had to get hold of himself. Ker would want him to.

"Toss these two over the side as well, Barrack Leader?"

Wynn's hands on his shoulders tightened, but Jerek swallowed the protest that rose in his throat and tried to stand straighter. If he told them who he was, would it save them? He had to stay alive, didn't he? He couldn't win if he was dead. He wasn't a coward for thinking that, was he? Wynn's hands tightened even more.

"What?" Tel turned to face the voice from behind them. "Of course not."

Jerek released the breath he was holding, forcing his fists to open and relax.

"We've no orders about them." This was Pella, the thickset man they'd left on the floor of their room. "I mean, no orders either way. The Shekayrin just wanted the Nast girl back. We could even let them go." He sounded remarkably reasonable, considering Wynn was still wearing his tunic.

Tel hesitated, and Jerek began to hope that he *was* just going to let them go—though how he and Wynn were supposed to find their way without Kerida— Jerek swallowed, blinking.

"Bring them along," Tel finally said. "We can't leave Wynn Martan to go back to her Wing," he added when Pella seemed about to disagree. "And it may be they'll draw the Miners out, and we can capture one of them."

Pella shrugged and gestured to the other soldiers, who moved into place around them. From the way the men were looking around, it was obvious that they'd been told *something* about who lived in the mine. Wynn took Jerek's hand, but Pella separated them.

"I don't think so. You'll be less likely to run on your own, so we'll keep the two of you apart."

Jerek was put between two other soldiers, men he didn't recognize from Gaena, but not before Wynn had given him a fierce look. He nodded his understanding. Pella thought they wouldn't try to escape alone, but he was wrong. Jerek had a reason to run these men didn't know about. That was what Wynn's look meant. She meant him to get away if he could, and not worry about her.

And that was what he *intended* to do, though the thought of running off into the dark with no idea of what might be out there twisted his guts. Ganni and Dersay and Anapola were the only Feelers he knew, or who knew him. Were they still alive? And . . .

Jerek let them take his knife and search through his belt pouch. They took Wynn's sword and removed her pouch completely, though they let him keep his.

"I told them you'd come here," Tel was saying now. "And I was right." He looked toward the chasm. "I would have brought her back."

"Tel." Pella cleared his throat. "Tel, we'd better get moving. That they were in here at all means they got past the Shekayrin."

"You won't be leaving here." Wynn sounded so calm. Jerek wished he could sound as calm as that.

Well, no. What he really wished was that the Halians had never come, and Ker was still alive and he was at home helping in the stable, and studying accounts and good stewardship of the land with Nessa. He sucked in a deep breath. Too late for that. What mattered now was doing what Ker wanted done. Escape. Get to the Wings. Be the Luqs.

"You're lucky." Tel glanced at Jerek and then back to Wynn. "You don't know what's in here. What we're saving you from."

Jerek took a last look at the black space that had swallowed his friend. "I know," he said. "It's you that's forgotten."

"If we tied their hands in front, it would make things easier."

"Easier for whom?" Tel's shoulders kept creeping up around his ears. Things certainly weren't easy for *him*. What was he going to tell the Shekayrin? He'd had the witch in his hands, for the Father's sake, and he'd lost her. *Curse* his luck.

"Easier for the men, is what I was thinking." Pella looked him up and down, his frown twisted to one side. "Sir."

Tel's ears flushed with heat. He heard the criticism in Pella's tone. He'd been a third officer, for the gods' sake. He shouldn't need Pella to tell him to consider the men. Tel nodded, his neck stiff. "You're right, but let's wait until we're outside."

The older man gave Tel a short salute and Tel's shoulders lowered, just a tiny bit. He couldn't remember when he'd last felt this angry. And what was it his mother used to tell him? Anger makes you stupid.

He took a deep breath and let it out slowly. Stupid officers killed themselves and their men. So he didn't take the lead himself as he wanted to, but assigned it to two of the others. One man walked next to the girl and he himself took charge of Jerek. That left Pella behind him—just where the older man liked to be—and two more to bring up the rear. Here in the middle, where he could keep an eye on everything, was where an officer should be.

They were headed back to the main tunnel, but quickly Tel began to wonder if he shouldn't have stayed in the lead after all. "Hold up." He handed the boy over to Pella and made his way to the front. "You must have taken a wrong turning."

"I couldn't have, sir. There aren't any."

"Pella?"

"He's correct, sir. The tunnel itself is turning."

That couldn't be right. Chasing the witch, they'd run down a straight tunnel with only one turning . . . or had it just seemed that way?

It would look bad if he went back and checked, as if he didn't trust his own men. But his sense of direction was like an arrow in his head, and that arrow said the opening they came from should be to the right, and the tunnel was definitely leading them away from it.

"Proceed, but half speed."

Now the tunnel *was* perfectly straight, though still leading them in what felt like the wrong direction. Tel started counting paces in his head. When he reached two hundred, he called another halt, strode up to where the girl was, and pushed her against the wall, his forearm across her throat.

"Who's doing this? Is it you?" He spoke through clenched teeth, quietly enough that the men couldn't overhear. The last thing they needed was panic.

Her dark eyes were wide, showing the whites. She blinked, looking scared, but he wouldn't be fooled by that. She'd probably learned that trick from the witch, playing helpless and lost. Her eyes swiveled sideways.

A large, meaty hand wrapped around Tel's upper arm, and a gruff voice murmured. "Just a second, Tel, wait now. What is it she's doing?"

Tel turned just his head to face Pella, without letting up the pressure on the girl. "She's done something to confuse us. We're not heading the right way. We should have come to the entrance tunnel long ago."

"Let her talk, man, see what she says."

Tel released the pressure of his forearm, and Wynn took a deep, gasping breath.

"Have you lost all the sense you ever had?" she rasped out.

He'd been holding her tighter than he'd realized. "How could *I* be doing anything?"

Tel swallowed. She was only a girl, after all. A good archer, but just an ordinary girl who couldn't change the direction of a tunnel made of rock.

An ordinary girl.

"It's *her*." Something tight in his chest loosened, and he felt like laughing aloud. Kerida Nast was alive. The witch was behind this. And now she was— "Tricking us," he said.

"Or maybe your sense of direction isn't working that well anymore." The girl was almost smiling. "Svann done any more trickery on you? Ooo, I forgot. He doesn't have his jewel."

Tel smiled. The girl's jaw set, and her eyes narrowed. He hadn't lost either the witch or the jewel. The Shekayrin would be pleased after all.

And the Shekayrin had been able to get the witch to do things she didn't want to do.

"Kerida." He raised his voice. He had to be right. When he had the witch, it wouldn't matter what the men thought. "We have Wynn, and the boy. If you don't show yourself . . ." He turned away from the girl as he spoke, grabbing the boy by the shoulder and dragging him forward. The look Jerek gave him made Tel grit his teeth. What had to be done, had to be done.

"Give up—" was all he managed to say when an arrow took him in the shoulder, spinning him halfway around and numbing his whole hand. He touched the shaft, falling to his knees. It wasn't the pain that shocked him, so much as the fact that the arrow had come out of the solid wall.

The scream forced its way out of Kerida's throat before she could stop it. Only when she realized what the sound was, did she manage to bite down on it. She wouldn't give Tel the satisfaction of knowing she was afraid. She fell so quickly that the light and Tel's silhouette were gone in the blink of an eye, and she had only the soft luminescence of her wristlet to keep her from total darkness. Automatically, she spread her arms and legs to slow her fall, though she had no idea why she bothered.

Every now and then she could see a patch of the fluorescent moss on the wall of the shaft. Watching these patches, Ker thought her fall might be slowing after all, as one particularly oddly shaped bit of moss got no farther away, and in fact seemed to come a bit closer, as if she was moving toward it.

"You fall so swift and quiet as a hawk, girl."

"Ganni?" Ker tried to roll toward his voice, but whatever power held her gave her no purchase.

"Ganni, quick, they've got Jerek and Wynn. We've got to stop them—"

"Softly, softly, my child. Give me a chance."

Ker could see movement, mere shadows in the soft light of the mosses, and felt hands on her wrists, and then her ankles. She was careful not to grab, reminded of the swimming training her brother had given her as a child. Don't clutch at the people saving you, or you might pull them under as well or, in this case, pull them over.

After all, there might be a limit to how many Ganni could hold. And they didn't all have the same Gift. *I can't stop you from falling.* That's what Ennick had said. So she forced herself to relax, to let the hands haul her onto a ledge she could barely make out. Only when she felt her entire weight on the rock beneath her did she finally grab hold of the hands helping her, unable to stifle the sob that rose in her throat.

"Sorry it took so long to reach you, girl. I had to get under you, you see, I might have snapped your neck stopping you from above."

"That doesn't matter—or yes, of course, thank you! But Tel was waiting for us and they have Jerek and—"

"And we have you, girl, which is what's important to me. Our people are tracking them, don't you worry." The old man was turning away from her. "Do we know where they are now, Ennick?"

"Tunnel seventeen, they should be."

"Good. You go join them, quick now. We'll follow in two shakes."

"Don't say anything to the soldiers about Jerek." Ker put her hand out in the direction of Ennick's voice. "Don't let them know who he is."

"Girl, we're not mouselings. And Ennick doesn't talk to outsiders at all."

Ker was never sure exactly how they got back to the entry tunnels so quickly. Tunnels and shafts seemed to appear where there hadn't been anything a moment before, and at one point Ganni "helped" them over a gap that was too wide for anyone except an athlete at the Harvest Games to leap over without help.

Not far beyond that gap they caught up with another group, this one armed with bows, spears, and swords. Ker thought she recognized some of the faces. There was Ennick, certainly, and there Norwil nodded at her, but before she could put names to any others there were shouts, and arrows flying. Ganni pushed her down as a spear came at them, and then stood, as he'd done outside, eyes closed, brow furrowed, flicking aside anything that came near them with short movements of his hands and fingers.

"Please, please, please," Ker murmured under her breath, hardly aware which god—or all of them—she was asking to help them. *Let Jerek be all right, and Wynn. And Tel.* She didn't know which one she cared most about. Her hand kept straying to the lump under her tunic, where the jewel waited.

At last the sounds of combat died away and the light of the glow stone dimmed, as though someone had thrown a cloth over it. A man she didn't know was cutting Jerek's bonds. As soon as he was freed, he launched himself at her, wrapping his arms around her tightly enough to cut off breath. She was pushed back against the wall, and a lucky thing, too, or they would have both gone down.

"Hey, it's all right. These are friends. Hey, Jerek."

"You're alive! You're—" The boy pulled back for just a second. "You *are* alive?" He gave her a bit of a shake. "I can feel you, so you can't be a spirit." He wrapped his arms around her again and she could feel him trembling, perhaps struggling not to cry. "I wouldn't have told," he said into her ear. She felt his shoulders straighten. "I wouldn't have told them who I am, not just to save myself. I wouldn't have."

"Of course not. I know. No one thought you would." Ker could see Wynn's anxious face peering from behind Ganni's shoulder. "Did we, Wynn?"

"Not me." Wynn's grin was a brave effort, but it was lucky Jerek wasn't looking at her. "I knew my Fa—my hero would tough it out."

"Here now, Jerek." Ker took careful hold of his arms. "You're stronger than you think, I can't breathe." Jerek loosened his hold enough for Ker to take a deep breath. He didn't release her entirely, however, and seeing the stiffness of his face Ker slipped her own arms back around him.

"We're safe now." She looked over at Ganni. "The others?"

The old man turned to one side and gestured with an open hand. Now that there was no one blocking her view, Kerida saw Tel lying on his side, his cheek pressed against the dirt, his mouth fallen open. Her heart hitched, then his eyes opened, and her heart started beating again.

As if he knew what she'd thought, Ganni patted her on the shoulder. "Alive as you or me, as the fact that we've got him trussed should have told you. Of the rest, two're dead, and two more bound."

One of the other Feelers had Tel's pouch open and was going through its contents. It was the same stiffened canvas satchel he'd had with him since they'd met in the kitchen of Questin Hall. Ker was turning away when something familiar and homely caught her eye.

A small clay jar, sealed shut by a wide wooden plug with a strip of linen to keep it tight. She blinked, knowing it immediately for the little jar of grease she'd given Tel when his harness had been new and stiff. The Feeler pried the plug loose to inspect the contents, and Ker could see the jar was empty. Tel had kept it all this time, carefully put away in his belt pouch, even though it was empty.

She glanced at him just in time to see him turn his eyes away.

She took a breath and squared her shoulders. "Jerek, this is Ennick. He's a good friend of mine. Ennick, would you guard Jerek for me?"

Jerek peered up at Ennick. The large man grinned down at the small one and, as Ker had thought, there was something in the simplicity of Ennick's expression that made Jerek nod, then smile and put out his hand.

"So why are we saving this man's life?" Norwil said. "Aren't they the enemy? Shouldn't we be killing him?" Give him his due, Ker thought, he didn't sound happy about it.

Ganni was shaking his head. "I'm afraid I'm on Norwil's side on this one, Kerida Griffin Girl. You yourself said he's been changed."

"That's just it." Ker loosened the fastenings of her tunic and pulled the jewel out of its wrapping. It looked darker in the light of the dimmed glow stone, more like jet or obsidian, less like a ruby. "Here."

A woman Ker didn't know cleared her throat. "It looks different from the one Luca had. More"—she hesitated—"more real somehow."

"Ask Tel Cursar how real it is." Ker looked at Tel again. He was lying limp and still, but she'd seen his eyes open once already, and now there was a gleam of light where his eyelashes met. "I think I can change him back." When she turned back, Ganni was studying her closely. "At least, I'd like to try."

"Worth a try, isn't it?" Norwil said. "If it kills him, it's no loss."

"No!" Tel began to struggle. "Keep her away from me! Keep the witch away! Kill me! Kill me first!"

66 L UCA Pa'narion went missing overnight, but I suppose you already knew that."

"The watch did not report seeing him leave." Juria Sweetwater turned her eyes away from the columns of Panthers lined up outside the main gates of Oste, to face their Faro. Tonia Nast was dressed for the cold morning and the biting wind that raked the battlements. There were fur-lined gloves on her hands, and the panther-skin cloak that marked her rank was wrapped closely around her.

Just as closely as Juria's own bear-skin cloak was wrapped.

"Well, I don't suppose either of us can tell a High Inquisitor of the Halls of Law where he may or may not go." Tonia Nast dropped her voice to a murmur no one else could possibly hear. "If I had to guess, I'd say that Luca Pa'narion has gone to place himself under the orders of our prince."

Juria smiled and shook her head.

The other woman grinned. "You're sure you don't want to borrow some of my Panthers?"

"I am sure. Thank you."

The Faro of Panthers nodded, started toward the stairs, but turned back. "Juria, I have no right to ask, but—how long after I leave will there be Bears in Oste?"

Juria bared her teeth. She didn't particularly care whether it looked much like a smile. "You may tell the Wings that I will hold the pass, Faro of Panthers, against the enemy crossing the Serpents Teeth. Those are my orders."

The Faro of Panthers shrugged her cloak a little closer around her, her eyes narrowing. "And if they say you're looking to set yourself up as Luqs?"

Juria blinked. Wasn't this the very thing that she and Luca had wondered about Tonia herself? "*They* say, or *you* say?"

This time it was Tonia Nast's turn to bare her teeth. She waved her gloved hand as if to shoo away an annoying insect. "'They say, they say, what say they?'" she said, quoting the famous playwright, and her smile turned genuine. "What do we care, you and I? I almost envy you, Juria. This is what the historians write their books about."

Juria found herself smiling back. "Only if we win."

For a moment the other woman's face turned serious, but the grin returned so quickly that Juria couldn't be sure she'd seen anything else. A whistle from below drew her attention to the assembled soldiers. The Laxtor of Panthers was holding up her left hand in signal. Juria turned back to Tonia.

"May the Mother hold you in her arms," she said.

"And you, as well." Suddenly Tonia held up her own arms and, more than a little surprised, Juria stepped into them, to give and receive the double kiss of family. "If you should see her, tell my sister I love her, and I think of her always."

Juria swallowed and blinked away the moisture in her eyes. "Which one?"

Tonia tilted her head to one side. "Whichever."

It wasn't until the last of the Panthers were almost out of

sight on the road away from the pass that Surm came up to the battlements and stood next to her.

"*Could* they have stopped us?" he said. "Are we doing the right thing?"

Juria answered without turning around. "'Perhaps' answers both your questions. But something is sure." She slipped her arm around Surm's waist. "We Sweetwaters have always been lucky, ever since my great-grandfather held the Gellas Bridge against Penvals. And the Nasts are luckier than most."

For the first time since she'd entered the mines, Kerida was in a real living space, not a meeting hall, not a sleeping alcove, but a room with a table and chairs, cupboards, and shelves filled with plates, dishes, and scrolls. There was even, against the north wall, a small shrine to the household gods, with the statue of the Mother well to the fore. Ker stroked her hand across the fine-grained wood of the tabletop.

"From one of my very first trading trips," Ganni said from his seat across the table. "My grandfather took me. I spotted this table and decided I couldn't go home without it."

The grain seemed to move in the shifting candlelight. "Do you remember what you traded for it?"

"Yes, I do, child. A pair of small candlesticks carved in the shape of griffins by Sendova himself. His work always fetched good prices. It still does, though he's long gone now."

"None of which brings us any closer to our business," Norwil said from where he leaned against the doorframe.

"Where are the others?" Ker, Wynn, and Jerek had been given a chance to wash up, but after that she'd been brought here alone.

"The young prince is off with Ennick, though he said he'd come if you feel he's needed," Ganni said. "And your Wynn's showing our archers a thing or two. They needn't hear all our business, need they? It's *you* the Prophecy and the griffin speak of, and it's you who're one of us, not those others. Time to talk to them when we have ourselves sorted out."

Ker leaned back in her chair, looking from one Feeler to the other. She could see nothing but kindness and concern on the old man's face, and though Norwil still seemed to think of her as some sort of prize that put the Feelers of the Mines and Tunnels ahead of the Springs and Pools Clan, she was at least valuable to him. She'd never thought of herself as fully "one of us," no matter where she'd been. Not at home, not in the military, even before the Halls of Law had taken them both away. When she'd made up her mind to be a Talent, the Halians had destroyed her chances. Whatever Ganni thought, and Ker was sure the old man meant well, she wasn't so sure she could be "one of us."

"You've done what you promised us you'd do," Norwil said. "You've brought us the prince. We've got a bargaining point now with the Wings and the Polity. We come to them from a position of strength."

"Is that still so?" Ganni said. "What with it being the boy?"

Ker shrugged. "The Faro of Bears was sure the Wings would be willing to follow his father . . . They should be just as willing to follow the son."

"Maybe even more so," Norwil pointed out. "They'll follow the family member they've got their hands on, as they did in Corwin's time, and appoint one of themselves regent, maybe. I can see them thinking a thirteen-year-old boy would be easier to control, especially when there's something as important as this invasion to deal with."

The old man rubbed his chin. "If the Wings acclaim the son, he's the Luqs, regardless of what the father might do."

"That's the way it's always been," Ker agreed.

"So that's our hope for pushing back the invaders? Get the boy to the Wings and the sooner the better?"

"I don't see any other way." Ker met first Norwil's eyes, then Ganni's.

"Yet you want to delay this to save your friend?" Norwil said.

Ker sat quiet, chewing her lower lip. "It's like there's two things going on." She took the jewel out of her pouch and set it down on the table. "The invasion and the Prophecy. The jewel might be the link between them, if I can figure out how it works. Back in Gaena, we didn't have time to find Tel, or see if we could use the jewel to change him back." *We had to leave him behind.* "If I can undo what's been done to him, I could help others. We could get our own people back."

"It *is* the Third Sign." Norwil had that calculating look again. "The Bone of the Griffin." He turned to Ganni. "She's the one who speaks with them, so maybe she's the one who uses their bones?"

Ganni and Norwil took Ker back to the meeting room. Off to one side, well away from the others, Tel, Pella, and the other remaining soldiers were seated with their backs against the wall, ankles and hands bound in front of them. Tel was watching her with narrowed eyes. Norwil signaled, and two of the Feelers guarding the soldiers pulled Tel to his feet and dragged him over to a seat on the dais, in clear view of the small council, and perhaps two score others, many of whom were armed. Dersay was sitting where Sala once sat.

Ker could also see the old lady, Ara, relaxed in a chair next to Jerek, with the child Larin standing on Ara's other side. Ara was holding each by the hand—which made Ker purse her lips in a silent whistle. It was one thing to see a dead woman, what did it mean that Jerek, like Larin, could touch her? They looked as though they'd known each other forever. Wynn stood at parade rest just behind Jerek, trying to watch everyone at once. As Ker moved up onto the raised area, Jerek came to her, touching her on the arm as if to be sure of her. "They told us you were all right," he said, as if to explain why he hadn't come looking for her.

"They told me the same about you." Ker bowed her head to the old woman, and got a head tilt and a toothy smile in return.

"She's amazing, isn't she?" Jerek looked to Ara and back again. "Do you know how old she is?"

Ker blinked, half smiling. "I wasn't sure it was all right to ask." He could speak to her as well as touch her. What with that, and his multicolored aura . . .

A cloud passed over Jerek's face, but cleared away quickly. "She seemed happy to tell me—" he began.

"Did she tell you she's dead? That no one else can see her?"

Both Ker and Jerek turned around. Tel was much closer to them than they'd realized. Jerek went pale, his eyes staring.

"They didn't tell you, did they? These are *Feelers*, boy. You know what that means?"

Jerek's face hardened. "They did tell me," he said. "And to you I'm not 'boy.' To you I'm 'Lord Brightwing.'" He glanced at the old woman. "I don't care if they *are* Feelers. Do you think I can't tell good people when I see them? The only person here who's tried to hurt anyone is you." Larin had come up next to him, and taken his hand. When he looked down at her, she smiled. Jerek nodded and smiled back at her before resuming his place.

A buzz of sound passed through the watchers like a wave. Tel spat on the floor. Someone laughed, but at a sign from Dersay, silence fell again.

Ganni beckoned to her. "As good a time as any, I would think."

Ker straightened her spine and forced her shoulders to relax. As they approached him, Tel threw himself off the seat, rolling to his knees to crawl away, a look of fierce determination on his face. His guards hauled him up again and set him back on the stool, keeping him there with a hand on each shoulder.

"You hold still, boy, or we hold you still." Without waiting for a response, Ganni reached out, his hands curved as if he cupped Tel's face in his palms. Tel's eyes grew wide.

"Don't." Ker put a hand on Ganni's forearm. "No need to frighten him. He'll sit still without that, won't you?"

Tel's breath shuddered noisily, but he nodded. "I'm not afraid. I'm under the hand of the Sunflower Shekayrin. You can't do anything to me."

Ker wasn't so very sure he was wrong. Her heart was pounding, and her palms were sweaty. She'd thought there couldn't be anything worse than the look of indifference that had been in Tel's eyes since he'd been changed in Gaena, but there was. Hate was worse than indifference, after all, no matter what the stories said. She could live with it if Tel didn't care about her. But to have him hate her was almost more than she could bear.

Except it wasn't him, it was the jewel. She had to believe that the old Tel, the real Tel, was in him somewhere—overlaid by the net cast by the jewel, but there just the same. And if he wasn't? Or if she wasn't able to remove the net and restore Tel's aura? Then she had nothing to lose, did she? She wiped her hands off on her trousers and took the jewel out of its wrapping. Its facets no longer held the light the way it had done even in the woods at night. She turned it this way and that, but could see no colors in it. *Paraste.*

Auras sprang up all around her, the colors bright and moving. She could see how the patterns of red lines that caged Tel's aura matched the faceted pattern of the jewel, but the jewel itself now seemed dead, with no light of its own. A niggle of doubt ran up Ker's spine. Had she somehow used it up?

The jewel had always been powerful, full of light, in Svann's hands. As if, she thought now, he'd been recharging it somehow. She thought of the red dust. Was there some connection? Whatever it was, the secret had stayed with Svann, unless there was some way *she* could repower it?

At that thought, lines of color began reaching out from her aura, and Ganni's and the others close to her, toward the jewel. She concentrated, and the movement stopped.

"Hah! You can't use it, can you?"

"What about it, girl? Is he right?" Ganni stood with his arms crossed across his chest.

"I *have* used it, so no. But it's empty, like a mill with no water or no wind. *We* could power it, I think, the magic's not *so* different, but—" Ker shook her head. "I'm afraid to experiment. I need something to either repower the jewel safely, or to let me into Tel's mind the same way I got into the mind of the griffin—"

"What *about* the griffin?" This was Dersay. "He certainly seems to be able to get into any mind he wants to."

The small council led everyone who wished to witness through a set of tunnels Ker had never seen before. Finally, the tunnel began to climb and the temperature to drop. When they got to a place where they actually had to scramble over a pile of rocks to get to a higher level, Ker decided she had to ask.

"Ganni, where are we going?"

<<You said you wanted me. Dersay called. I come.>>

"Weimerk," Ker said aloud. This was the first time she'd heard him when she wasn't tired, or in pain.

<<Yes.>>

Ganni grinned. "You hear him, don't you? Just as you can see Ara. Can you hear the other Far-thinkers as well?"

"No—"

<<Not yet.>>

Ker moved ahead of Ganni, the griffin's voice in her head like a line of color leading her toward him. The new level spilled out into a cavelike room open on one side to the cold winter sky. Squinting against the increase of light and wind, she ran toward the griffin preening himself in a sheltered corner.

"Kerida. Nast. It. Has. Been. Too. Long."

Suddenly, she was enveloped in a sweep of feathers and fur.

"Weimerk." She coughed as she tried to dislodge a bit of down. The griffin smelled of snow and cold air. "We've been speaking for days."

"But. I. Could. Not. Embrace. You." His wings unfolded, exposing Ker to the cold air. "Here. Is. Your. Friend. Tel. Cursar." Weimerk's tail slashed. "Oh. This. Is. Quite. Bad. He. Tastes. And. Smells. Quite. Wrongly. I'm. Afraid."

"That's what I hope you can help me with." She held out the jewel. "Can you see the pattern of the facets?"

"Of. Course."

"And you see how the same pattern traps Tel's aura?"

"Naturally."

"Can you get it off? Can you free him?"

"It. Is. Not. For. Me. We. Do. Not. Use. Such. Things. You. Must. Do. It. You. Must. Learn. The. Paths. Of. The. Jewel. That. Is. The. Prophecy."

Ker shut her mouth before her teeth could freeze. "I must do it." She drew cold air deep into her lungs. "Of course." Weimerk's large right eye studied her as she shut her teeth on any further protest. She could see there was no point in arguing with him—and even less in being angry. She didn't have time.

Ker drummed her fingers on her thigh, and turned to Ganni. "If you helped me, I could show you what to move . . ."

Ganni's brow furrowed. "With it not physical, I'm not so very sure I can move it. What about Hitterol?"

Hitterol looked intrigued and Midon, normally so quiet, raised two fingers for her attention. "It seems to me—" he began.

"Just a minute." Norwil held up his hands. "The agreement was we let you try your jewel. Well, we've let you, and now it doesn't work, you want to use *us*. What does your soldier—what does *any* of this have to do with the Prophecy?"

Now even Ganni looked uncertain. Ker turned to Ara and Larin, but all she found there were smiles. She clenched her fists, and realized she was still holding the jewel.

"This is the Third Sign," she said. "This." She held up the jewel for everyone to see. "*This* is part of the Prophecy. You heard Weimerk. I have to learn to use it."

"'Bone of the griffin,'" Dersay said, smiling and nodding. "That's what it is. And it's here, in the Mines and Tunnels." At this, Norwil's frown disappeared, and he looked around, smiling.

"If I can restore Tel, I learn how the jewel works, I learn the magic of the Shekayrin, if you help me—" Ker broke off. She wasn't a Wing Faro, she wasn't even a full Talent. What could she promise them in exchange for helping Tel?

"I will restore your citizenship."

With everyone else in the cave she turned and looked at Jerek, standing quietly off to one side with Larin. Now, stepping forward, he looked taller somehow, the planes of his face squarer, more mature. Jerek was right; that *was* something the Luqs could do. This moment was a turning point for him, Ker realized, as Flashing the body in Camp Oste had been for her. She'd taken on the responsibilities of a Full Talent then, even if she didn't have the full knowledge and experience.

By stepping forward, Jerek was taking on the weight of the adult world. He glanced at her, and she could see in his eyes that he understood what he was doing. He was the prince. It was his responsibility, his life. She inclined her head in a shallow bow.

"Help us, and you'll receive full citizenship, with all its rights and privileges," he said. "You'll be free, and safe from any kind of persecution."

"You can give us this?"

Jerek looked around at all the faces. "I'm Jerek Brightwing. Cousin to the late Luqs, Ruarel the Third, grandchild, like her, to Rolian the Ninth. You help Kerida Nast break the magic of the Shekayrin, and I'll make you full citizens of the Faraman Polity. What one Luqs can take away, another can restore."

Ganni took a deep breath and looked around at the small council. Even Midon was smiling.

"What will you need us to do?" Ganni asked.

———

When Luca Pa'narion and his Feeler companion wandered up to the road from the ruins of what must have been Temlin Hall, Juria Sweetwater raised her arm in acknowledgment of their approach. "Just as I was beginning to wonder if I had to go all the way to the pass before we found you."

"Took you long enough. I've been Flashing you on the road for the last three days."

"It takes more time to move a Battle Wing than two people."

"Did the Panther give you any trouble?"

"None. I've yet to decide whether that is a good or bad thing."

"We've news. Our girl has succeeded; the prince is free and in the mines."

The vise that had been squeezing Juria's heart since she'd closed the gates of Oste behind her released, and she took the first easy breath she'd taken in days. Vindication. For the decision she'd made almost two months ago, when she'd sent her Bears into the Peninsula, and a month ago in sending her people for the prince. For the decision she'd made only days ago.

"We can rest your troops overnight, if you'd like. The griffin tells us there's now no hurry."

"The *griffin*? *Tells* us?"

"There may be a few things we neglected to mention, yes."

"Perhaps you should mention them now."

Paraste.

Ker steeled herself, almost overwhelmed by the colors of Weimerk's aura. She felt Ganni take her left hand, Hitterol her right. Beyond them, Larin and the others of the small council made up the circle. The world steadied. Ker concentrated on distinguishing between the mass of colors that was Weimerk, and the auras of the others. First, she sorted out the five basic colors of the Gifted—yellow, green, blue, purple, and orange—and the individual colors that marked their Gifts. Her own turquoise, Ganni's pink, Hitterol's silver, Midon's gold, Dersay's black, Larin's indigo. The extra coppery sheen she alone shared with Weimerk. Now it was easy to see Tel's three-colored aura—and even easier to see how it was caged and subdued by the net enclosing it. She wasn't sure how much the others could see, but that they could see *something* was obvious.

"It's not dampening." Hitterol's voice seemed to float in Ker's mind. She felt it as the Mind-healer's shudder of fear and disgust touched the others. "It's like it, but . . . no, not exactly the same. But there could be real, permanent damage if we're not successful."

Perhaps because Ker's Flash was strengthened by the others' Gifts, the net's light was bright enough to obscure rather than illuminate. In fact, now that she was concentrating on it, the net was all she could see. "It's too bright." Now there were hands on her shoulders and fingers gripping her elbows, and Midon's was the voice in her mind.

"See around the web, see into the through and the beyond." She let Midon take the lead and the brightness dimmed. But she still couldn't see where the net was fastened.

"It isn't really a net," Midon said. "That's just the way your mind makes sense of it. Don't be limited by these images, approach from all sides."

Ker staggered backward, but warm hands kept her from going down. They had dimmed the brightness of the net, but it seemed that by touching it, by manipulating it, they had made it aware of them. Lines of light reformed, almost like the stiff antennas of insects, and began to reach out from the net that held Tel.

"Quick, quick! Can you see it?" It was her special Talent to see, to understand the nature and purpose of something, of someone. The griffin's gift allowed her to do that without having to touch the object—something that Ker thought might be a very lucky thing right now. Something told her that if she had to touch that net of light, it might be the last thing the real Kerida Nast would ever do.

But now it was reaching out, not just for her, but for the people helping her. As Hitterol and Midon had done for her, she showed them what she was seeing, shared her Gift with them, gave them her understanding of the light. She felt someone lift her arms and, suddenly knowing what was wanted, she held out her hands, palms flat toward the spears of light that threatened them. The closest one stopped moving, even began to retreat, and Ker saw her own aura, wrapped and braided tight by the auras of the Feelers, pushing back on it. But shafts of red still approached, growing like icicles.

As they shoved and parried, Ker realized they weren't going to win. They could only stop one or two of the light spears at a time. There were too many. Eventually, one would break through and touch them. What would happen then? Would they remember who and what they'd been before the net captured them?

She felt a little push at her inner spaces, where blocks and barriers still lived. She'd felt this push before. Weimerk!

"Go," she called to him. "Escape while you can!"

Instead, the push continued. *He doesn't understand*, she

thought. He didn't see the danger he was in. He'd helped her once before, brushing her blocks aside to help her in her first encounter with the auras. For the first time, Ker deliberately dropped her blocks herself, allowing the griffin to see what she saw, sense what she sensed.

And this time, Weimerk showed her not just what *she* could do, but what all of them together could do. Their auras intensified, fed by the colors of the griffin, their light blazing, brighter, brighter still, the lines of the net curling back from them now, dimming, shriveling smaller and smaller, until it was once again just a net trapping Tel Cursar's aura, patterned like the facets of Svann's jewel.

<<Brush it off,>> came the griffin's instruction.

Together, Ker and the Feelers focused their auras on the net, concentrated as it unraveled and unwove, until they brushed it away like a cobweb.

Ker took a deep breath. Felt how the auras around her calmed, the colors steadied, no longer swirling and spiking into waves, but flowing gently. She felt hands tighten on her arms and blinked, looking up.

"Kerida? Ker? Is that you?"

That was a look she hadn't seen on Tel's face for some time. He leaned forward and kissed her, just before collapsing to the floor.

When Ker entered the room they'd been given, Wynn was sitting on a three-legged stool next to Tel's bed, watching over him as he slept.

"How is he?"

"Better than you, it seems." Wynn's smile twisted when Ker pushed her hair off her forehead with trembling hands. "You look ready to drop. Here." She stood and gave her seat to Ker.

Ker sank onto the stool, feeling the strain in her knees for the first time.

"You know, I used to think it might be nice to have the Talent." Wynn's voice was quiet as air.

Ker pressed her hands together between her knees. It was hard to keep herself from touching Tel. "It's useful. I'm not so sure about 'nice.'"

"Well, I mean, you'd be able to tell, wouldn't you? You'd know if someone really loved you. Whether it was real."

Ker had overheard some of the other Candidates talking about things like this when she was in the Hall. It had seemed important then. "Not everyone can Flash something like that, but yes, it can be done." She pulled her focus from Tel's face. "Was there someone?"

"No. At least, no one in particular." Wynn still spoke quietly, and Ker guessed that she wasn't telling the whole truth.

"Maybe one of your 'aunties'?"

Wynn looked sideways at her. "You don't miss much, do you?"

"Well, I figured no one could have as many aunts and uncles as you claimed, and so, I thought . . ." Ker let her voice trail off. What she thought sounded rude, now that she was about to say it out loud.

"You thought I didn't have any real family, just people on the street I did things for." A flash of white as Wynn smiled. "You'd be right."

Suddenly Tel's soft snoring broke off as he rolled to his side, facing away. The two girls fell silent, but he made no other move. Wynn wrinkled her nose.

"Talents almost always get used for criminal cases," Ker said, lowering her voice still further. "You know, finding evidence. Questions of Law. Not so much for people's feelings. That may change now, though." She gestured with her head toward the world of Feelers outside the door of the room.

"I've been working with the people they call Lifters, people like Ganni. He can move and manipulate anything he can see. Rocks, people—"

"Arrows in flight."

"Well, yes. But there's so much more. They brought me a baby who couldn't keep his food down and we fixed him. I could Flash that he had a hole here, where he swallowed." Ker tapped the base of her throat. "Linking auras, I could show Ganni and then he could move the baby's throat so the hole closed. I think maybe, one day, we might be able to help Ennick understand more than maps."

They'd be able to reverse dampening, she thought.

"Could you have done that before?"

"Before the griffin? Before I could see the auras and manipulate them? No. No, I couldn't."

"Could anyone else?"

Ker shook her head. "No one else has even mentioned the auras."

"So are they right? Are you the one in the Prophecy?"

Ker took in a deep lungful of air and let it out slowly. "Not *the* one, no, I don't think so. I'm already the Second Sign. I don't think I can be more than that." Ker motioned Wynn closer, waiting to speak until she could murmur in the other girl's ear. "I think it might be Jerek."

"Well, now." Wynn shook her head, her lips in a twisted smile. "That's either wonderful, or it's a disaster." Ker shrugged, her eyes drifting back to Tel Cursar.

"I suppose we'll see, won't we?" Wynn said. "Larin's seen it already, and she's just not saying." Wynn patted Ker on the arm. "In the meantime, I'm off to get some sleep. Watching this one here"—she pointed at Tel with her chin—"it's a wonder I didn't drop off myself." The curtains rustled closed behind her.

"I thought she'd never leave." Tel rolled over again until he was facing her, propped up on one elbow.

"How long have you been awake?"

"Since you came in. I dreamed you were here, and you were." His smile was gentle, though it had no humor in it. "I need to apologize."

Ker's throat clenched. "You mean for kissing me in front of all those people? I should think so." She could tell her tone wasn't as light as she meant it to be. "Are you all right?" How would he react to everything that had happened to him—the things that he'd thought, and done—

"I remember it," he admitted. "I remember what happened. Things I said—things I *felt*. It's like it happened a long time ago, or as though it's only a story I know really well. Almost. I'll never be free of it, though." His smile was painful to see. "And I'll never apologize for kissing you."

Ker smiled before she could stop herself, hoped that hers looked better than his.

"You're free of the jewel's web. That much I know for sure."

"How could it happen? How could he do that to me? Make me forget everything I knew and everything I felt—even what I felt about you?"

Ker thought about the empty jar of grease Tel had kept in his satchel. "I don't think you did. Not completely. Judging by everything I Flashed, Svann *was* using some of what you really felt—"

When he jerked away, she sat down on the edge of his pallet and took his free hand in both of hers. "No, listen. It's better if you know." She waited until he was looking at her again. "You remember how you reacted when you first learned I was a Talent? That's how the military thinks—that's how *I* thought, once. It doesn't take much manipulation to take that genuine feeling, a flame that exists, however small, and fan it into a blaze. So much of what they're saying, the Halians, is a little bit true." She thought about what she'd heard Jak, and others, say. "The Halls *do* take children away from their families. There *are* more women than men in positions of power and status, inside the military and out. The fact is he *had* to use the jewel on you, to make you behave the way you did. There are many who didn't—don't—need that much persuasion. Think of that." She took a deep breath.

"People like Pella?"

"People like Pella. Willing to stand on the stronger side. Willing to stand with us, now that we're safe away from Svann."

"You can't trust him!"

"You forget, I can Flash him." She brushed his face with her fingertips. She knew what was really troubling him. "The same as I can Flash you. I know I can trust you. I can tell if someone's been jeweled just by looking at their aura, and now I can fix it. What are you smiling about?"

"I'm remembering Svann telling Jak that 'the word jewel is not a verb.'" He sobered. "Can you save Jak?"

"I hope so. I hope it isn't already too late. There are Far-seers looking." Ker took another deep breath.

"You're exhausted, let's worry about Jak tomorrow. Here." Tel shifted over on the pallet. "Lie down. I'll watch over you for a change. Let's not worry about what comes next."

———

What came next, according to the Feelers, was Jerek's formal acceptance as their Luqs. Though, as Tel pointed out, the Clan of the Mines and Tunnels had strange ideas of formality. Shortly after breakfast—a meal spent, on Ker's part, in avoiding Tel's eyes and trying not to smile—Ennick came to fetch them, along with Wynn and Jerek.

"What about Weimerk?" Ker said. She pulled the edge of her tunic straight, wishing it was cleaner.

"Can't get through the tunnels," Ennick said. "Small council says the great hall. Up this tunnel, second left, across the mushroom space and then third right."

<<If you are there, I am there also. Meanwhile, I will feed.>>

Ker rubbed her forehead. Would she ever get used to this?

Ennick led them along the route he'd outlined, giving them little running descriptions of where each crossing tunnel went, and what could be found there.

"I'll never remember all of this," Wynn whispered.

"I don't think we're supposed to," Ker said. "But it's distracting Jerek, so let Ennick be."

Once they arrived at the great hall, Ennick ushered them to one side of the dais like a herd dog bringing in his sheep, and stood protectively in front of them.

"Are you nervous?" Ker could have bitten her tongue. What a ridiculous thing to say, but the words were out before she could stop them.

Jerek nodded, his eyes on the Lifters who were hanging baskets of the green fluorescent moss throughout the huge room. "Not as much as I thought I'd be," he added. "But I'm only nervous, not afraid."

"No one would blame you if you were," Ker said.

Jerek shook his head. "It's not shameful to be afraid. When Nessa was teaching me the sword, she used to say it was often sensible. The trick is not to let it stop you from doing what needs to be done."

Tel caught Ker's gaze over the boy's head and raised his eyebrows, grinning. "She sounds sensible herself," he said. "I'd like to meet Nessa one day."

Jerek glanced upward. "She might be in Gaena. I never got a chance to ask."

"We can ask now," Tel said. "You can send for her." When Jerek frowned, Tel added, "You're the prince. You'll be Luqs. If you want someone to go, they'll go."

As they were talking, the room was filling up. In addition to the baskets of moss, Tel's glow stone had been set in a basket on the dais, where it provided light without blinding anyone. Jerek looked at the people gathering and swallowed. Ker put a hand on his shoulder. He was just a boy raised in a vineyard, a country holding. Had he even seen this many people, all in one place, before?

They were joined on the dais by the small council. Norwil UnGifted, Ganni Lifter, Dersay Far-thinker, Midon Far-seer, Hitterol Mind-healer, holding the hand of Larin. The little Time-seer looked a bit lonely without Ara standing somewhere near. Ker wondered where the old woman was.

Ganni looked toward them and made a beckoning gesture with his hand.

"Shall I come with you?" she said to Jerek. The boy hesitated, his lip between his teeth. "No, thank you," he said. "They should see me as myself."

He was right, Ker thought. He was thinking like a leader.

"Attention, everyone." Norwil clapped his hands. "You all know me, I speak here for the UnGifted. Is there anyone who doesn't know why we're here?"

He waited a moment, but—if anything—the hall grew quieter. He turned to Jerek. "If you would. Please take the Speaker's seat."

Ker looked up—and caught Dersay looking up also.

<<Come outside. Quickly. Soldiers come.>>

Ker leaped to her feet, gripping the plaque she still wore around her neck. Nate Primo was alive, well, and *here*. But before she could say anything to reassure the Feelers who were already on their feet, Dersay spoke up.

"It's Cuarel, and the Inquisitor. They're here. Everyone, they're here. It's the Bears. We won't have to take the prince to them. They've come to us."

<<Come out.>>

This time Ker could hear Weimerk both in her head and with her ears. With a shiver, she realized that this was the same entrance that she and Tel and Wynn had blocked, almost unrecognizable now. It hadn't taken much for Lifters to clear it. And it had taken less time to reach it than she remembered. Luca Pa'narion and Cuarel were waiting when they arrived. Ker wondered how long the Inquisitor had been wearing his black tunic. Cuarel nodded at her absently, looking beyond everyone until she saw Dersay, and ran to her.

"Well, Talent Nast, a job well done, it appears." Luca's grin was bigger than his face, and his aura sparkled. "Come out when you're ready." He inclined his head to Jerek, and returned outside.

"*Are* you ready?" Ker said to Jerek. "That's the Bear Wing out there."

"This is why you brought me here." Jerek flexed his hands.

"You'll have to go out to meet them. They won't come in. It's safe, though. Weimerk's out there."

Jerek hesitated, glancing between Ker and Ennick.

"Shall I come with you this time? Or Tel? A soldier might be better, to meet soldiers."

Jerek furrowed his brow, as if uncertain of her reaction. "I'd like it to be Ennick."

Ker blinked. The boy was a genius to have thought of that. Every Feeler present today—every Bear for that matter— would remember the image of their prince walking out to greet his Battle Wing hand in hand with the giant boy, the damaged one. They would remember it their whole lives, and they would tell their children. Jerek was thinking like a Luqs. Ker swallowed, unable to decide whether she was proud of him, or sorry for him.

"Would you walk out with me, Ennick?" Jerek held out his hand to the big man.

"Sure, Jerek, I can go outside with *you*. But you know, you can't get lost here."

"I know, Ennick, but I'd feel better if you were with me."

The big man took Jerek's offered hand. Jerek nodded,

touched Ker once on the arm, smiled at Wynn, and stepped outside. Ker and Tel let them advance a few paces into the cold winter sunlight, before following.

Outside, waiting for them, were three familiar figures, Luca Pa'narion, Juria Sweetwater, and her Laxtor, Surm Barlot. Half a Company of Bears were drawn up in the space outside the exit, but when Ker looked up, every crest and ridge was lined with soldiers, their purple tunics, with a scattering of green, glowing in the sunlight. She thought about Flashing, to see what all the auras would look like, but she resisted.

"I greet you, my prince." Luca came forward and folded himself to both knees on the stony ground. "I am the Talent High Inquisitor Luca Pa'narion, at your service."

"Thank you, Talent Inquisitor." Jerek managed a small smile, as Luca waggled his eyebrows. "Please rise."

"Thank you, my prince. May I present—" Before Luca could continue, a muted scream drew every eye upward. The griffin, feathers and fur sparkling in the sunshine, circled the clearing three times before coming in for a landing, scattering soldiers right and left. Only Juria Sweetwater stood her ground, her eyes narrowed and her lips parted. Surm Barlot shouted orders, and the Company began to reform, leaving Weimerk a clear space.

"This is Weimerk, the griffin," Jerek said.

Luca nodded. "It certainly is." He looked at Ker, and she smiled back. "As I was saying, may I present, my lord prince, my lord griffin, the Faro of Bears, Juria Sweetwater. Faro, our prince, Jerek Firoxi."

"Jerek Brightwing," the boy corrected.

"A. Name. Of. Good. Omen," Weimerk said, preening the feathers on his right wing.

The Faro bowed again, and waited courteously for the griffin to speak again before she came forward, hitching her bearskin cloak a little higher on her shoulders. She glanced at Ker, and Ker nodded back. Juria Sweetwater inclined her head to Jerek.

"I have brought my Bears to your service, Jerek Bright-wing. May I shelter them here?"

Ennick stepped up. "Plenty of room, Jerek. Section Clover and Section Honeysuckle have been empty for ages."

Norwil coughed, and both Jerek and Juria turned their heads to him. "As Speaker for the Mines and Tunnels, I welcome you, Faro of Bears. If you come in, we can see about finding accommodation for yourself and your soldiers. Like Ennick said, there's plenty of room."

Juria turned her eyes to Jerek, though she still addressed Norwil. "A Faro cannot enter, nor pass the range of the Serpents Teeth, without the permission of the Luqs of Farama," Juria said.

The muscles in Jerek's face tightened as he clenched his teeth. He took a deep breath, raising his chin.

"You may enter."

Ker held her breath as the Faro of Bears kneeled and put her face into Jerek's hands.

Epilogue

ENNICK found the strange man exactly where Griffin Girl told him the man would be. Tunnel one hundred and seventy-three, just past the Cherry Blossom Shaft, and before where it crossed with tunnel five hundred and fifty-seven. The man was standing, with his arms spread out and his cheek pressed tight against the wall of the tunnel, his hands twitching. His blue tunic was very dirty. Ennick's mother would have made him change and wash if he was as dirty as that. And his black cloak was covered with dust. There were tiny, tiny lines of red rock in the tunnel wall just there, like the tiny, tiny wrinkles around Ennick's mother's eyes. Only red.

Close around where the man was pressing himself against the rock, the tiny, tiny lines were flashing, a little bit like sparks from a fire. Ennick wasn't afraid. Griffin Girl had told him to come here. He put his hand on the man's shoulder, and the man's eyes opened to look at him. The pupils were so big Ennick could hardly see any color in the man's eyes at all.

"My name's Ennick," he told the man. "Kerida Griffin Girl said you should come with me."

The man swallowed and licked his lips. Ennick could see the man's lips were dry. He was probably thirsty. Ennick would give him some of his water when they were moving.

"There's a griffin," the man whispered. Now Ennick could see he had the griffin's old claw in his hand, and he'd been scratching at the surface of the rock face with it.

"That's right." Ennick laid his hand on the man's wrist and made him be still. "His name is Weimerk, and he's my friend. He says one day he'll be big enough to carry me, if Kerida says it's all right."

"I saw him," the man said. He shut his eyes again. "I saw the griffin. He showed me the way here."

"That's right," Ennick said. "You left all your friends, but don't worry, we found them. Don't you want to come where your friends are?"

"The griffin." The tiny, tiny red lines flickered again.

"Weimerk's there, too, or he will be if Kerida asks him to come. Do you want to see him?"

The eyes opened again. This time Ennick could see that there seemed to be red lines in the man's eyes, too. "I can see him? Yes," the man said. "I want to see him."

"Come on, then."

When the man pushed himself away from the wall, he wavered for a moment, and before Ennick could catch him, crumpled to the ground. Ennick tsked and looked at him, hands on his hips, shaking his head. Then he stooped and gathered the man up in his arms.

"This is going to take a while," he told the man. "Just you rest."

———

The Sky Emperor, Guon Kar Lyn, Son of the Sun, and Father of the Moon, regarded with distaste the man lying prostrate on the marble floor in front of the Sky Throne. Guon Kar Lyn stroked the tricolor cat sitting in his lap and composed his face. "Rise."

The Poppy Shekayrin was young enough to get to his feet quite quickly and without the use of his hands. Once standing, he clasped his hands in front of him and focused his attention on the Sky Emperor's left slipper. As was proper. The eye embroidered on the slipper's toe undoubtedly peered back.

"You have a report for me?" Sometimes Guon Kar Lyn tired of the protocols that prevented people from speaking to him until he had first addressed them. Sometimes.

"I do, Sky Emperor. I fear, however, that it will displease you."

Guon Kar Lyn grimaced. At least this one was honest enough to say so. "Nevertheless, you must speak."

"Yes, Sky Emperor." The man shivered, as if he had been about to move, but changed his mind. "It is as you feared, Son of the Sun. Your sister the Princess Imperial Bakura Kar Luyn has . . ."

Guon Kar Lyn stifled a sigh. "You have my permission to say it."

Nevertheless, the Shekayrin had to clear his throat before he could speak. "She has the taint, my emperor. The jewels spark in her presence."

He must have made some movement, for the cat on his lap looked up at him and blinked with disapproval.

"I assure you she is safe for the moment, Father of the Moon. She has been well netted, and her magic will not work, nor will any other Shekayrin be able to detect her condition."

"Thank you, Quo Dval. You have done well. I know it has cost you much to speak. Are there others who know of the Princess Imperial's condition?"

"No one, my Emperor. I followed your instructions most closely."

Strange, Guon thought, how no one ever seemed to see the danger in that. Somehow, no one ever thought the worst would happen to them.

Except Baku. As a mere toddler she had crawled into the lap of her favorite older brother and told him that he would be Sky Emperor one day, and that she would be dead. At that time, there had been eleven people between him and the Sky Throne he now occupied.

Well, he had been Emperor now for seven years. But Baku would not die. He loved her. Taint or no taint, she was his sister, and the sister of the Sky Emperor was too valuable to destroy, even though she could not now be given as wife to anyone here, no matter how badly an alliance was wanted—tentative plans forming in that direction would be immediately scrapped.

"You have done well," he repeated, gesturing the man forward. The cat, now thoroughly offended, leaped down from his lap. Or perhaps the keen-witted animal knew what was coming?

"Come, I would reward you." From his headdress he pulled a long thin metal pin, and freed the thumb-sized golden bell it affixed to the headdress. The mage mounted to the second step of the throne and Guon descended two steps to meet him. He might as well overwhelm the man with honors, it cost nothing. The man took the golden bell in both hands, bowing his head. Guon leaned to give him the ritual embrace, and thrust the long pin through the man's clothing on his left side. The pin slipped between two ribs and pierced the man's heart, which stopped beating almost immediately.

Guon stood motionless, bearing the man's weight in his arms until he could be sure there would be no flow of blood, whereupon he slowly removed the pin. He allowed the body to sink to its knees, and slump to its right. He recovered the golden bell from where the man's dead hand had let it fall, and restored it and its fastener to his headdress. He took the man's soul stone and tucked it into one of the many pockets in his left sleeve. Now he would not have to wait until one was brought back for him. He returned to his throne. After a few minutes, the cat resumed its place on his lap.

He would call his attendants soon, and they would come with their customary efficiency to deal with the poor Shekayrin, taken so suddenly and so fatally ill, perhaps—who knew?—from the anxiety of having lost his soul stone. Which was why, he would tell anyone intrepid enough to ask him, the Poppy Shekayrin had asked for this audience.

Once the remains were removed, he would have his little sister brought to him, his precious Baku, who had loved him when he was no one, long before anyone else believed he would become Son of the Sun and Father of the Moon.

She was not safe here. Though he was Sky Emperor, though she was Princess Imperial, she was not above the law, and the law said that witches could not live. Netted or not, she could not live.

The cat in his lap rolled over, presenting its belly for his hand. Every time he was surprised by the softness of its fur.

He would send his sister to the new province of Farama as wife to the new ruler there. It would cement his grip on the place. And Baku would be safer than she could be here, away from anyone who might suspect—or know. Away from the hot scrutiny of this court, her taint might never be discovered.

It would break his heart to part with her, but she would live.